JOHN C. FREMO[NT]
EL DORADO CITY CA.

TEACHER JOHN KEATING
SUBJECT ENGLISH
STUDENT ID

1. SECTION 1 Directions: This section is about Out There "The Evil Within" TPB. Please read carefully every question and answer wisely. Good Luck!

1. Who wrote this collection?
   - Brian Augustyn
2. It was pencilled by?
   - Humberto Ramos
3. The inker was?
   - Sandra Hope
4. Who colored it?
   - Studio F's ~~Edg~~ Edgar Delgado
5. Lettering was handled by?
   - Ryan Cline
   - Gus Hartman
   - Jenna Garcia
   - Robbie Robbins for IDW
   - Sergio Garcia
6. Who created **Out There**?
   - Brian Augustyn and Humberto Ramos
7. This edition and the **Out there** logo were designed by?
   - Leonardo Olea
8. There are 2 variant covers in this volume. Name the creative teams who did them and the issues they appeared in.
   - Carlos Meglia did issue #1 variant cover
   - Bruce Timm did issue #3 variant cover
   - Both colored by Edgar Delgado

OUT THERE: The Evil Within. ISBN: 1-56389-893-4 Published by WildStorm Productions, 888 Prospect St. #240, La Jolla, CA 92037. Cover and compilation copyright © 2002 WildStorm Productions, an imprint of DC Comics. All rights reserved. Originally published in single magazine form as OUT THERE #1-6, copyright © 2001, 2002 Humberto Ramos. OUT THERE is (tm) and © Humberto Ramos.

Cliffhanger! is a trademark of DC Comics. The stories, characters, and incidents mentioned in this magazine are entirely fictional. Printed on recyclable paper. WildStorm does not read or accept unsolicited submissions of ideas, stories or artwork.

PRINTED IN CANADA

DC Comics. A division of Warner Bros. --An AOL Time Warner Company

Wait

GO ON TO THE NEXT PAGE

Hey wax lips
Giv me the answers
or I'll kick your lousy nerdy butt
Loomis

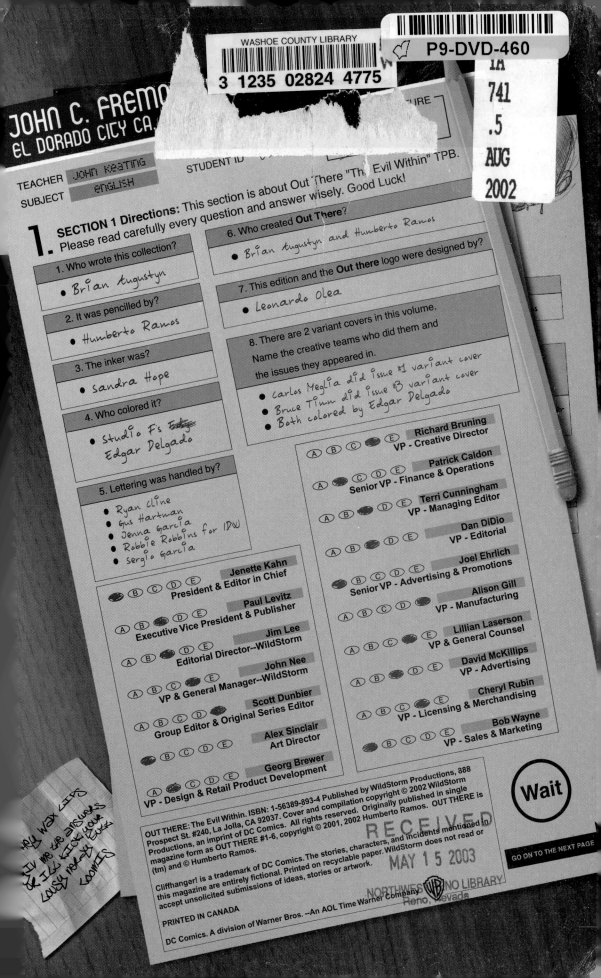

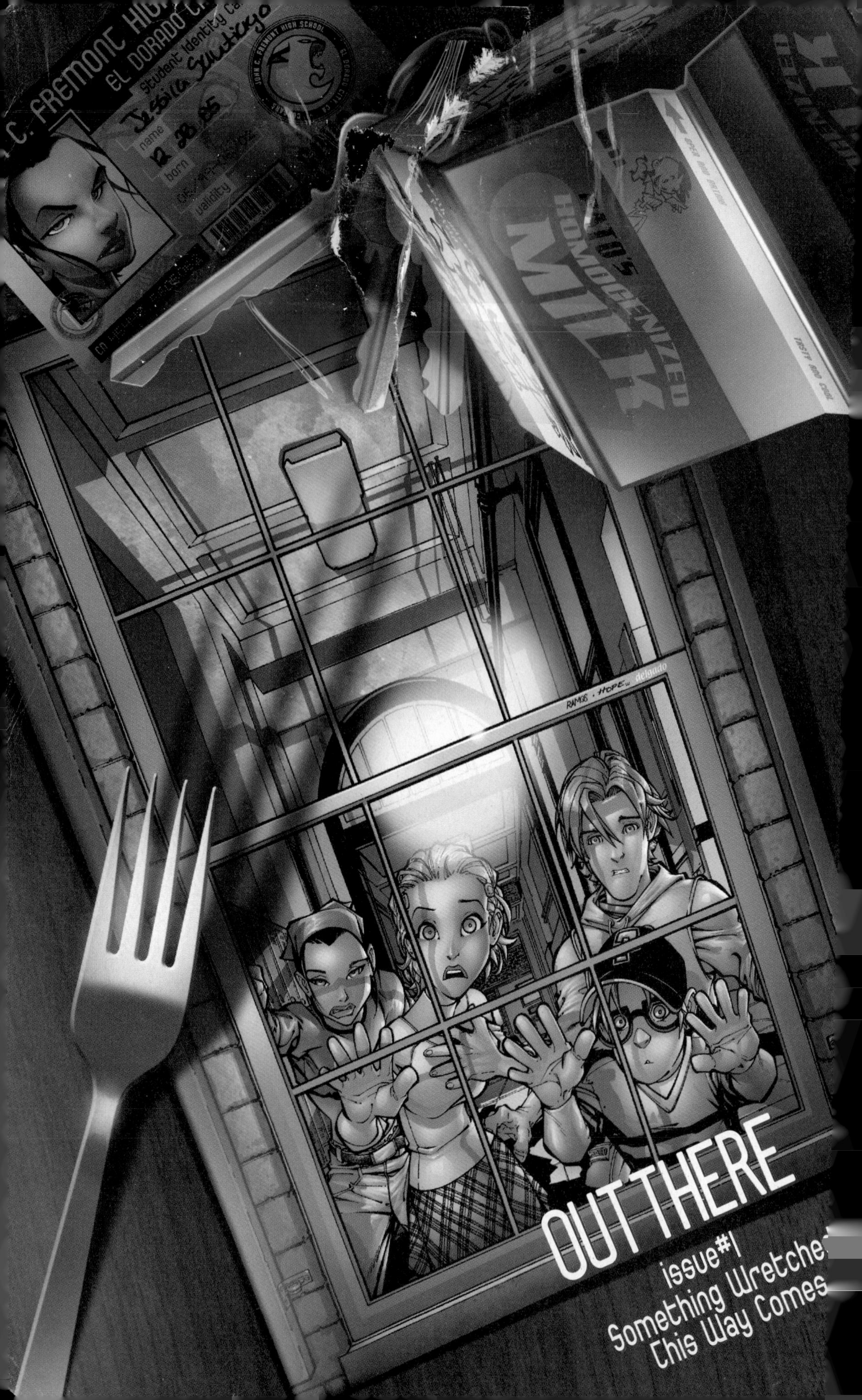

OUT THERE
issue#1
Something Wretche
This Way Comes
RAMOS · HOPE · delgado
HOMOGENIZED
MILK
EL DORADO
Student Identity Card
name
born
validity

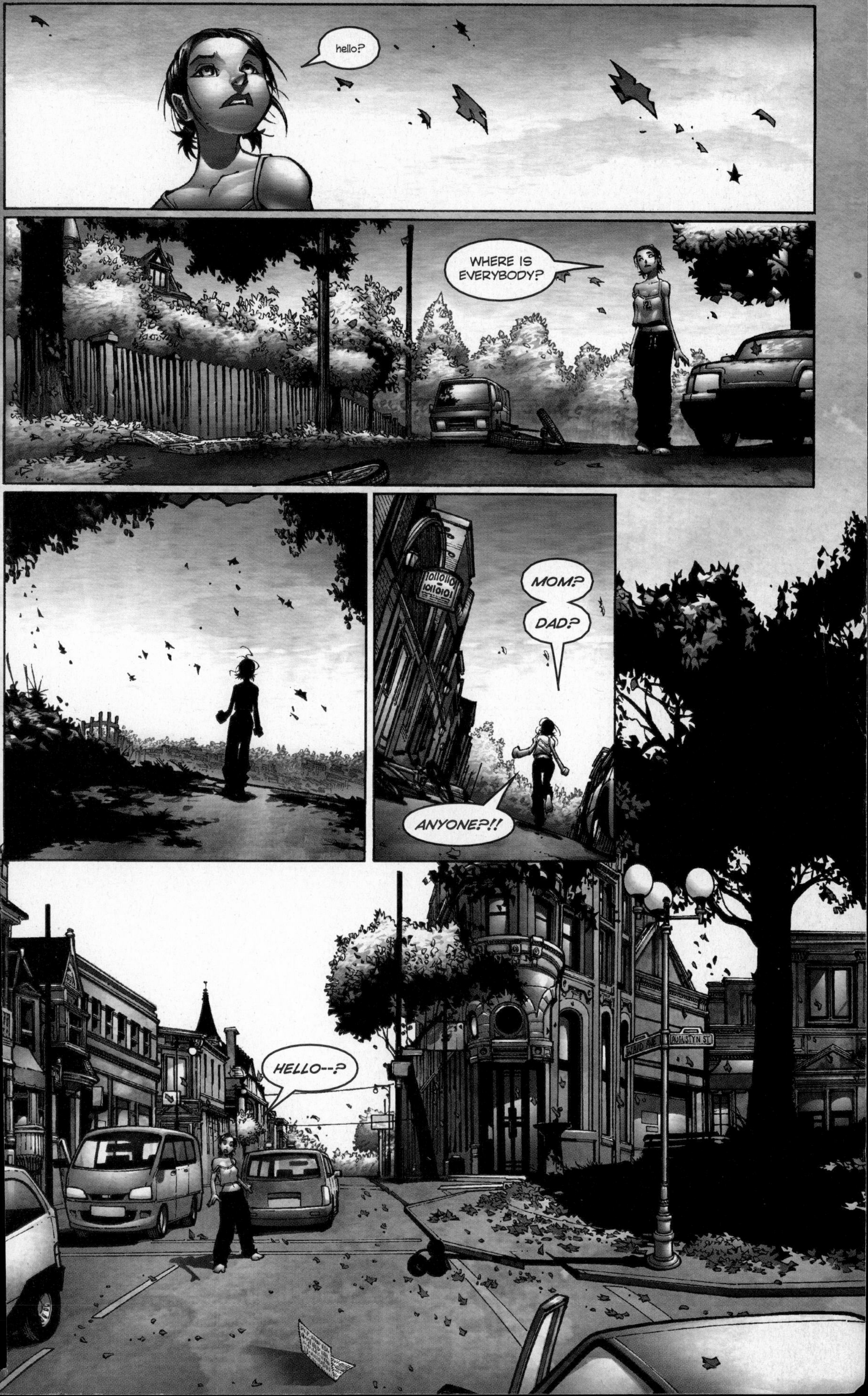
hello?
WHERE IS EVERYBODY?
MOM?
DAD?
ANYONE?!!
AUGUSTYN ST
HELLO--?

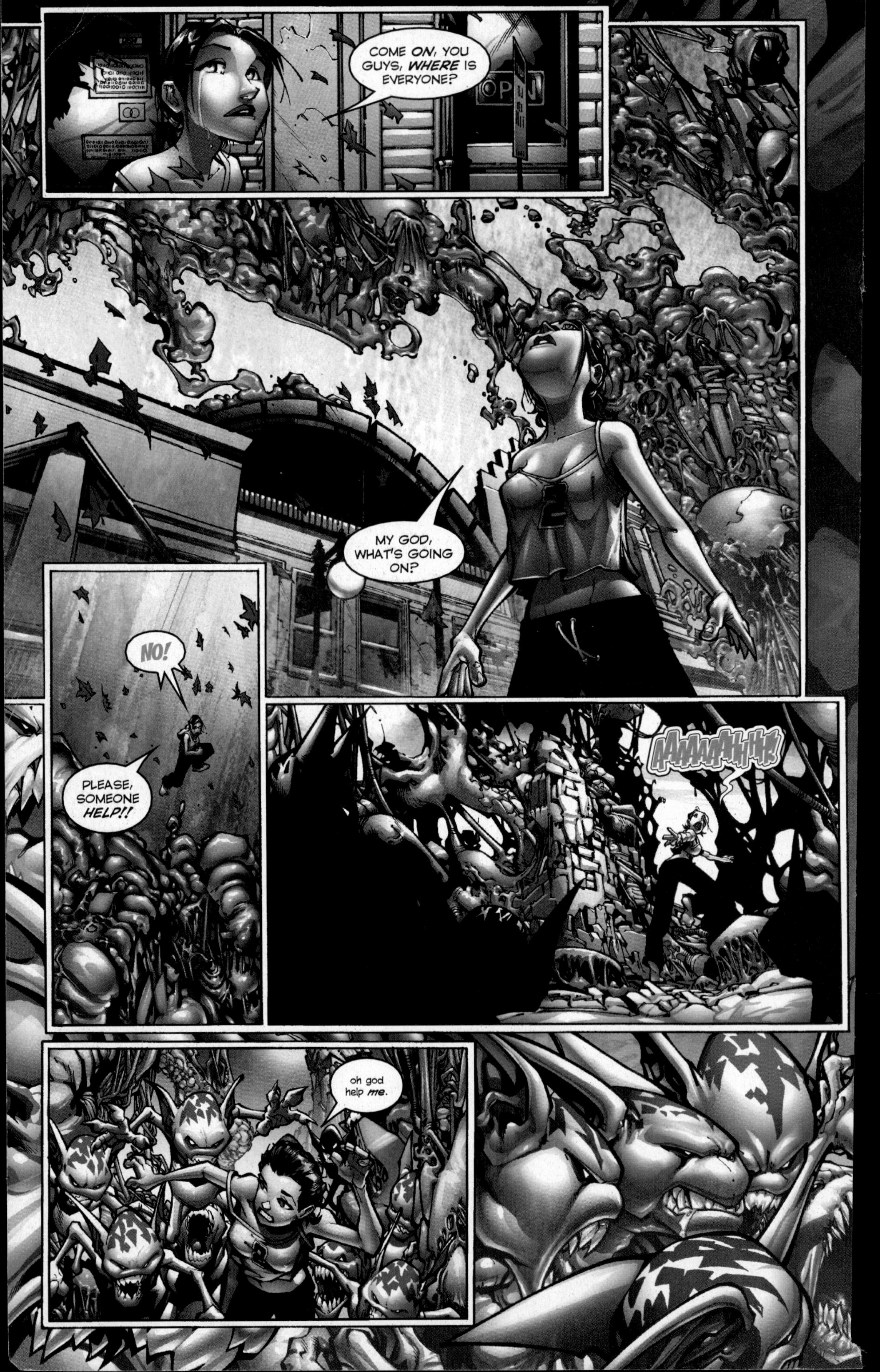
COME *ON*, YOU GUYS, ***WHERE*** IS EVERYONE?
MY GOD, WHAT'S GOING ON?
NO!
PLEASE, SOMEONE ***HELP!!***
AAAAAAAHHHH!
oh god help *me*.

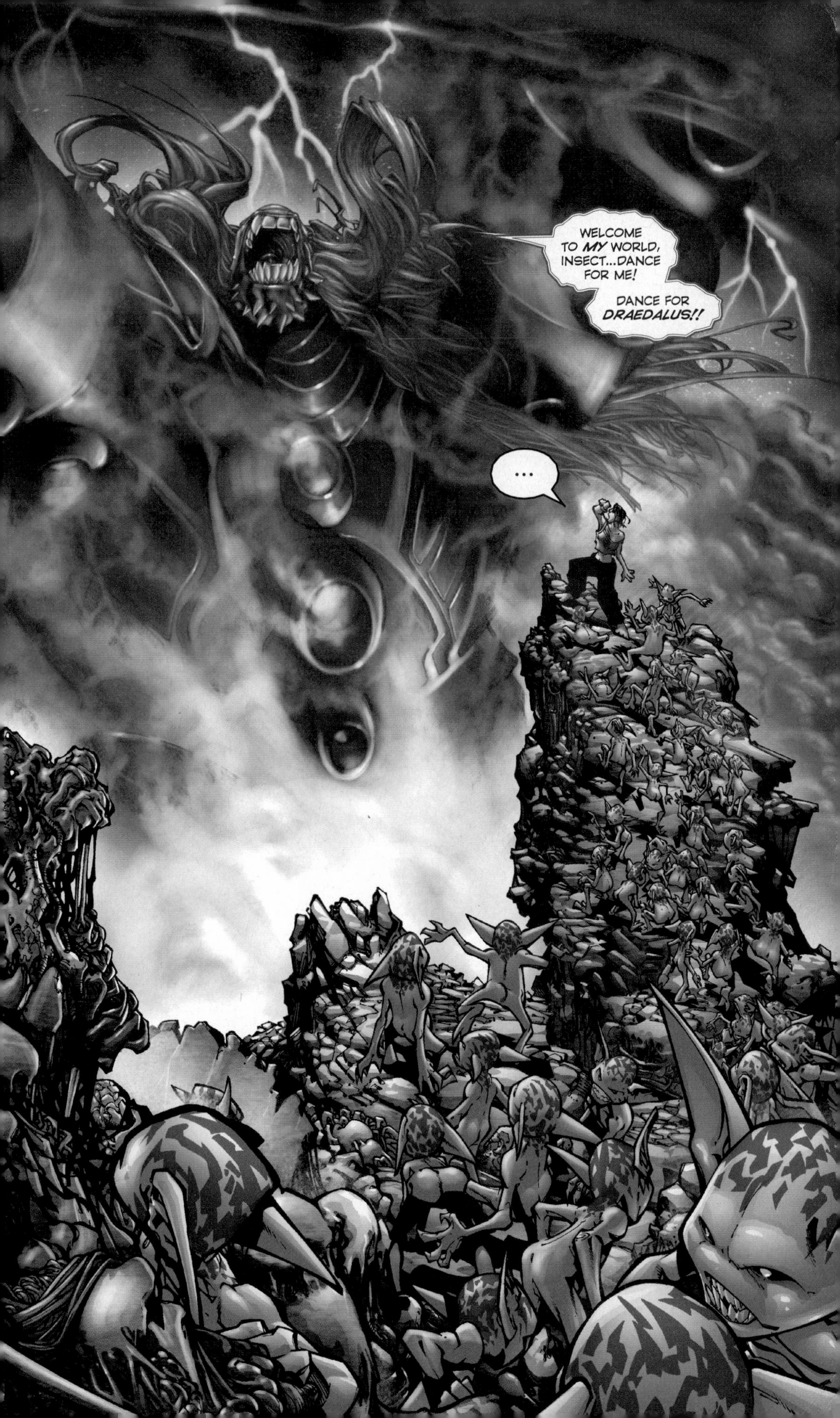
WELCOME TO MY WORLD, INSECT...DANCE FOR ME!
DANCE FOR DRAEDALUS!!
...

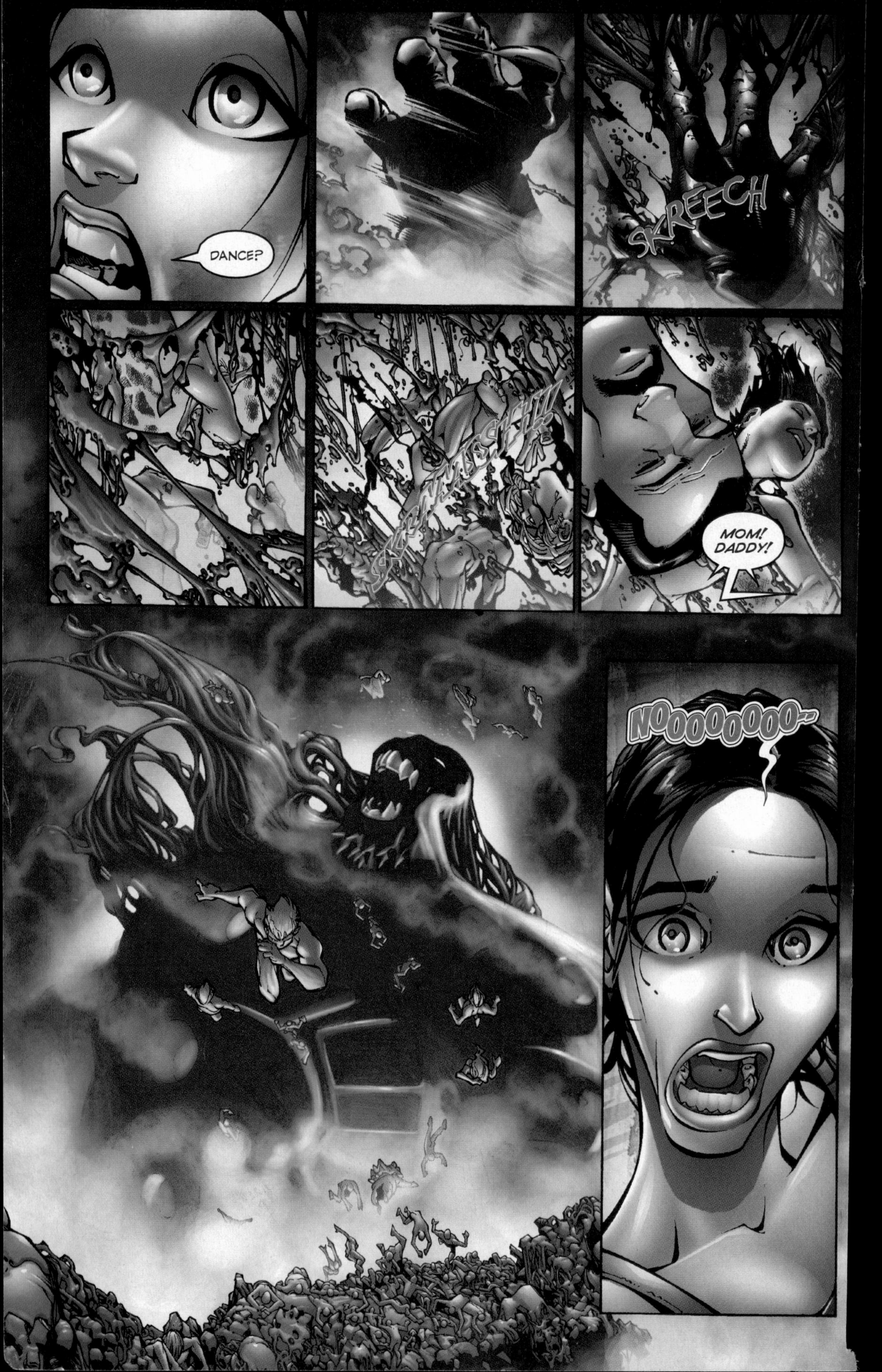
DANCE?
SKREECH
MOM! DADDY!
NOOOOOOOO--

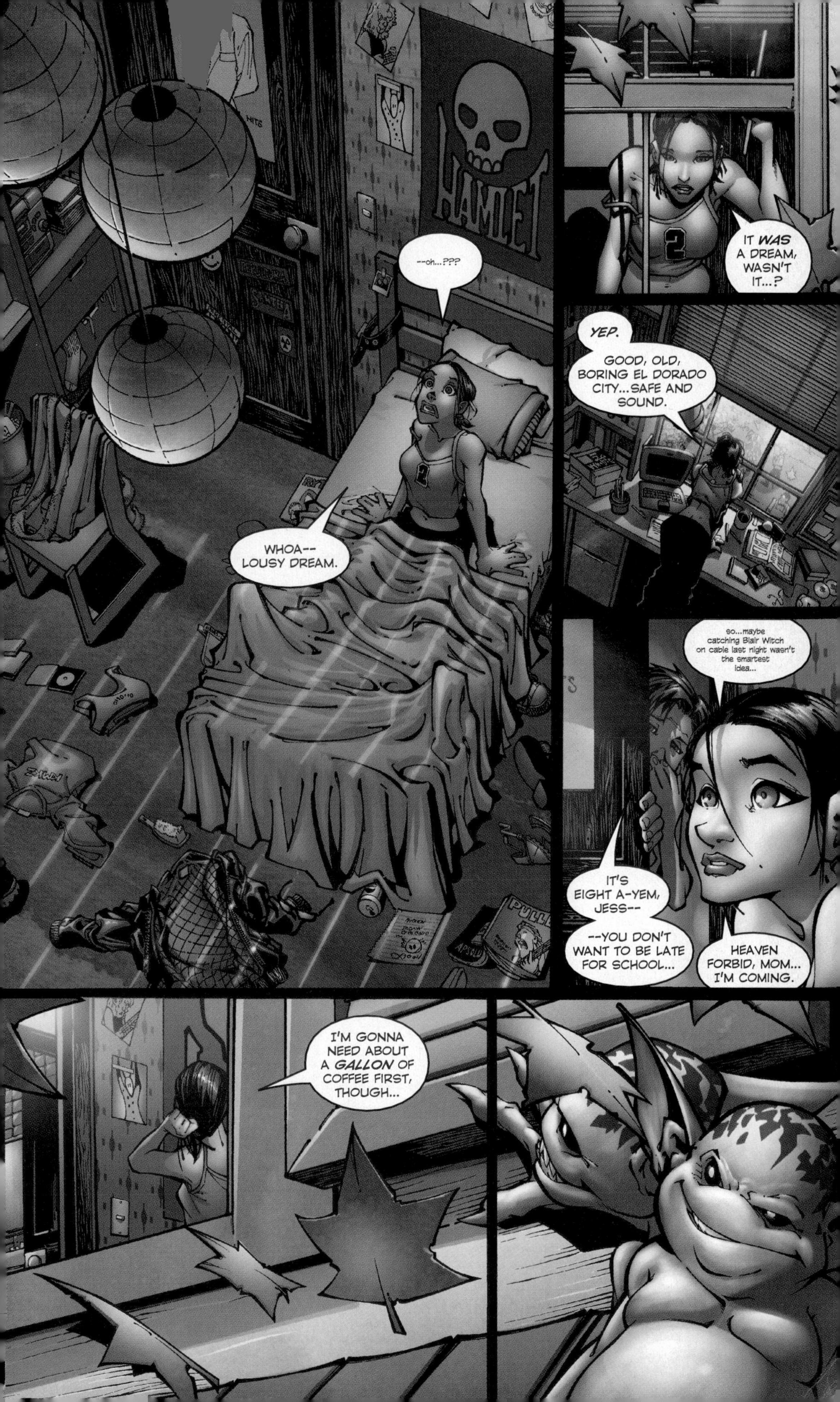
--oh...???
WHOA-- LOUSY DREAM.
IT WAS A DREAM, WASN'T IT...?
YEP.
GOOD, OLD, BORING EL DORADO CITY...SAFE AND SOUND.
so...maybe catching Blair Witch on cable last night wasn't the smartest idea...
IT'S EIGHT A-YEM, JESS--
--YOU DON'T WANT TO BE LATE FOR SCHOOL...
HEAVEN FORBID, MOM... I'M COMING.
I'M GONNA NEED ABOUT A GALLON OF COFFEE FIRST, THOUGH...

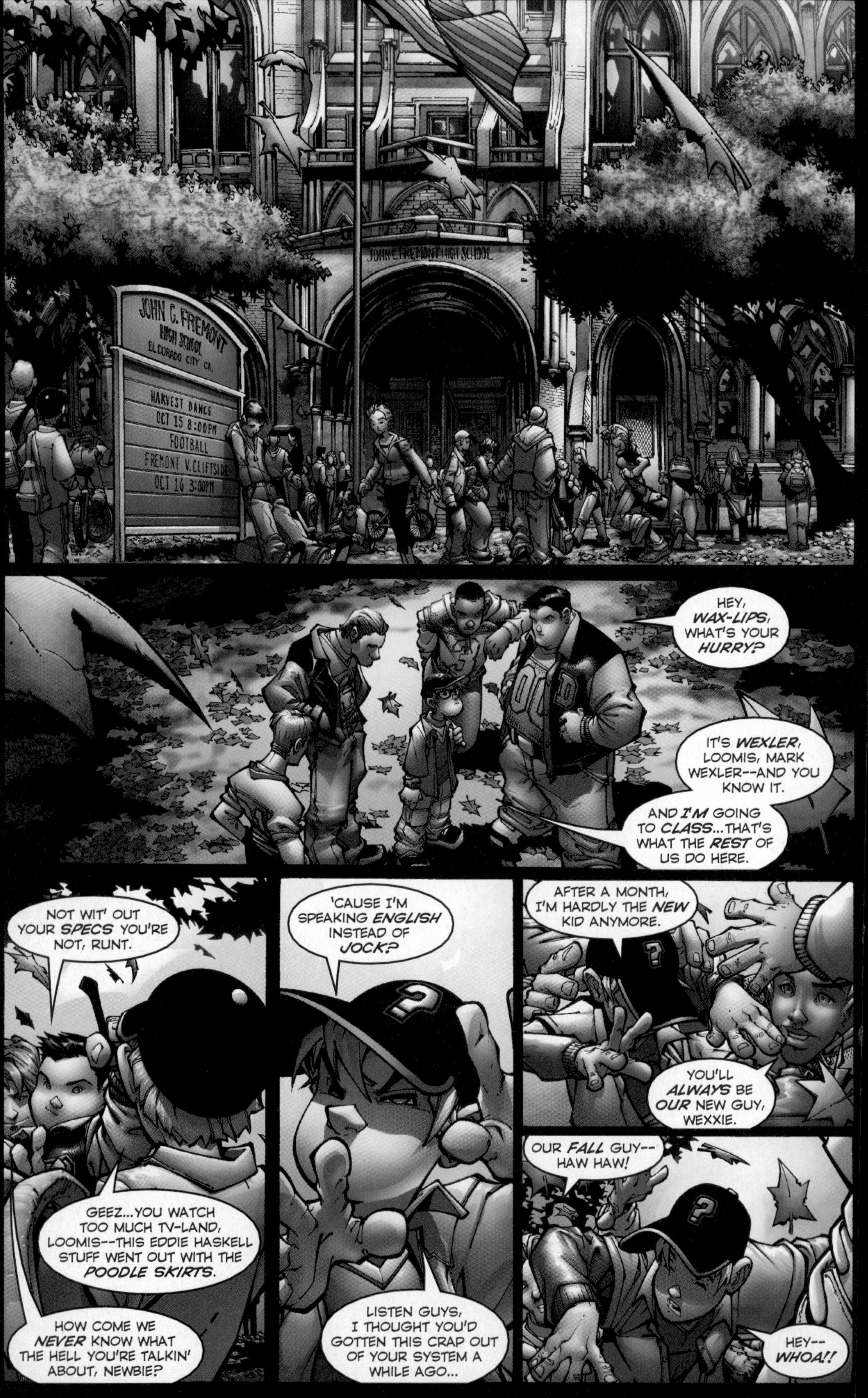
JOHN C. FREMONT HIGH SCHOOL
JOHN C. FREMONT HIGH SCHOOL EL DORADO CITY CA.
HARVEST DANCE OCT 15 8:00PM
FOOTBALL FREMONT V. CLIFFSIDE OCT 16 3:00PM
HEY, WAX-LIPS, WHAT'S YOUR HURRY?
IT'S WEXLER, LOOMIS, MARK WEXLER--AND YOU KNOW IT.
AND I'M GOING TO CLASS...THAT'S WHAT THE REST OF US DO HERE.
NOT WIT' OUT YOUR SPECS YOU'RE NOT, RUNT.
GEEZ...YOU WATCH TOO MUCH TV-LAND, LOOMIS--THIS EDDIE HASKELL STUFF WENT OUT WITH THE POODLE SKIRTS.
HOW COME WE NEVER KNOW WHAT THE HELL YOU'RE TALKIN' ABOUT, NEWBIE?
'CAUSE I'M SPEAKING ENGLISH INSTEAD OF JOCK?
LISTEN GUYS, I THOUGHT YOU'D GOTTEN THIS CRAP OUT OF YOUR SYSTEM A WHILE AGO...
AFTER A MONTH, I'M HARDLY THE NEW KID ANYMORE.
YOU'LL ALWAYS BE OUR NEW GUY, WEXXIE.
OUR FALL GUY--HAW HAW!
HEY--WHOA!!

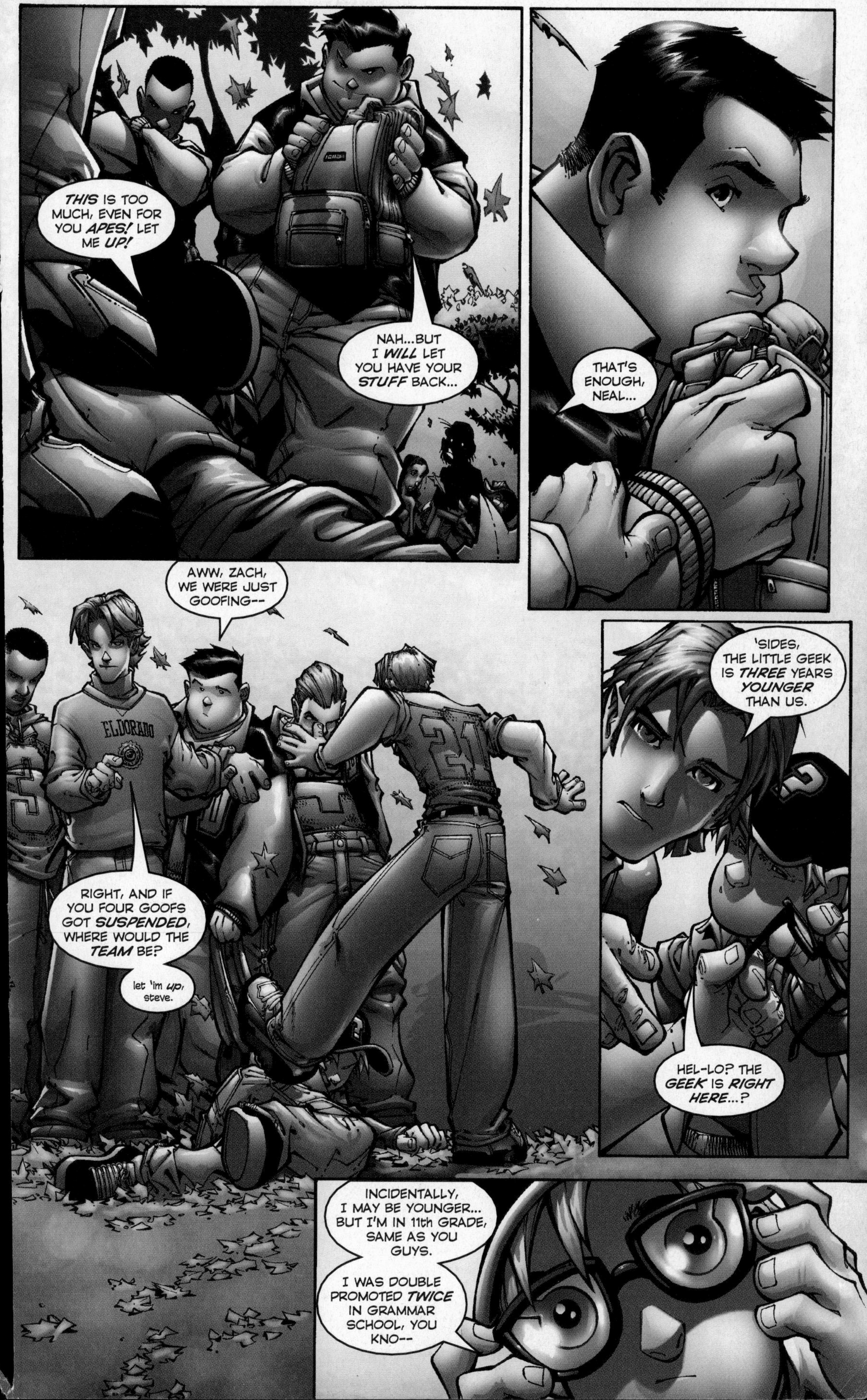
THIS IS TOO MUCH, EVEN FOR YOU APES! LET ME UP!
NAH...BUT I WILL LET YOU HAVE YOUR STUFF BACK...
THAT'S ENOUGH, NEAL...
AWW, ZACH, WE WERE JUST GOOFING--
RIGHT, AND IF YOU FOUR GOOFS GOT SUSPENDED, WHERE WOULD THE TEAM BE?
let 'im up, steve.
ELDORADO
'SIDES, THE LITTLE GEEK IS THREE YEARS YOUNGER THAN US.
HEL-LO? THE GEEK IS RIGHT HERE...?
INCIDENTALLY, I MAY BE YOUNGER... BUT I'M IN 11th GRADE, SAME AS YOU GUYS.
I WAS DOUBLE PROMOTED TWICE IN GRAMMAR SCHOOL, YOU KNO--

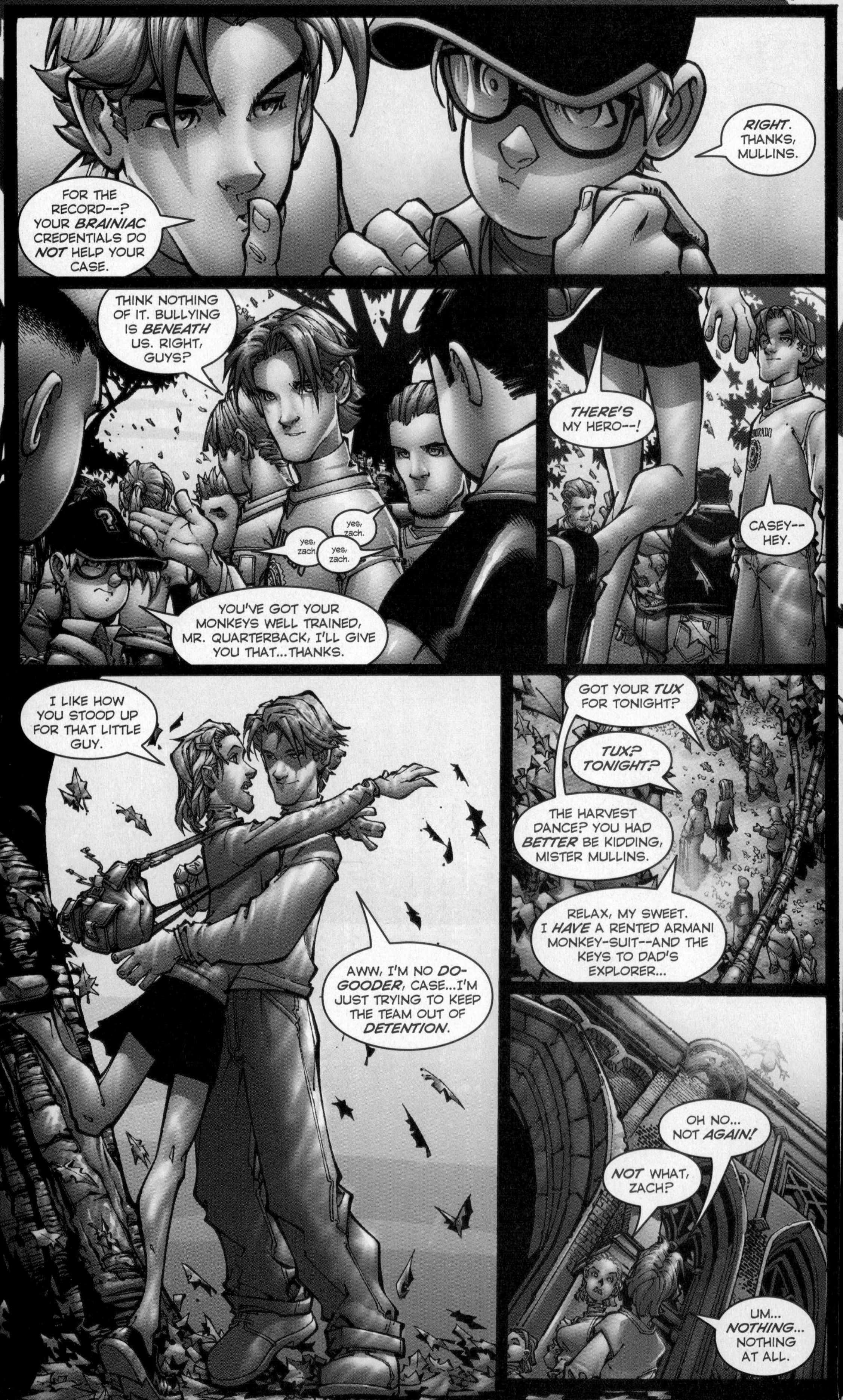
FOR THE RECORD--? YOUR BRAINIAC CREDENTIALS DO NOT HELP YOUR CASE.
RIGHT. THANKS, MULLINS.
THINK NOTHING OF IT. BULLYING IS BENEATH US. RIGHT, GUYS?
yes, zach.
yes, zach.
yes, zach.
YOU'VE GOT YOUR MONKEYS WELL TRAINED, MR. QUARTERBACK, I'LL GIVE YOU THAT...THANKS.
THERE'S MY HERO--!
CASEY-- HEY.
I LIKE HOW YOU STOOD UP FOR THAT LITTLE GUY.
AWW, I'M NO DO-GOODER, CASE...I'M JUST TRYING TO KEEP THE TEAM OUT OF DETENTION.
GOT YOUR TUX FOR TONIGHT?
TUX? TONIGHT?
THE HARVEST DANCE? YOU HAD BETTER BE KIDDING, MISTER MULLINS.
RELAX, MY SWEET. I HAVE A RENTED ARMANI MONKEY-SUIT--AND THE KEYS TO DAD'S EXPLORER...
OH NO... NOT AGAIN!
NOT WHAT, ZACH?
UM... NOTHING... NOTHING AT ALL.

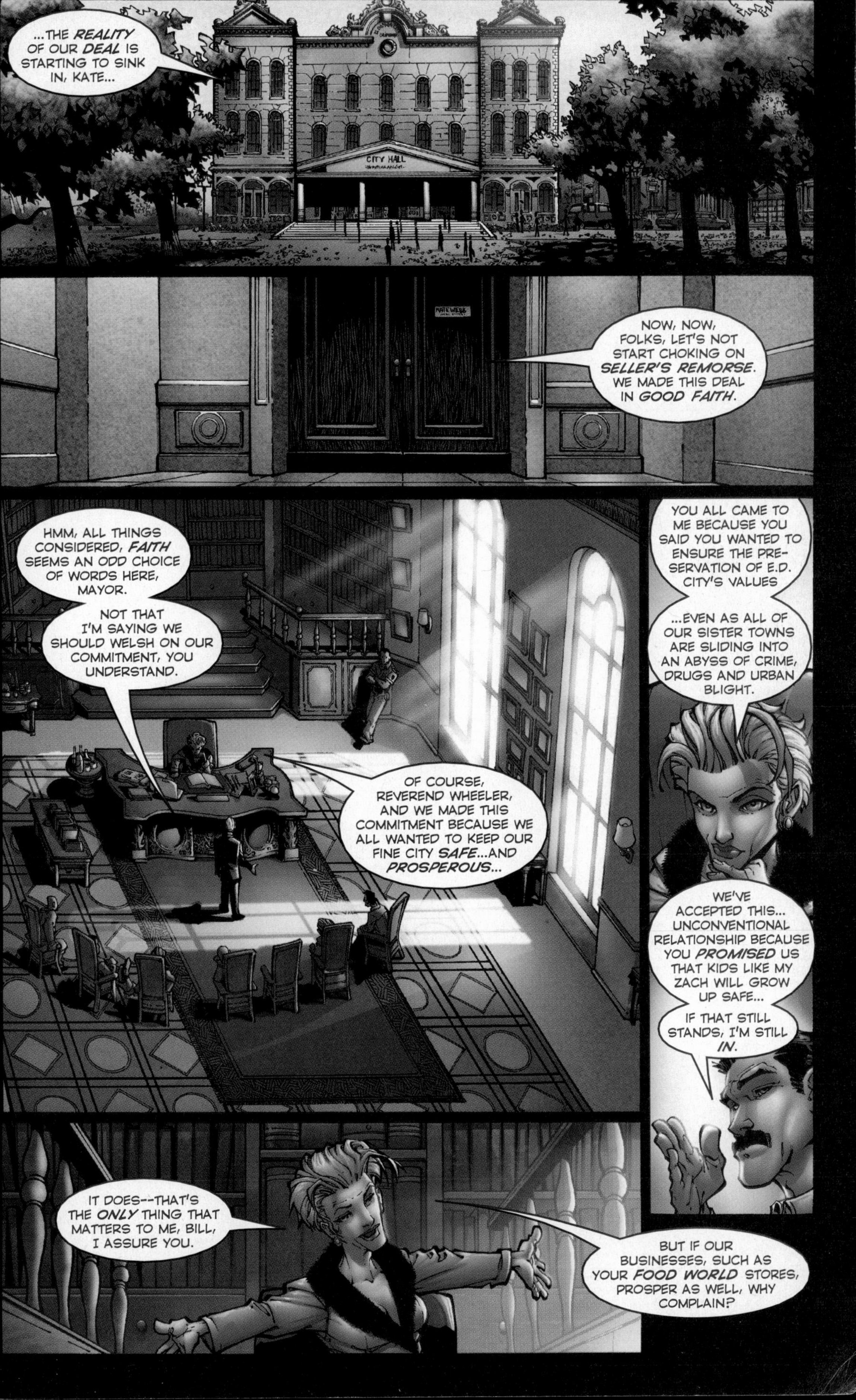
...THE REALITY OF OUR DEAL IS STARTING TO SINK IN, KATE...
CITY HALL
NOW, NOW, FOLKS, LET'S NOT START CHOKING ON SELLER'S REMORSE. WE MADE THIS DEAL IN GOOD FAITH.
HMM, ALL THINGS CONSIDERED, FAITH SEEMS AN ODD CHOICE OF WORDS HERE, MAYOR.
NOT THAT I'M SAYING WE SHOULD WELSH ON OUR COMMITMENT, YOU UNDERSTAND.
OF COURSE, REVEREND WHEELER, AND WE MADE THIS COMMITMENT BECAUSE WE ALL WANTED TO KEEP OUR FINE CITY SAFE...AND PROSPEROUS...
YOU ALL CAME TO ME BECAUSE YOU SAID YOU WANTED TO ENSURE THE PRESERVATION OF E.D. CITY'S VALUES
...EVEN AS ALL OF OUR SISTER TOWNS ARE SLIDING INTO AN ABYSS OF CRIME, DRUGS AND URBAN BLIGHT.
WE'VE ACCEPTED THIS... UNCONVENTIONAL RELATIONSHIP BECAUSE YOU PROMISED US THAT KIDS LIKE MY ZACH WILL GROW UP SAFE...
IF THAT STILL STANDS, I'M STILL IN.
IT DOES--THAT'S THE ONLY THING THAT MATTERS TO ME, BILL, I ASSURE YOU.
BUT IF OUR BUSINESSES, SUCH AS YOUR FOOD WORLD STORES, PROSPER AS WELL, WHY COMPLAIN?

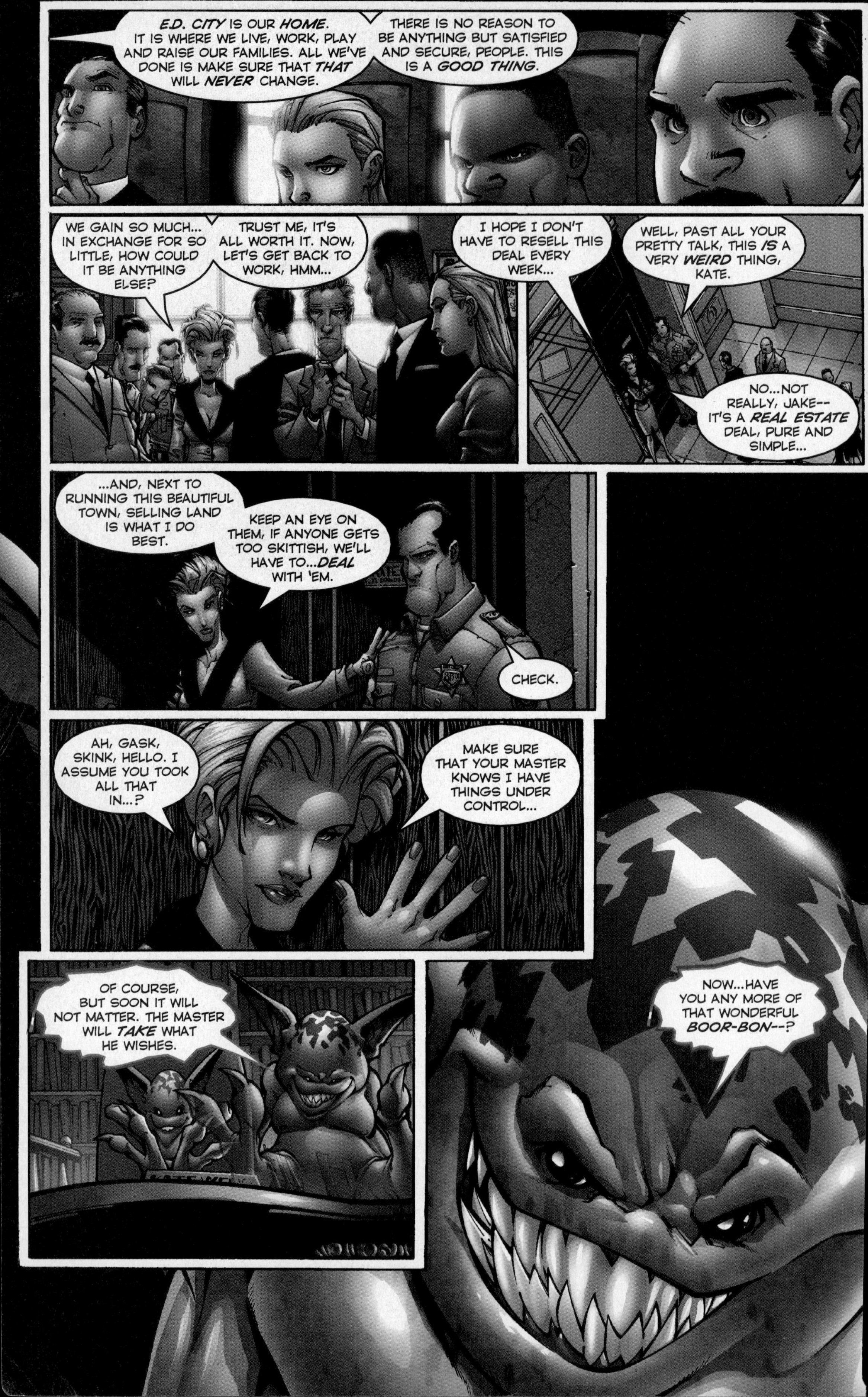
E.D. CITY IS OUR HOME. IT IS WHERE WE LIVE, WORK, PLAY AND RAISE OUR FAMILIES. ALL WE'VE DONE IS MAKE SURE THAT THAT WILL NEVER CHANGE.
THERE IS NO REASON TO BE ANYTHING BUT SATISFIED AND SECURE, PEOPLE. THIS IS A GOOD THING.
WE GAIN SO MUCH... IN EXCHANGE FOR SO LITTLE, HOW COULD IT BE ANYTHING ELSE?
TRUST ME, IT'S ALL WORTH IT. NOW, LET'S GET BACK TO WORK, HMM...
I HOPE I DON'T HAVE TO RESELL THIS DEAL EVERY WEEK...
WELL, PAST ALL YOUR PRETTY TALK, THIS IS A VERY WEIRD THING, KATE.
NO...NOT REALLY, JAKE-- IT'S A REAL ESTATE DEAL, PURE AND SIMPLE...
...AND, NEXT TO RUNNING THIS BEAUTIFUL TOWN, SELLING LAND IS WHAT I DO BEST.
KEEP AN EYE ON THEM, IF ANYONE GETS TOO SKITTISH, WE'LL HAVE TO...DEAL WITH 'EM.
CHECK.
AH, GASK, SKINK, HELLO. I ASSUME YOU TOOK ALL THAT IN...?
MAKE SURE THAT YOUR MASTER KNOWS I HAVE THINGS UNDER CONTROL...
OF COURSE, BUT SOON IT WILL NOT MATTER. THE MASTER WILL TAKE WHAT HE WISHES.
NOW...HAVE YOU ANY MORE OF THAT WONDERFUL BOOR-BON--?

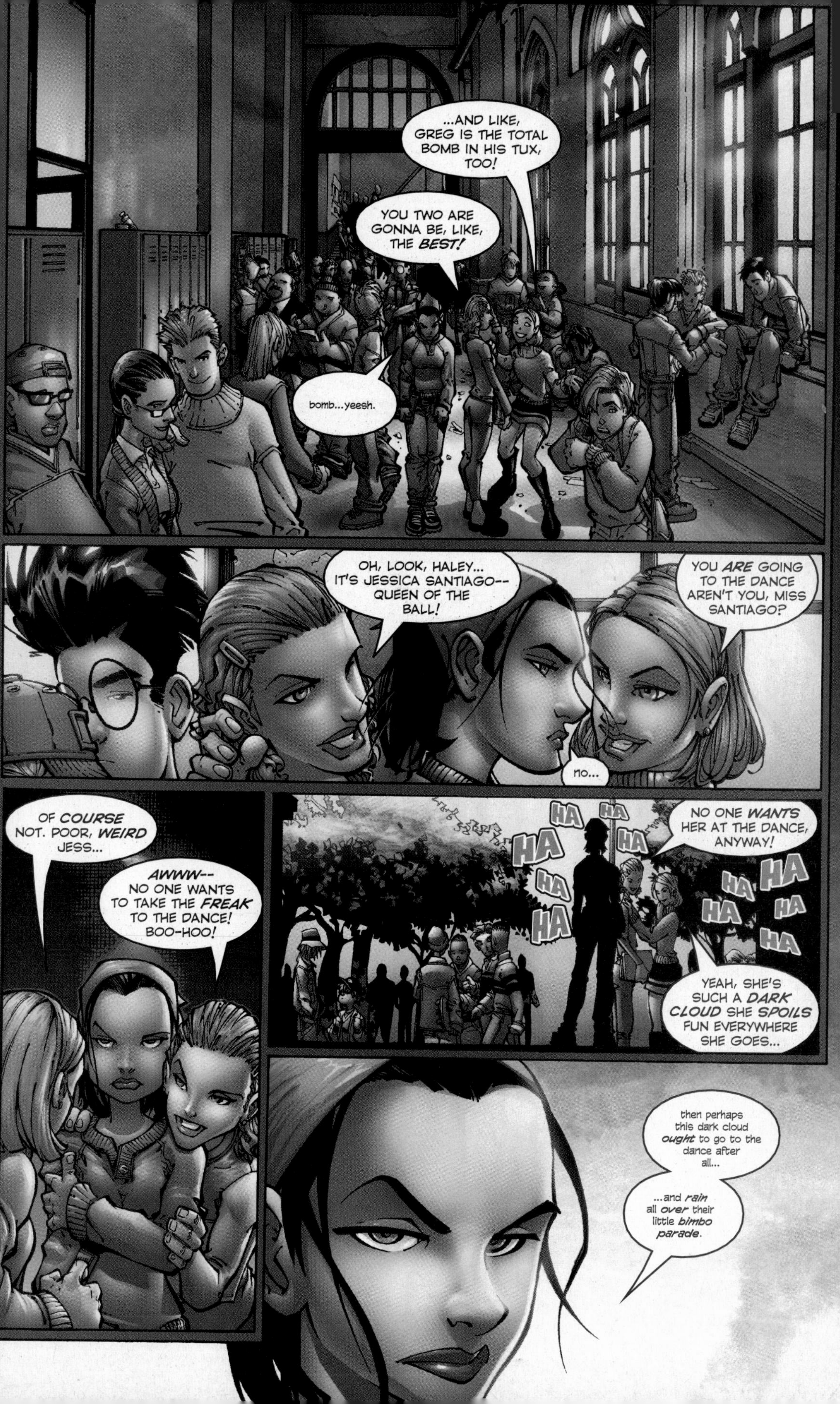

...AND LIKE, GREG IS THE TOTAL BOMB IN HIS TUX, TOO!
YOU TWO ARE GONNA BE, LIKE, THE BEST!
bomb...yeesh.
OH, LOOK, HALEY... IT'S JESSICA SANTIAGO-- QUEEN OF THE BALL!
YOU ARE GOING TO THE DANCE AREN'T YOU, MISS SANTIAGO?
no...
OF COURSE NOT. POOR, WEIRD JESS...
AWWW-- NO ONE WANTS TO TAKE THE FREAK TO THE DANCE! BOO-HOO!
HA HA HA HA HA HA
NO ONE WANTS HER AT THE DANCE, ANYWAY!
HA HA HA HA HA HA
YEAH, SHE'S SUCH A DARK CLOUD SHE SPOILS FUN EVERYWHERE SHE GOES...
then perhaps this dark cloud ought to go to the dance after all...
...and rain all over their little bimbo parade.

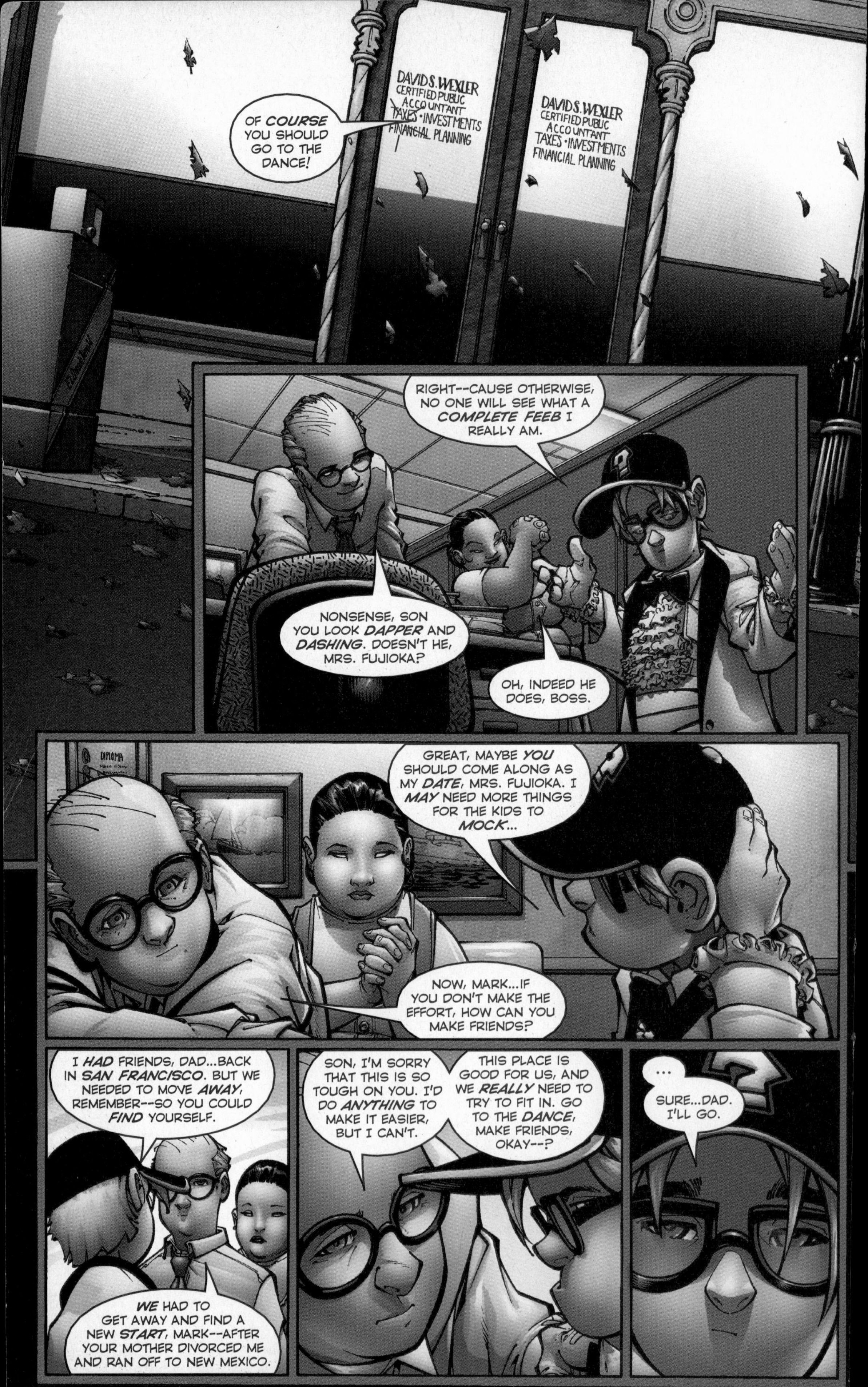
DAVID S. WEXLER CERTIFIED PUBLIC ACCOUNTANT TAXES • INVESTMENTS FINANCIAL PLANNING
DAVID S. WEXLER CERTIFIED PUBLIC ACCOUNTANT TAXES • INVESTMENTS FINANCIAL PLANNING
OF COURSE YOU SHOULD GO TO THE DANCE!
RIGHT--CAUSE OTHERWISE, NO ONE WILL SEE WHAT A COMPLETE FEEB I REALLY AM.
NONSENSE, SON YOU LOOK DAPPER AND DASHING. DOESN'T HE, MRS. FUJIOKA?
OH, INDEED HE DOES, BOSS.
DIPLOMA
GREAT, MAYBE YOU SHOULD COME ALONG AS MY DATE, MRS. FUJIOKA. I MAY NEED MORE THINGS FOR THE KIDS TO MOCK...
NOW, MARK...IF YOU DON'T MAKE THE EFFORT, HOW CAN YOU MAKE FRIENDS?
I HAD FRIENDS, DAD...BACK IN SAN FRANCISCO. BUT WE NEEDED TO MOVE AWAY, REMEMBER--SO YOU COULD FIND YOURSELF.
WE HAD TO GET AWAY AND FIND A NEW START, MARK--AFTER YOUR MOTHER DIVORCED ME AND RAN OFF TO NEW MEXICO.
SON, I'M SORRY THAT THIS IS SO TOUGH ON YOU. I'D DO ANYTHING TO MAKE IT EASIER, BUT I CAN'T.
THIS PLACE IS GOOD FOR US, AND WE REALLY NEED TO TRY TO FIT IN. GO TO THE DANCE, MAKE FRIENDS, OKAY--?
...
SURE...DAD. I'LL GO.

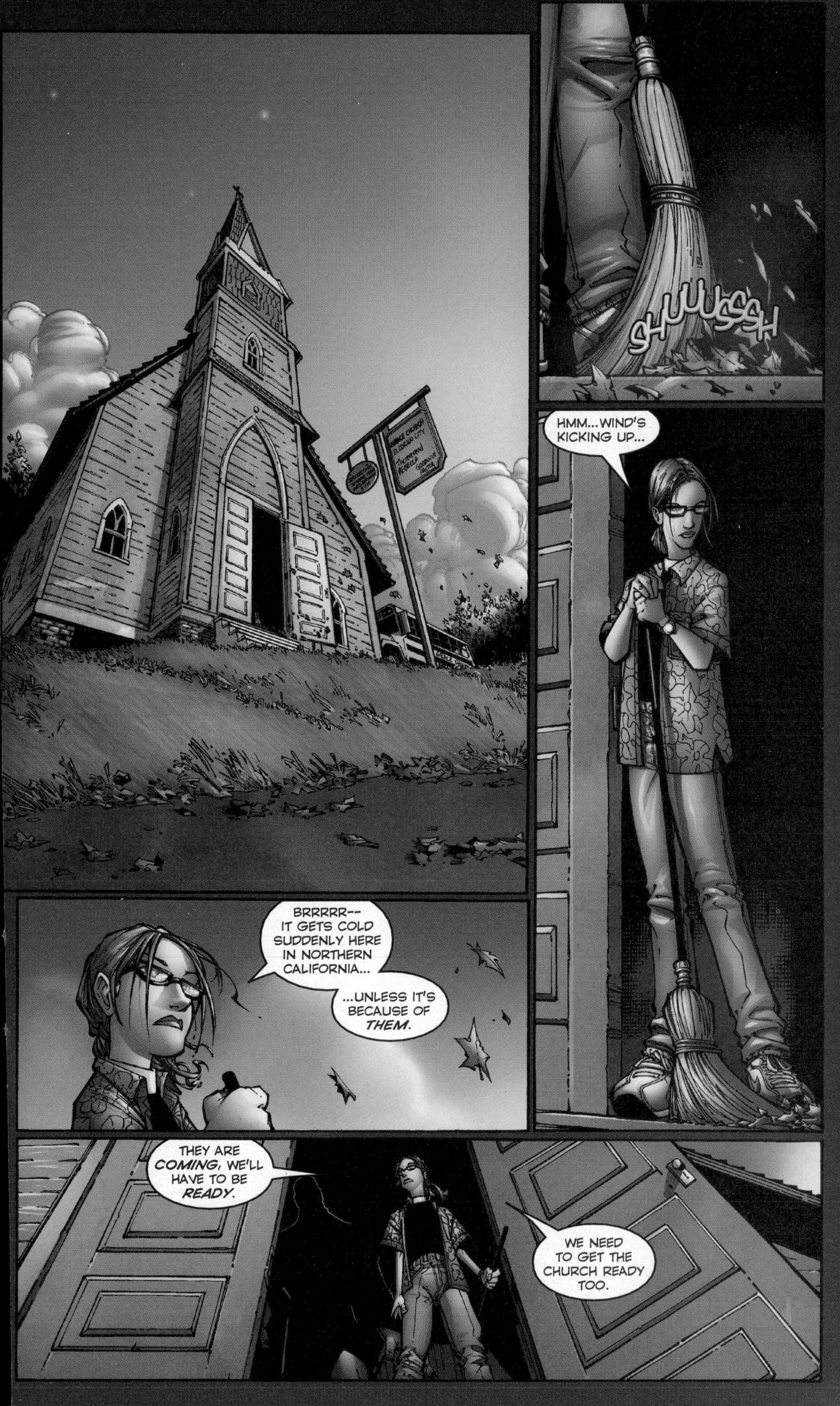
SHUUUSSSH
HMM...WIND'S KICKING UP...
BRRRRR-- IT GETS COLD SUDDENLY HERE IN NORTHERN CALIFORNIA...
...UNLESS IT'S BECAUSE OF THEM.
THEY ARE COMING, WE'LL HAVE TO BE READY.
WE NEED TO GET THE CHURCH READY TOO.

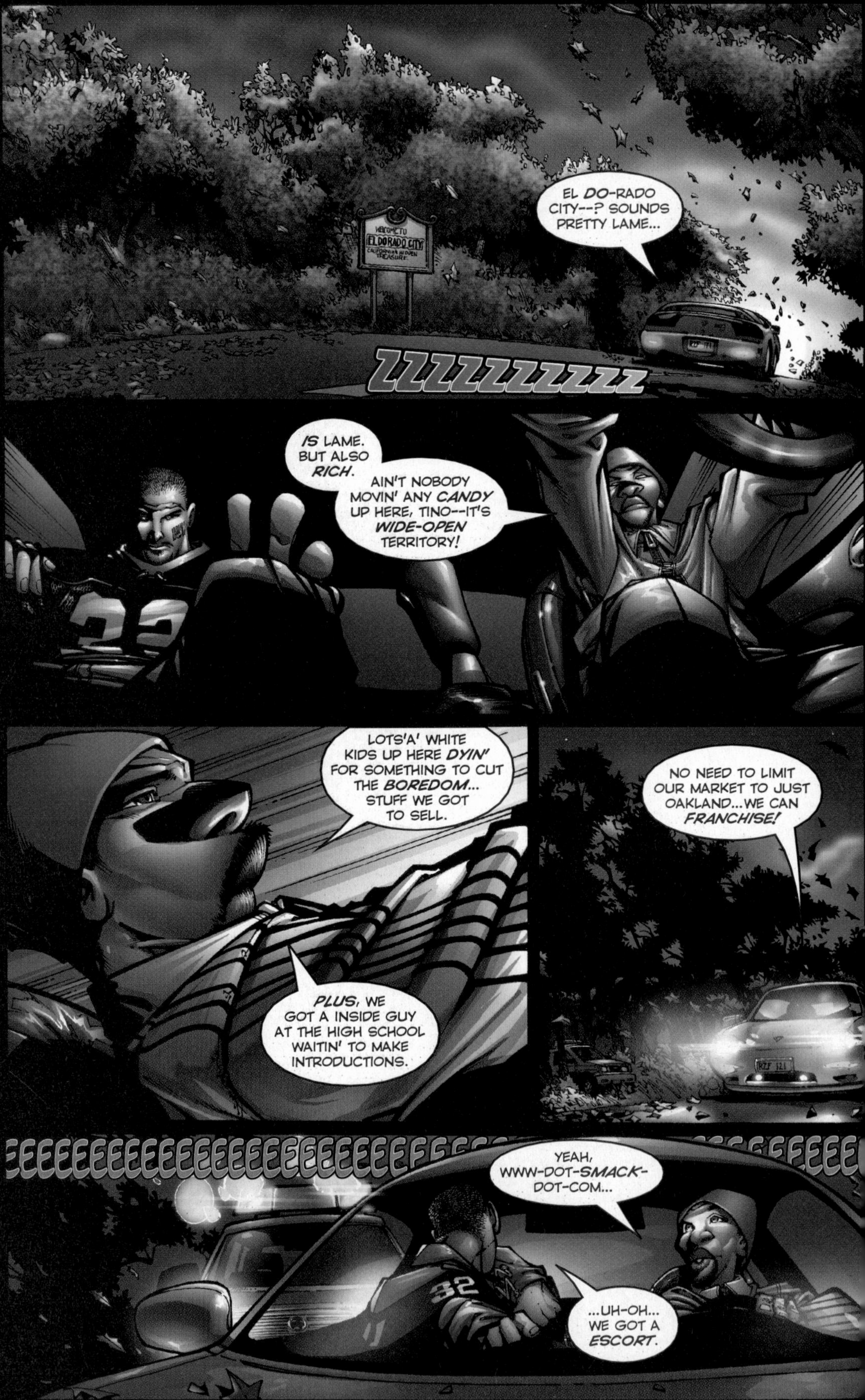
WELCOME TO
EL DORADO CITY
CALIFORNIA'S HIDDEN TREASURE
EL DO-RADO CITY--? SOUNDS PRETTY LAME...
ZZZZZZZZZZZZ
IS LAME. BUT ALSO RICH.
AIN'T NOBODY MOVIN' ANY CANDY UP HERE, TINO--IT'S WIDE-OPEN TERRITORY!
LOTS'A' WHITE KIDS UP HERE DYIN' FOR SOMETHING TO CUT THE BOREDOM... STUFF WE GOT TO SELL.
PLUS, WE GOT A INSIDE GUY AT THE HIGH SCHOOL WAITIN' TO MAKE INTRODUCTIONS.
NO NEED TO LIMIT OUR MARKET TO JUST OAKLAND...WE CAN FRANCHISE!
EEEEEEEEEEEEEEEEEEEEEEEEEEEEEEE
YEAH, WWW-DOT-SMACK-DOT-COM...
...UH-OH... WE GOT A ESCORT.

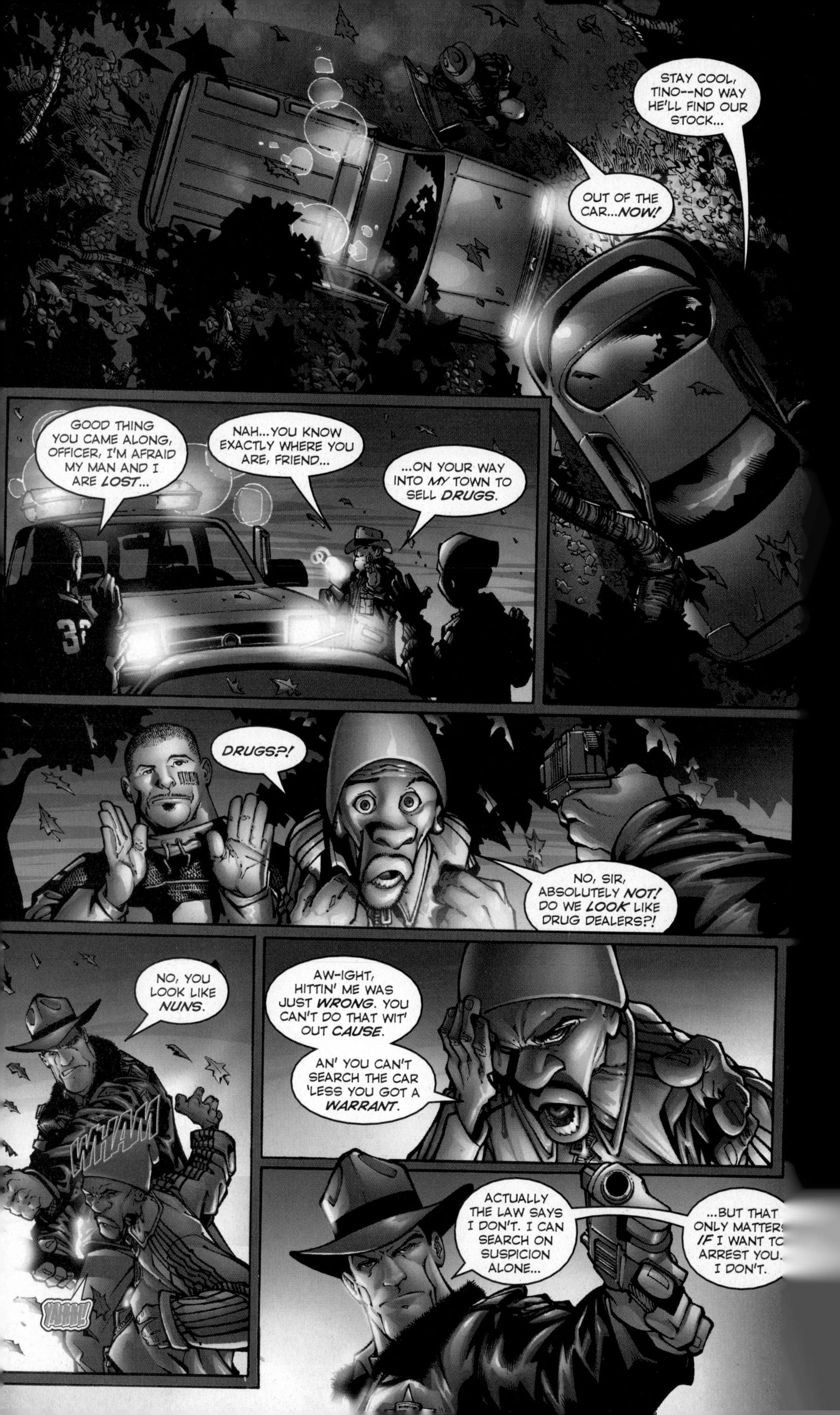
STAY COOL, TINO--NO WAY HE'LL FIND OUR STOCK...
OUT OF THE CAR...NOW!
GOOD THING YOU CAME ALONG, OFFICER, I'M AFRAID MY MAN AND I ARE LOST...
NAH...YOU KNOW EXACTLY WHERE YOU ARE, FRIEND...
...ON YOUR WAY INTO MY TOWN TO SELL DRUGS.
DRUGS?!
NO, SIR, ABSOLUTELY NOT! DO WE LOOK LIKE DRUG DEALERS?!
NO, YOU LOOK LIKE NUNS.
WHAM
YAHHH!
AW-IGHT, HITTIN' ME WAS JUST WRONG. YOU CAN'T DO THAT WIT' OUT CAUSE.
AN' YOU CAN'T SEARCH THE CAR 'LESS YOU GOT A WARRANT.
ACTUALLY THE LAW SAYS I DON'T. I CAN SEARCH ON SUSPICION ALONE...
...BUT THAT ONLY MATTERS IF I WANT TO ARREST YOU. I DON'T.

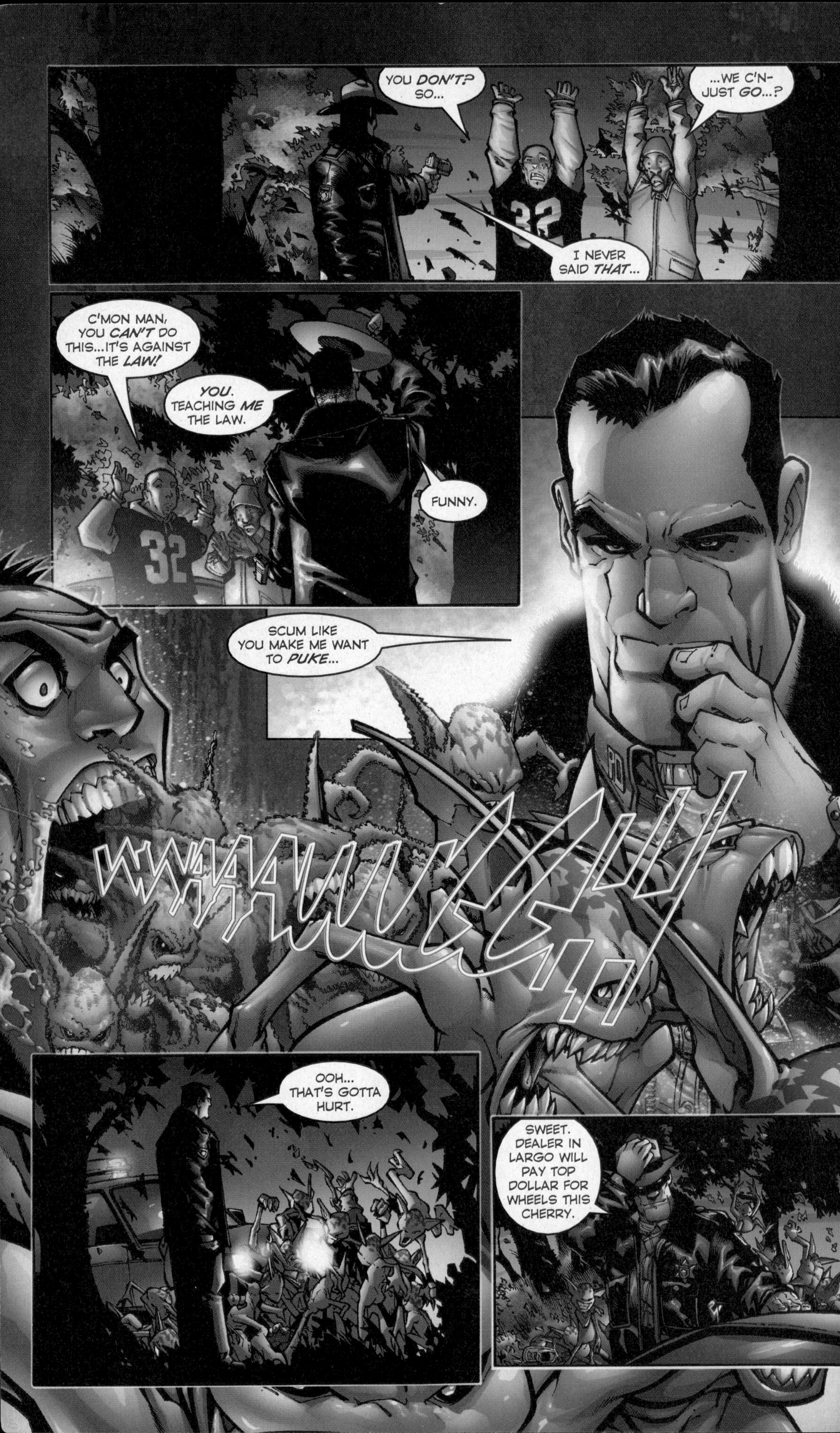
YOU DON'T? SO...
...WE C'N- JUST GO...?
I NEVER SAID THAT...
C'MON MAN, YOU CAN'T DO THIS...IT'S AGAINST THE LAW!
YOU. TEACHING ME THE LAW.
FUNNY.
SCUM LIKE YOU MAKE ME WANT TO PUKE...
WWAAUUUGGHH
OOH... THAT'S GOTTA HURT.
SWEET. DEALER IN LARGO WILL PAY TOP DOLLAR FOR WHEELS THIS CHERRY.

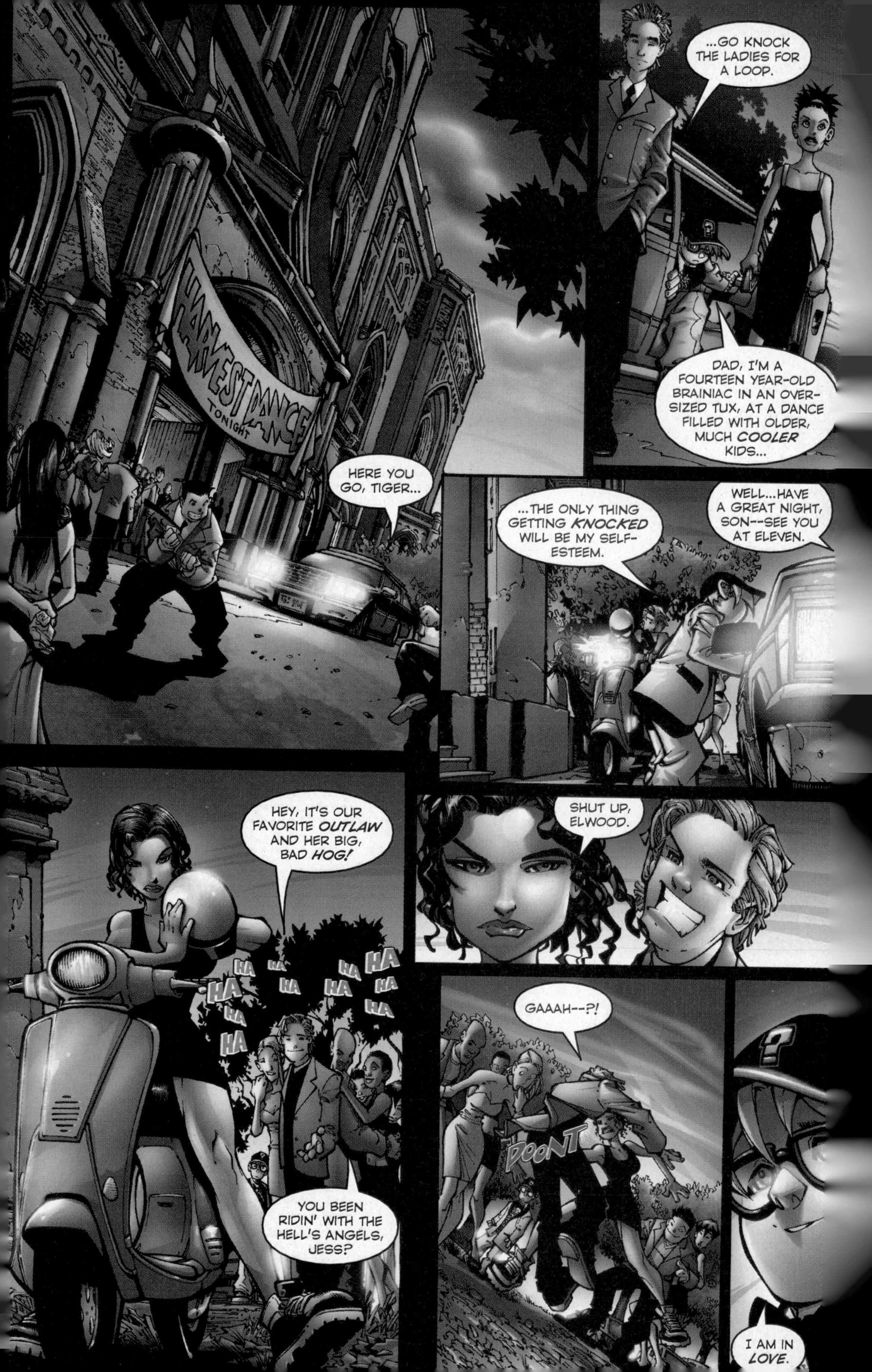

HARVEST DANCE TONIGHT
HERE YOU GO, TIGER...
...GO KNOCK THE LADIES FOR A LOOP.
DAD, I'M A FOURTEEN YEAR-OLD BRAINIAC IN AN OVER-SIZED TUX, AT A DANCE FILLED WITH OLDER, MUCH COOLER KIDS...
...THE ONLY THING GETTING KNOCKED WILL BE MY SELF-ESTEEM.
WELL...HAVE A GREAT NIGHT, SON--SEE YOU AT ELEVEN.
HEY, IT'S OUR FAVORITE OUTLAW AND HER BIG, BAD HOG!
HA HA HA HA HA HA HA HA HA HA HA HA
YOU BEEN RIDIN' WITH THE HELL'S ANGELS, JESS?
SHUT UP, ELWOOD.
GAAAH--?!
DOONT
I AM IN LOVE.

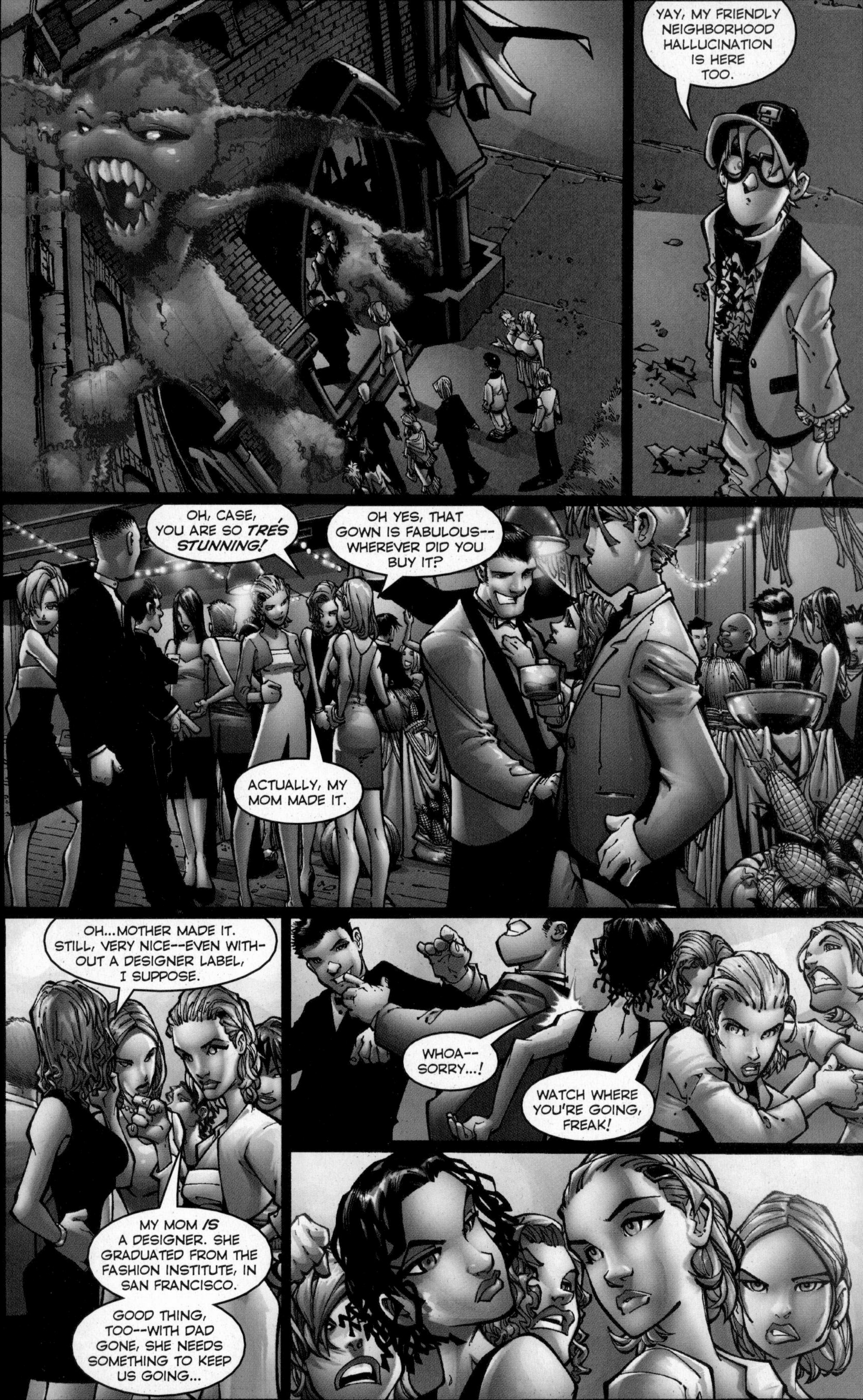
YAY, MY FRIENDLY NEIGHBORHOOD HALLUCINATION IS HERE TOO.
OH, CASE, YOU ARE SO TRÈS STUNNING!
OH YES, THAT GOWN IS FABULOUS-- WHEREVER DID YOU BUY IT?
ACTUALLY, MY MOM MADE IT.
OH...MOTHER MADE IT. STILL, VERY NICE--EVEN WITH-OUT A DESIGNER LABEL, I SUPPOSE.
MY MOM IS A DESIGNER. SHE GRADUATED FROM THE FASHION INSTITUTE, IN SAN FRANCISCO.
GOOD THING, TOO--WITH DAD GONE, SHE NEEDS SOMETHING TO KEEP US GOING...
WHOA-- SORRY...!
WATCH WHERE YOU'RE GOING, FREAK!

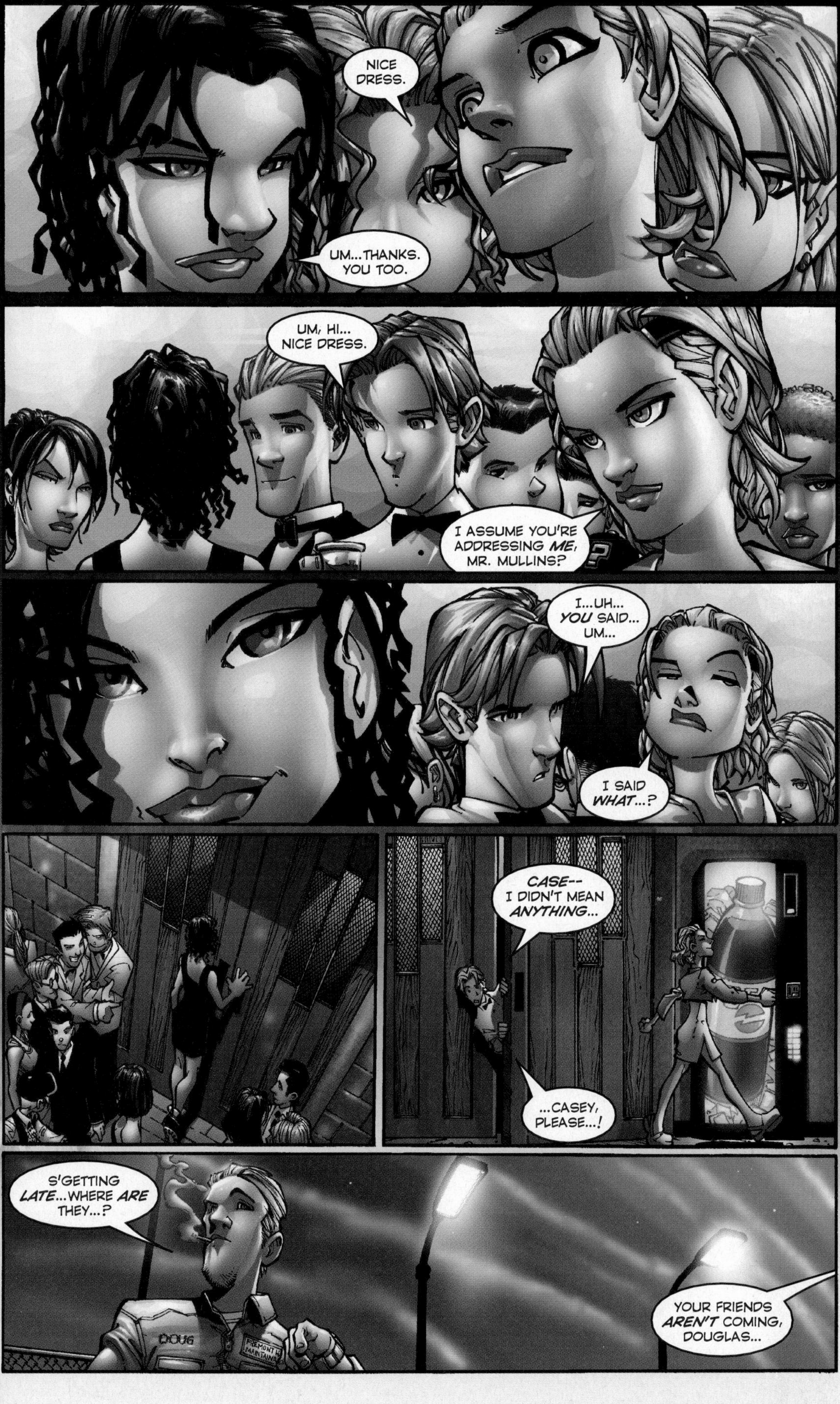
NICE DRESS.
UM...THANKS. YOU TOO.
UM, HI... NICE DRESS.
I ASSUME YOU'RE ADDRESSING *ME*, MR. MULLINS?
I...UH... *YOU* SAID... UM...
I SAID *WHAT*...?
CASE-- I DIDN'T MEAN *ANYTHING*...
...CASEY, PLEASE...!
S'GETTING *LATE*...WHERE *ARE* THEY...?
YOUR FRIENDS *AREN'T* COMING, DOUGLAS...

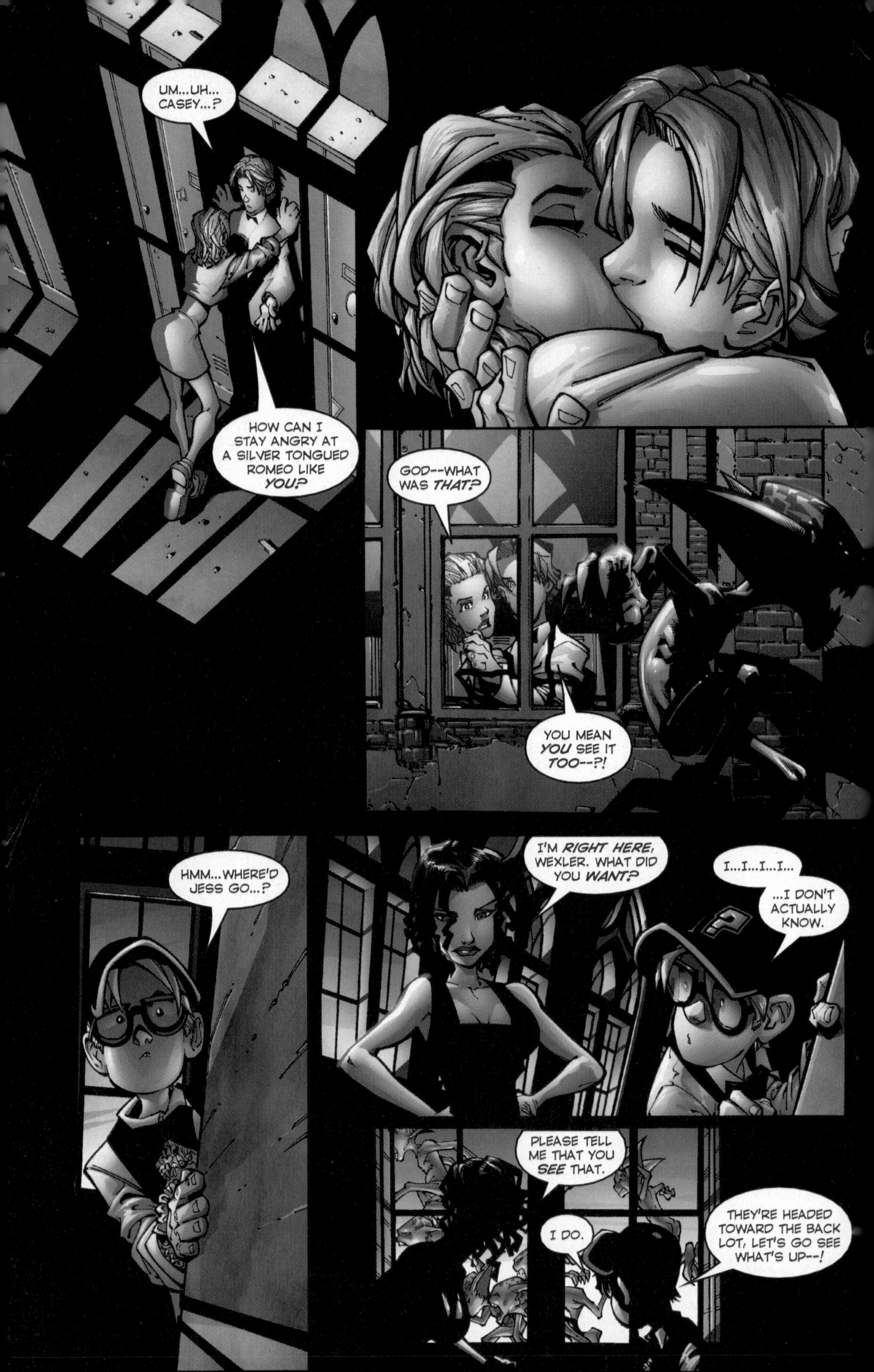
UM...UH... CASEY...?
HOW CAN I STAY ANGRY AT A SILVER TONGUED ROMEO LIKE YOU?
GOD--WHAT WAS THAT?
YOU MEAN YOU SEE IT TOO--?!
HMM...WHERE'D JESS GO...?
I'M RIGHT HERE, WEXLER. WHAT DID YOU WANT?
I...I...I...I...
...I DON'T ACTUALLY KNOW.
PLEASE TELL ME THAT YOU SEE THAT.
I DO.
THEY'RE HEADED TOWARD THE BACK LOT, LET'S GO SEE WHAT'S UP--!

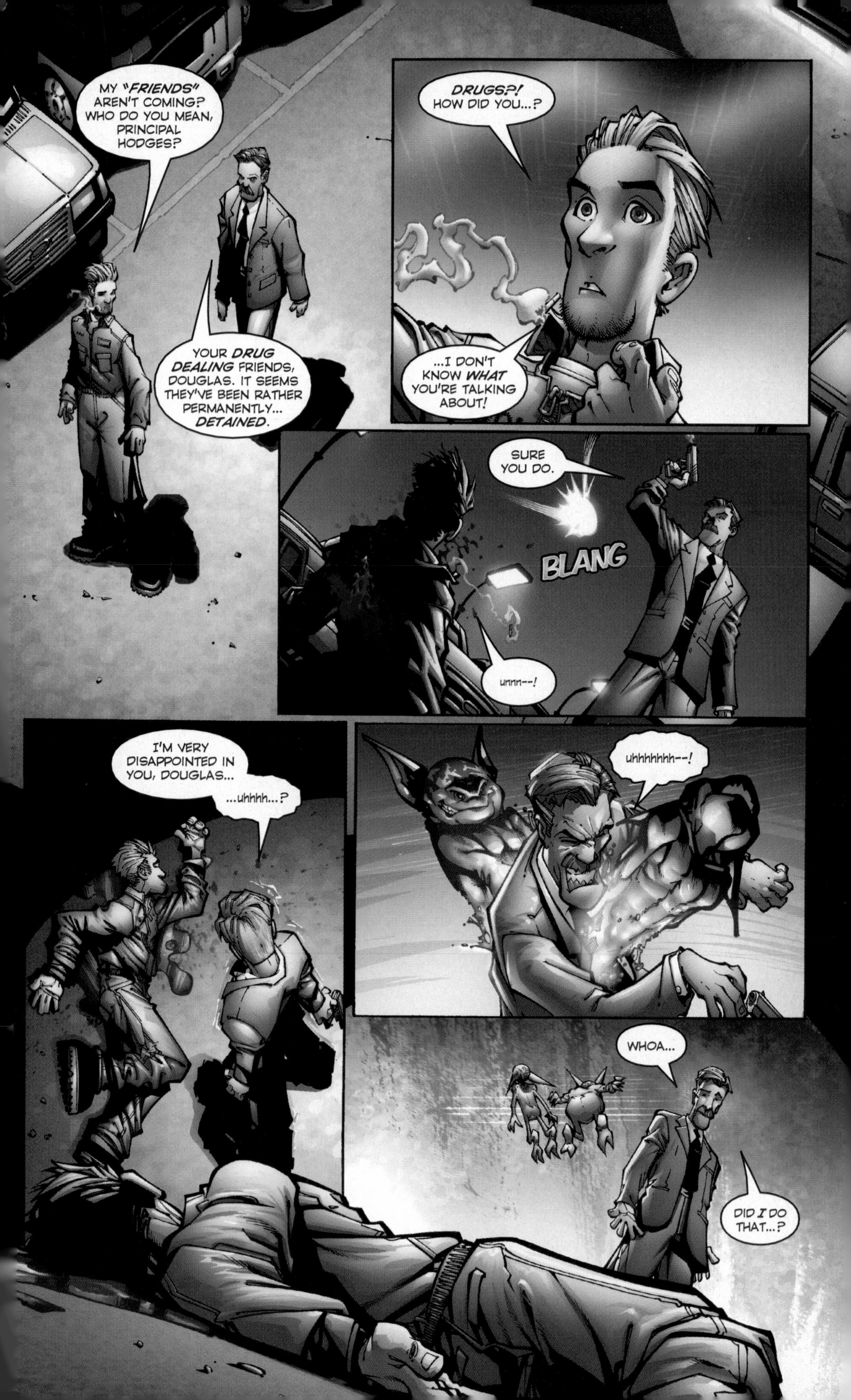
MY "FRIENDS" AREN'T COMING? WHO DO YOU MEAN, PRINCIPAL HODGES?
YOUR DRUG DEALING FRIENDS, DOUGLAS. IT SEEMS THEY'VE BEEN RATHER PERMANENTLY... DETAINED.
DRUGS?! HOW DID YOU...?
...I DON'T KNOW WHAT YOU'RE TALKING ABOUT!
SURE YOU DO.
BLANG
unnn--!
I'M VERY DISAPPOINTED IN YOU, DOUGLAS...
...uhhhh...?
uhhhhhhh--!
WHOA...
DID I DO THAT...?

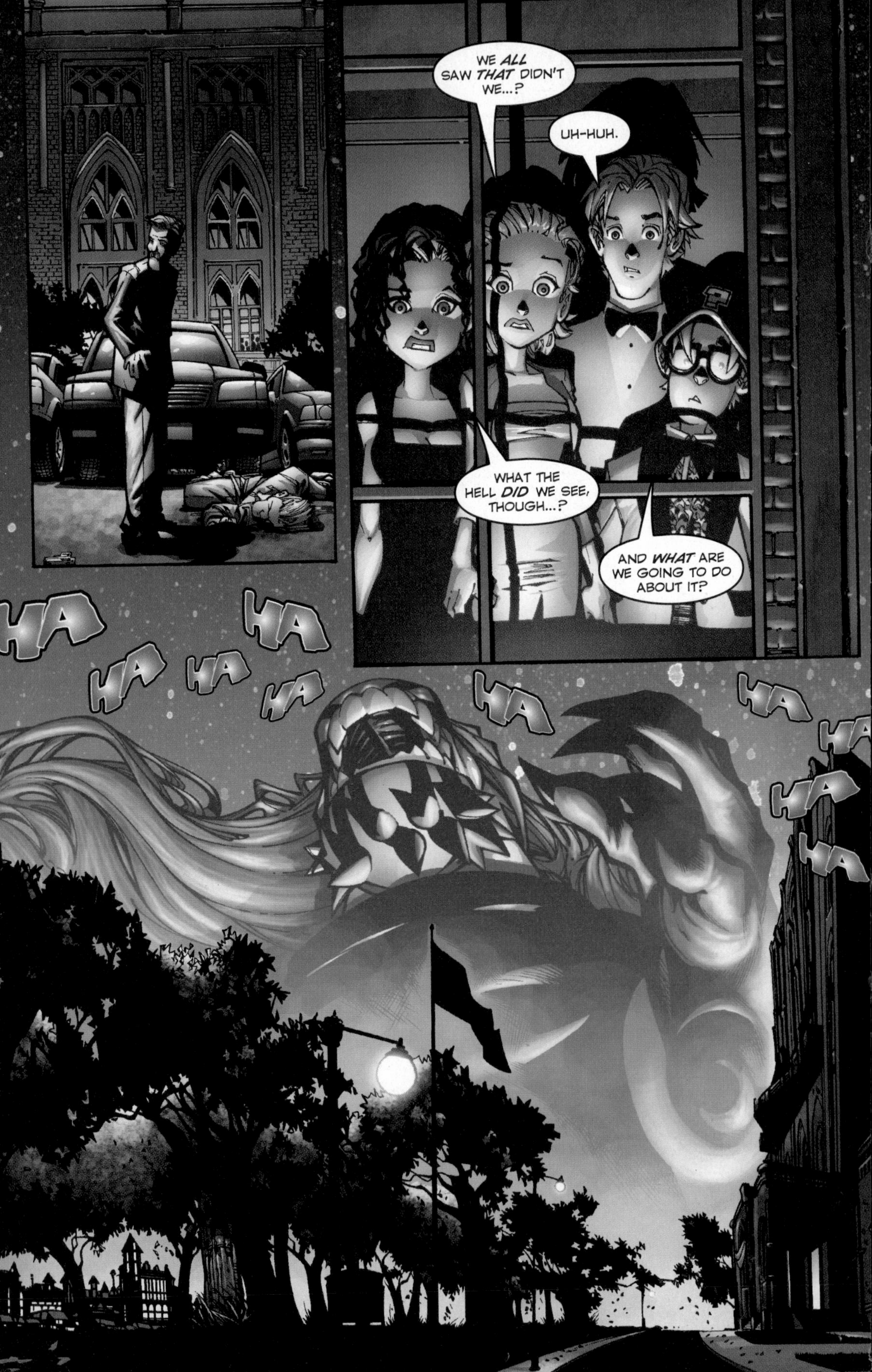
WE ALL SAW THAT DIDN'T WE...?
UH-HUH.
WHAT THE HELL DID WE SEE, THOUGH...?
AND WHAT ARE WE GOING TO DO ABOUT IT?
HA HA HA HA HA HA HA HA HA HA

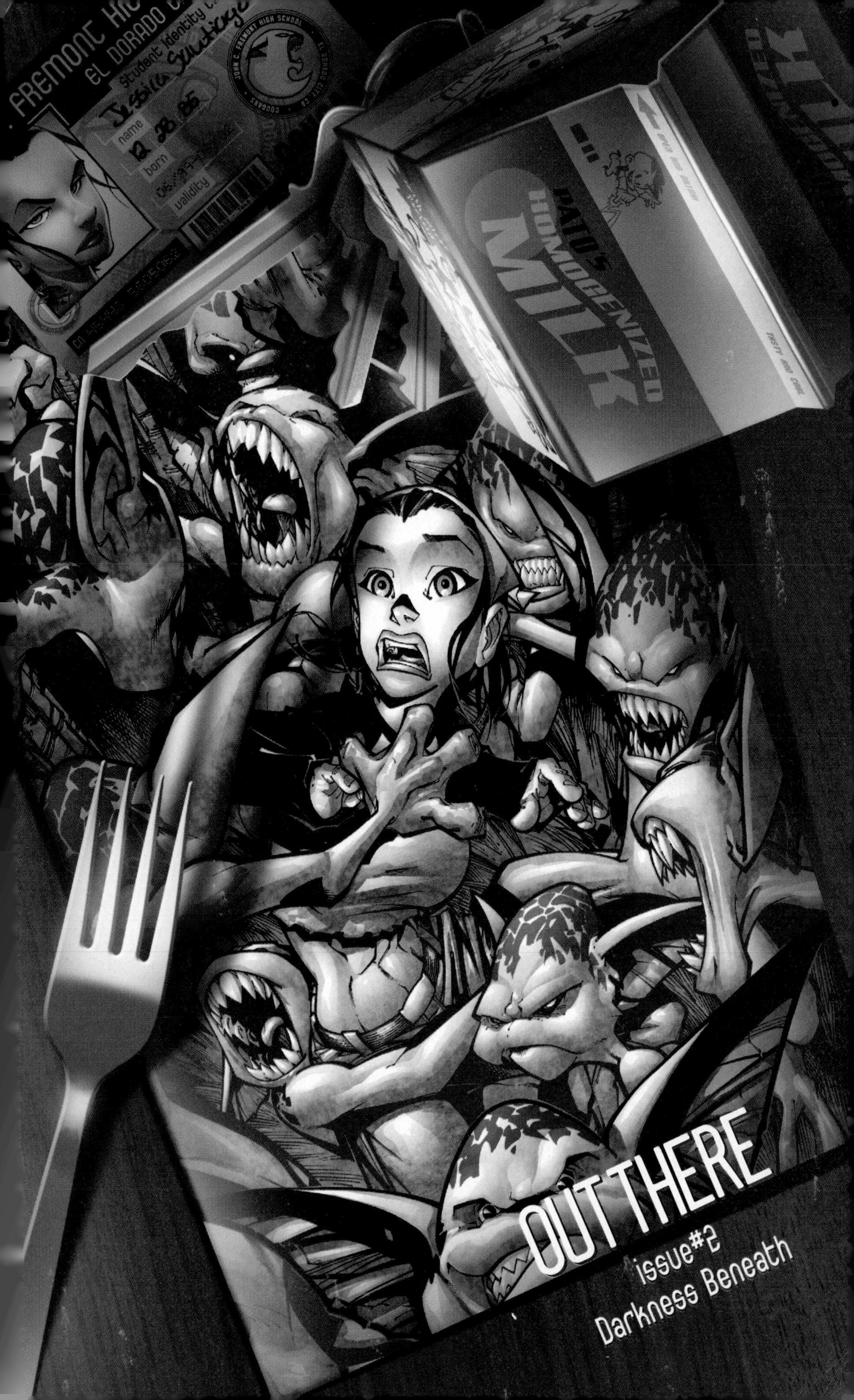
OUT THERE
issue#2
Darkness Beneath

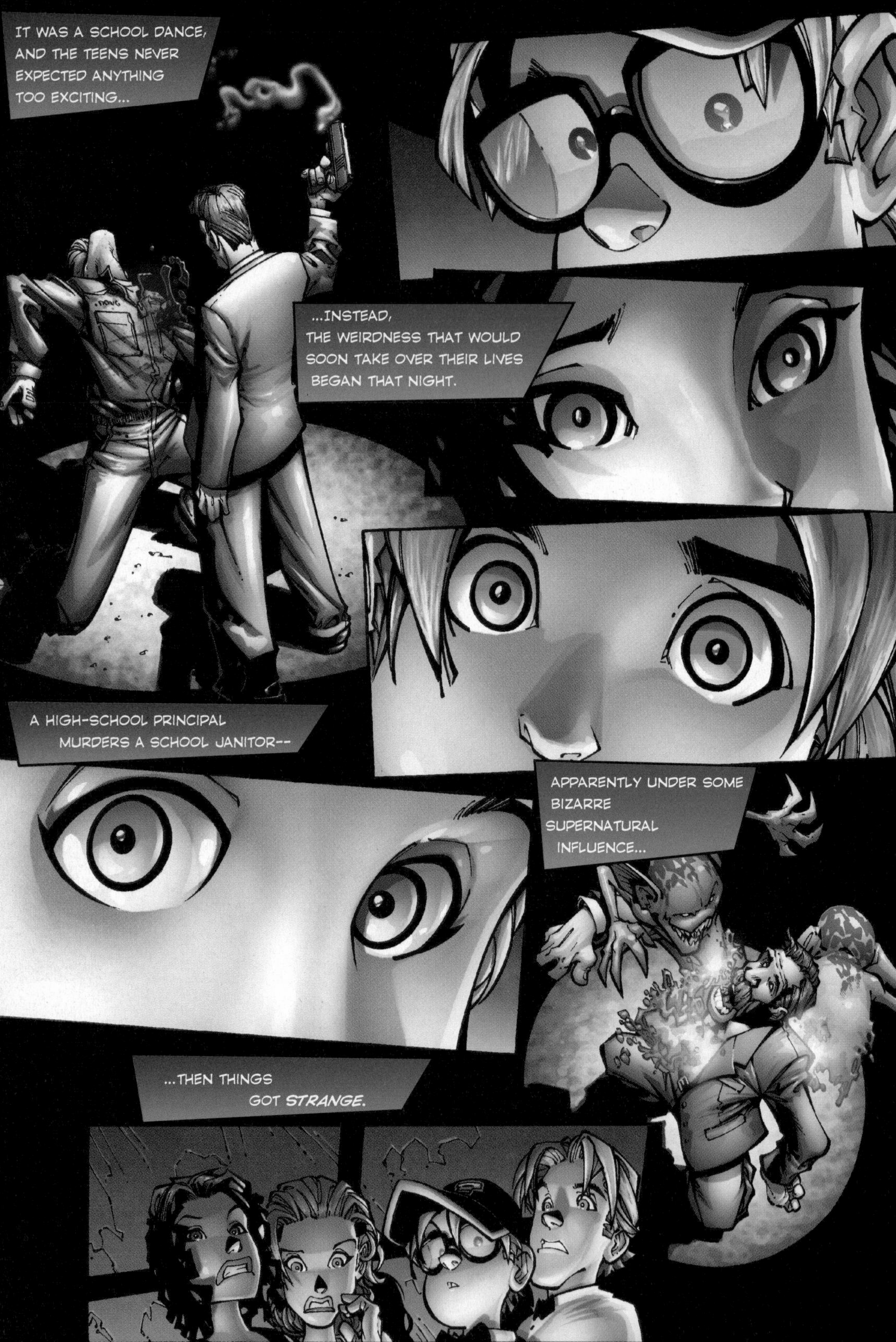
IT WAS A SCHOOL DANCE, AND THE TEENS NEVER EXPECTED ANYTHING TOO EXCITING...
...INSTEAD, THE WEIRDNESS THAT WOULD SOON TAKE OVER THEIR LIVES BEGAN THAT NIGHT.
A HIGH-SCHOOL PRINCIPAL MURDERS A SCHOOL JANITOR--
APPARENTLY UNDER SOME BIZARRE SUPERNATURAL INFLUENCE...
...THEN THINGS GOT *STRANGE*.

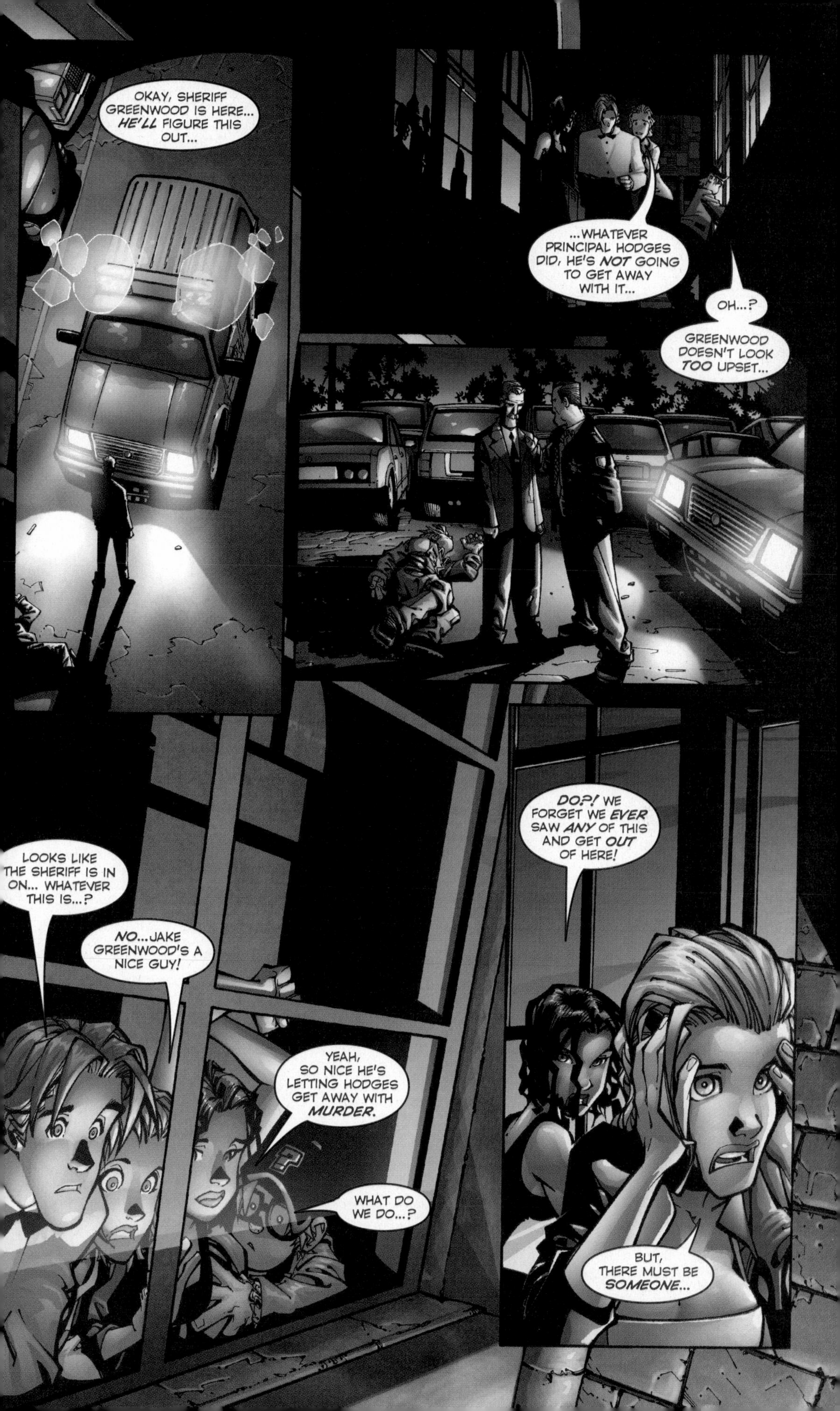
OKAY, SHERIFF GREENWOOD IS HERE... HE'LL FIGURE THIS OUT...
...WHATEVER PRINCIPAL HODGES DID, HE'S NOT GOING TO GET AWAY WITH IT...
OH...?
GREENWOOD DOESN'T LOOK TOO UPSET...
LOOKS LIKE THE SHERIFF IS IN ON... WHATEVER THIS IS...?
NO...JAKE GREENWOOD'S A NICE GUY!
YEAH, SO NICE HE'S LETTING HODGES GET AWAY WITH MURDER.
WHAT DO WE DO...?
DO?! WE FORGET WE EVER SAW ANY OF THIS AND GET OUT OF HERE!
BUT, THERE MUST BE SOMEONE...

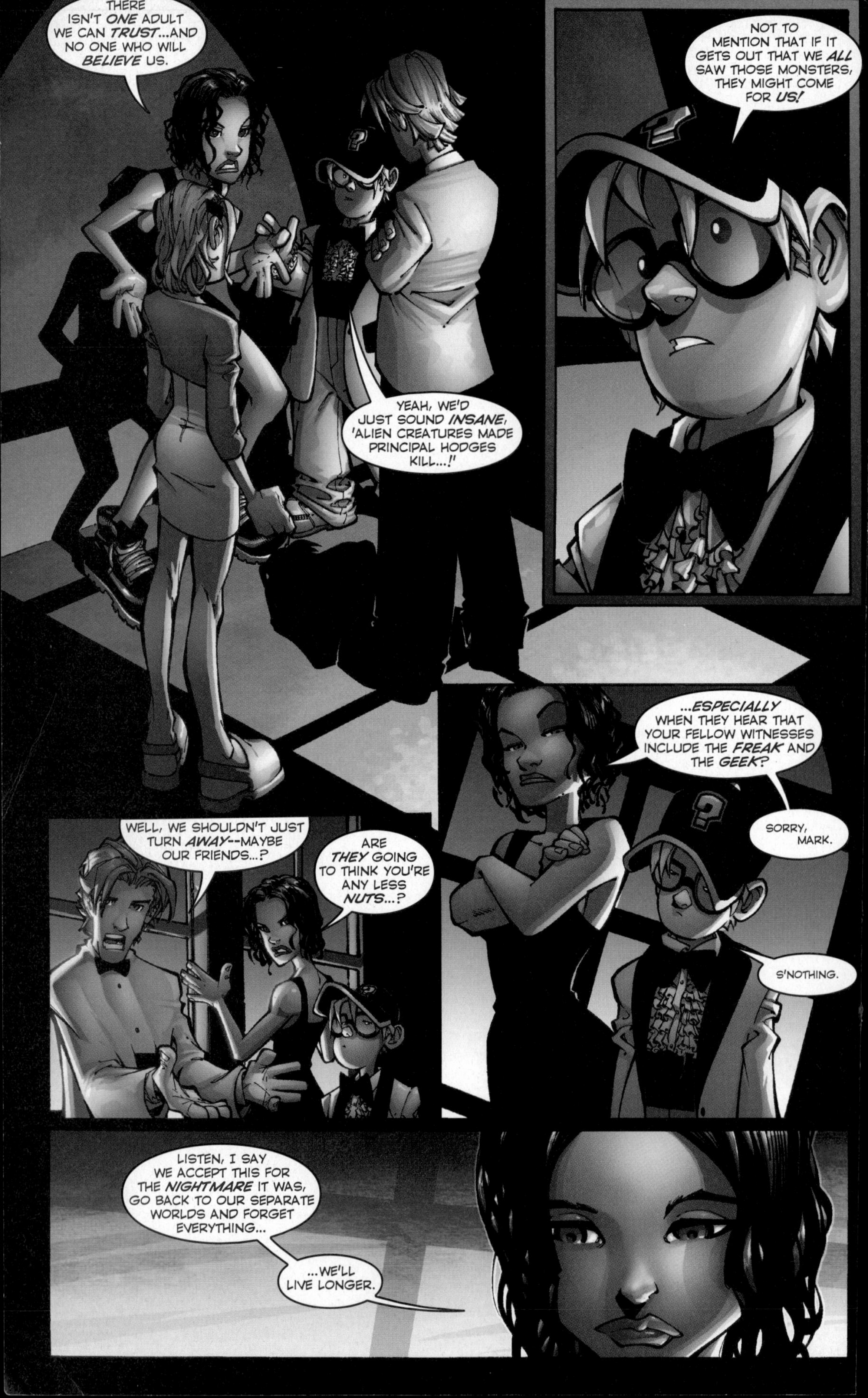
THERE ISN'T *ONE* ADULT WE CAN *TRUST*...AND NO ONE WHO WILL *BELIEVE* US.
YEAH, WE'D JUST SOUND *INSANE*, 'ALIEN CREATURES MADE PRINCIPAL HODGES KILL...!'
NOT TO MENTION THAT IF IT GETS OUT THAT WE *ALL* SAW THOSE MONSTERS, THEY MIGHT COME FOR *US!*
...*ESPECIALLY* WHEN THEY HEAR THAT YOUR FELLOW WITNESSES INCLUDE THE *FREAK* AND THE *GEEK*?
SORRY, MARK.
S'NOTHING.
WELL, WE SHOULDN'T JUST TURN *AWAY*--MAYBE OUR FRIENDS...?
ARE *THEY* GOING TO THINK YOU'RE ANY LESS *NUTS*...?
LISTEN, I SAY WE ACCEPT THIS FOR THE *NIGHTMARE* IT WAS, GO BACK TO OUR SEPARATE WORLDS AND FORGET EVERYTHING...
...WE'LL LIVE LONGER.

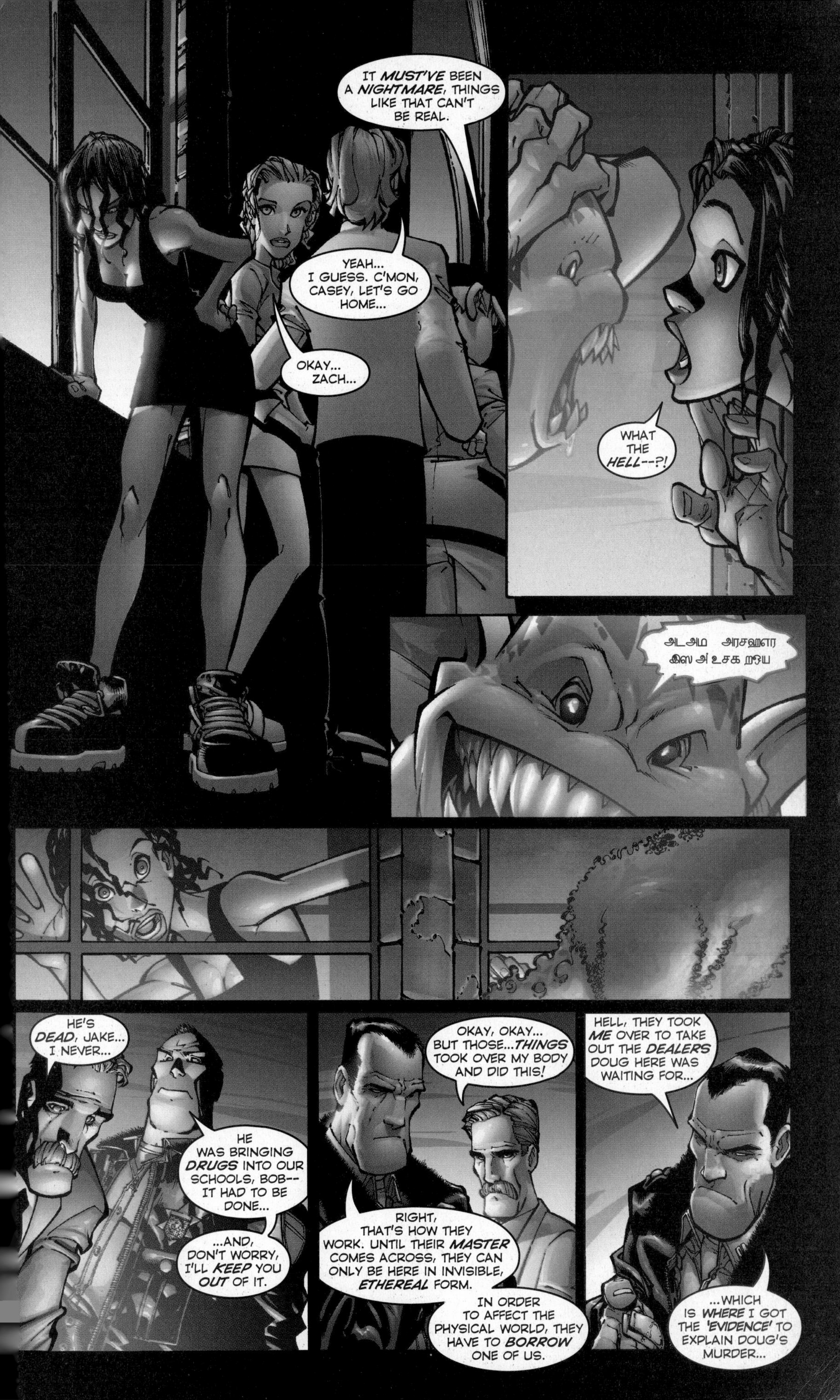
IT MUST'VE BEEN A NIGHTMARE, THINGS LIKE THAT CAN'T BE REAL.
YEAH... I GUESS. C'MON, CASEY, LET'S GO HOME...
OKAY... ZACH...
WHAT THE HELL--?!
அடஅம அரசஹுளர இஸ அ் உசக றூய
HE'S DEAD, JAKE... I NEVER...
HE WAS BRINGING DRUGS INTO OUR SCHOOLS, BOB-- IT HAD TO BE DONE...
...AND, DON'T WORRY, I'LL KEEP YOU OUT OF IT.
OKAY, OKAY... BUT THOSE...THINGS TOOK OVER MY BODY AND DID THIS!
RIGHT, THAT'S HOW THEY WORK. UNTIL THEIR MASTER COMES ACROSS, THEY CAN ONLY BE HERE IN INVISIBLE, ETHEREAL FORM.
IN ORDER TO AFFECT THE PHYSICAL WORLD, THEY HAVE TO BORROW ONE OF US.
HELL, THEY TOOK ME OVER TO TAKE OUT THE DEALERS DOUG HERE WAS WAITING FOR...
...WHICH IS WHERE I GOT THE 'EVIDENCE' TO EXPLAIN DOUG'S MURDER...

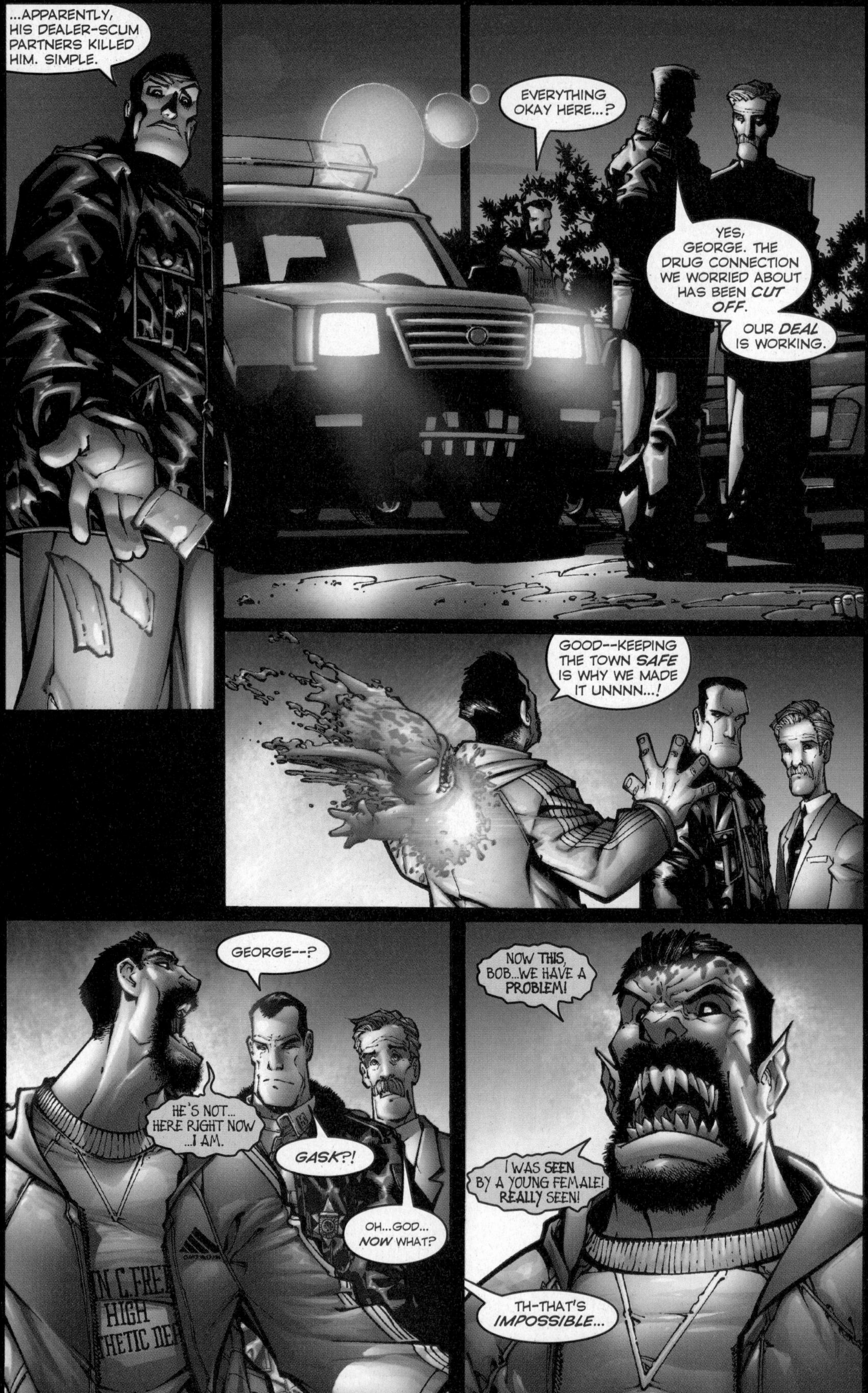

...APPARENTLY, HIS DEALER-SCUM PARTNERS KILLED HIM. SIMPLE.
EVERYTHING OKAY HERE...?
YES, GEORGE. THE DRUG CONNECTION WE WORRIED ABOUT HAS BEEN CUT OFF.
OUR DEAL IS WORKING.
GOOD--KEEPING THE TOWN SAFE IS WHY WE MADE IT UNNNN...!
GEORGE--?
HE'S NOT... HERE RIGHT NOW ...I AM.
GASK?!
OH...GOD... NOW WHAT?
NOW THIS, BOB...WE HAVE A PROBLEM!
I WAS SEEN BY A YOUNG FEMALE! REALLY SEEN!
TH-THAT'S IMPOSSIBLE...

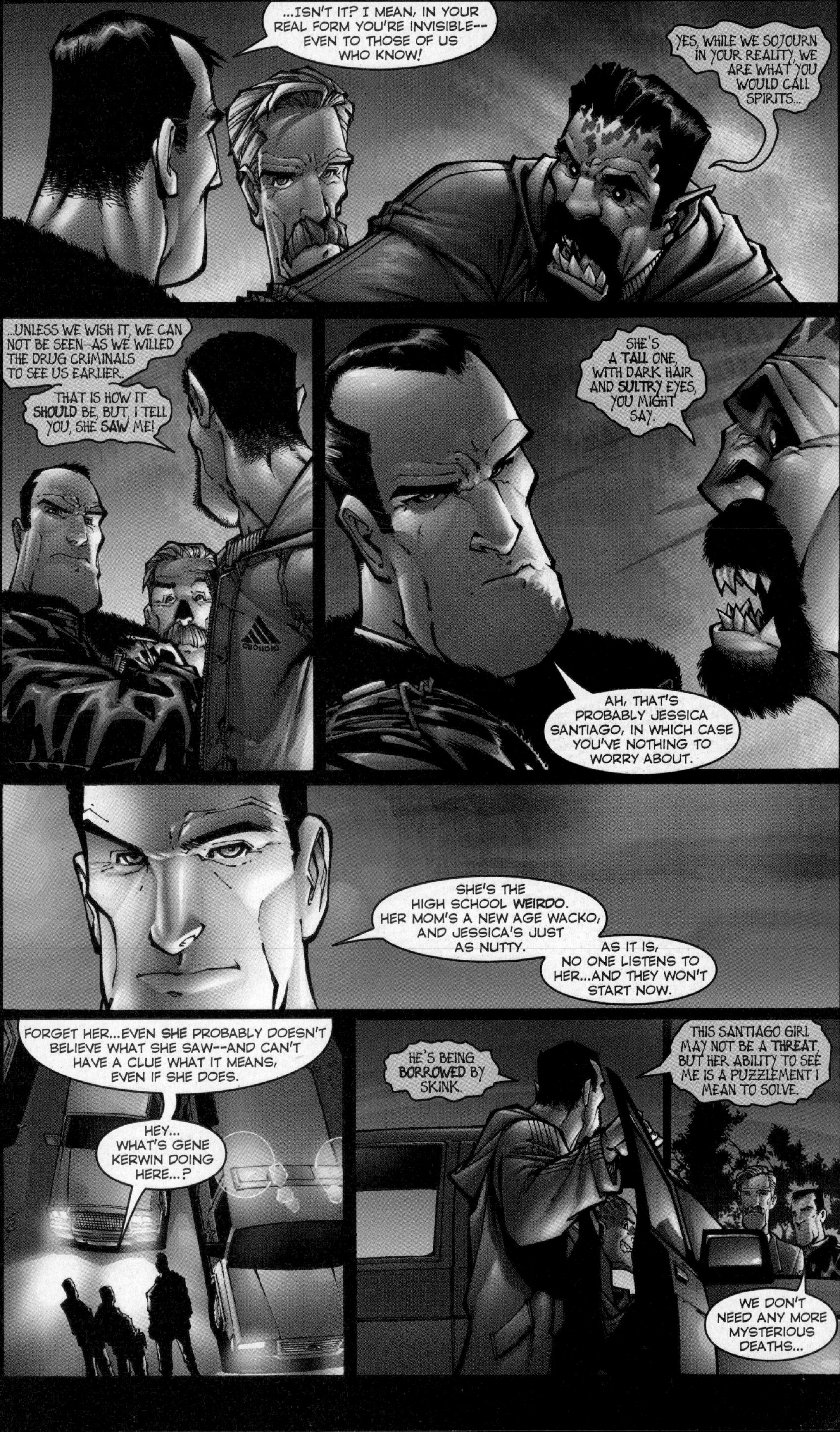
...ISN'T IT? I MEAN, IN YOUR REAL FORM YOU'RE INVISIBLE-- EVEN TO THOSE OF US WHO KNOW!
YES, WHILE WE SOJOURN IN YOUR REALITY, WE ARE WHAT YOU WOULD CALL SPIRITS...
...UNLESS WE WISH IT, WE CAN NOT BE SEEN--AS WE WILLED THE DRUG CRIMINALS TO SEE US EARLIER.
THAT IS HOW IT SHOULD BE, BUT, I TELL YOU, SHE SAW ME!
SHE'S A TALL ONE, WITH DARK HAIR AND SULTRY EYES, YOU MIGHT SAY.
AH, THAT'S PROBABLY JESSICA SANTIAGO, IN WHICH CASE YOU'VE NOTHING TO WORRY ABOUT.
SHE'S THE HIGH SCHOOL WEIRDO. HER MOM'S A NEW AGE WACKO, AND JESSICA'S JUST AS NUTTY.
AS IT IS, NO ONE LISTENS TO HER...AND THEY WON'T START NOW.
FORGET HER...EVEN SHE PROBABLY DOESN'T BELIEVE WHAT SHE SAW--AND CAN'T HAVE A CLUE WHAT IT MEANS, EVEN IF SHE DOES.
HEY... WHAT'S GENE KERWIN DOING HERE...?
HE'S BEING BORROWED BY SKINK.
THIS SANTIAGO GIRL MAY NOT BE A THREAT, BUT HER ABILITY TO SEE ME IS A PUZZLEMENT I MEAN TO SOLVE.
WE DON'T NEED ANY MORE MYSTERIOUS DEATHS...

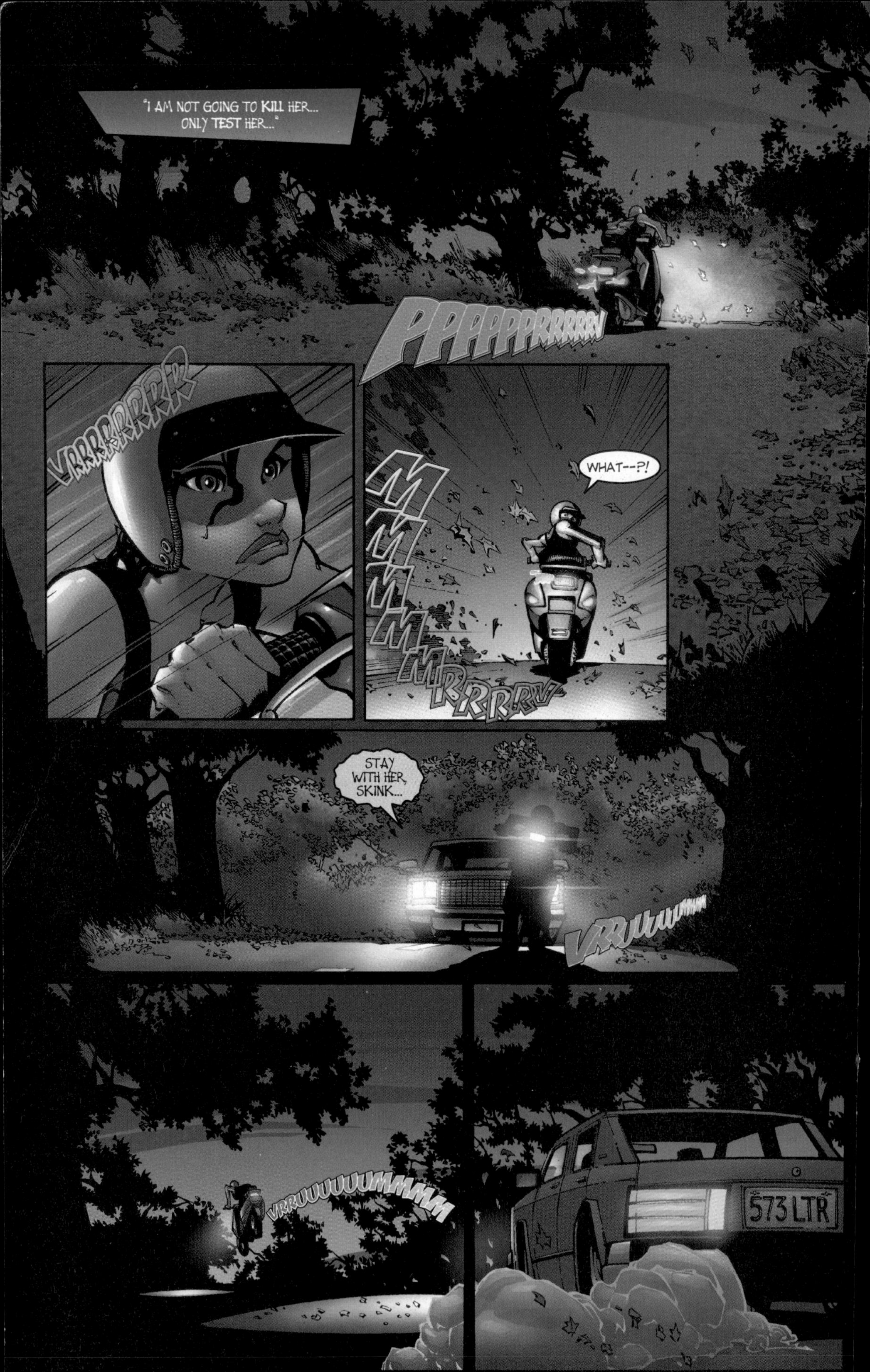
"I AM NOT GOING TO KILL HER... ONLY TEST HER..."
PPPPPPRRRRRV
VRRRRRRRR
WHAT--?!
MMMMMMRRRRV
STAY WITH HER, SKINK...
VRUUUUMMM
VRUUUUUUMMMM
573 LTR

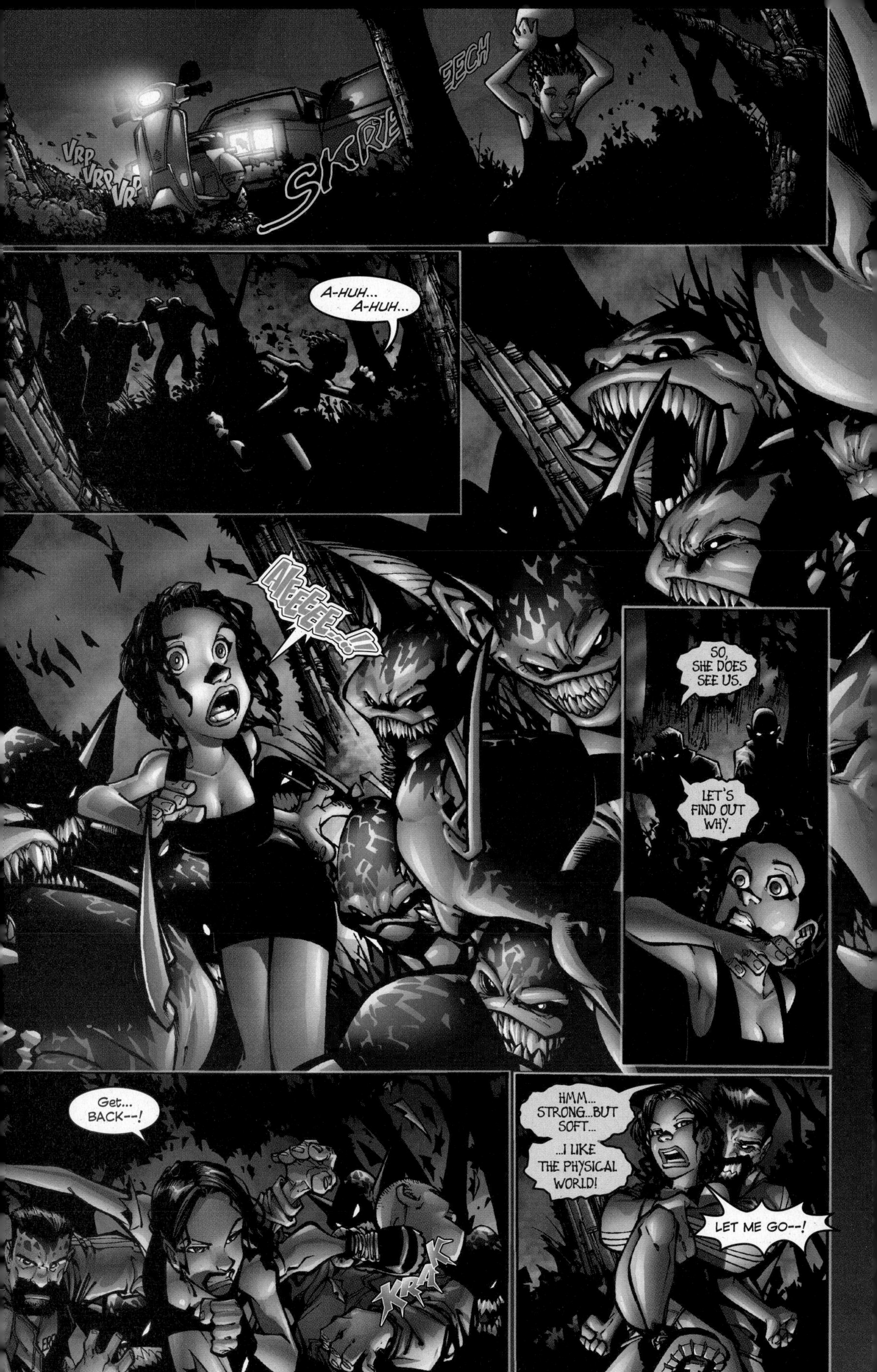
VRP VRP VRP
SKREEEECH
A-HUH... A-HUH...
AIEEEEE...!!
SO, SHE DOES SEE US.
LET'S FIND OUT WHY.
Get... BACK--!
KRAK
HMM... STRONG...BUT SOFT...
...I LIKE THE PHYSICAL WORLD!
LET ME GO--!

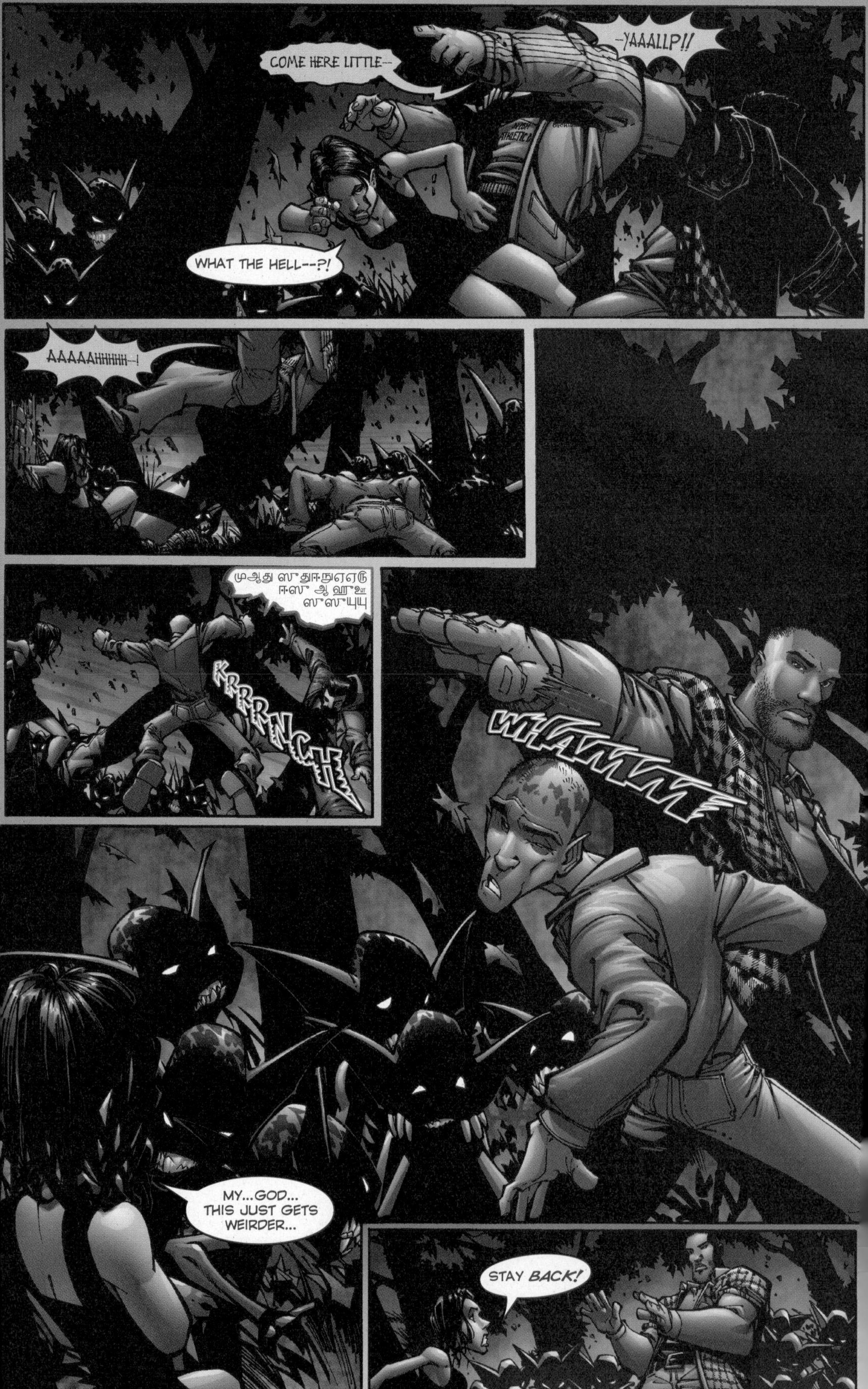
COME HERE LITTLE--
--YAAALLP!!
WHAT THE HELL--?!
AAAAAHHHHH--!
KRRRNCH
MY...GOD...
THIS JUST GETS
WEIRDER...
STAY BACK!

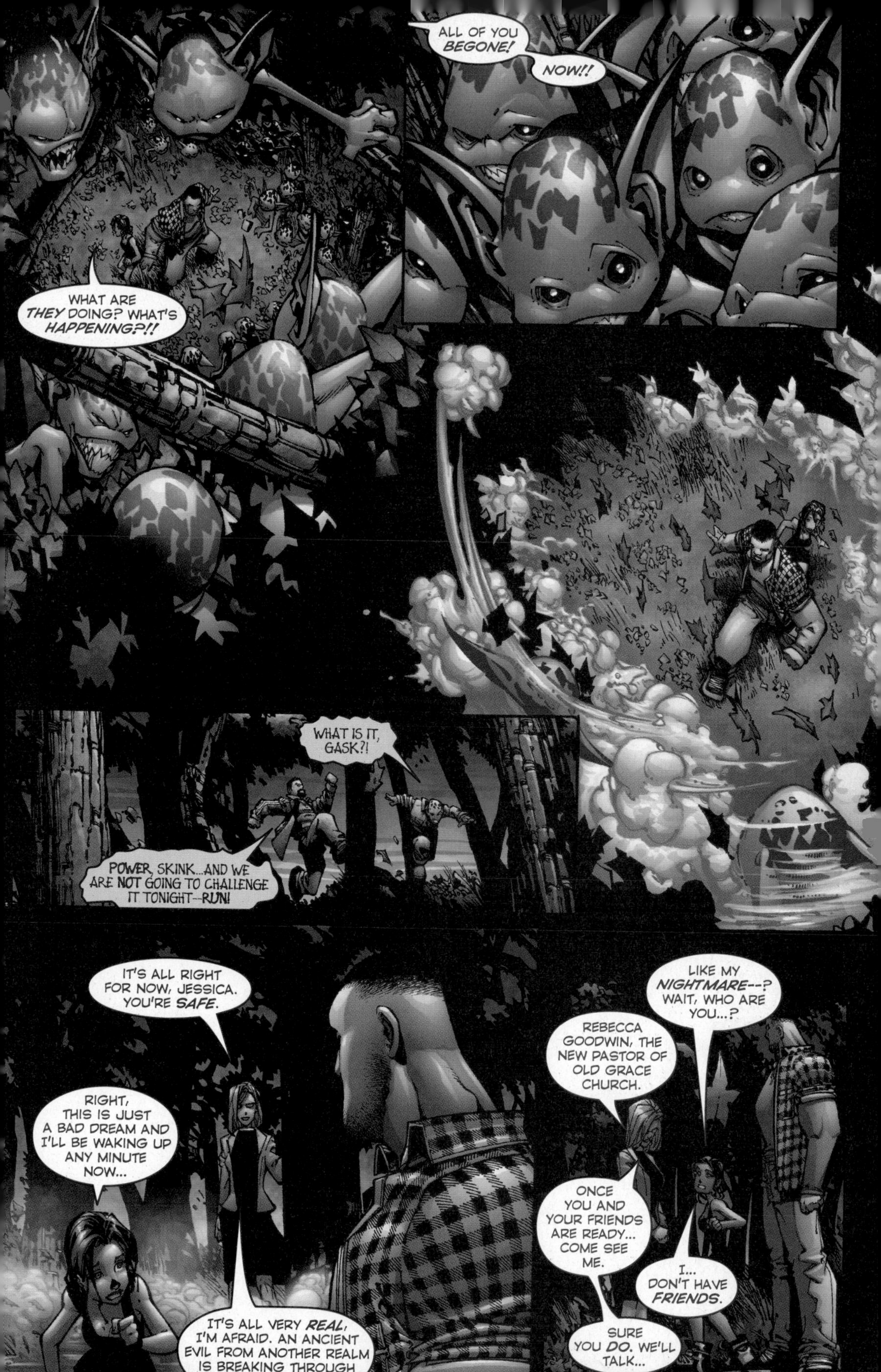
ALL OF YOU BEGONE!
NOW!!
WHAT ARE THEY DOING? WHAT'S HAPPENING?!!
WHAT IS IT, GASK?!
POWER, SKINK...AND WE ARE NOT GOING TO CHALLENGE IT TONIGHT--RUN!
IT'S ALL RIGHT FOR NOW, JESSICA. YOU'RE SAFE.
RIGHT, THIS IS JUST A BAD DREAM AND I'LL BE WAKING UP ANY MINUTE NOW...
IT'S ALL VERY REAL, I'M AFRAID. AN ANCIENT EVIL FROM ANOTHER REALM IS BREAKING THROUGH TO OUR WORLD...
LIKE MY NIGHTMARE--? WAIT, WHO ARE YOU...?
REBECCA GOODWIN, THE NEW PASTOR OF OLD GRACE CHURCH.
ONCE YOU AND YOUR FRIENDS ARE READY... COME SEE ME.
I... DON'T HAVE FRIENDS.
SURE YOU DO. WE'LL TALK...

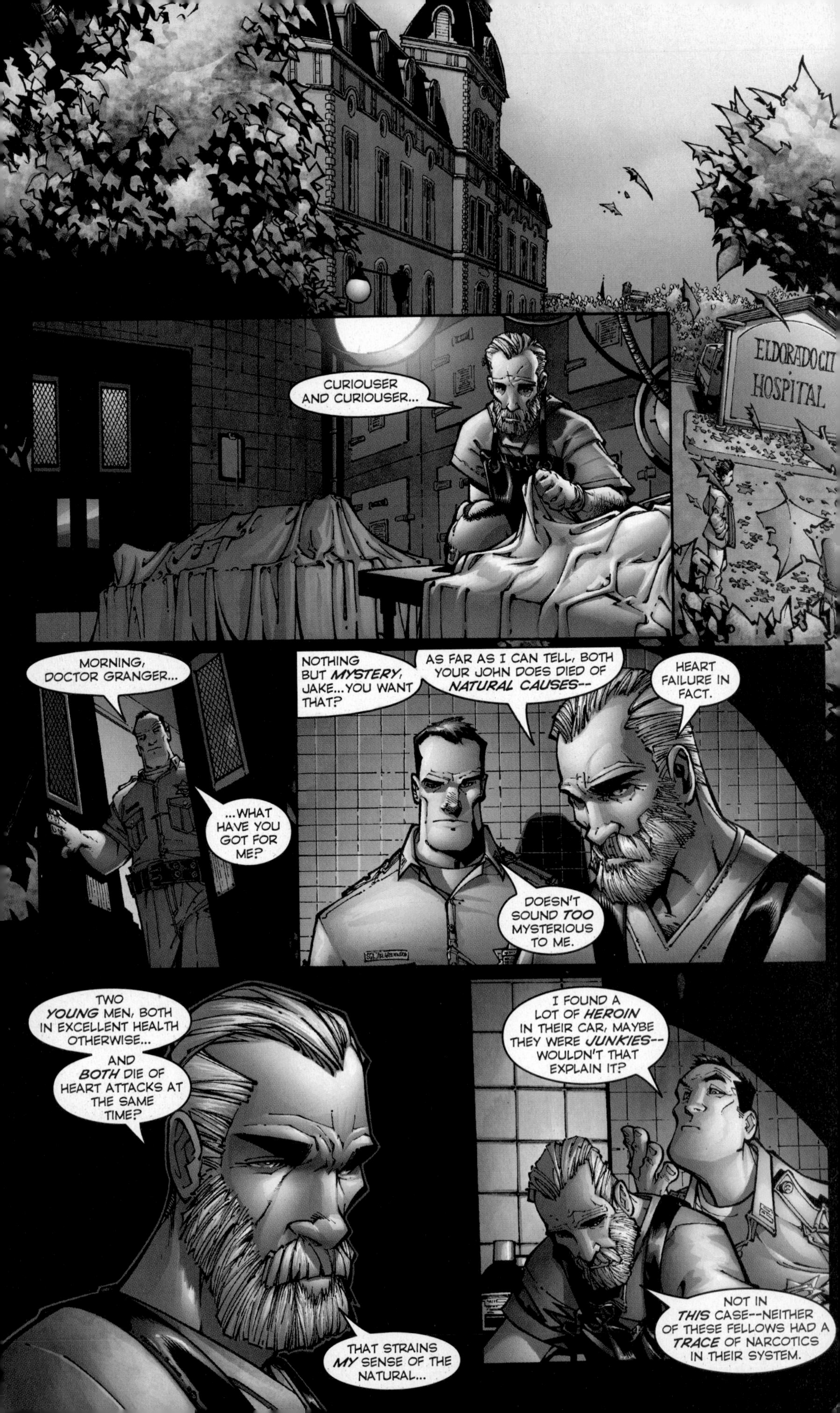
ELDORADO CITY HOSPITAL
CURIOUSER AND CURIOUSER...
MORNING, DOCTOR GRANGER...
...WHAT HAVE YOU GOT FOR ME?
NOTHING BUT MYSTERY, JAKE...YOU WANT THAT?
AS FAR AS I CAN TELL, BOTH YOUR JOHN DOES DIED OF NATURAL CAUSES--
HEART FAILURE IN FACT.
DOESN'T SOUND TOO MYSTERIOUS TO ME.
TWO YOUNG MEN, BOTH IN EXCELLENT HEALTH OTHERWISE...
AND BOTH DIE OF HEART ATTACKS AT THE SAME TIME?
THAT STRAINS MY SENSE OF THE NATURAL...
I FOUND A LOT OF HEROIN IN THEIR CAR, MAYBE THEY WERE JUNKIES--WOULDN'T THAT EXPLAIN IT?
NOT IN THIS CASE--NEITHER OF THESE FELLOWS HAD A TRACE OF NARCOTICS IN THEIR SYSTEM.

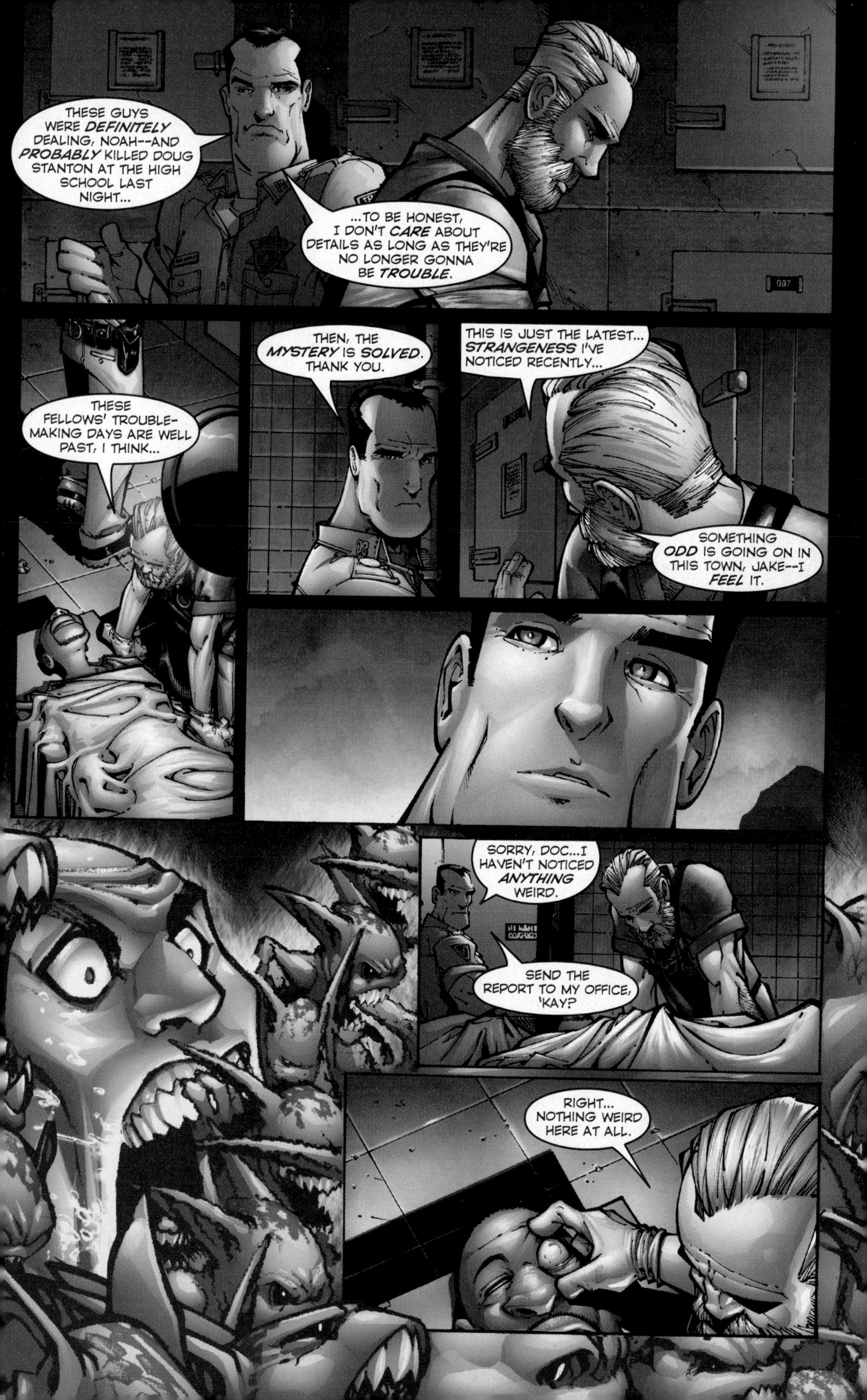
THESE GUYS WERE DEFINITELY DEALING, NOAH--AND PROBABLY KILLED DOUG STANTON AT THE HIGH SCHOOL LAST NIGHT...
...TO BE HONEST, I DON'T CARE ABOUT DETAILS AS LONG AS THEY'RE NO LONGER GONNA BE TROUBLE.
THESE FELLOWS' TROUBLE-MAKING DAYS ARE WELL PAST, I THINK...
THEN, THE MYSTERY IS SOLVED. THANK YOU.
THIS IS JUST THE LATEST... STRANGENESS I'VE NOTICED RECENTLY...
SOMETHING ODD IS GOING ON IN THIS TOWN, JAKE--I FEEL IT.
SORRY, DOC...I HAVEN'T NOTICED ANYTHING WEIRD.
SEND THE REPORT TO MY OFFICE, 'KAY?
RIGHT... NOTHING WEIRD HERE AT ALL.

THE WELL ROUNDED UNICORN
COMICS · SCI · FI · GAMES · TOYS · CARDS

IS EVERYTHING OKAY, ZACH...?

WHAT DO YOU MEAN, DAD...?

YOU'VE BEEN PRETTY...I DON'T KNOW, *WITHDRAWN* ALL MORNING. WHAT'S UP, SPORT?

NOTHING DAD, *REALLY.* I GOTTA GO.

OKAY, THEN...HAVE FUN.

BE... SAFE.

WHAT IS IT THAT HAS YOU DIGGING SO ASSIDUOUSLY THROUGH MY *INDEPENDENT COMICS* ARCHIVES, WEXLER, M'MAN?

AH...WRITER-ARTIST MAX OSTROW'S TRAGICALLY OVER-LOOKED, THREE-ISSUE MASTER-PIECE OF MURDER, MAGIC AND MALEVOLENCE...

...EXCELLENT TASTE, M'MAN.

DAMN NATION, OLIVER... DO YOU HAVE IT?

HERE IT IS...

WE HAVE *EVERYTHING,* MARK.

DAMN NATION

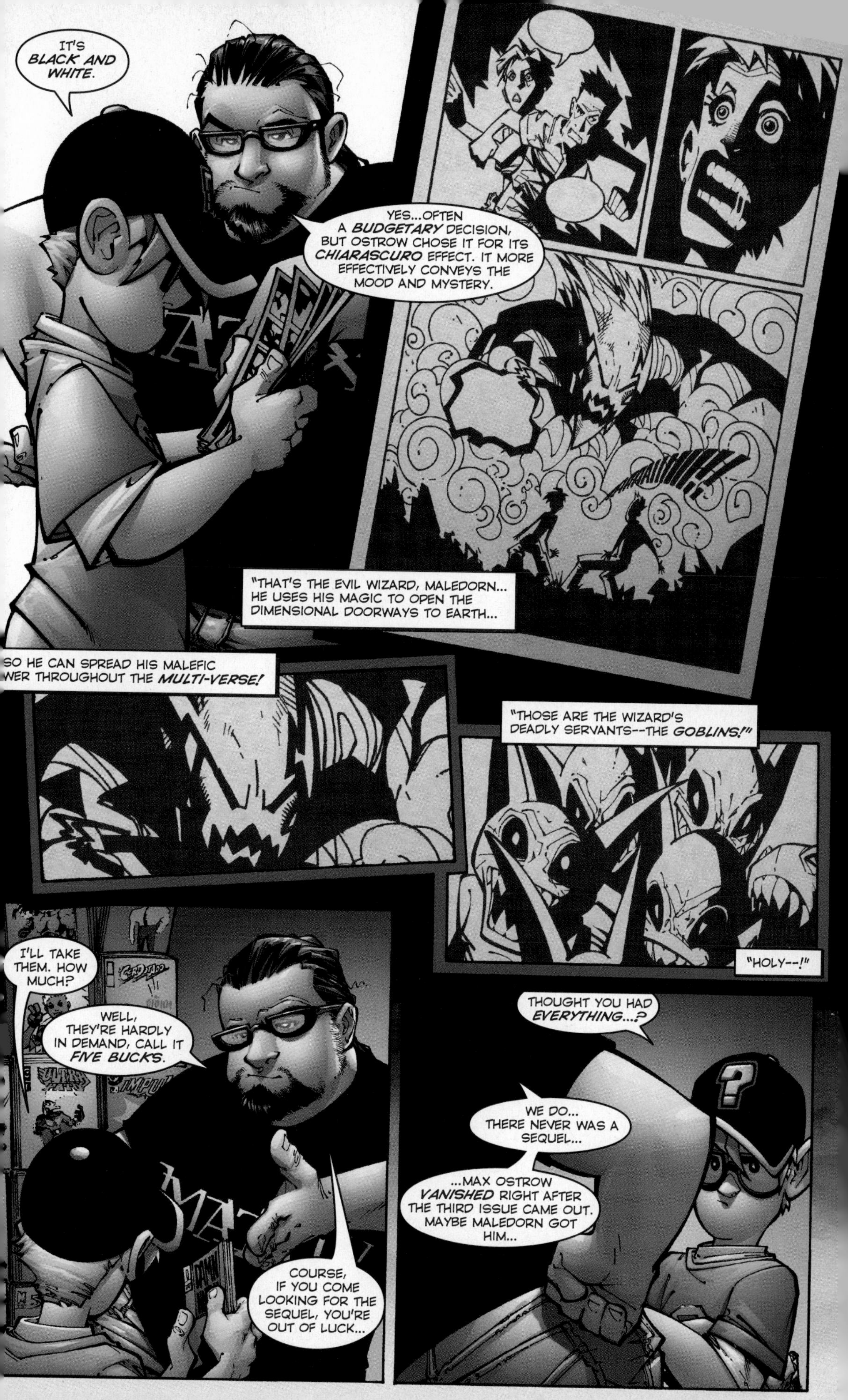

IT'S BLACK AND WHITE.
YES...OFTEN A BUDGETARY DECISION, BUT OSTROW CHOSE IT FOR ITS CHIAROSCURO EFFECT. IT MORE EFFECTIVELY CONVEYS THE MOOD AND MYSTERY.
"THAT'S THE EVIL WIZARD, MALEDORN... HE USES HIS MAGIC TO OPEN THE DIMENSIONAL DOORWAYS TO EARTH...
SO HE CAN SPREAD HIS MALEFIC
WER THROUGHOUT THE MULTI-VERSE!
"THOSE ARE THE WIZARD'S DEADLY SERVANTS--THE GOBLINS!"
"HOLY--!"
I'LL TAKE THEM. HOW MUCH?
WELL, THEY'RE HARDLY IN DEMAND, CALL IT FIVE BUCKS.
COURSE, IF YOU COME LOOKING FOR THE SEQUEL, YOU'RE OUT OF LUCK...
THOUGHT YOU HAD EVERYTHING...?
WE DO... THERE NEVER WAS A SEQUEL...
...MAX OSTROW VANISHED RIGHT AFTER THE THIRD ISSUE CAME OUT. MAYBE MALEDORN GOT HIM...

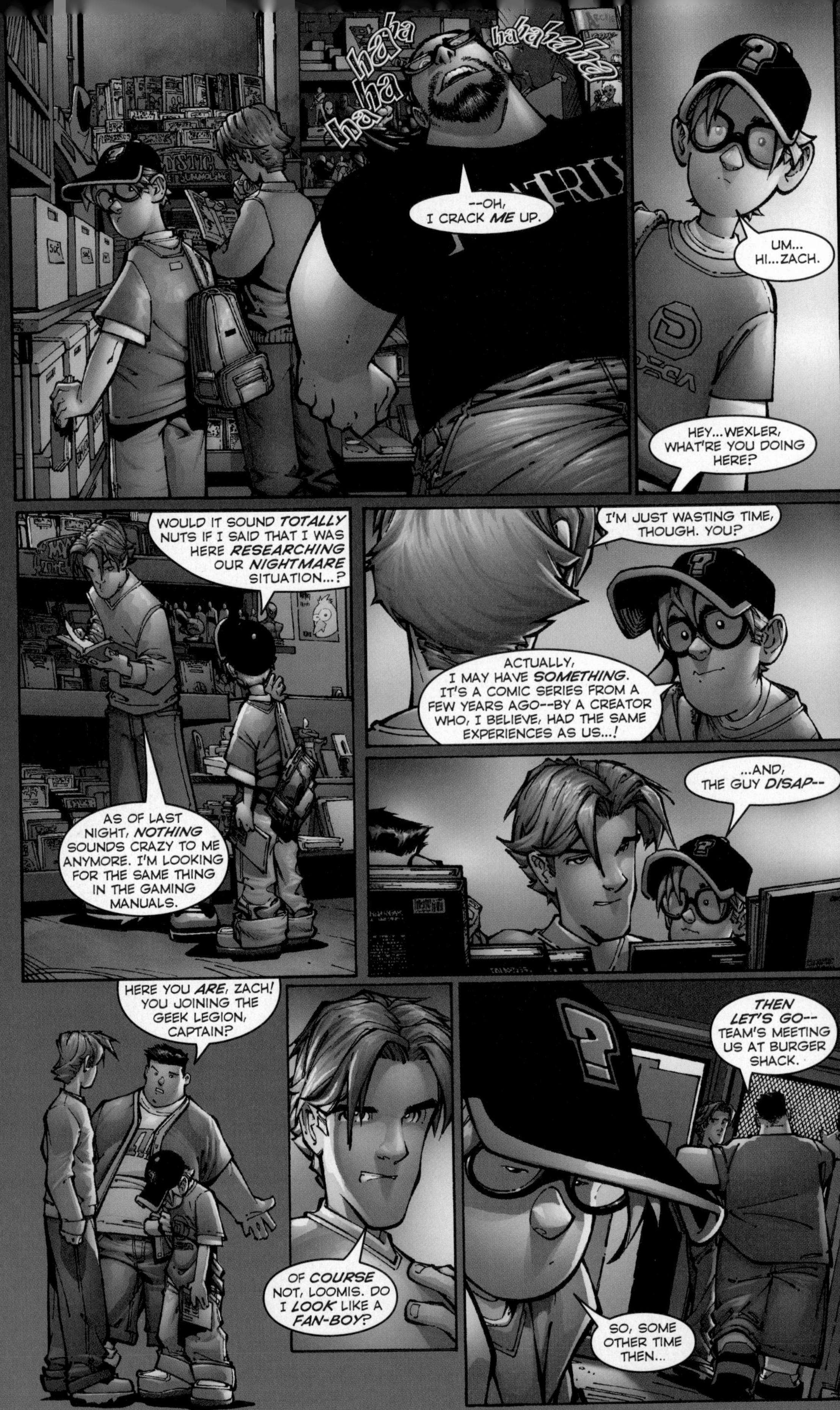
haha ha ha
hahahahaha
--OH, I CRACK ME UP.
UM... HI...ZACH.
HEY...WEXLER, WHAT'RE YOU DOING HERE?
WOULD IT SOUND TOTALLY NUTS IF I SAID THAT I WAS HERE RESEARCHING OUR NIGHTMARE SITUATION...?
AS OF LAST NIGHT, NOTHING SOUNDS CRAZY TO ME ANYMORE. I'M LOOKING FOR THE SAME THING IN THE GAMING MANUALS.
I'M JUST WASTING TIME, THOUGH. YOU?
ACTUALLY, I MAY HAVE SOMETHING. IT'S A COMIC SERIES FROM A FEW YEARS AGO--BY A CREATOR WHO, I BELIEVE, HAD THE SAME EXPERIENCES AS US...!
...AND, THE GUY DISAP--
HERE YOU ARE, ZACH! YOU JOINING THE GEEK LEGION, CAPTAIN?
OF COURSE NOT, LOOMIS. DO I LOOK LIKE A FAN-BOY?
THEN LET'S GO-- TEAM'S MEETING US AT BURGER SHACK.
SO, SOME OTHER TIME THEN...

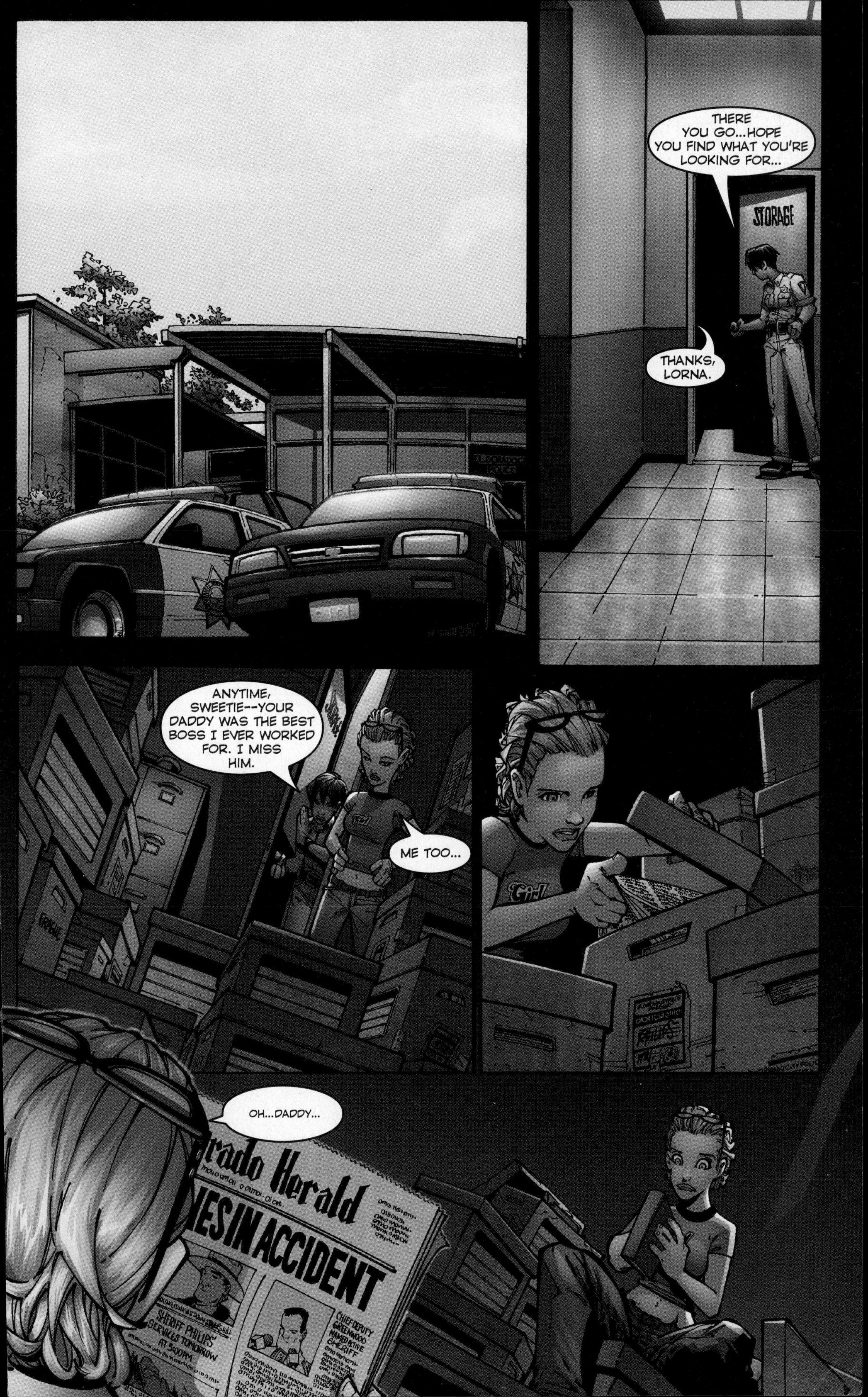
THERE YOU GO...HOPE YOU FIND WHAT YOU'RE LOOKING FOR...
STORAGE
THANKS, LORNA.
ANYTIME, SWEETIE--YOUR DADDY WAS THE BEST BOSS I EVER WORKED FOR. I MISS HIM.
ME TOO...
OH...DADDY...
rado Herald
IES IN ACCIDENT
SHERIFF PHILIPS SERVICES TOMORROW AT 5:00PM

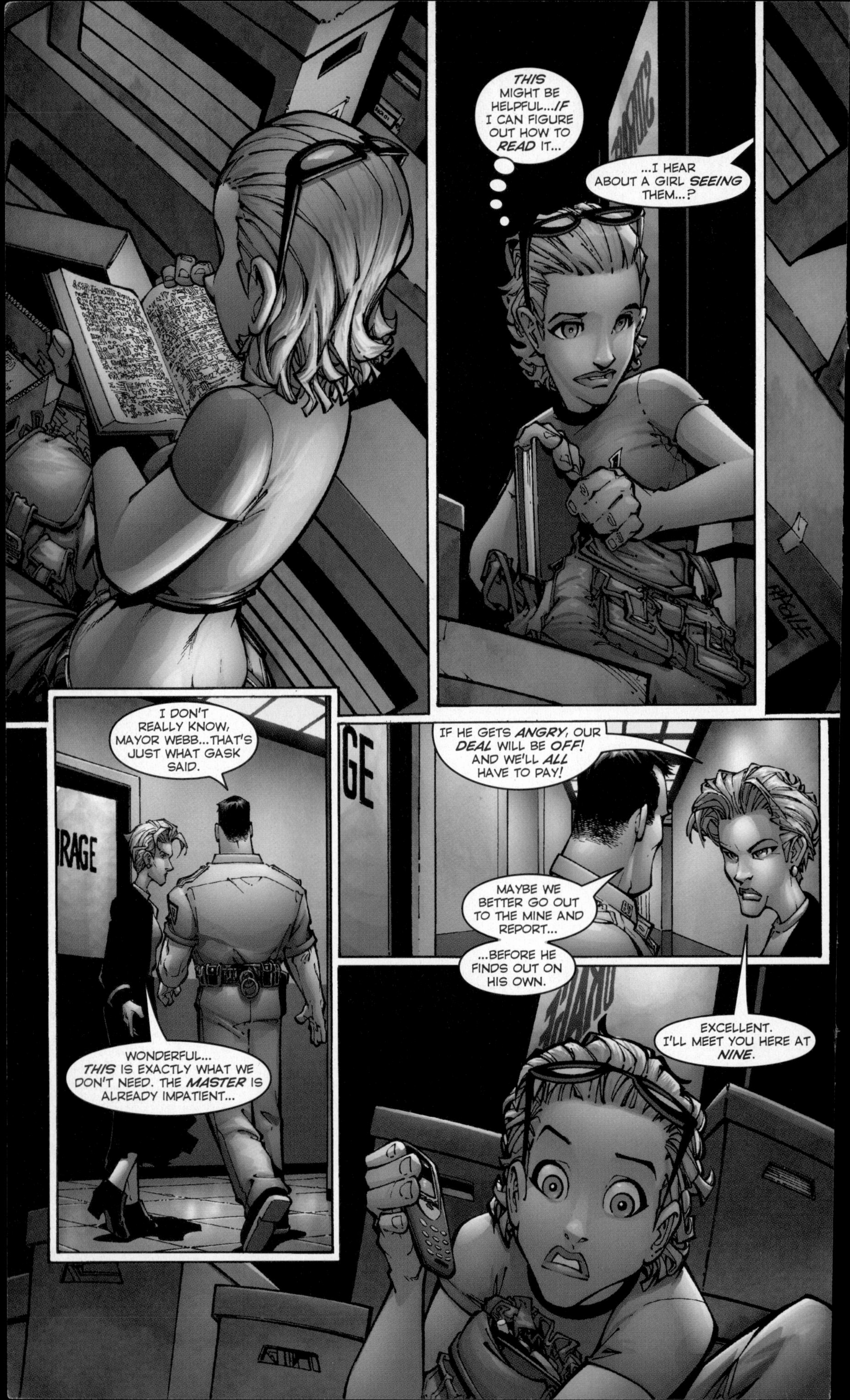
THIS MIGHT BE HELPFUL...IF I CAN FIGURE OUT HOW TO READ IT...
...I HEAR ABOUT A GIRL SEEING THEM...?
I DON'T REALLY KNOW, MAYOR WEBB...THAT'S JUST WHAT GASK SAID.
IRAGE
GE
IF HE GETS ANGRY, OUR DEAL WILL BE OFF! AND WE'LL ALL HAVE TO PAY!
MAYBE WE BETTER GO OUT TO THE MINE AND REPORT...
...BEFORE HE FINDS OUT ON HIS OWN.
WONDERFUL... THIS IS EXACTLY WHAT WE DON'T NEED. THE MASTER IS ALREADY IMPATIENT...
EXCELLENT. I'LL MEET YOU HERE AT NINE.

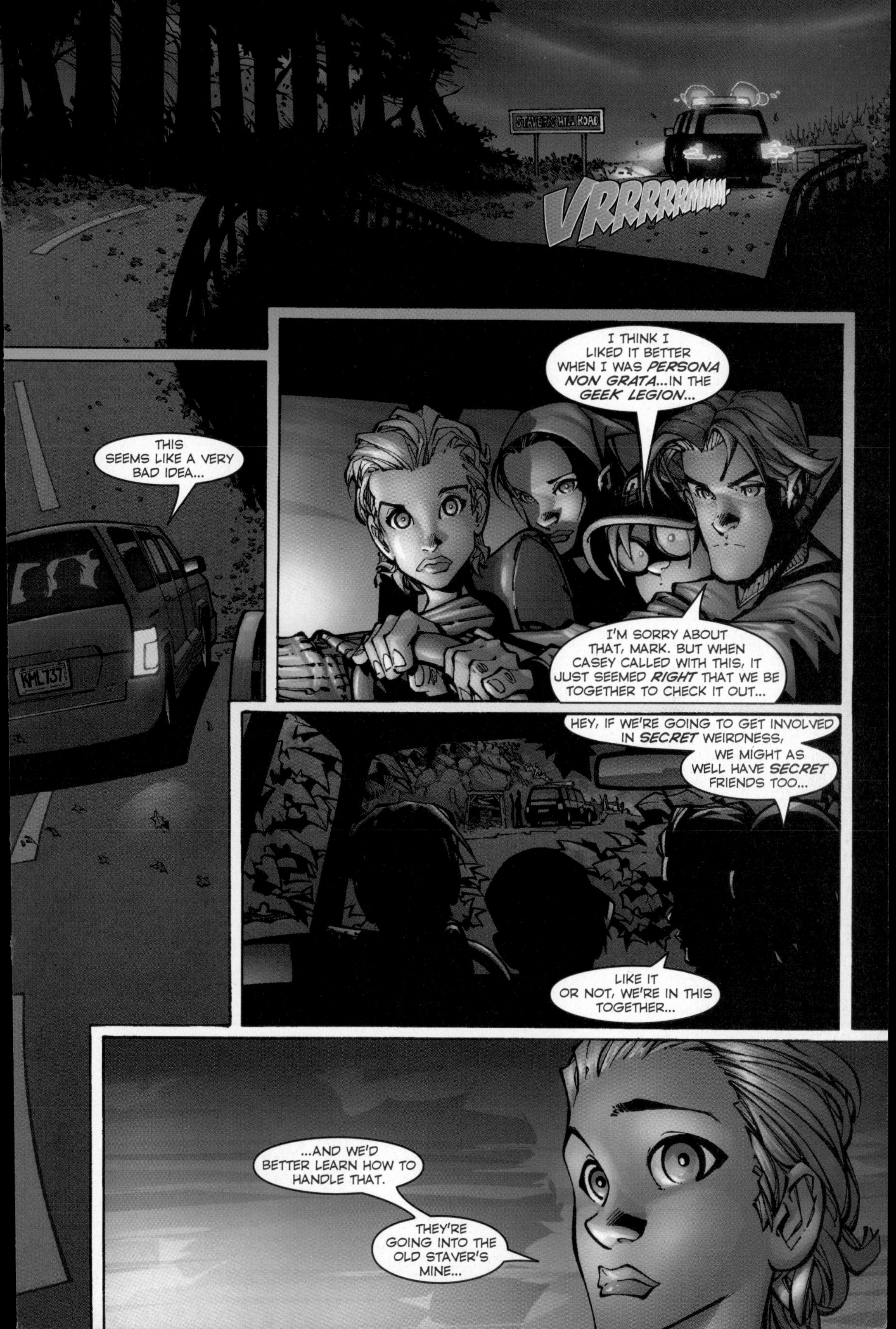
STAVER'S HILL ROAD
VRRRRRMMM
THIS SEEMS LIKE A VERY BAD IDEA...
I THINK I LIKED IT BETTER WHEN I WAS *PERSONA NON GRATA*...IN THE *GEEK LEGION*...
I'M SORRY ABOUT THAT, MARK. BUT WHEN CASEY CALLED WITH THIS, IT JUST SEEMED *RIGHT* THAT WE BE TOGETHER TO CHECK IT OUT...
HEY, IF WE'RE GOING TO GET INVOLVED IN *SECRET* WEIRDNESS, WE MIGHT AS WELL HAVE *SECRET* FRIENDS TOO...
LIKE IT OR NOT, WE'RE IN THIS TOGETHER...
...AND WE'D BETTER LEARN HOW TO HANDLE THAT.
THEY'RE GOING INTO THE OLD STAVER'S MINE...

I'M ALMOST CERTAIN THAT THIS IS A TRULY *STUPID* IDEA, BUT I THINK WE SHOULD FOLLOW THEM.

MY...GOD... THIS IS WHERE MY DAD DIED.

IT...IT PROBABLY WASN'T AN *ACCIDENT* AT ALL...OH LORD, WHAT'S GOING ON?!

MAYBE WE'LL FIND OUT...*IN THERE.*

ஏஹ்ʾ அத த துஹ்ʾஎ வாʾஎலுலு ஈஸ்ʾ ஈஇஓஈநுங ஒரு வாʾடு ∴ஒரு துஹ்ʾஎ ருஏநுஈநுநுஈநுங ?∴ ஈத சுஷ்ʾமு முகுலு;முஸ்ʾலுகு

...*DRAEDELUS!!*

WELCOME... *MASTER!*

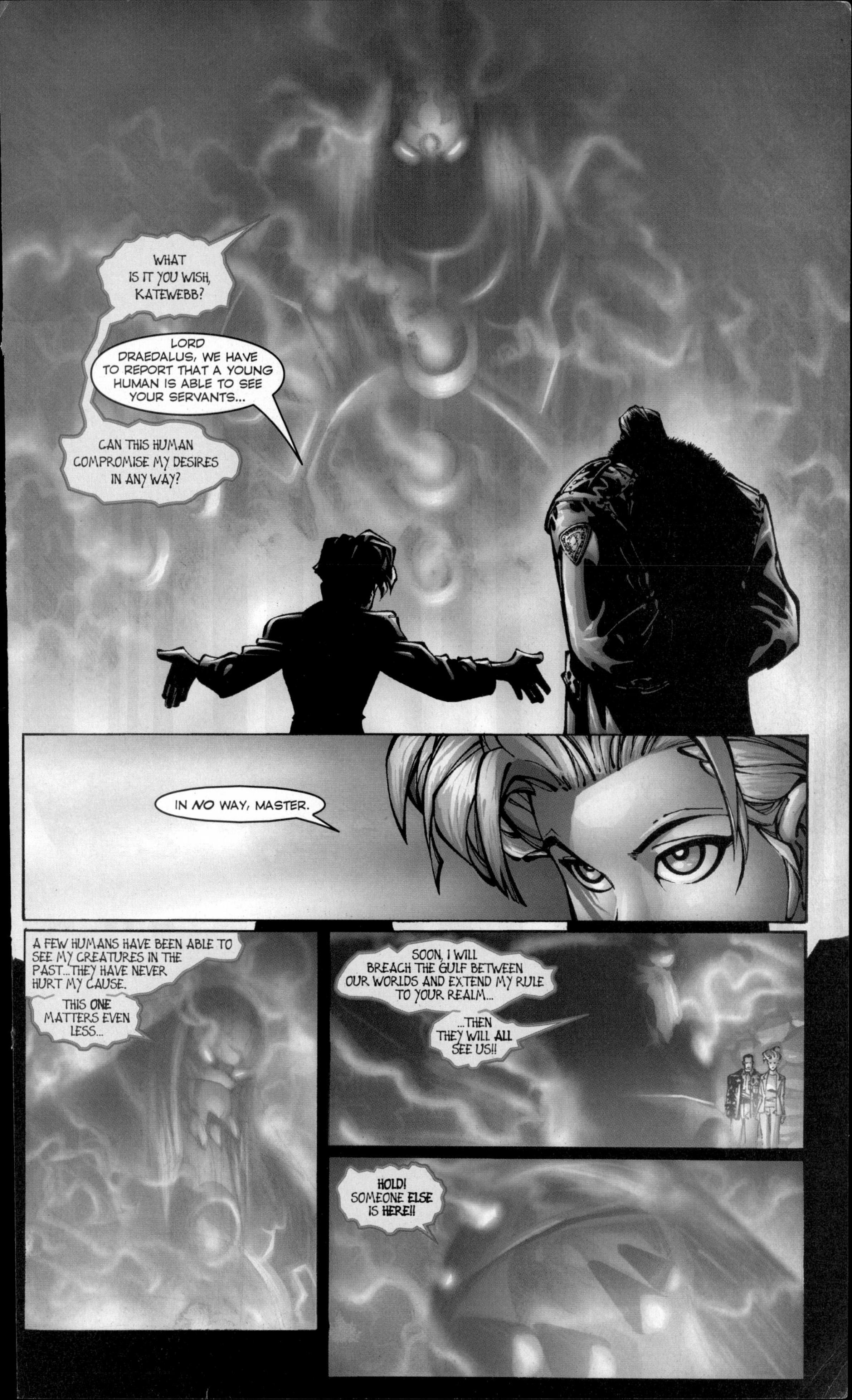
WHAT IS IT YOU WISH, KATEWEBB?
LORD DRAEDALUS, WE HAVE TO REPORT THAT A YOUNG HUMAN IS ABLE TO SEE YOUR SERVANTS...
CAN THIS HUMAN COMPROMISE MY DESIRES IN ANY WAY?
IN NO WAY, MASTER.
A FEW HUMANS HAVE BEEN ABLE TO SEE MY CREATURES IN THE PAST...THEY HAVE NEVER HURT MY CAUSE.
THIS ONE MATTERS EVEN LESS...
SOON, I WILL BREACH THE GULF BETWEEN OUR WORLDS AND EXTEND MY RULE TO YOUR REALM...
...THEN THEY WILL ALL SEE US!!
HOLD! SOMEONE ELSE IS HERE!!

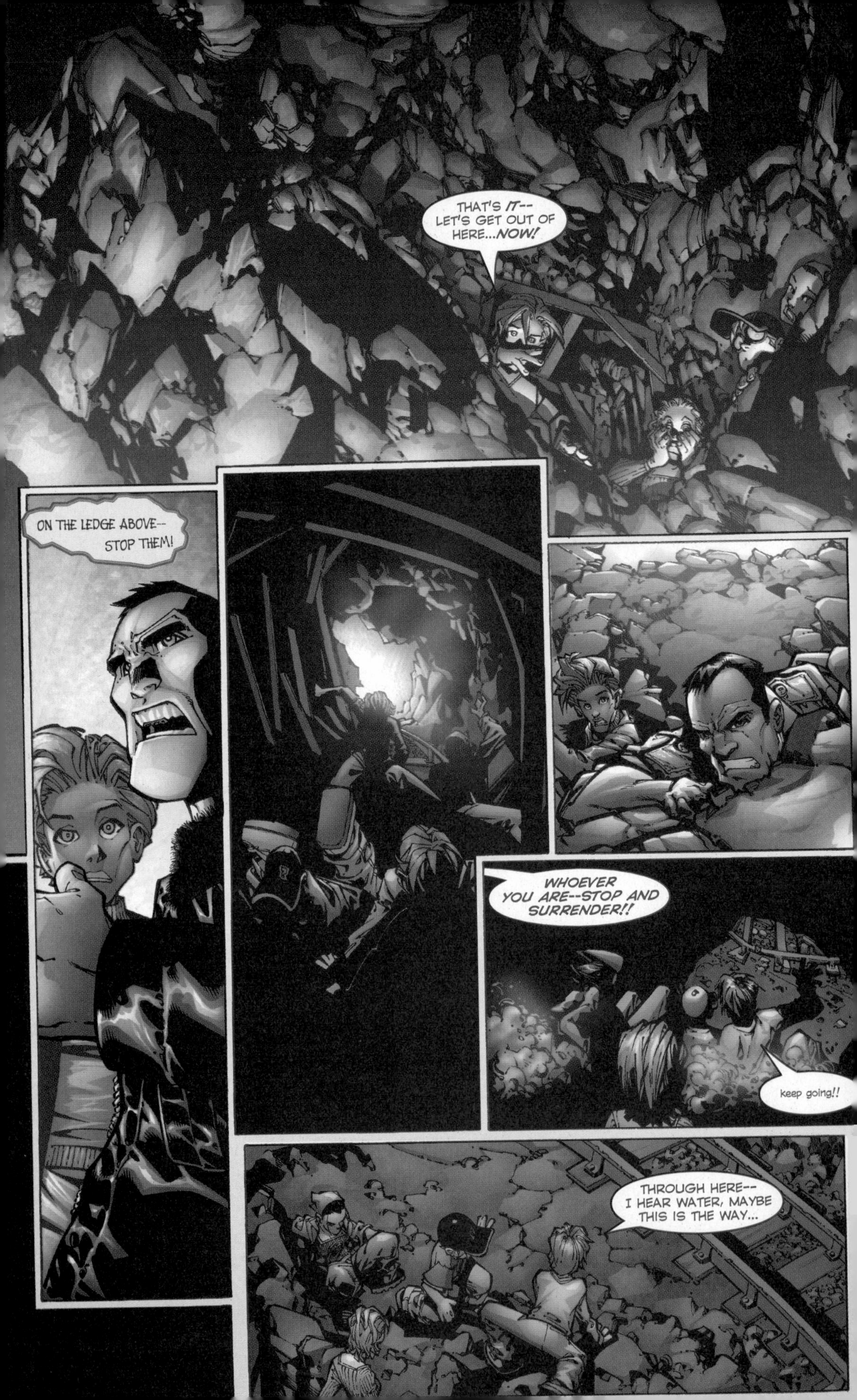
THAT'S IT--
LET'S GET OUT OF HERE...NOW!
ON THE LEDGE ABOVE--
STOP THEM!
WHOEVER YOU ARE--STOP AND SURRENDER!!
keep going!!
THROUGH HERE--
I HEAR WATER, MAYBE THIS IS THE WAY...

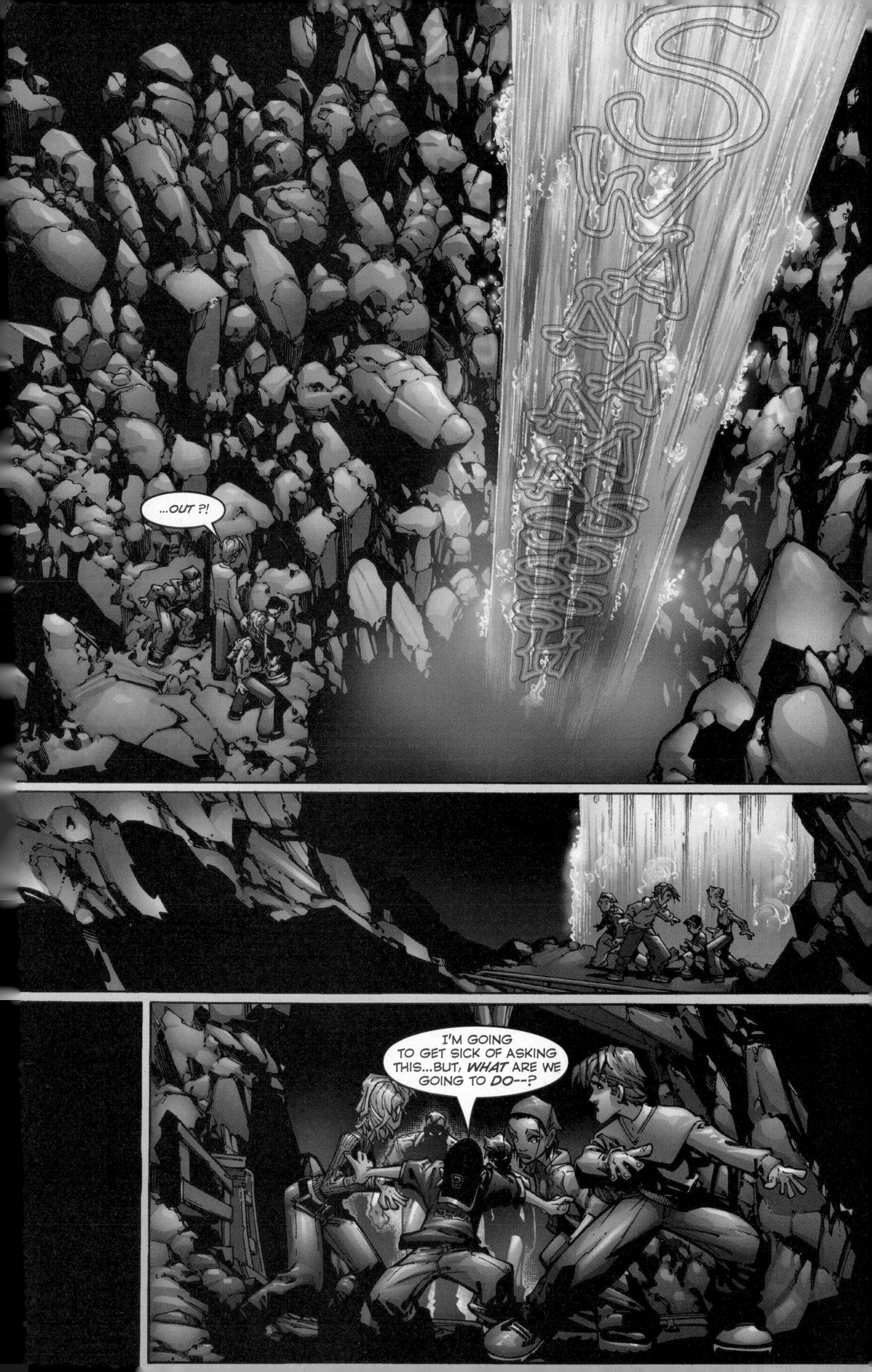
SWAAAASSOOOOH
...OUT ?!
I'M GOING TO GET SICK OF ASKING THIS...BUT, *WHAT* ARE WE GOING TO *DO*--?

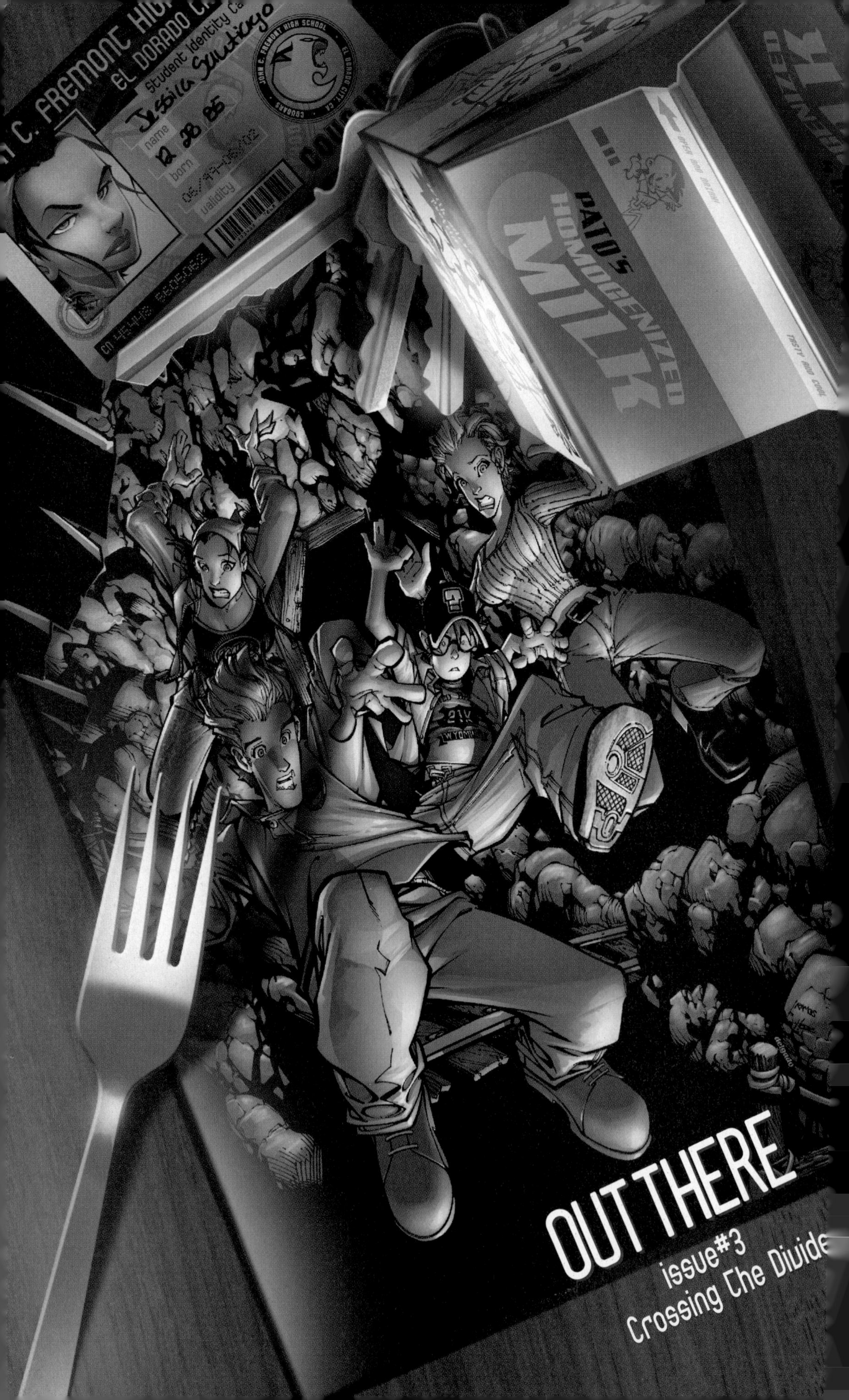
PATO'S
HOMOGENIZED
MILK
OUT THERE
issue#3
Crossing The Divide

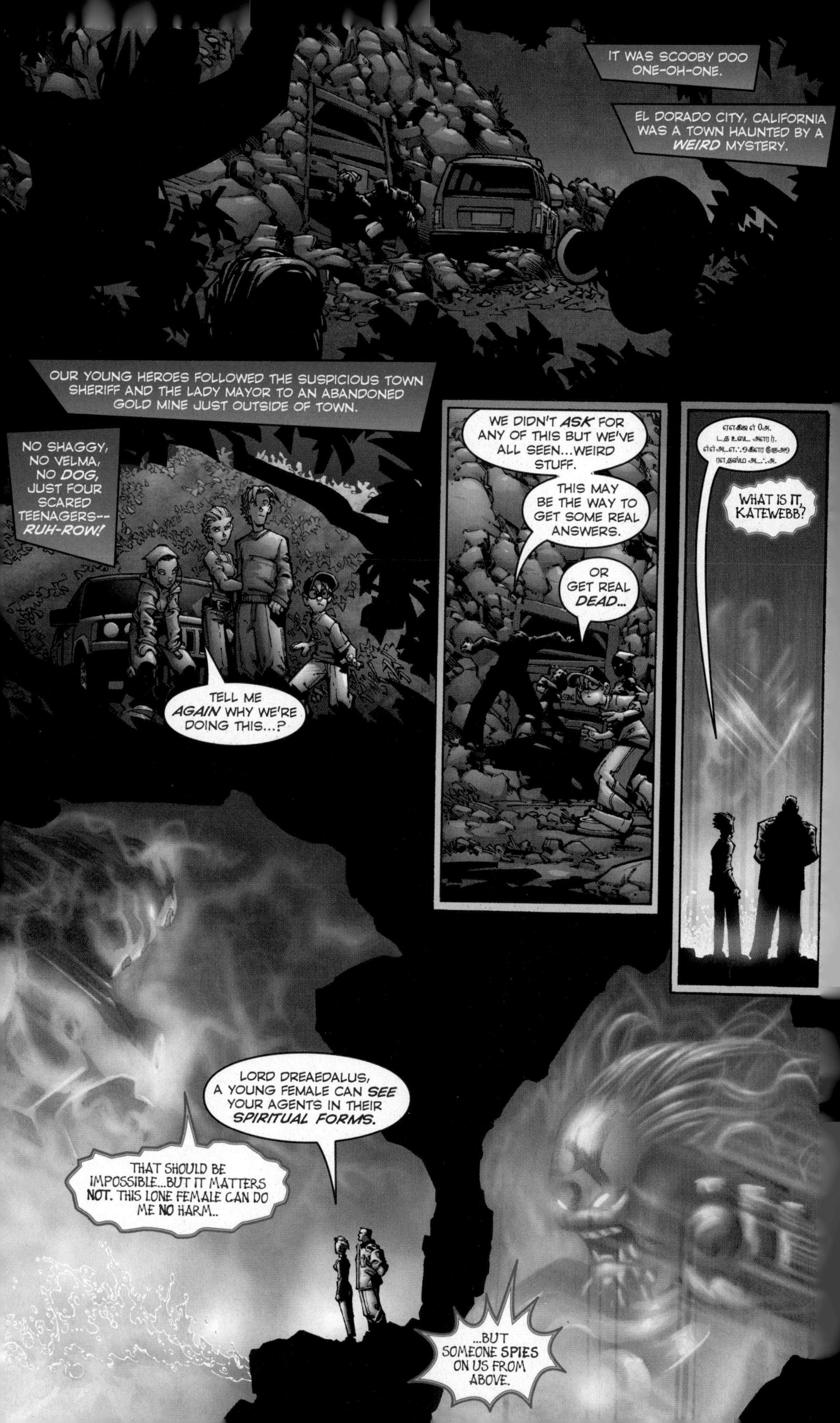
IT WAS SCOOBY DOO ONE-OH-ONE.
EL DORADO CITY, CALIFORNIA WAS A TOWN HAUNTED BY A WEIRD MYSTERY.
OUR YOUNG HEROES FOLLOWED THE SUSPICIOUS TOWN SHERIFF AND THE LADY MAYOR TO AN ABANDONED GOLD MINE JUST OUTSIDE OF TOWN.
NO SHAGGY, NO VELMA, NO DOG, JUST FOUR SCARED TEENAGERS-- RUH-ROW!
TELL ME AGAIN WHY WE'RE DOING THIS...?
WE DIDN'T ASK FOR ANY OF THIS BUT WE'VE ALL SEEN...WEIRD STUFF.
THIS MAY BE THE WAY TO GET SOME REAL ANSWERS.
OR GET REAL DEAD...
WHAT IS IT, KATEWEBB?
LORD DREAEDALUS, A YOUNG FEMALE CAN SEE YOUR AGENTS IN THEIR SPIRITUAL FORMS.
THAT SHOULD BE IMPOSSIBLE...BUT IT MATTERS NOT. THIS LONE FEMALE CAN DO ME NO HARM..
...BUT SOMEONE SPIES ON US FROM ABOVE.

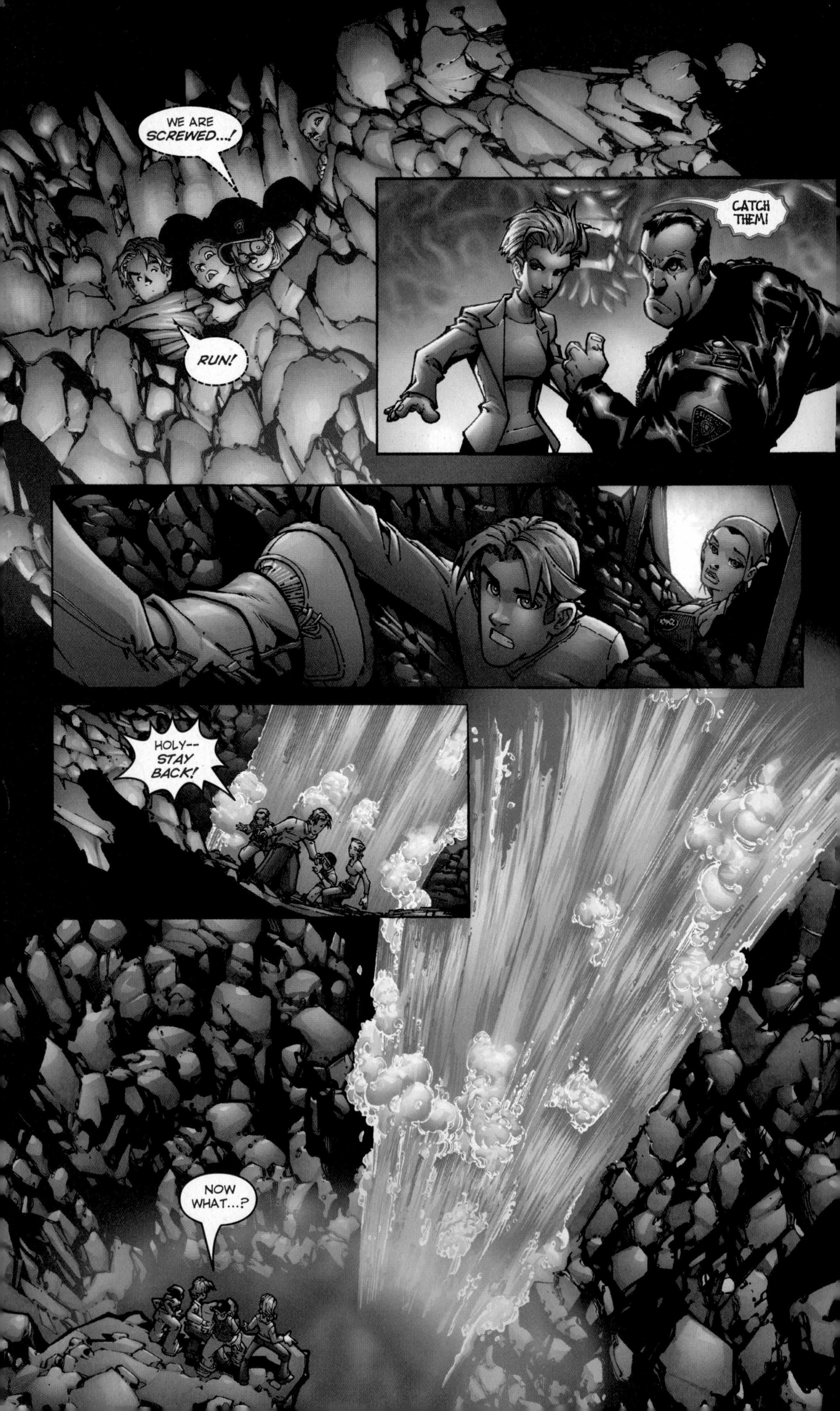

WE ARE SCREWED...!
RUN!
CATCH THEM!
HOLY-- STAY BACK!
NOW WHAT...?

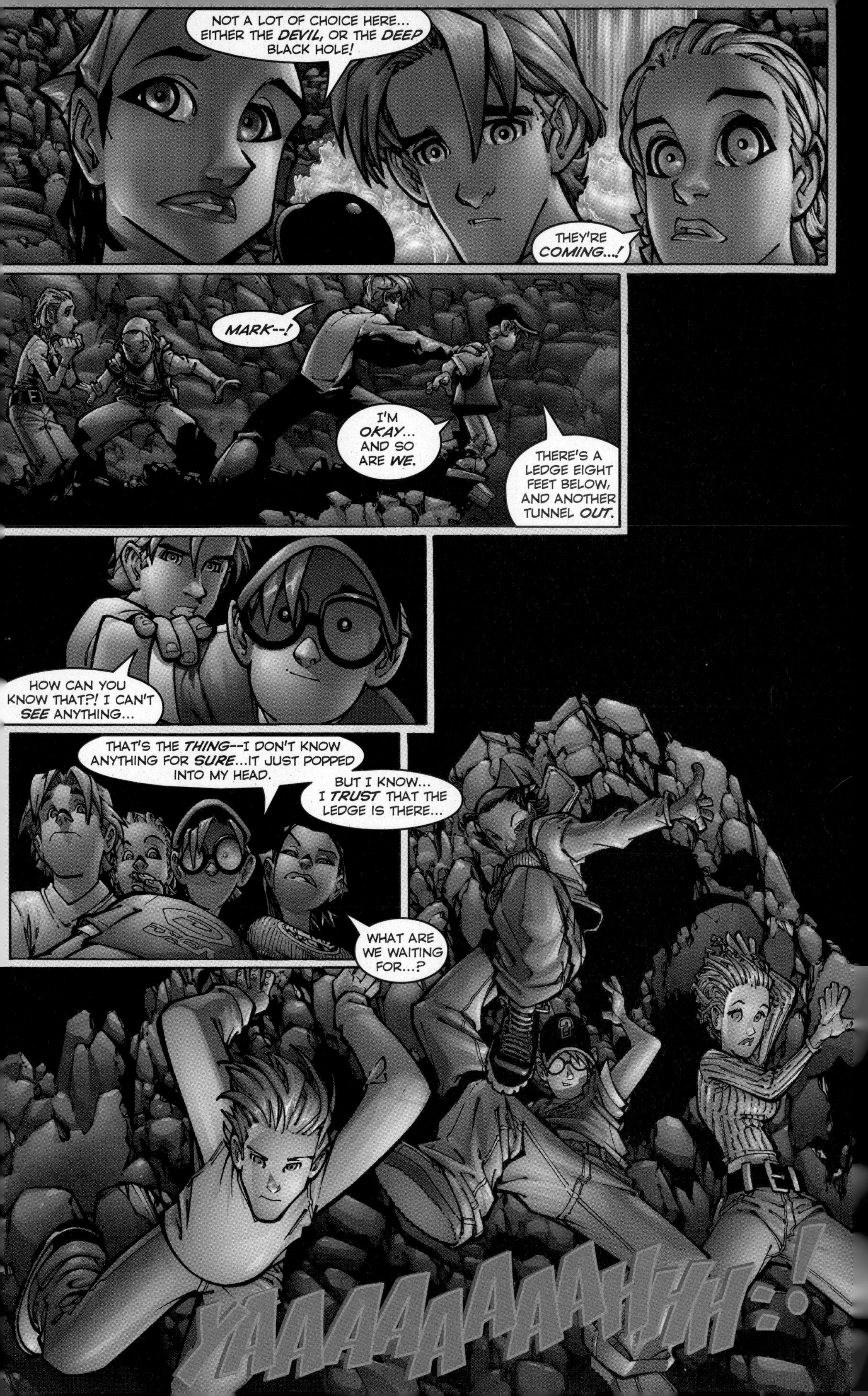
NOT A LOT OF CHOICE HERE... EITHER THE *DEVIL*, OR THE *DEEP* BLACK HOLE!
THEY'RE *COMING*...!
MARK--!
I'M *OKAY*... AND SO ARE *WE*.
THERE'S A LEDGE EIGHT FEET BELOW, AND ANOTHER TUNNEL *OUT*.
HOW CAN YOU KNOW THAT?! I CAN'T *SEE* ANYTHING...
THAT'S THE *THING*--I DON'T KNOW ANYTHING FOR *SURE*...IT JUST POPPED INTO MY HEAD.
BUT I KNOW... I *TRUST* THAT THE LEDGE IS THERE...
WHAT ARE WE WAITING FOR...?
YAAAAAAAAAHHH--!

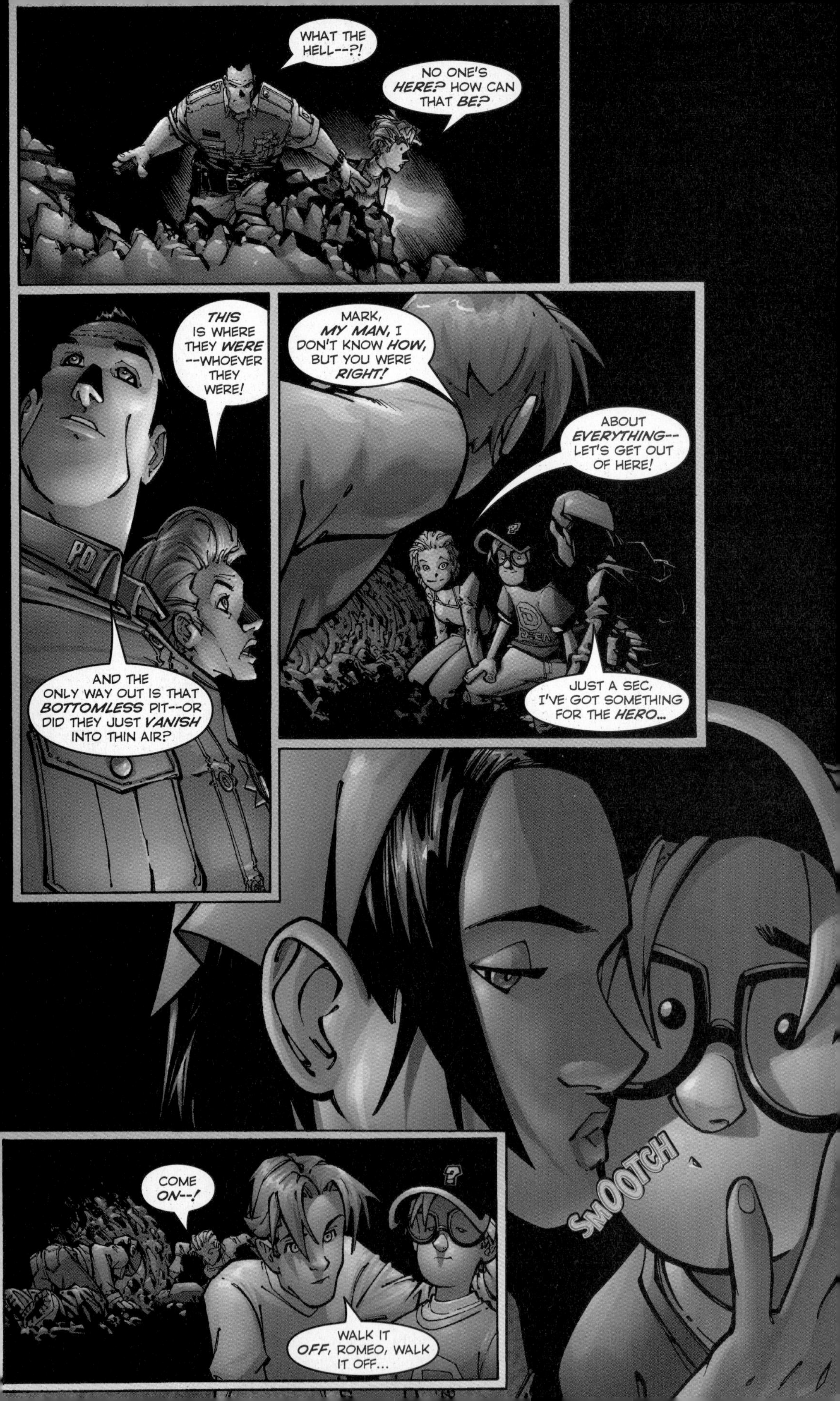
WHAT THE HELL--?!
NO ONE'S *HERE?* HOW CAN THAT *BE?*
THIS IS WHERE THEY *WERE* --WHOEVER THEY WERE!
AND THE ONLY WAY OUT IS THAT *BOTTOMLESS* PIT--OR DID THEY JUST *VANISH* INTO THIN AIR?
MARK, *MY MAN,* I DON'T KNOW *HOW,* BUT YOU WERE *RIGHT!*
ABOUT *EVERYTHING*-- LET'S GET OUT OF HERE!
JUST A SEC, I'VE GOT SOMETHING FOR THE *HERO...*
SMOOTCH
?
COME *ON--!*
WALK IT *OFF,* ROMEO, WALK IT OFF...

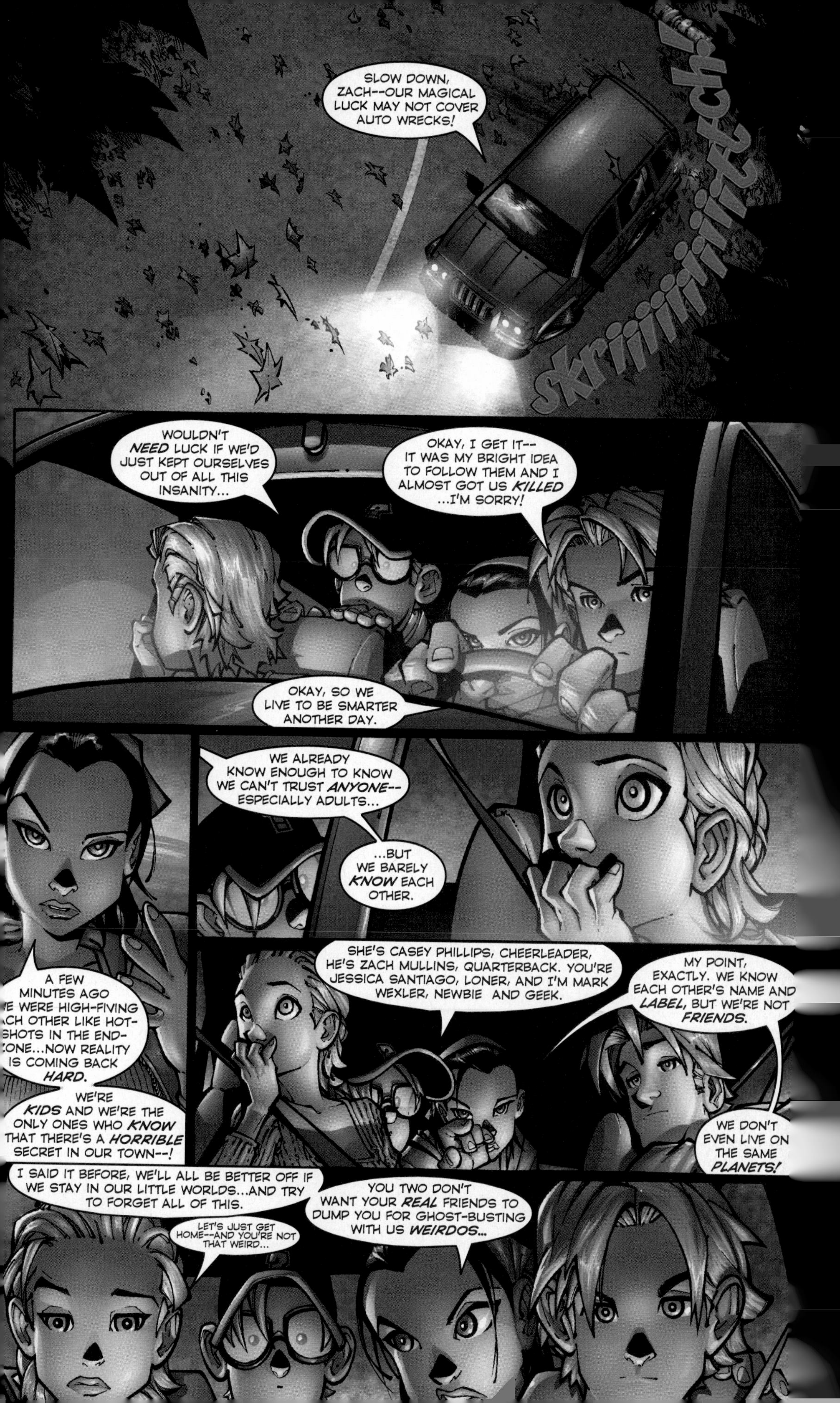
SLOW DOWN, ZACH--OUR MAGICAL LUCK MAY NOT COVER AUTO WRECKS!
SKRIIIIIIIITCH!
WOULDN'T NEED LUCK IF WE'D JUST KEPT OURSELVES OUT OF ALL THIS INSANITY...
OKAY, I GET IT--IT WAS MY BRIGHT IDEA TO FOLLOW THEM AND I ALMOST GOT US KILLED ...I'M SORRY!
OKAY, SO WE LIVE TO BE SMARTER ANOTHER DAY.
WE ALREADY KNOW ENOUGH TO KNOW WE CAN'T TRUST ANYONE--ESPECIALLY ADULTS...
...BUT WE BARELY KNOW EACH OTHER.
A FEW MINUTES AGO WE WERE HIGH-FIVING EACH OTHER LIKE HOT-SHOTS IN THE END-ZONE...NOW REALITY IS COMING BACK HARD.
WE'RE KIDS AND WE'RE THE ONLY ONES WHO KNOW THAT THERE'S A HORRIBLE SECRET IN OUR TOWN--!
SHE'S CASEY PHILLIPS, CHEERLEADER, HE'S ZACH MULLINS, QUARTERBACK. YOU'RE JESSICA SANTIAGO, LONER, AND I'M MARK WEXLER, NEWBIE AND GEEK.
MY POINT, EXACTLY. WE KNOW EACH OTHER'S NAME AND LABEL, BUT WE'RE NOT FRIENDS.
WE DON'T EVEN LIVE ON THE SAME PLANETS!
I SAID IT BEFORE, WE'LL ALL BE BETTER OFF IF WE STAY IN OUR LITTLE WORLDS...AND TRY TO FORGET ALL OF THIS.
YOU TWO DON'T WANT YOUR REAL FRIENDS TO DUMP YOU FOR GHOST-BUSTING WITH US WEIRDOS...
LET'S JUST GET HOME--AND YOU'RE NOT THAT WEIRD...

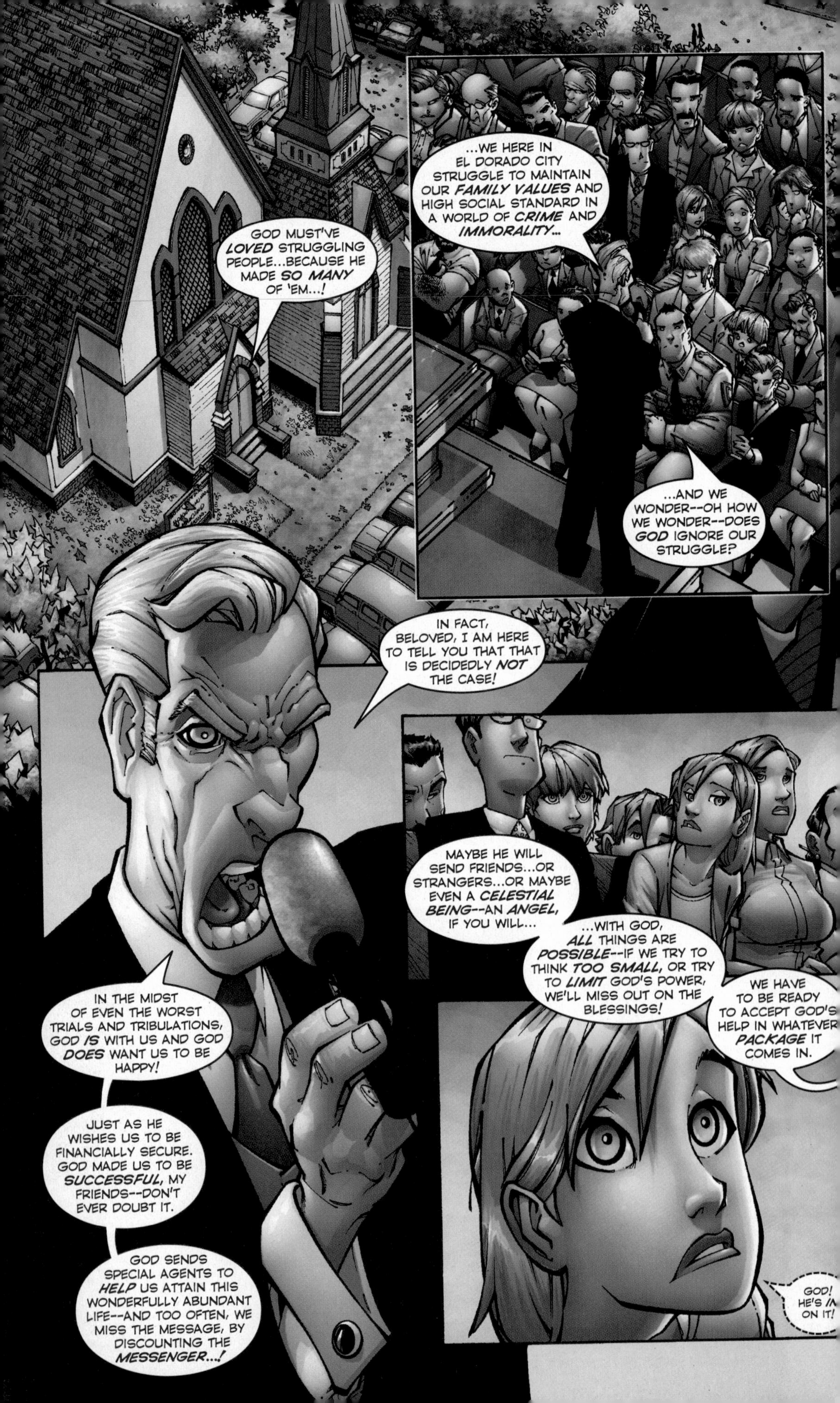
GOD MUST'VE LOVED STRUGGLING PEOPLE...BECAUSE HE MADE SO MANY OF 'EM...!
...WE HERE IN EL DORADO CITY STRUGGLE TO MAINTAIN OUR FAMILY VALUES AND HIGH SOCIAL STANDARD IN A WORLD OF CRIME AND IMMORALITY...
...AND WE WONDER--OH HOW WE WONDER--DOES GOD IGNORE OUR STRUGGLE?
IN FACT, BELOVED, I AM HERE TO TELL YOU THAT THAT IS DECIDEDLY NOT THE CASE!
IN THE MIDST OF EVEN THE WORST TRIALS AND TRIBULATIONS, GOD IS WITH US AND GOD DOES WANT US TO BE HAPPY!
JUST AS HE WISHES US TO BE FINANCIALLY SECURE. GOD MADE US TO BE SUCCESSFUL, MY FRIENDS--DON'T EVER DOUBT IT.
GOD SENDS SPECIAL AGENTS TO HELP US ATTAIN THIS WONDERFULLY ABUNDANT LIFE--AND TOO OFTEN, WE MISS THE MESSAGE, BY DISCOUNTING THE MESSENGER...!
MAYBE HE WILL SEND FRIENDS...OR STRANGERS...OR MAYBE EVEN A CELESTIAL BEING--AN ANGEL, IF YOU WILL...
...WITH GOD, ALL THINGS ARE POSSIBLE--IF WE TRY TO THINK TOO SMALL, OR TRY TO LIMIT GOD'S POWER, WE'LL MISS OUT ON THE BLESSINGS!
WE HAVE TO BE READY TO ACCEPT GOD'S HELP IN WHATEVER PACKAGE IT COMES IN.
GOD! HE'S IN ON IT!

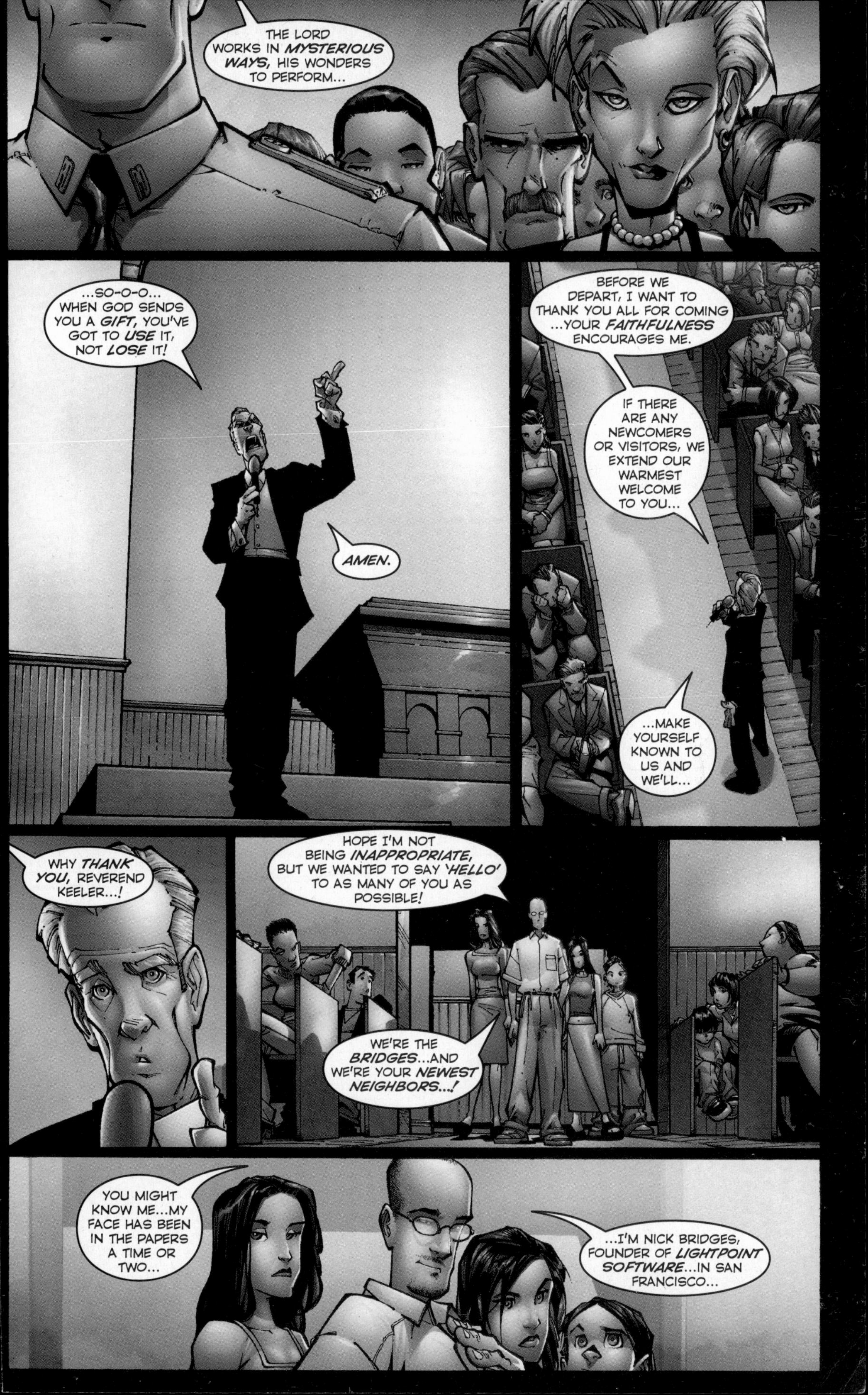
THE LORD WORKS IN MYSTERIOUS WAYS, HIS WONDERS TO PERFORM...
...SO-O-O... WHEN GOD SENDS YOU A GIFT, YOU'VE GOT TO USE IT, NOT LOSE IT!
AMEN.
BEFORE WE DEPART, I WANT TO THANK YOU ALL FOR COMING ...YOUR FAITHFULNESS ENCOURAGES ME.
IF THERE ARE ANY NEWCOMERS OR VISITORS, WE EXTEND OUR WARMEST WELCOME TO YOU...
...MAKE YOURSELF KNOWN TO US AND WE'LL...
WHY THANK YOU, REVEREND KEELER...!
HOPE I'M NOT BEING INAPPROPRIATE, BUT WE WANTED TO SAY 'HELLO' TO AS MANY OF YOU AS POSSIBLE!
WE'RE THE BRIDGES...AND WE'RE YOUR NEWEST NEIGHBORS...!
YOU MIGHT KNOW ME...MY FACE HAS BEEN IN THE PAPERS A TIME OR TWO...
...I'M NICK BRIDGES, FOUNDER OF LIGHTPOINT SOFTWARE...IN SAN FRANCISCO...

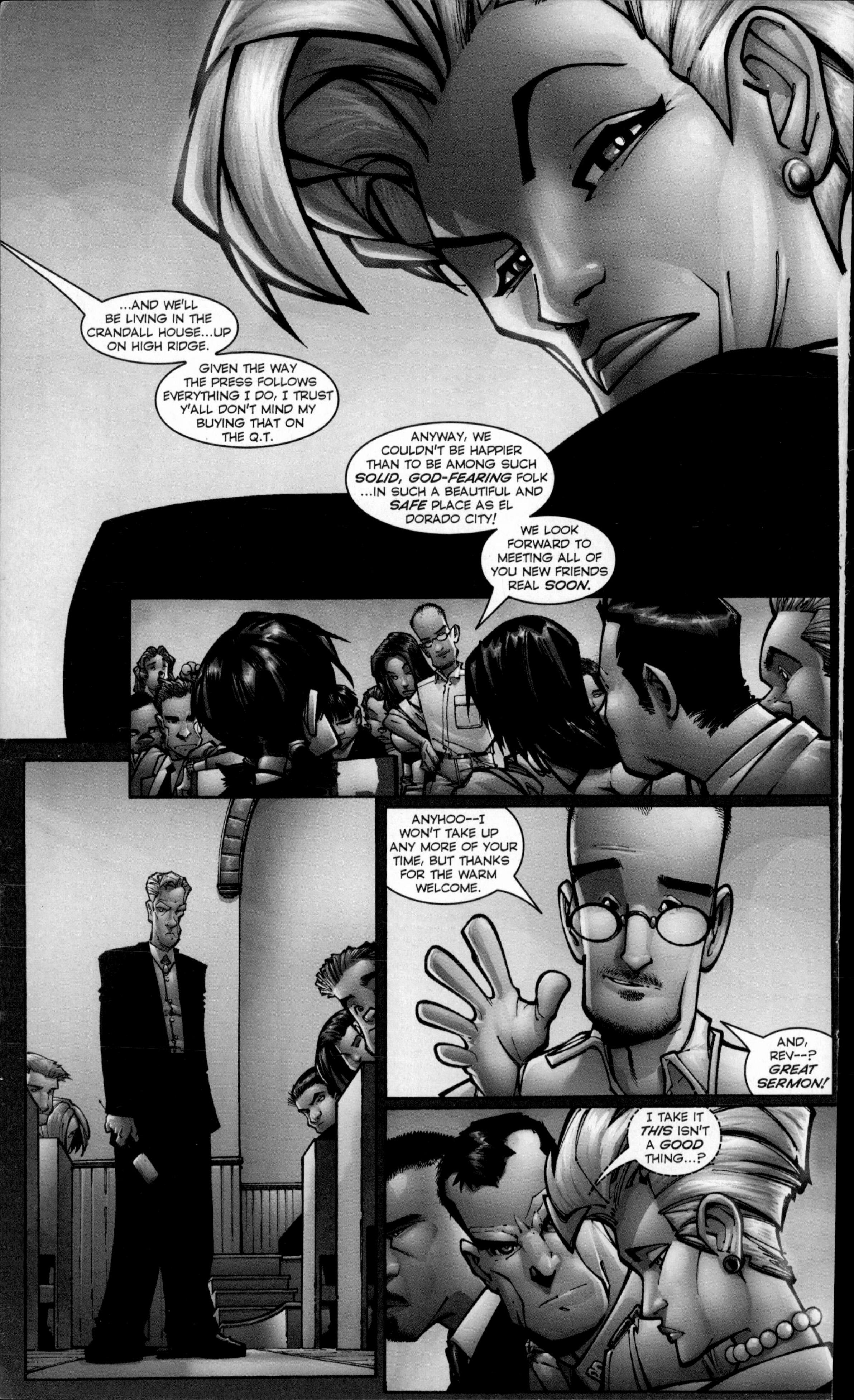
...AND WE'LL BE LIVING IN THE CRANDALL HOUSE...UP ON HIGH RIDGE.
GIVEN THE WAY THE PRESS FOLLOWS EVERYTHING I DO, I TRUST Y'ALL DON'T MIND MY BUYING THAT ON THE Q.T.
ANYWAY, WE COULDN'T BE HAPPIER THAN TO BE AMONG SUCH SOLID, GOD-FEARING FOLK ...IN SUCH A BEAUTIFUL AND SAFE PLACE AS EL DORADO CITY!
WE LOOK FORWARD TO MEETING ALL OF YOU NEW FRIENDS REAL SOON.
ANYHOO--I WON'T TAKE UP ANY MORE OF YOUR TIME, BUT THANKS FOR THE WARM WELCOME.
AND, REV--? GREAT SERMON!
I TAKE IT THIS ISN'T A GOOD THING...?

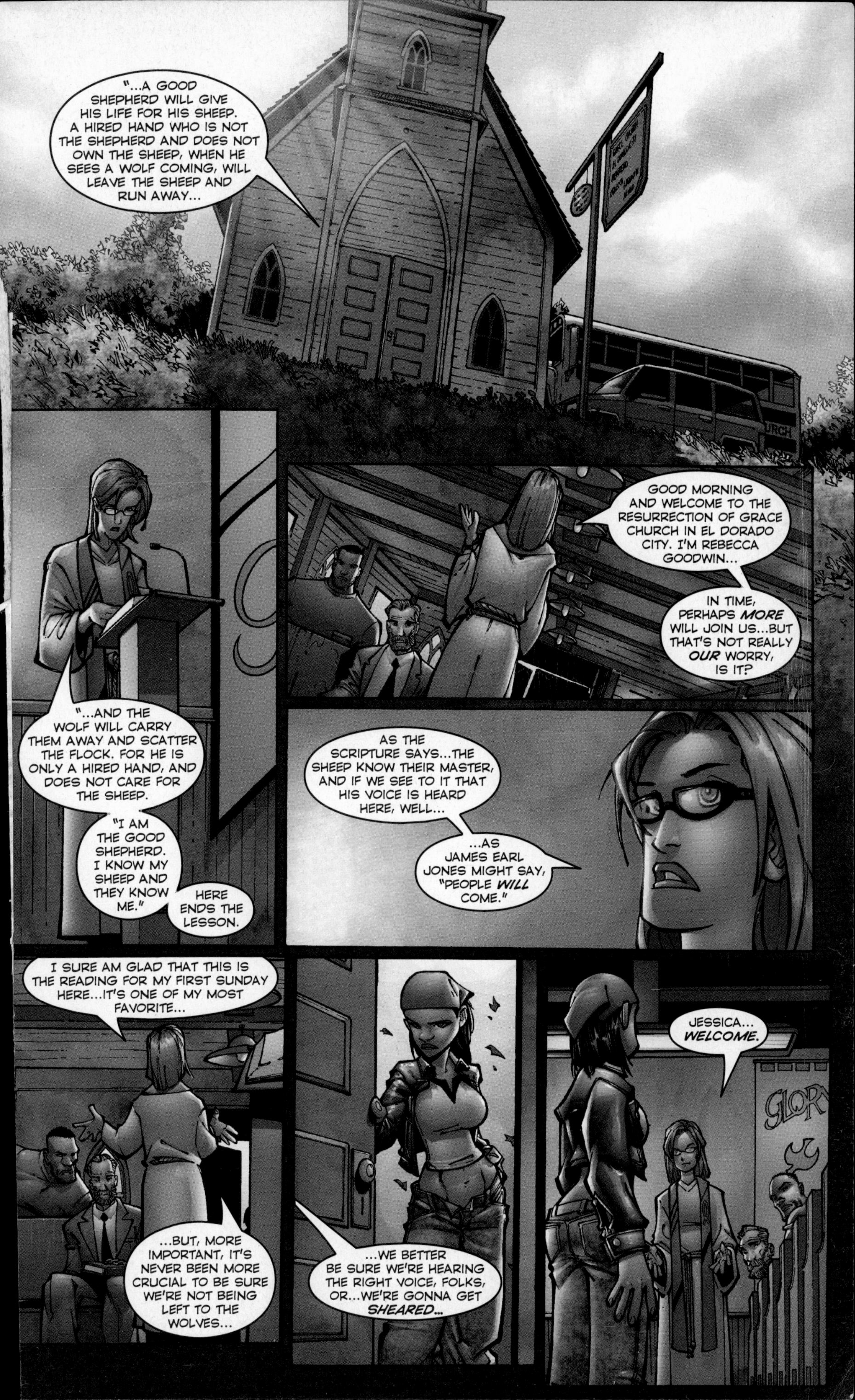
"...A GOOD SHEPHERD WILL GIVE HIS LIFE FOR HIS SHEEP. A HIRED HAND WHO IS NOT THE SHEPHERD AND DOES NOT OWN THE SHEEP, WHEN HE SEES A WOLF COMING, WILL LEAVE THE SHEEP AND RUN AWAY...
"...AND THE WOLF WILL CARRY THEM AWAY AND SCATTER THE FLOCK. FOR HE IS ONLY A HIRED HAND, AND DOES NOT CARE FOR THE SHEEP.
"I AM THE GOOD SHEPHERD. I KNOW MY SHEEP AND THEY KNOW ME."
HERE ENDS THE LESSON.
GOOD MORNING AND WELCOME TO THE RESURRECTION OF GRACE CHURCH IN EL DORADO CITY. I'M REBECCA GOODWIN...
IN TIME, PERHAPS MORE WILL JOIN US...BUT THAT'S NOT REALLY OUR WORRY, IS IT?
AS THE SCRIPTURE SAYS...THE SHEEP KNOW THEIR MASTER, AND IF WE SEE TO IT THAT HIS VOICE IS HEARD HERE, WELL...
...AS JAMES EARL JONES MIGHT SAY, "PEOPLE WILL COME."
I SURE AM GLAD THAT THIS IS THE READING FOR MY FIRST SUNDAY HERE...IT'S ONE OF MY MOST FAVORITE...
...BUT, MORE IMPORTANT, IT'S NEVER BEEN MORE CRUCIAL TO BE SURE WE'RE NOT BEING LEFT TO THE WOLVES...
...WE BETTER BE SURE WE'RE HEARING THE RIGHT VOICE, FOLKS, OR...WE'RE GONNA GET SHEARED...
JESSICA... WELCOME.
GLORY

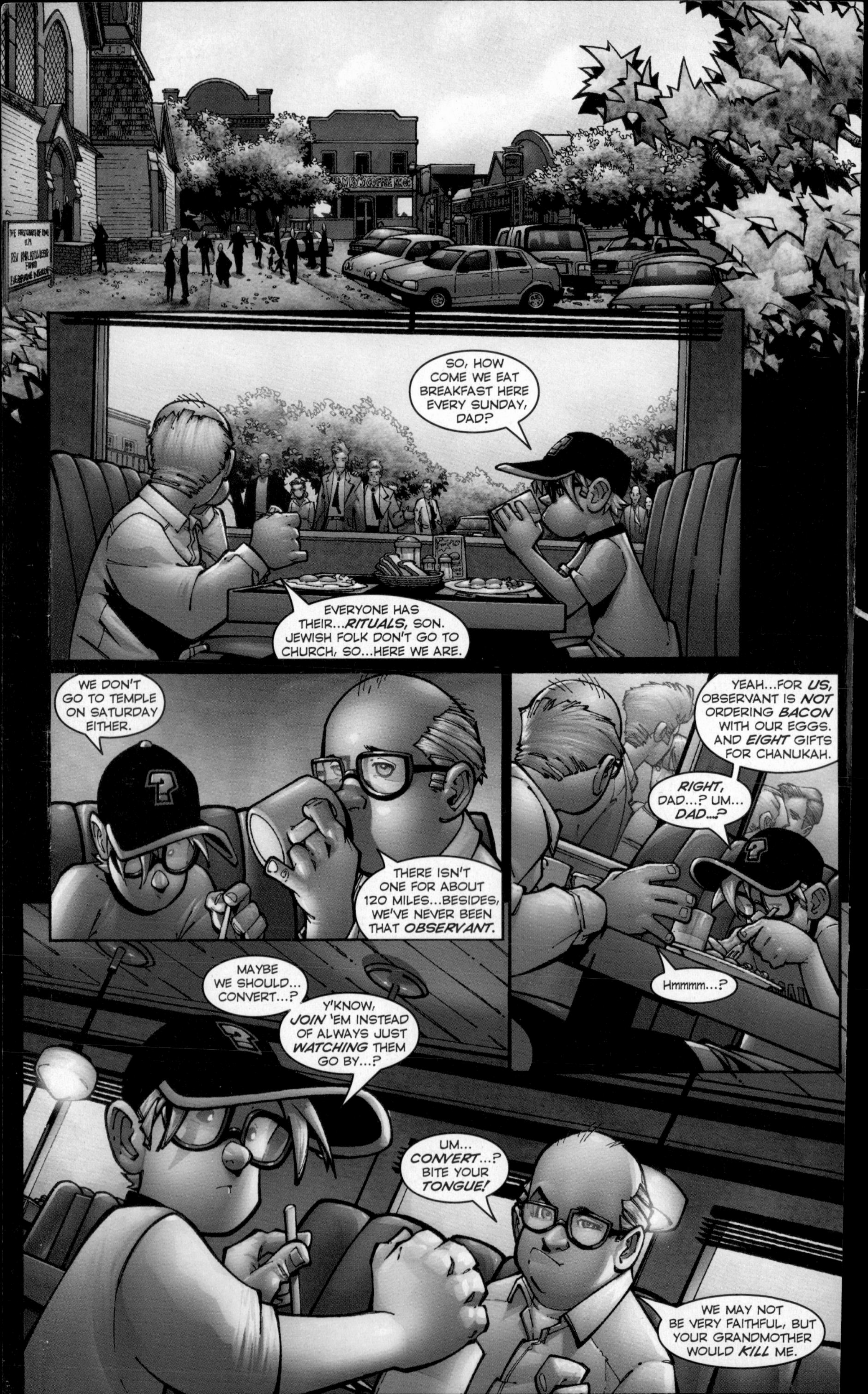
SO, HOW COME WE EAT BREAKFAST HERE EVERY SUNDAY, DAD?
EVERYONE HAS THEIR...RITUALS, SON. JEWISH FOLK DON'T GO TO CHURCH, SO...HERE WE ARE.
WE DON'T GO TO TEMPLE ON SATURDAY EITHER.
THERE ISN'T ONE FOR ABOUT 120 MILES...BESIDES, WE'VE NEVER BEEN THAT OBSERVANT.
YEAH...FOR US, OBSERVANT IS NOT ORDERING BACON WITH OUR EGGS. AND EIGHT GIFTS FOR CHANUKAH.
RIGHT, DAD...? UM... DAD...?
Hmmmm...?
MAYBE WE SHOULD... CONVERT...?
Y'KNOW, JOIN 'EM INSTEAD OF ALWAYS JUST WATCHING THEM GO BY...?
UM... CONVERT...? BITE YOUR TONGUE!
WE MAY NOT BE VERY FAITHFUL, BUT YOUR GRANDMOTHER WOULD KILL ME.

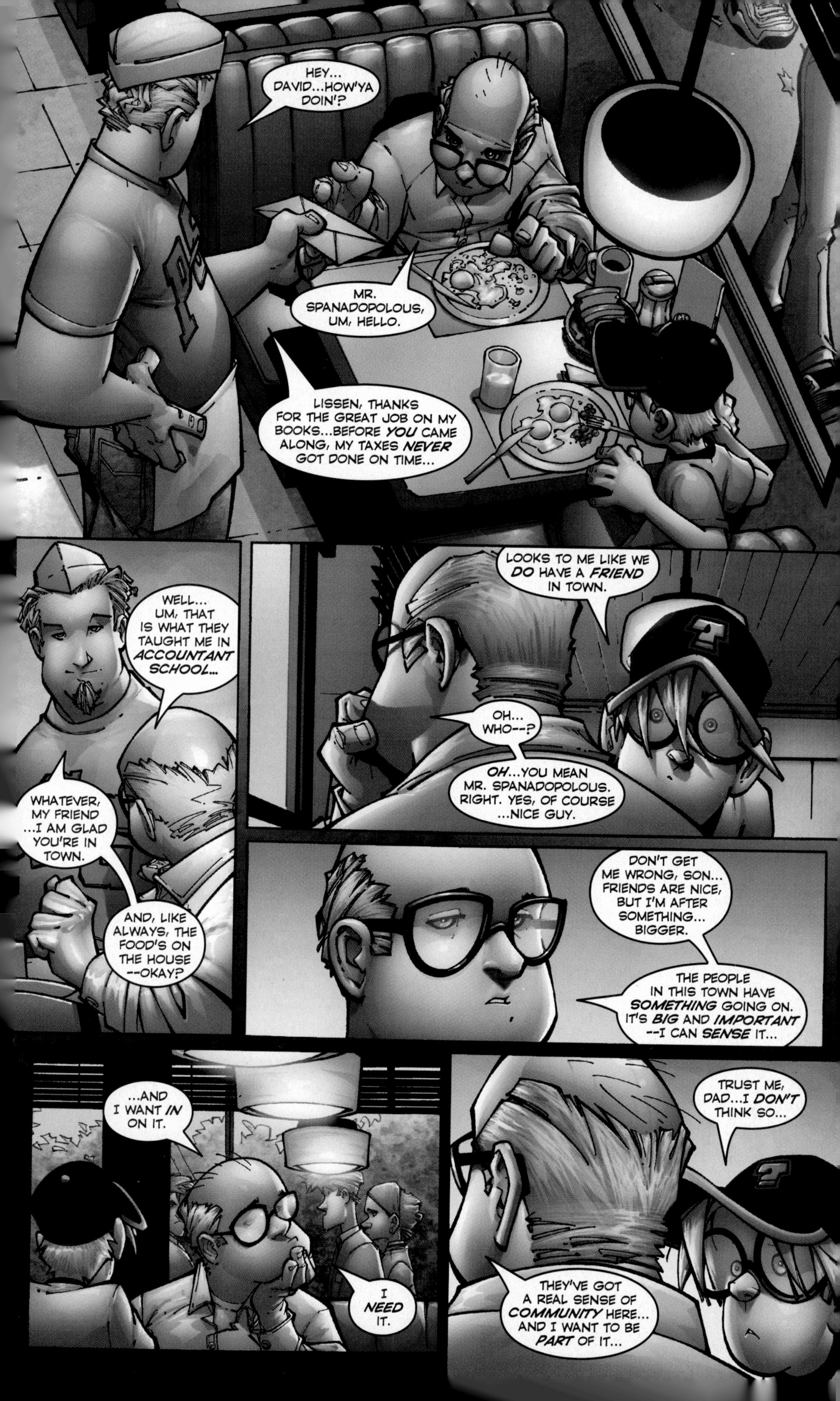

HEY... DAVID...HOW'YA DOIN'?
MR. SPANADOPOLOUS, UM, HELLO.
LISSEN, THANKS FOR THE GREAT JOB ON MY BOOKS...BEFORE YOU CAME ALONG, MY TAXES NEVER GOT DONE ON TIME...
WELL... UM, THAT IS WHAT THEY TAUGHT ME IN ACCOUNTANT SCHOOL...
WHATEVER, MY FRIEND ...I AM GLAD YOU'RE IN TOWN.
AND, LIKE ALWAYS, THE FOOD'S ON THE HOUSE --OKAY?
LOOKS TO ME LIKE WE DO HAVE A FRIEND IN TOWN.
OH... WHO--?
OH...YOU MEAN MR. SPANADOPOLOUS. RIGHT. YES, OF COURSE ...NICE GUY.
DON'T GET ME WRONG, SON... FRIENDS ARE NICE, BUT I'M AFTER SOMETHING... BIGGER.
THE PEOPLE IN THIS TOWN HAVE SOMETHING GOING ON. IT'S BIG AND IMPORTANT --I CAN SENSE IT...
...AND I WANT IN ON IT.
I NEED IT.
TRUST ME, DAD...I DON'T THINK SO...
THEY'VE GOT A REAL SENSE OF COMMUNITY HERE... AND I WANT TO BE PART OF IT...

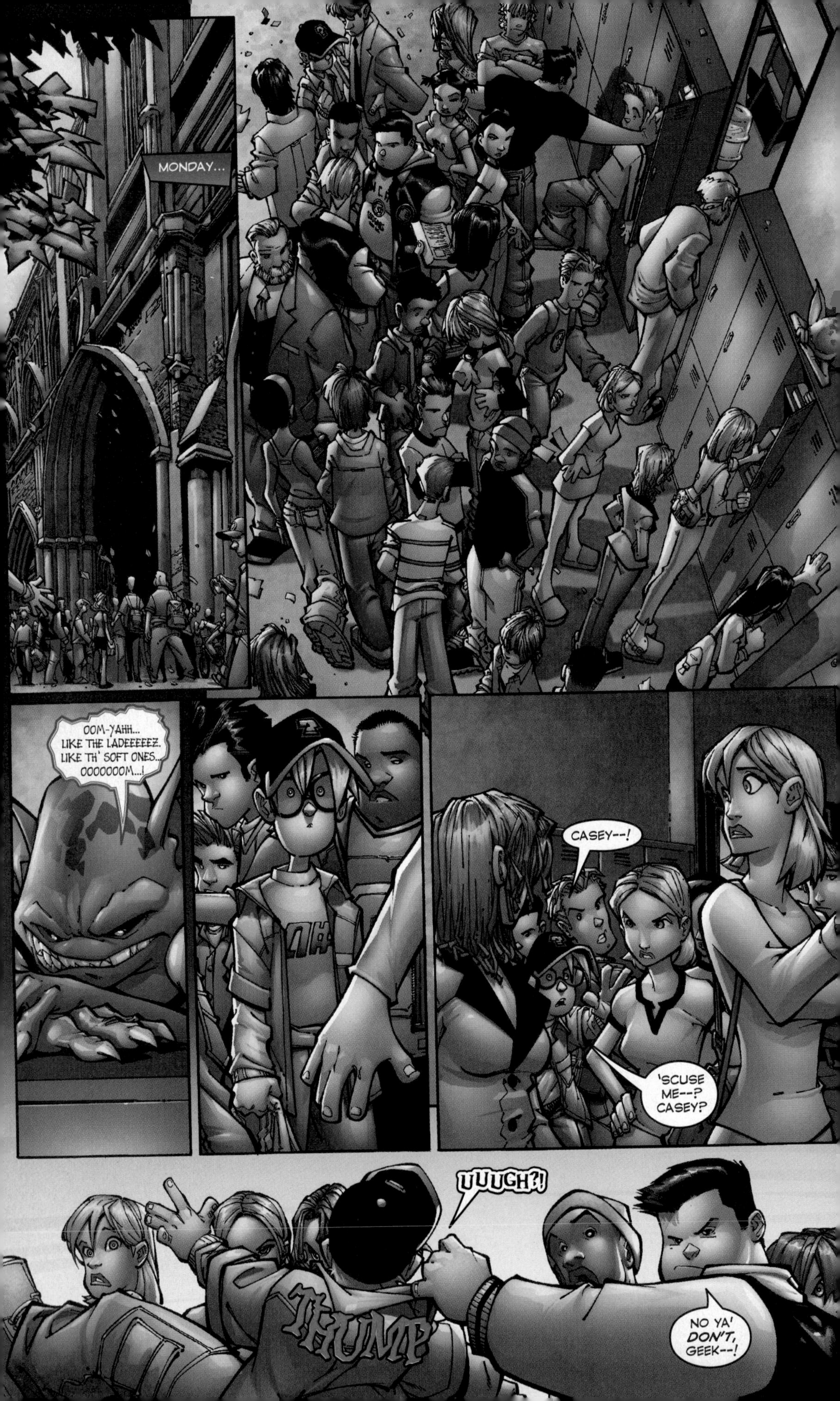
MONDAY...
OOM-YAHH... LIKE THE LADEEEEEZ. LIKE TH' SOFT ONES... OOOOOOOM...!
CASEY--!
'SCUSE ME--? CASEY?
UUUGH?!
THUMP
NO YA' DON'T, GEEK--!

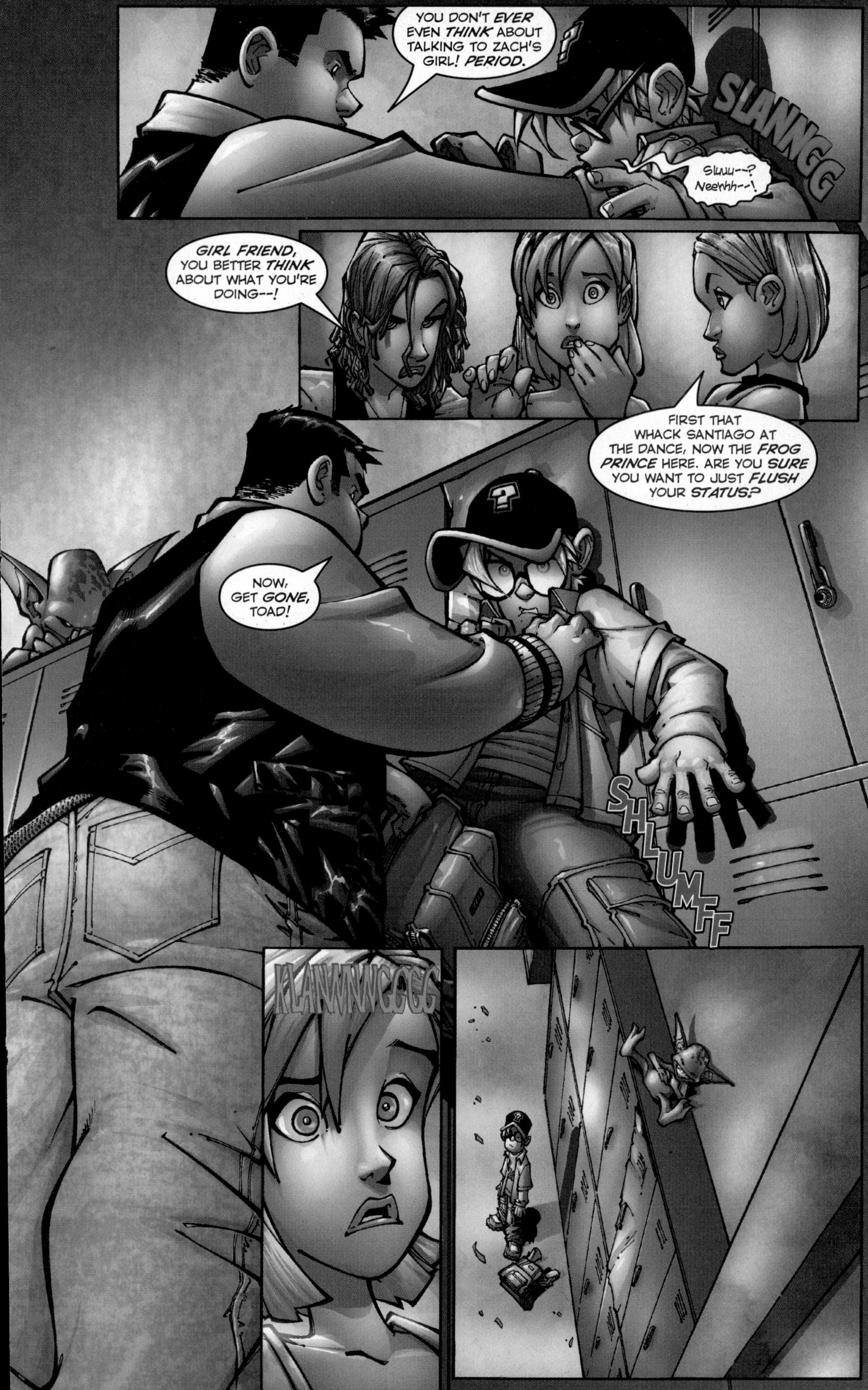
YOU DON'T *EVER* EVEN *THINK* ABOUT TALKING TO ZACH'S GIRL! *PERIOD.*
SLANNGG
Sluuu--? Neewhh--!
GIRL FRIEND, YOU BETTER *THINK* ABOUT WHAT YOU'RE DOING--!
FIRST THAT WHACK SANTIAGO AT THE DANCE, NOW THE *FROG PRINCE* HERE. ARE YOU *SURE* YOU WANT TO JUST *FLUSH* YOUR *STATUS?*
NOW, GET *GONE,* TOAD!
SHLUMFF
KLANWNNGGGG

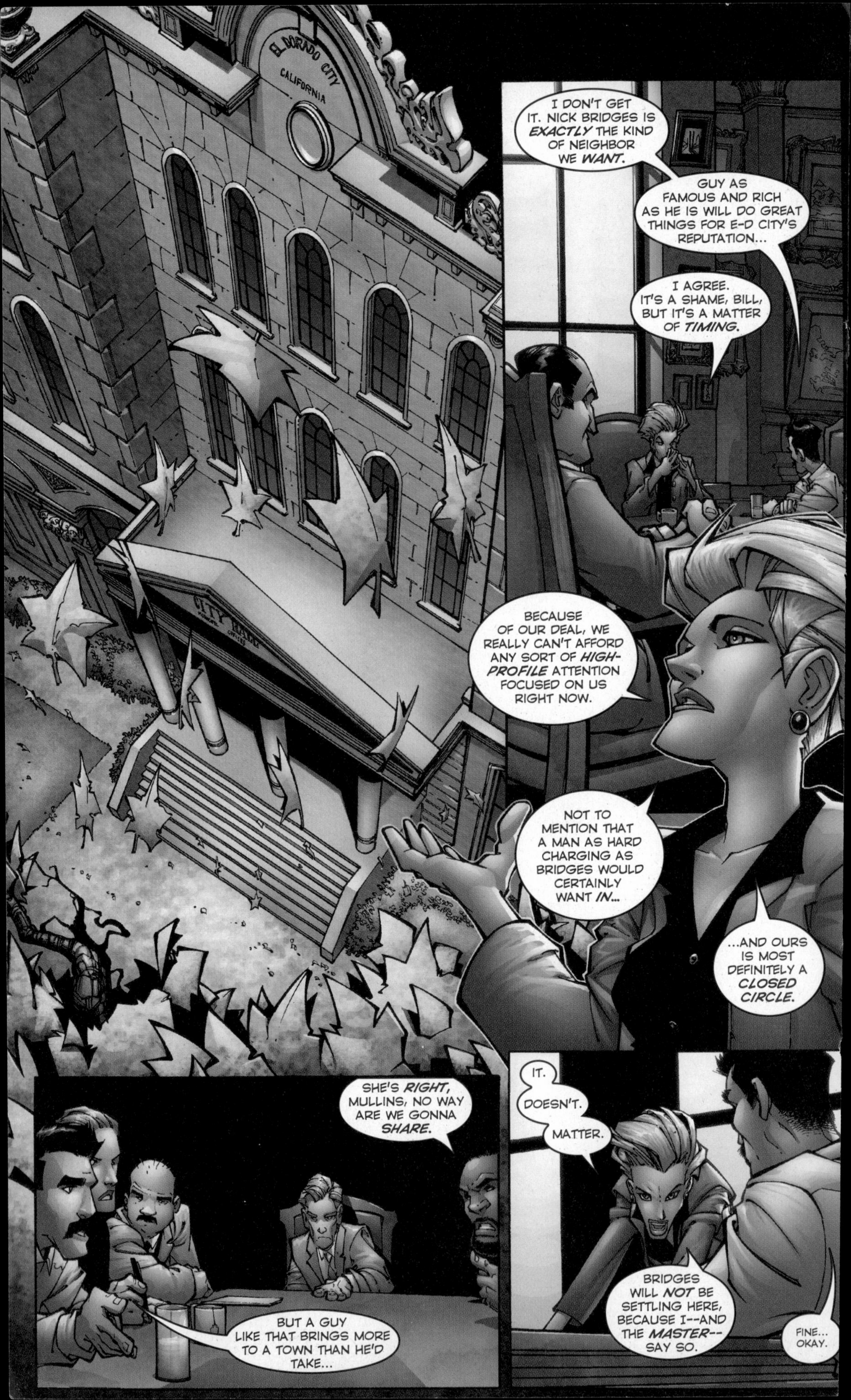
EL DORADO CITY
CALIFORNIA
CITY HALL
I DON'T GET IT. NICK BRIDGES IS *EXACTLY* THE KIND OF NEIGHBOR WE *WANT*.
GUY AS FAMOUS AND RICH AS HE IS WILL DO GREAT THINGS FOR E-D CITY'S REPUTATION...
I AGREE. IT'S A SHAME, BILL, BUT IT'S A MATTER OF *TIMING*.
BECAUSE OF OUR DEAL, WE REALLY CAN'T AFFORD ANY SORT OF *HIGH-PROFILE* ATTENTION FOCUSED ON US RIGHT NOW.
NOT TO MENTION THAT A MAN AS HARD CHARGING AS BRIDGES WOULD CERTAINLY WANT *IN*...
...AND OURS IS MOST DEFINITELY A *CLOSED CIRCLE*.
SHE'S *RIGHT*, MULLINS, NO WAY ARE WE GONNA *SHARE*.
BUT A GUY LIKE THAT BRINGS MORE TO A TOWN THAN HE'D TAKE...
IT.
DOESN'T.
MATTER.
BRIDGES WILL *NOT* BE SETTLING HERE, BECAUSE I--AND THE *MASTER*--SAY SO.
FINE... OKAY.

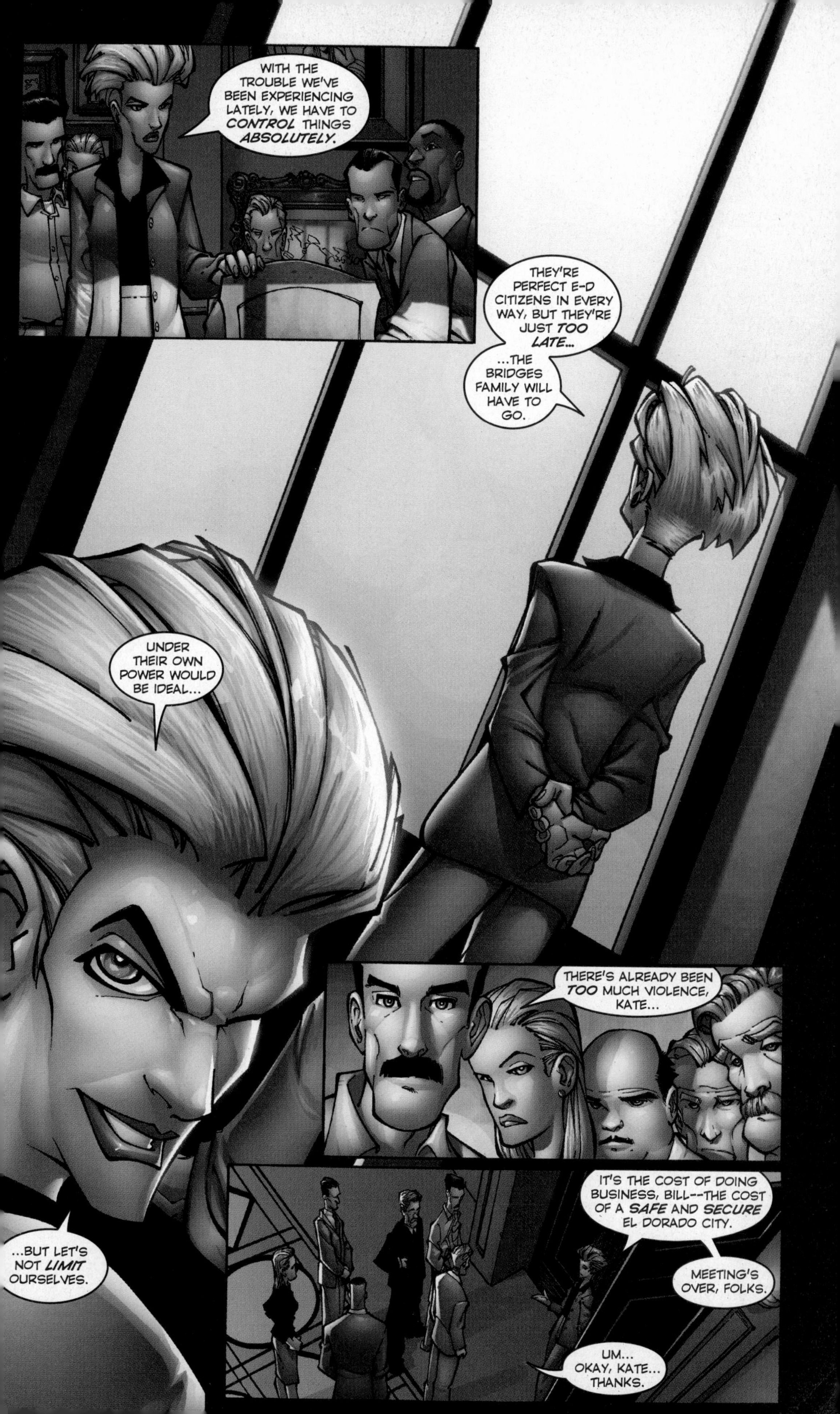
WITH THE TROUBLE WE'VE BEEN EXPERIENCING LATELY, WE HAVE TO CONTROL THINGS ABSOLUTELY.
THEY'RE PERFECT E-D CITIZENS IN EVERY WAY, BUT THEY'RE JUST TOO LATE...
...THE BRIDGES FAMILY WILL HAVE TO GO.
UNDER THEIR OWN POWER WOULD BE IDEAL...
...BUT LET'S NOT LIMIT OURSELVES.
THERE'S ALREADY BEEN TOO MUCH VIOLENCE, KATE...
IT'S THE COST OF DOING BUSINESS, BILL--THE COST OF A SAFE AND SECURE EL DORADO CITY.
MEETING'S OVER, FOLKS.
UM... OKAY, KATE... THANKS.

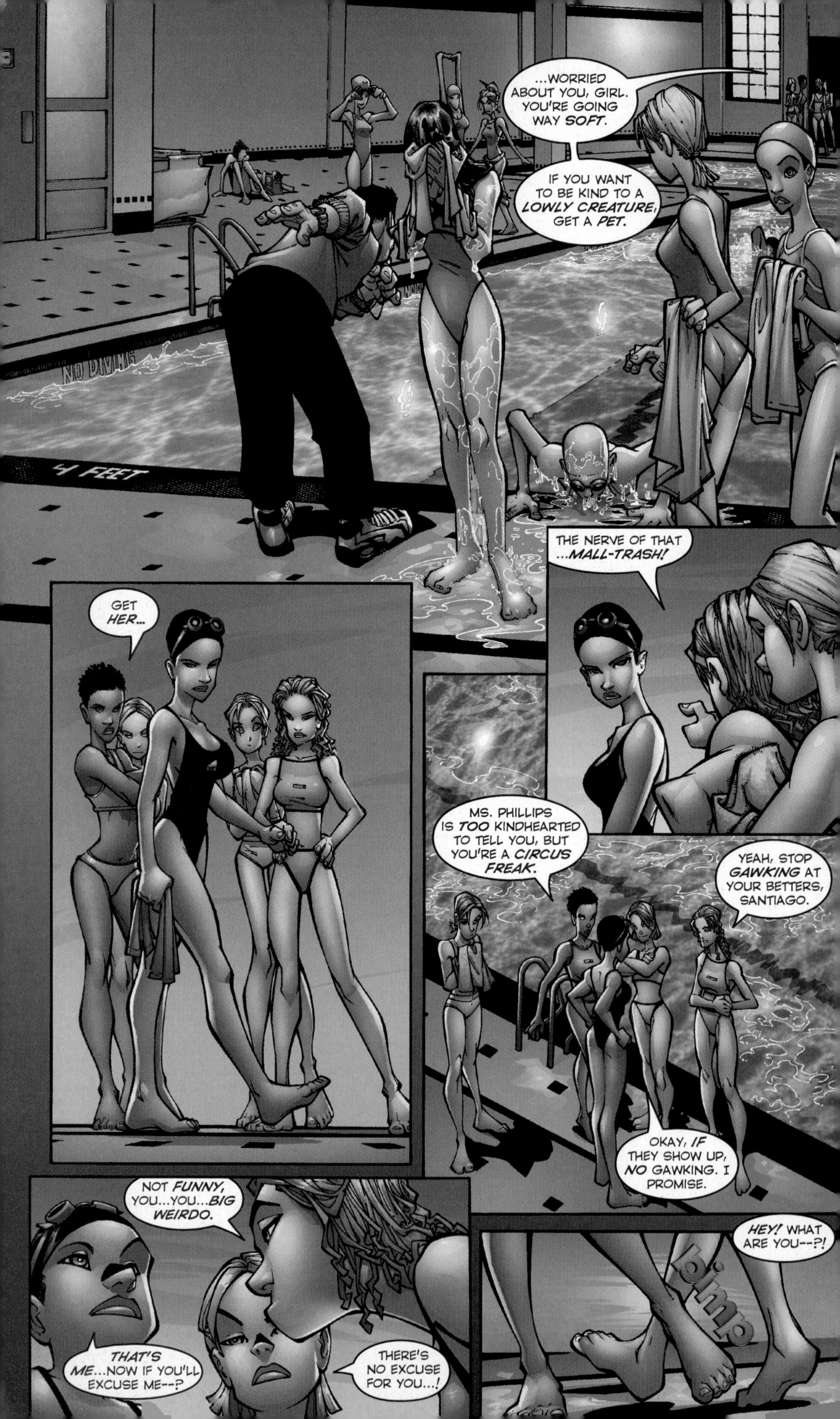
...WORRIED ABOUT YOU, GIRL. YOU'RE GOING WAY SOFT.
IF YOU WANT TO BE KIND TO A LOWLY CREATURE, GET A PET.
NO DIVING
4 FEET
THE NERVE OF THAT ...MALL-TRASH!
GET HER...
MS. PHILLIPS IS TOO KINDHEARTED TO TELL YOU, BUT YOU'RE A CIRCUS FREAK.
YEAH, STOP GAWKING AT YOUR BETTERS, SANTIAGO.
OKAY, IF THEY SHOW UP, NO GAWKING. I PROMISE.
NOT FUNNY, YOU...YOU...BIG WEIRDO.
THAT'S ME...NOW IF YOU'LL EXCUSE ME--?
THERE'S NO EXCUSE FOR YOU...!
HEY! WHAT ARE YOU--?!
bimp

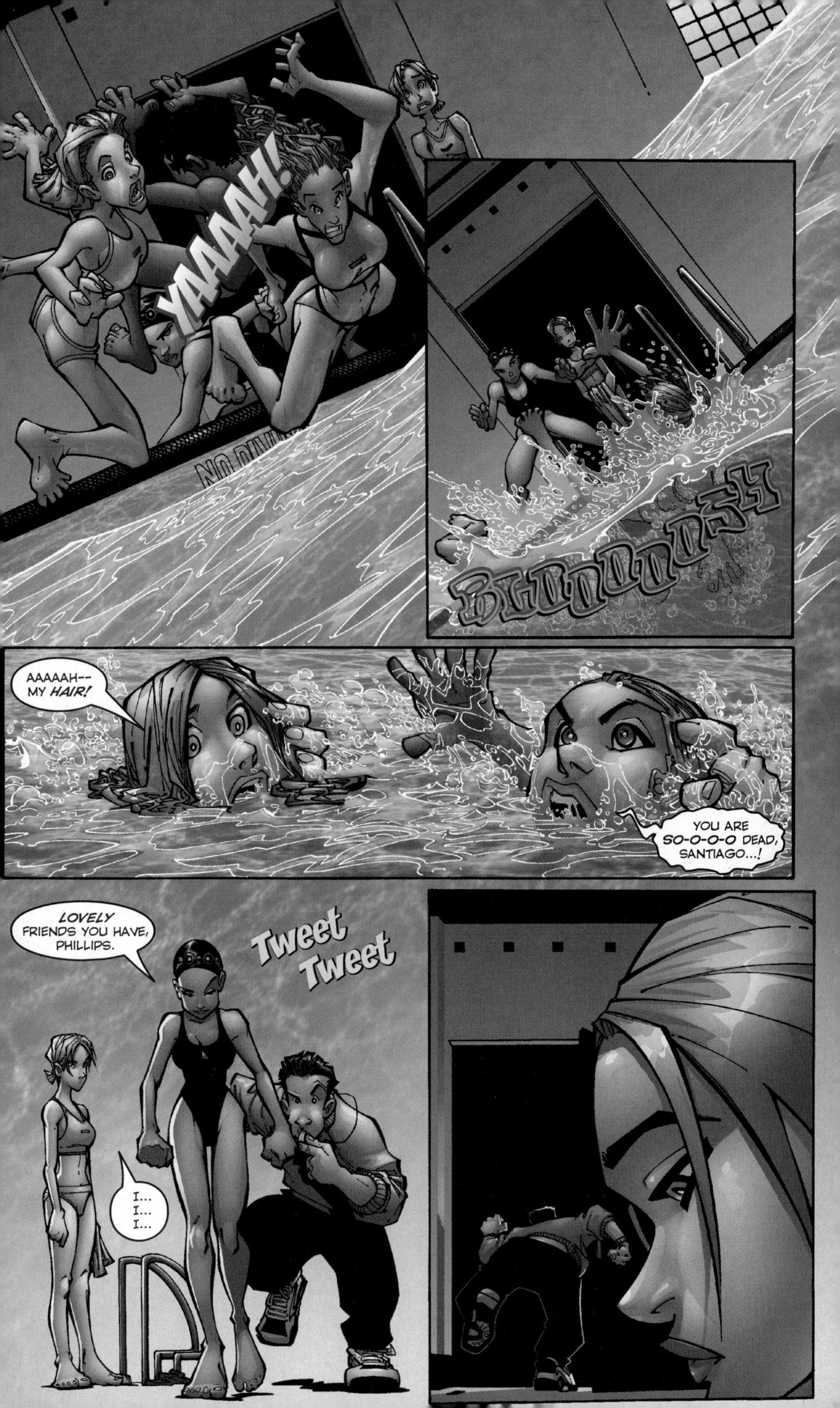
YAAAAH!
NO DIVI
BLOOOOOSH
AAAAAH-- MY HAIR!
YOU ARE SO-O-O-O DEAD, SANTIAGO...!
LOVELY FRIENDS YOU HAVE, PHILLIPS.
Tweet Tweet
I... I... I...

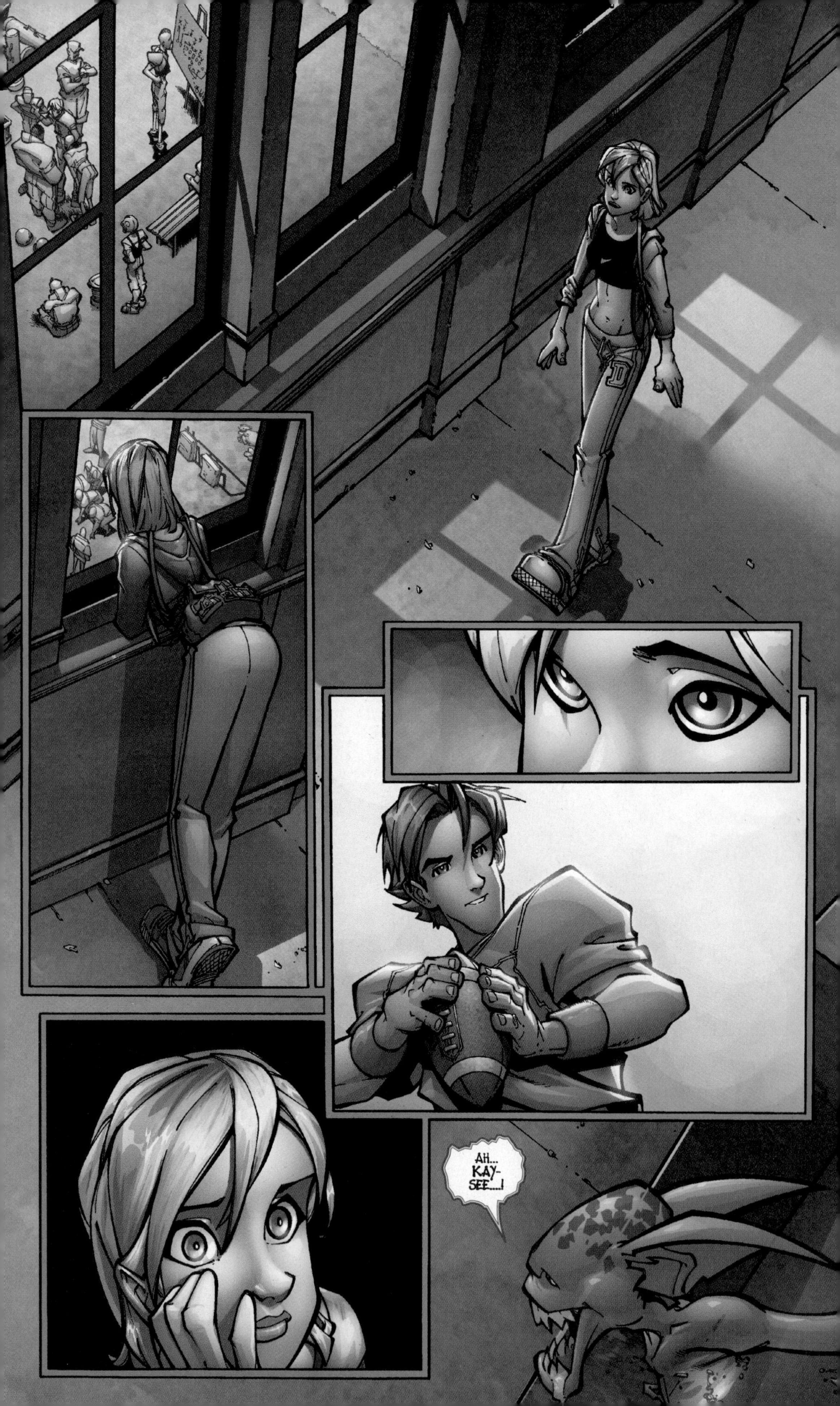
AH...
KAY-
SEE...!

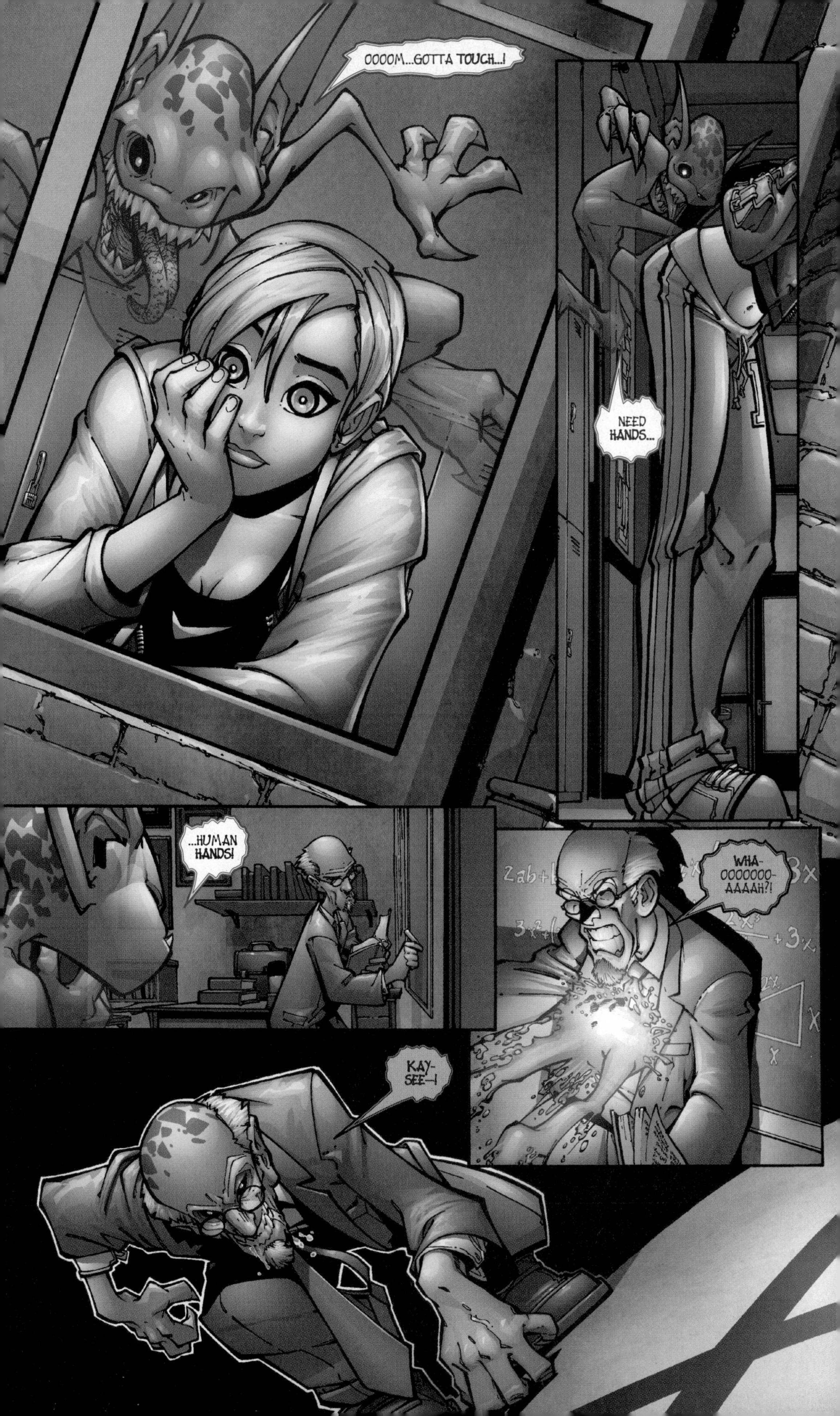
OOOOM...GOTTA TOUCH...!
NEED HANDS...
...HUMAN HANDS!
WHA-OOOOOOO-AAAAH?!
KAY-SEE--!

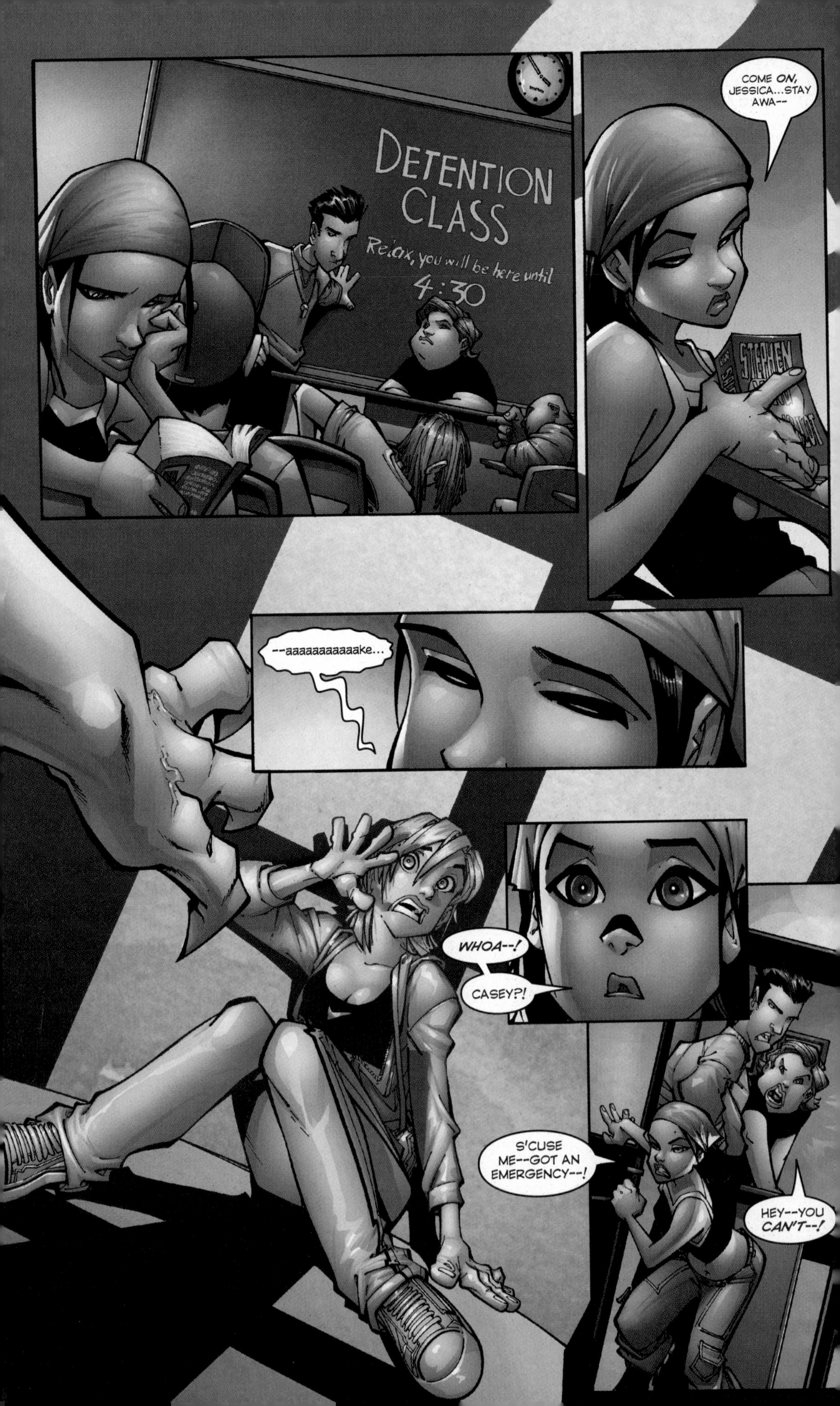
DETENTION CLASS
Relax, you will be here until 4:30
COME ON, JESSICA...STAY AWA--
--aaaaaaaaaaaake...
WHOA--!
CASEY?!
S'CUSE ME--GOT AN EMERGENCY--!
HEY--YOU CAN'T--!

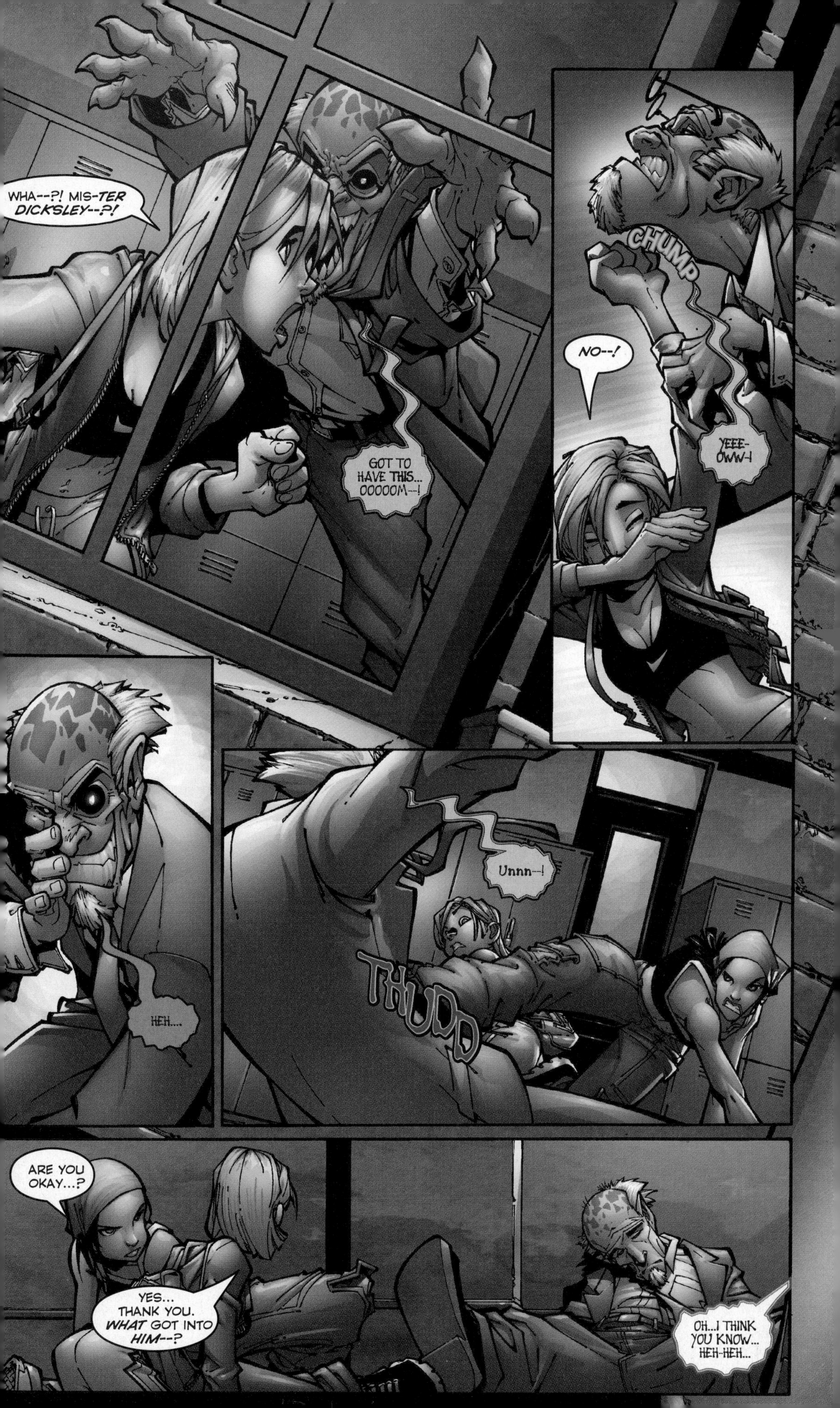
WHA--?! MIS-TER DICKSLEY--?!
GOT TO HAVE THIS... OOOOOM--!
CHUMP
NO--!
YEEE-OWW-!
HEH....
Unnn--!
THUDD
ARE YOU OKAY...?
YES... THANK YOU. WHAT GOT INTO HIM--?
OH...I THINK YOU KNOW... HEH-HEH...

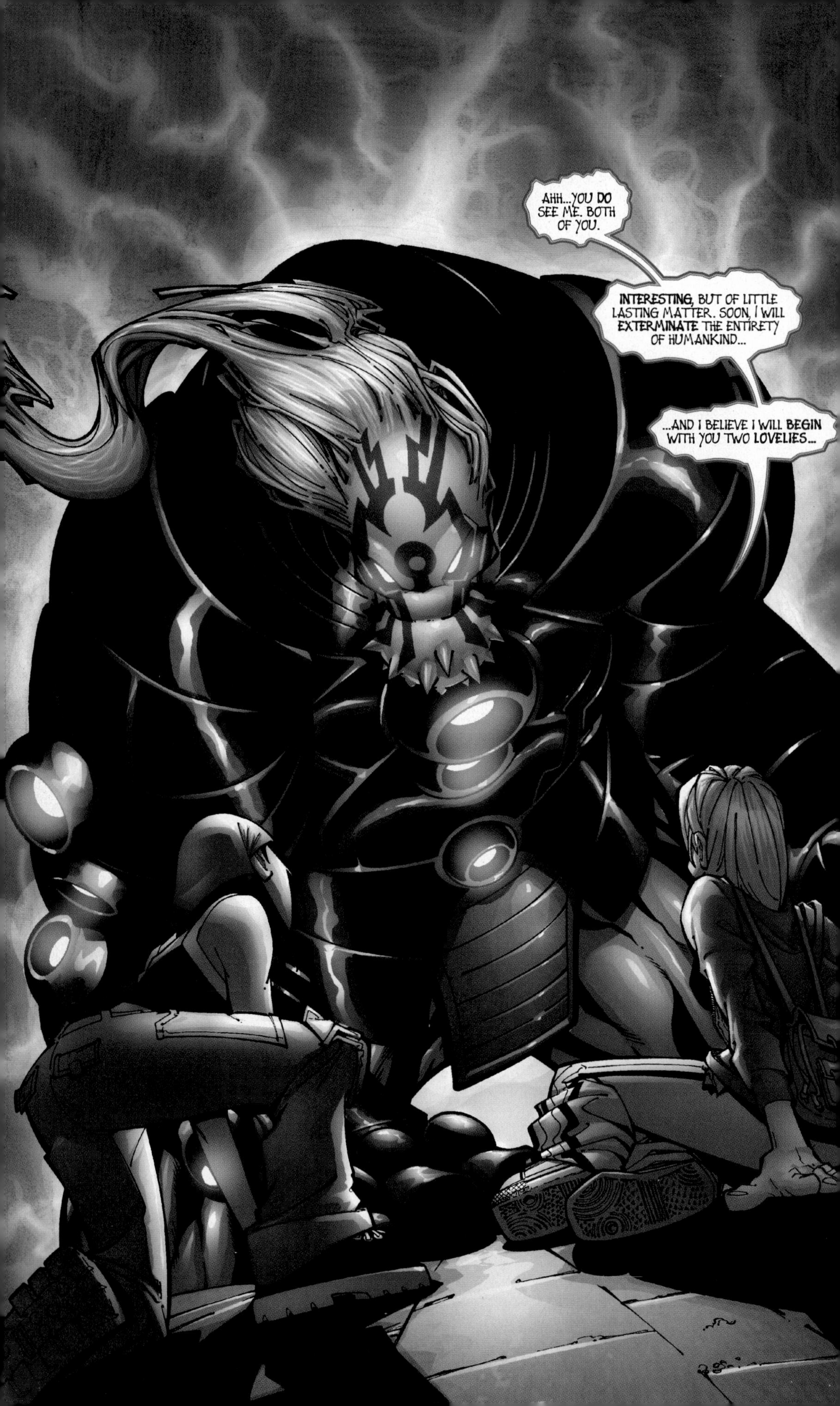
AHH...YOU DO SEE ME. BOTH OF YOU.
INTERESTING, BUT OF LITTLE LASTING MATTER. SOON, I WILL EXTERMINATE THE ENTIRETY OF HUMANKIND...
...AND I BELIEVE I WILL BEGIN WITH YOU TWO LOVELIES...

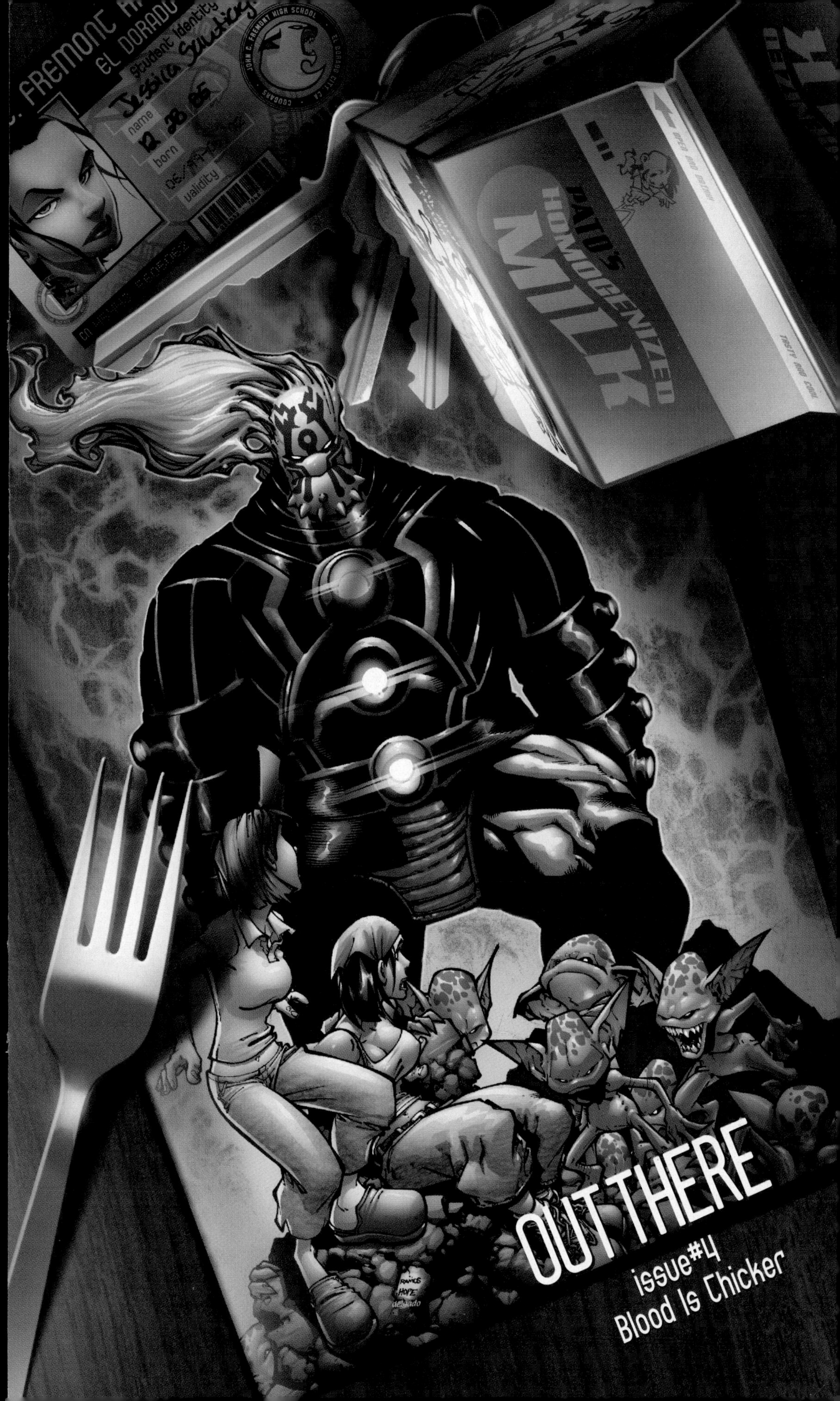
OUT THERE
issue#4
Blood Is Thicker

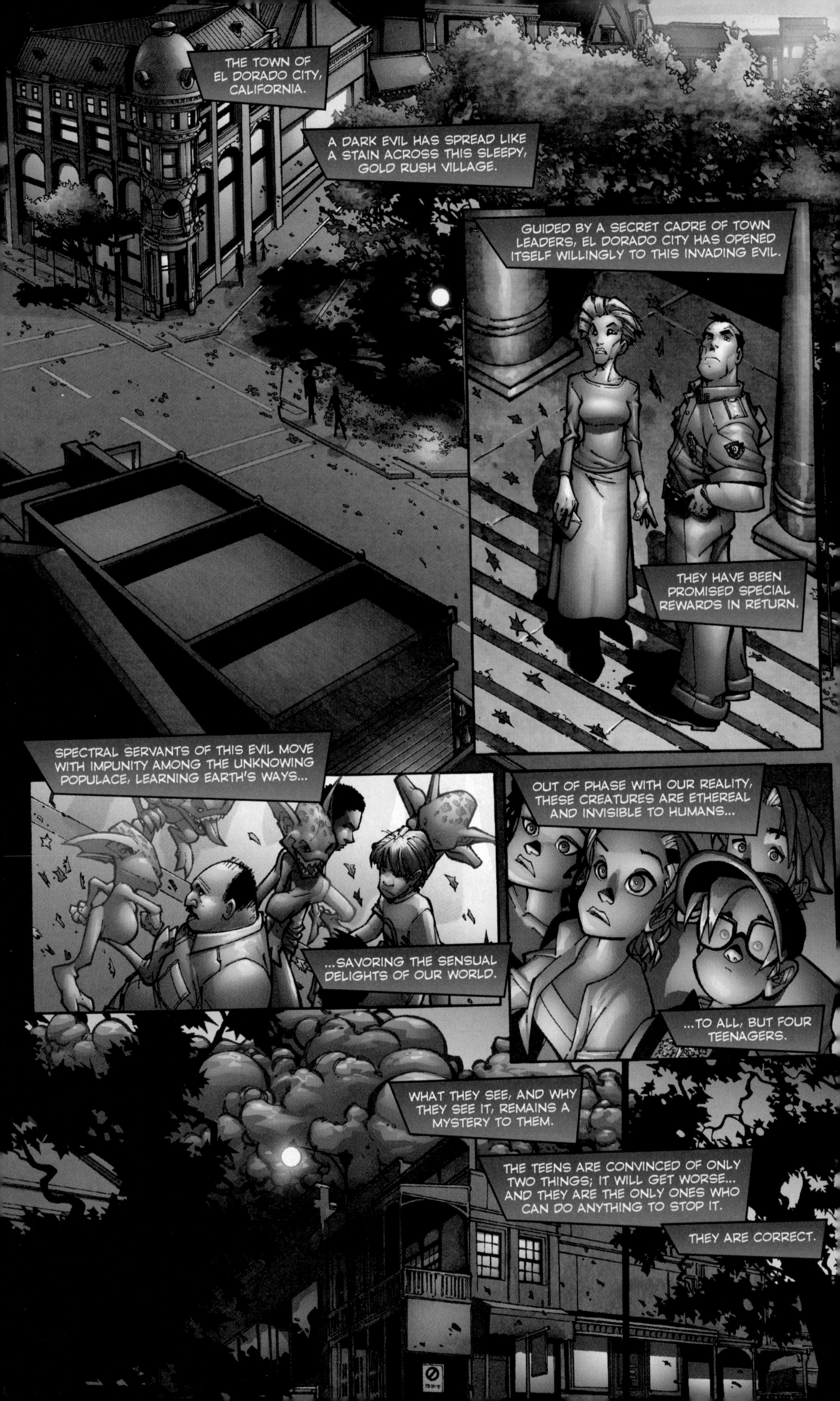

THE TOWN OF EL DORADO CITY, CALIFORNIA.
A DARK EVIL HAS SPREAD LIKE A STAIN ACROSS THIS SLEEPY, GOLD RUSH VILLAGE.
GUIDED BY A SECRET CADRE OF TOWN LEADERS, EL DORADO CITY HAS OPENED ITSELF WILLINGLY TO THIS INVADING EVIL.
THEY HAVE BEEN PROMISED SPECIAL REWARDS IN RETURN.
SPECTRAL SERVANTS OF THIS EVIL MOVE WITH IMPUNITY AMONG THE UNKNOWING POPULACE, LEARNING EARTH'S WAYS...
...SAVORING THE SENSUAL DELIGHTS OF OUR WORLD.
OUT OF PHASE WITH OUR REALITY, THESE CREATURES ARE ETHEREAL AND INVISIBLE TO HUMANS...
...TO ALL, BUT FOUR TEENAGERS.
WHAT THEY SEE, AND WHY THEY SEE IT, REMAINS A MYSTERY TO THEM.
THE TEENS ARE CONVINCED OF ONLY TWO THINGS; IT WILL GET WORSE... AND THEY ARE THE ONLY ONES WHO CAN DO ANYTHING TO STOP IT.
THEY ARE CORRECT.

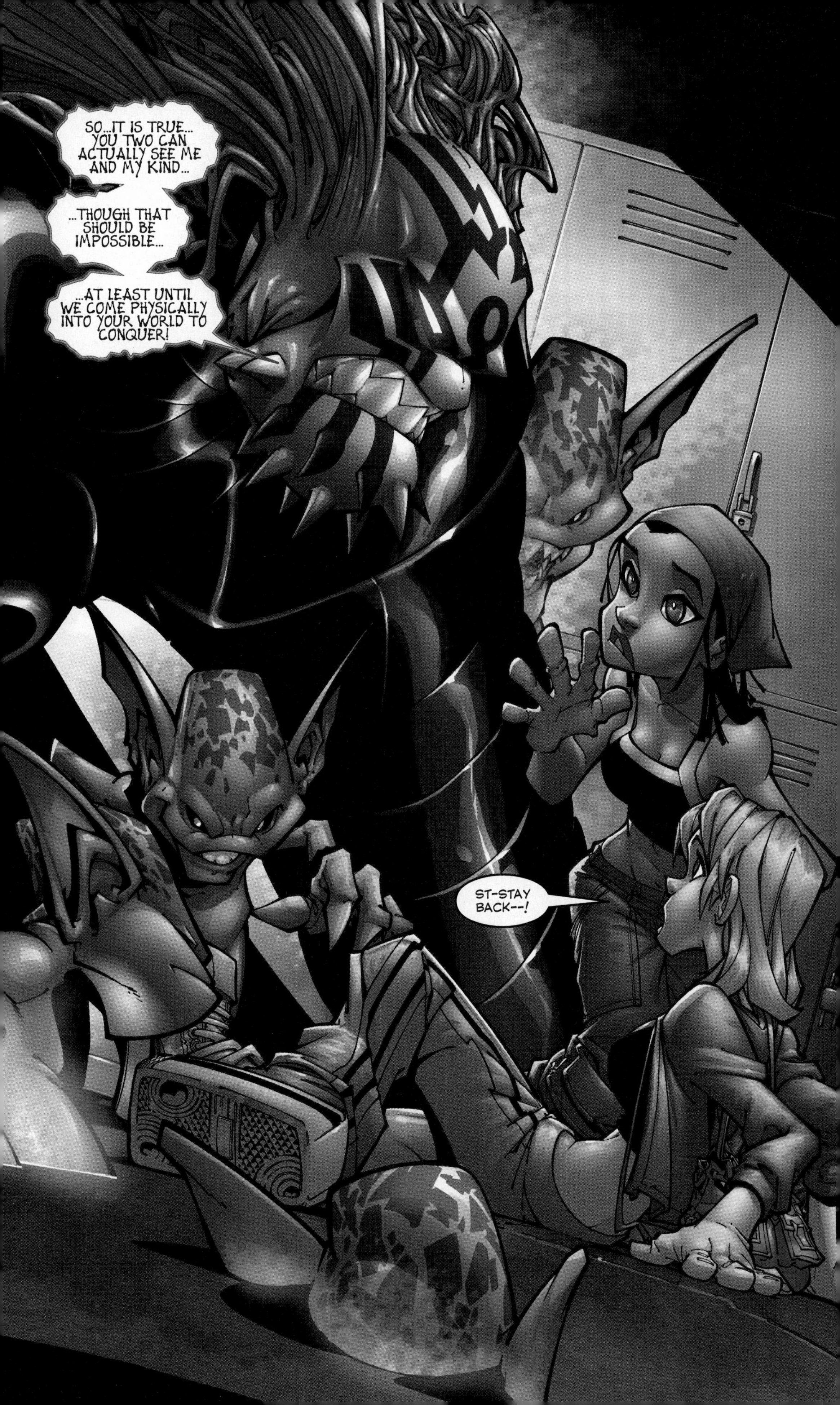
SO...IT IS TRUE... YOU TWO CAN ACTUALLY SEE ME AND MY KIND...
...THOUGH THAT SHOULD BE IMPOSSIBLE...
...AT LEAST UNTIL WE COME PHYSICALLY INTO YOUR WORLD TO CONQUER!
ST-STAY BACK--!

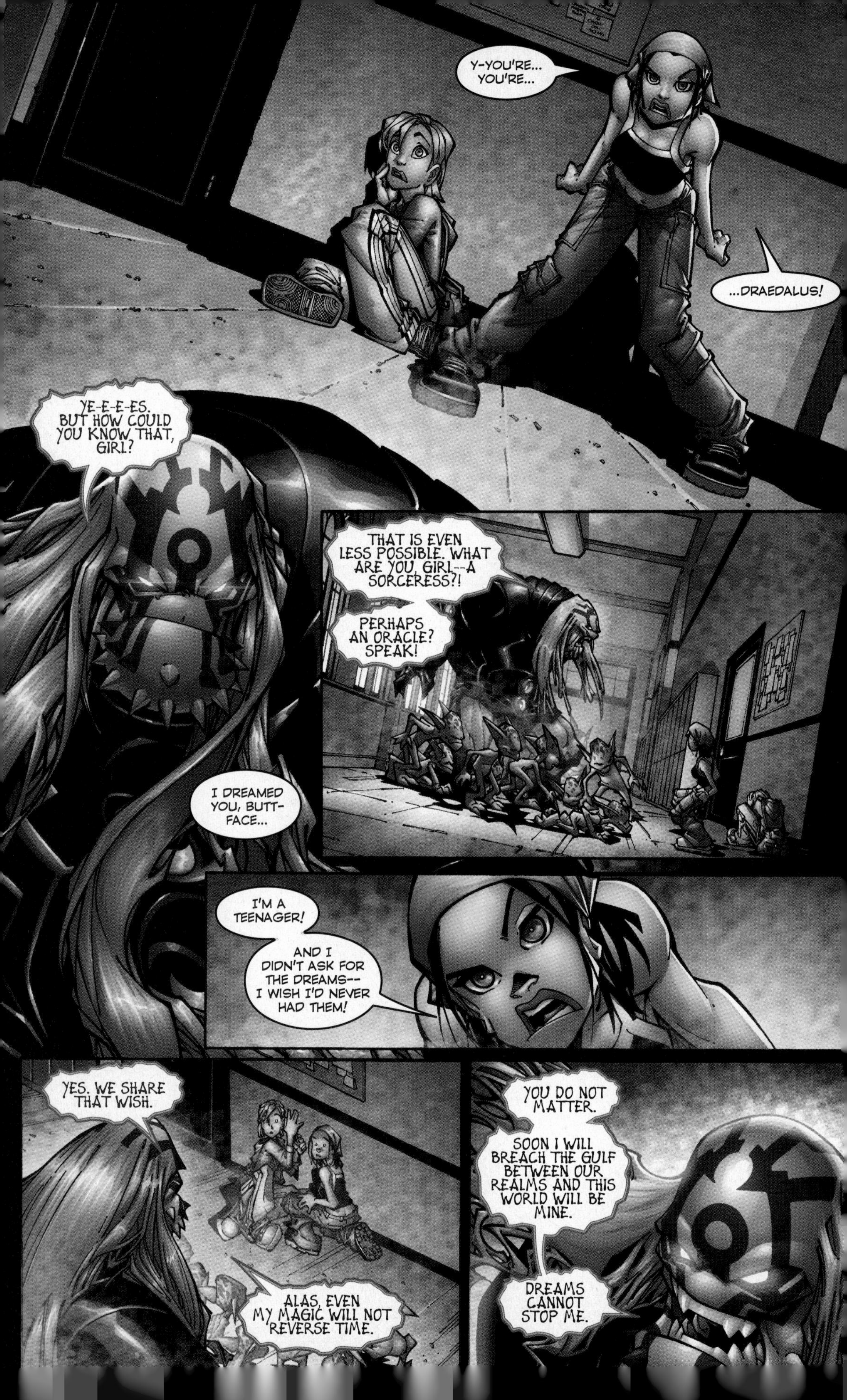
Y-YOU'RE... YOU'RE...
...DRAEDALUS!
YE-E-E-ES. BUT HOW COULD YOU KNOW THAT, GIRL?
I DREAMED YOU, BUTT-FACE...
THAT IS EVEN LESS POSSIBLE. WHAT ARE YOU, GIRL--A SORCERESS?!
PERHAPS AN ORACLE? SPEAK!
I'M A TEENAGER!
AND I DIDN'T ASK FOR THE DREAMS-- I WISH I'D NEVER HAD THEM!
YES. WE SHARE THAT WISH.
ALAS, EVEN MY MAGIC WILL NOT REVERSE TIME.
YOU DO NOT MATTER.
SOON I WILL BREACH THE GULF BETWEEN OUR REALMS AND THIS WORLD WILL BE MINE.
DREAMS CANNOT STOP ME.

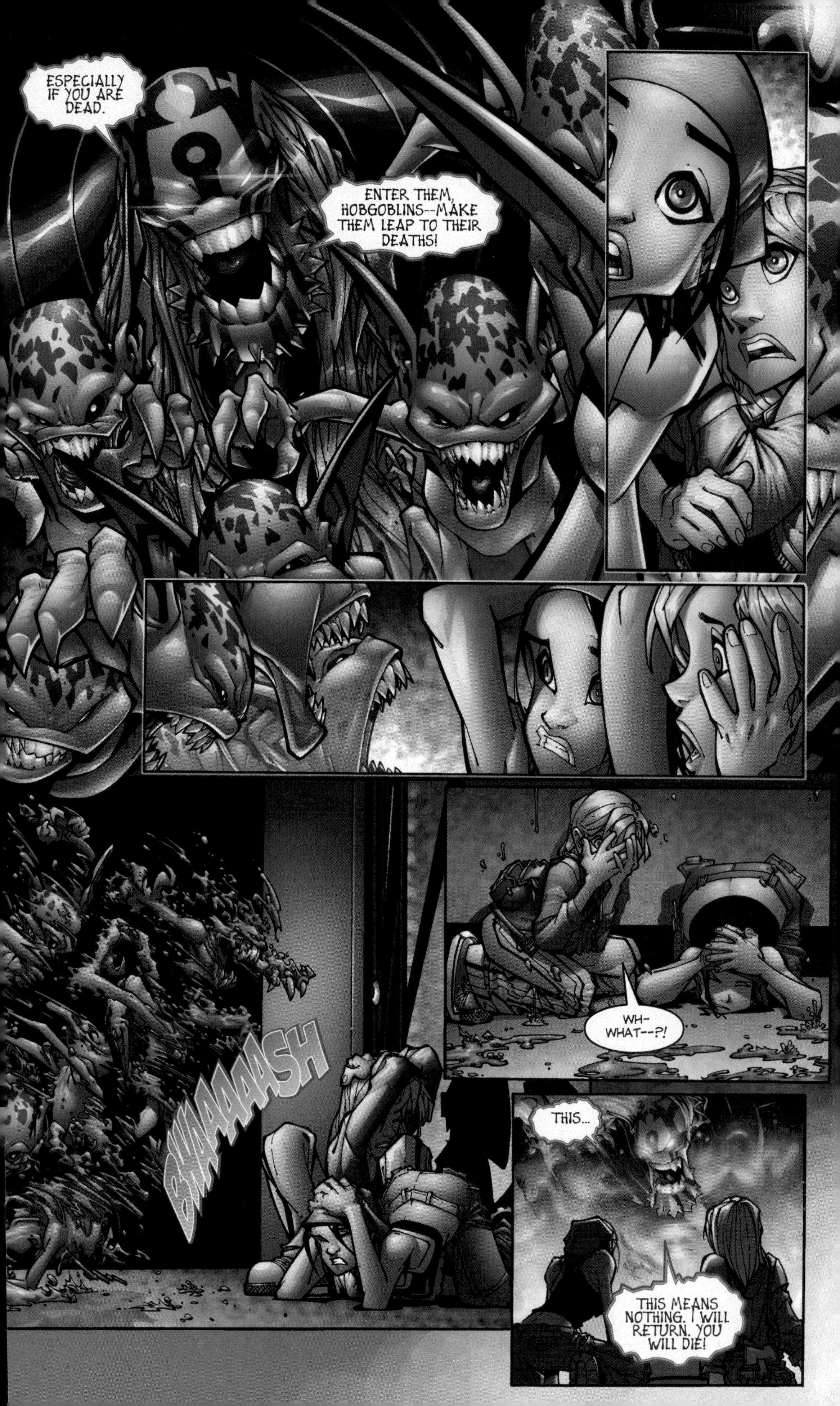
ESPECIALLY IF YOU ARE DEAD.
ENTER THEM, HOBGOBLINS--MAKE THEM LEAP TO THEIR DEATHS!
BWAAAAASH
WH- WHAT--?!
THIS...
THIS MEANS NOTHING. I WILL RETURN. YOU WILL DIE!

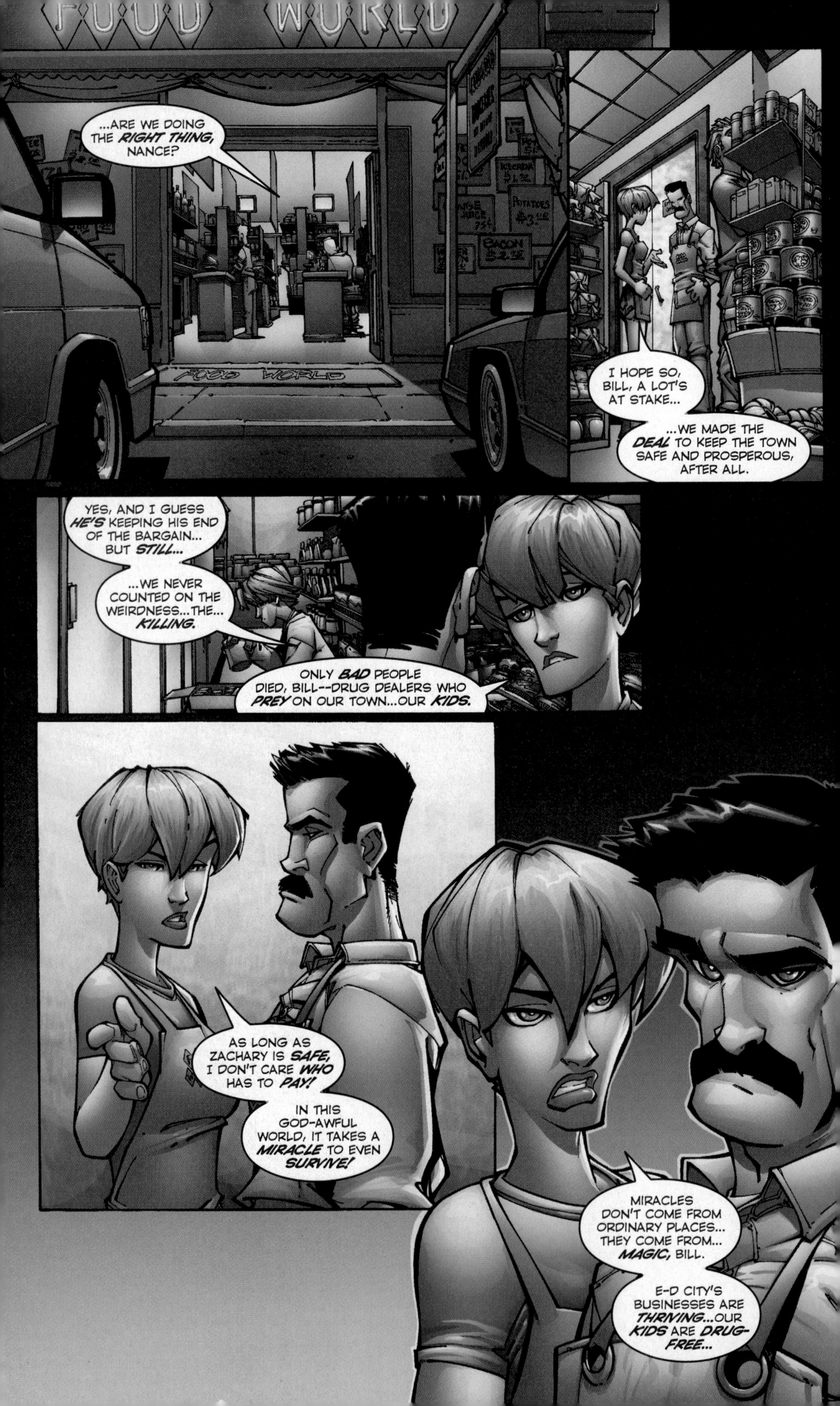
FOOD WORLD
...ARE WE DOING THE RIGHT THING, NANCE?
I HOPE SO, BILL, A LOT'S AT STAKE...
...WE MADE THE DEAL TO KEEP THE TOWN SAFE AND PROSPEROUS, AFTER ALL.
YES, AND I GUESS HE'S KEEPING HIS END OF THE BARGAIN... BUT STILL...
...WE NEVER COUNTED ON THE WEIRDNESS...THE... KILLING.
ONLY BAD PEOPLE DIED, BILL--DRUG DEALERS WHO PREY ON OUR TOWN...OUR KIDS.
AS LONG AS ZACHARY IS SAFE, I DON'T CARE WHO HAS TO PAY!
IN THIS GOD-AWFUL WORLD, IT TAKES A MIRACLE TO EVEN SURVIVE!
MIRACLES DON'T COME FROM ORDINARY PLACES... THEY COME FROM... MAGIC, BILL.
E-D CITY'S BUSINESSES ARE THRIVING...OUR KIDS ARE DRUG-FREE...

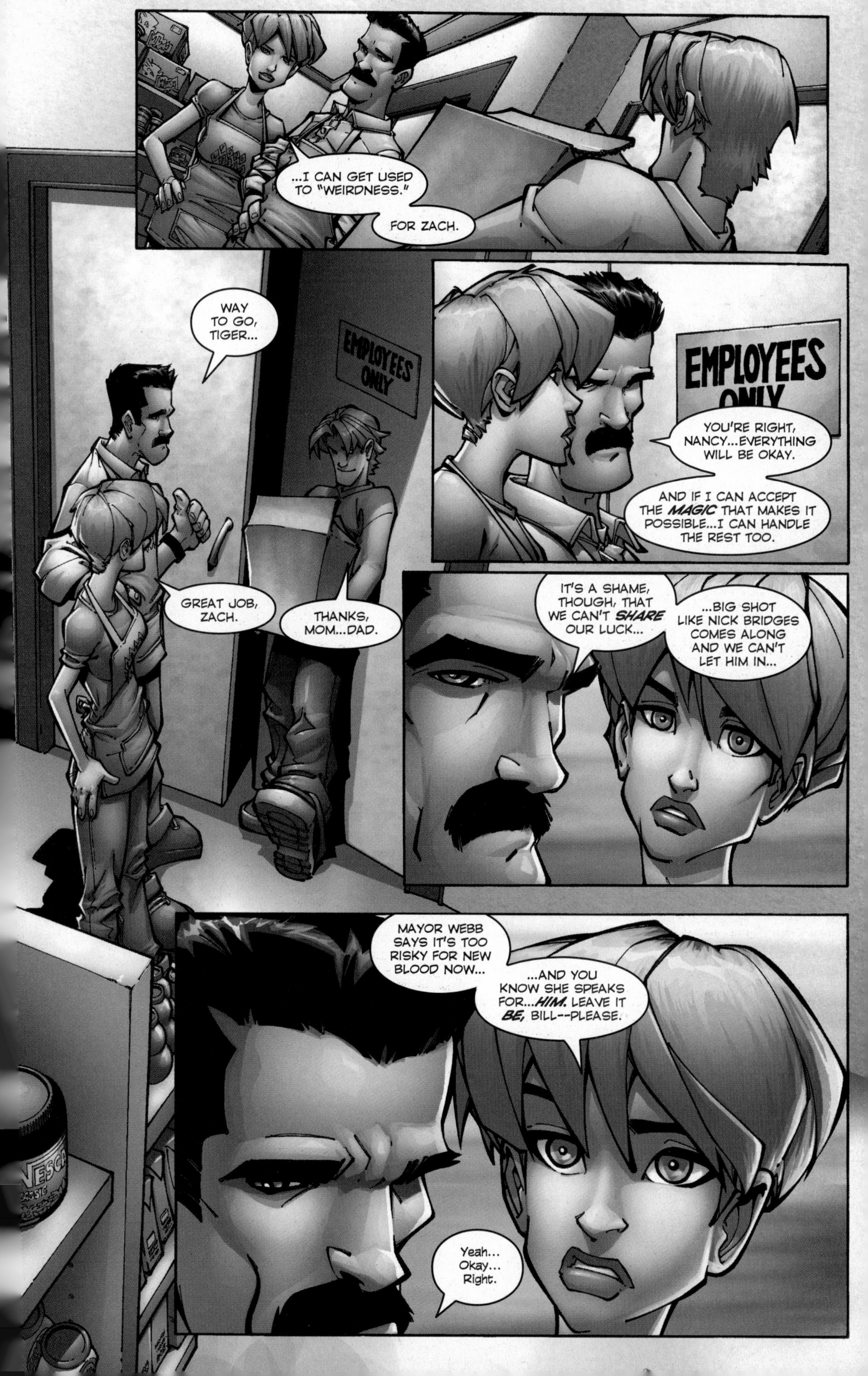
...I CAN GET USED TO "WEIRDNESS."
FOR ZACH.
WAY TO GO, TIGER...
EMPLOYEES ONLY
GREAT JOB, ZACH.
THANKS, MOM...DAD.
EMPLOYEES ONLY
YOU'RE RIGHT, NANCY...EVERYTHING WILL BE OKAY.
AND IF I CAN ACCEPT THE MAGIC THAT MAKES IT POSSIBLE...I CAN HANDLE THE REST TOO.
IT'S A SHAME, THOUGH, THAT WE CAN'T SHARE OUR LUCK...
...BIG SHOT LIKE NICK BRIDGES COMES ALONG AND WE CAN'T LET HIM IN...
MAYOR WEBB SAYS IT'S TOO RISKY FOR NEW BLOOD NOW...
...AND YOU KNOW SHE SPEAKS FOR...HIM. LEAVE IT BE, BILL--PLEASE.
Yeah... Okay... Right.

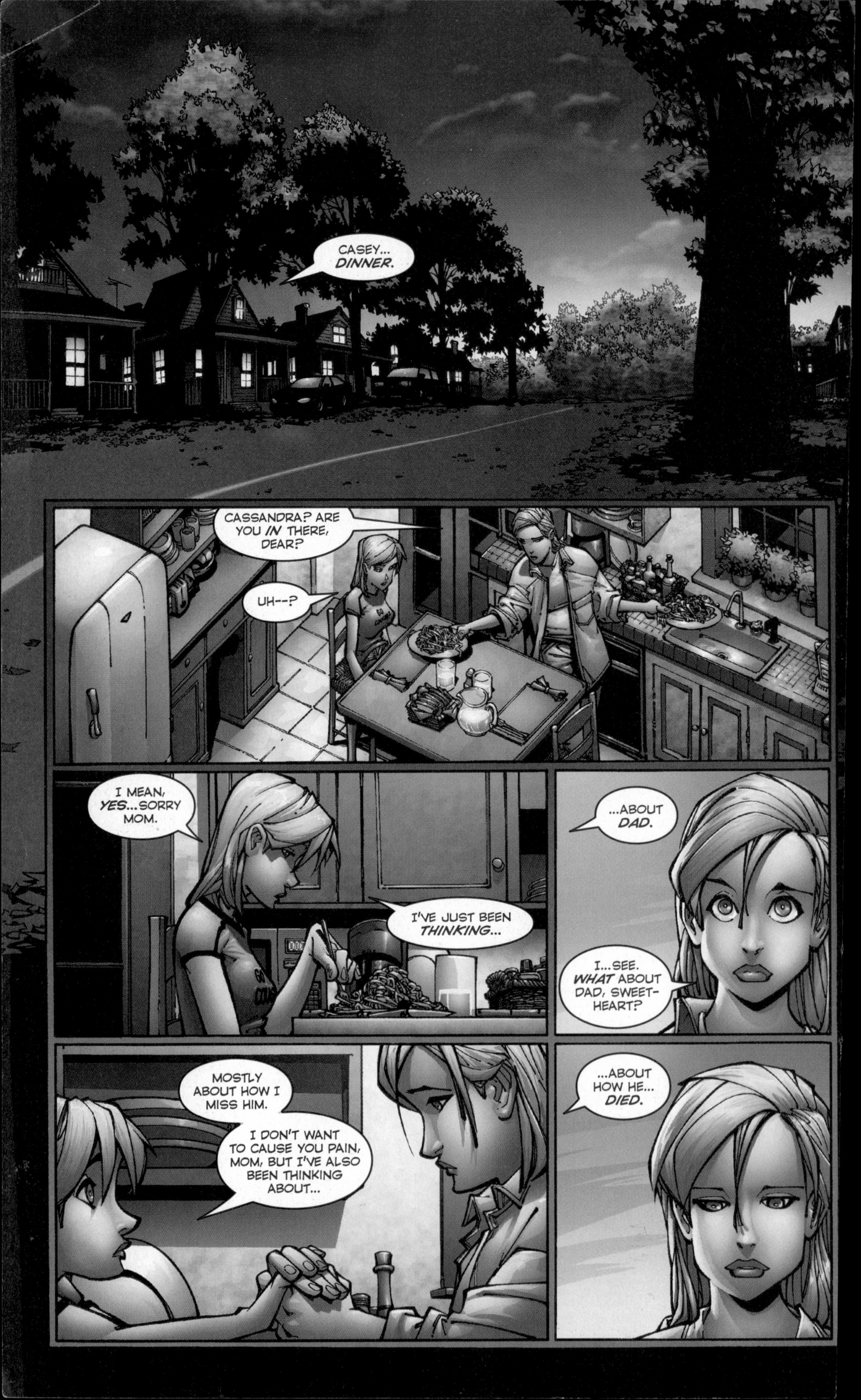
CASEY... DINNER.
CASSANDRA? ARE YOU IN THERE, DEAR?
UH--?
I MEAN, YES... SORRY MOM.
I'VE JUST BEEN THINKING...
...ABOUT DAD.
I... SEE. WHAT ABOUT DAD, SWEET-HEART?
MOSTLY ABOUT HOW I MISS HIM.
I DON'T WANT TO CAUSE YOU PAIN, MOM, BUT I'VE ALSO BEEN THINKING ABOUT...
...ABOUT HOW HE... DIED.

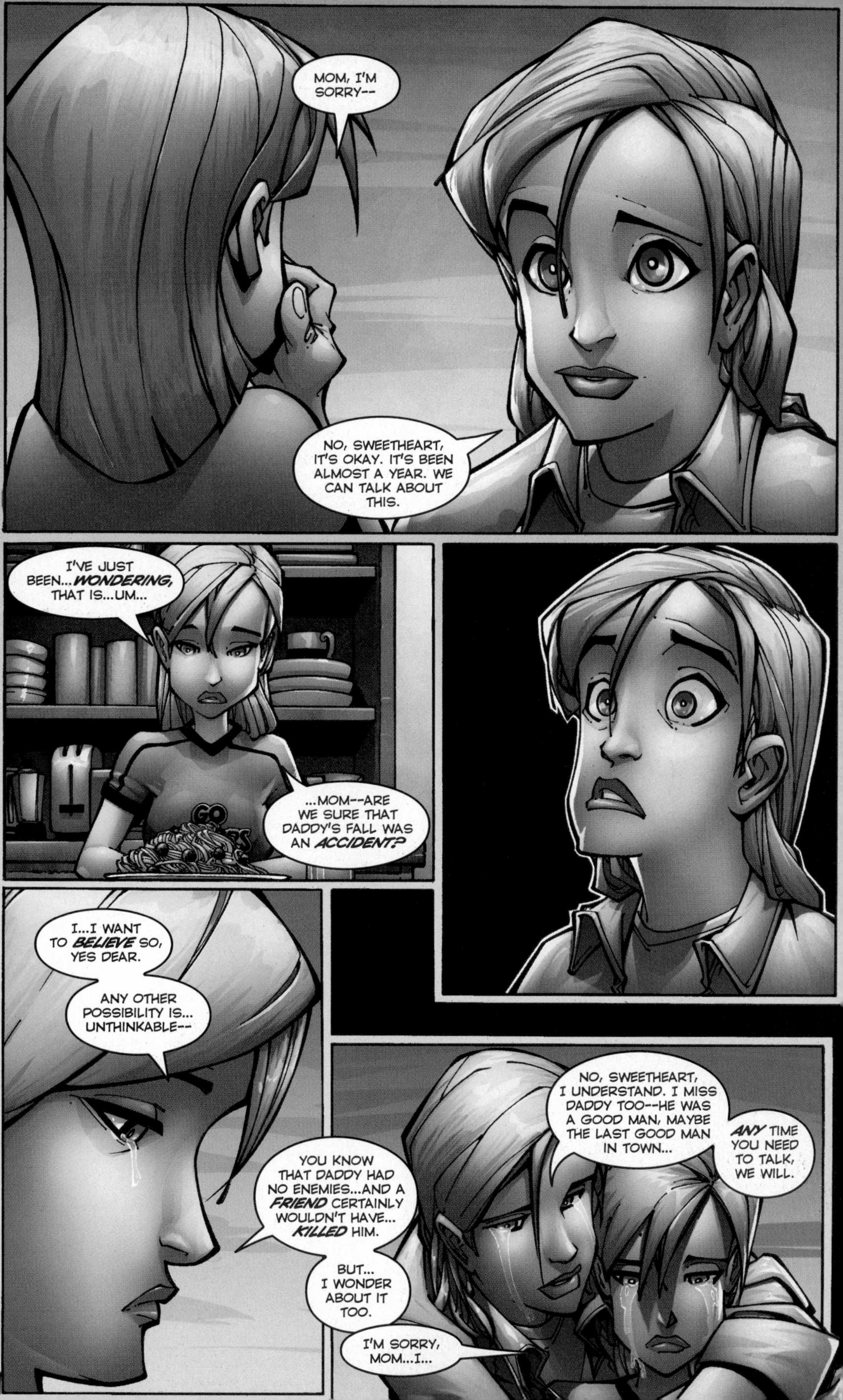
MOM, I'M SORRY--
NO, SWEETHEART, IT'S OKAY. IT'S BEEN ALMOST A YEAR. WE CAN TALK ABOUT THIS.
I'VE JUST BEEN...WONDERING, THAT IS...UM...
...MOM--ARE WE SURE THAT DADDY'S FALL WAS AN ACCIDENT?
GO
I...I WANT TO BELIEVE SO, YES DEAR.
ANY OTHER POSSIBILITY IS... UNTHINKABLE--
YOU KNOW THAT DADDY HAD NO ENEMIES...AND A FRIEND CERTAINLY WOULDN'T HAVE... KILLED HIM.
BUT... I WONDER ABOUT IT TOO.
I'M SORRY, MOM...I...
NO, SWEETHEART, I UNDERSTAND. I MISS DADDY TOO--HE WAS A GOOD MAN, MAYBE THE LAST GOOD MAN IN TOWN...
ANY TIME YOU NEED TO TALK, WE WILL.

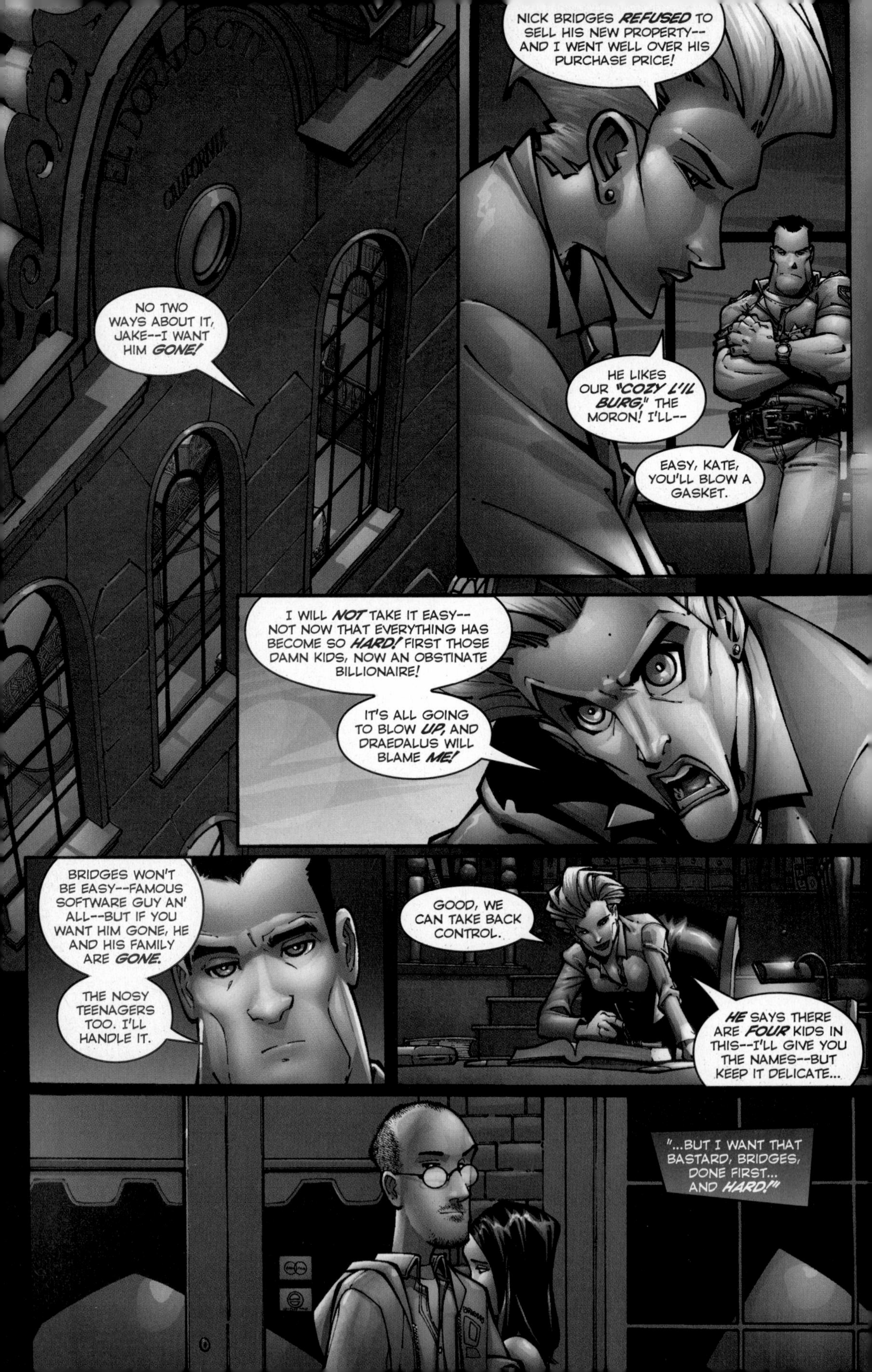
NICK BRIDGES REFUSED TO SELL HIS NEW PROPERTY-- AND I WENT WELL OVER HIS PURCHASE PRICE!
NO TWO WAYS ABOUT IT, JAKE--I WANT HIM GONE!
HE LIKES OUR "COZY L'IL BURG," THE MORON! I'LL--
EASY, KATE, YOU'LL BLOW A GASKET.
I WILL NOT TAKE IT EASY-- NOT NOW THAT EVERYTHING HAS BECOME SO HARD! FIRST THOSE DAMN KIDS, NOW AN OBSTINATE BILLIONAIRE!
IT'S ALL GOING TO BLOW UP, AND DRAEDALUS WILL BLAME ME!
BRIDGES WON'T BE EASY--FAMOUS SOFTWARE GUY AN' ALL--BUT IF YOU WANT HIM GONE, HE AND HIS FAMILY ARE GONE.
THE NOSY TEENAGERS TOO. I'LL HANDLE IT.
GOOD, WE CAN TAKE BACK CONTROL.
HE SAYS THERE ARE FOUR KIDS IN THIS--I'LL GIVE YOU THE NAMES--BUT KEEP IT DELICATE...
"...BUT I WANT THAT BASTARD, BRIDGES, DONE FIRST... AND HARD!"

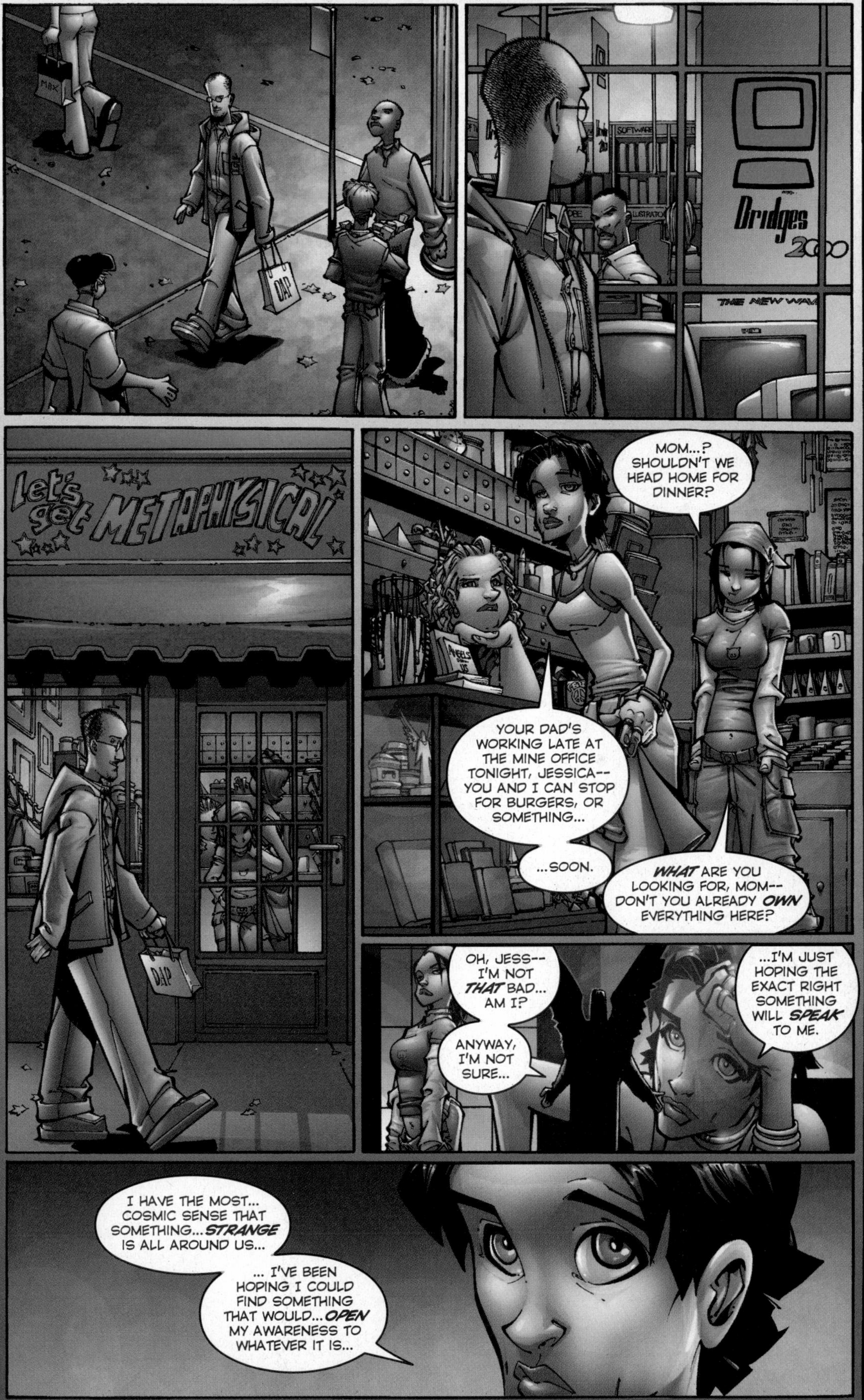
MAX
DAP
SOFTWARE
Dridges 2000
THE NEW WAV
Let's get METAPHYSICAL
MOM...? SHOULDN'T WE HEAD HOME FOR DINNER?
YOUR DAD'S WORKING LATE AT THE MINE OFFICE TONIGHT, JESSICA-- YOU AND I CAN STOP FOR BURGERS, OR SOMETHING...
...SOON.
WHAT ARE YOU LOOKING FOR, MOM-- DON'T YOU ALREADY OWN EVERYTHING HERE?
DAP
OH, JESS-- I'M NOT THAT BAD... AM I?
ANYWAY, I'M NOT SURE...
...I'M JUST HOPING THE EXACT RIGHT SOMETHING WILL SPEAK TO ME.
I HAVE THE MOST... COSMIC SENSE THAT SOMETHING... STRANGE IS ALL AROUND US...
... I'VE BEEN HOPING I COULD FIND SOMETHING THAT WOULD... OPEN MY AWARENESS TO WHATEVER IT IS...

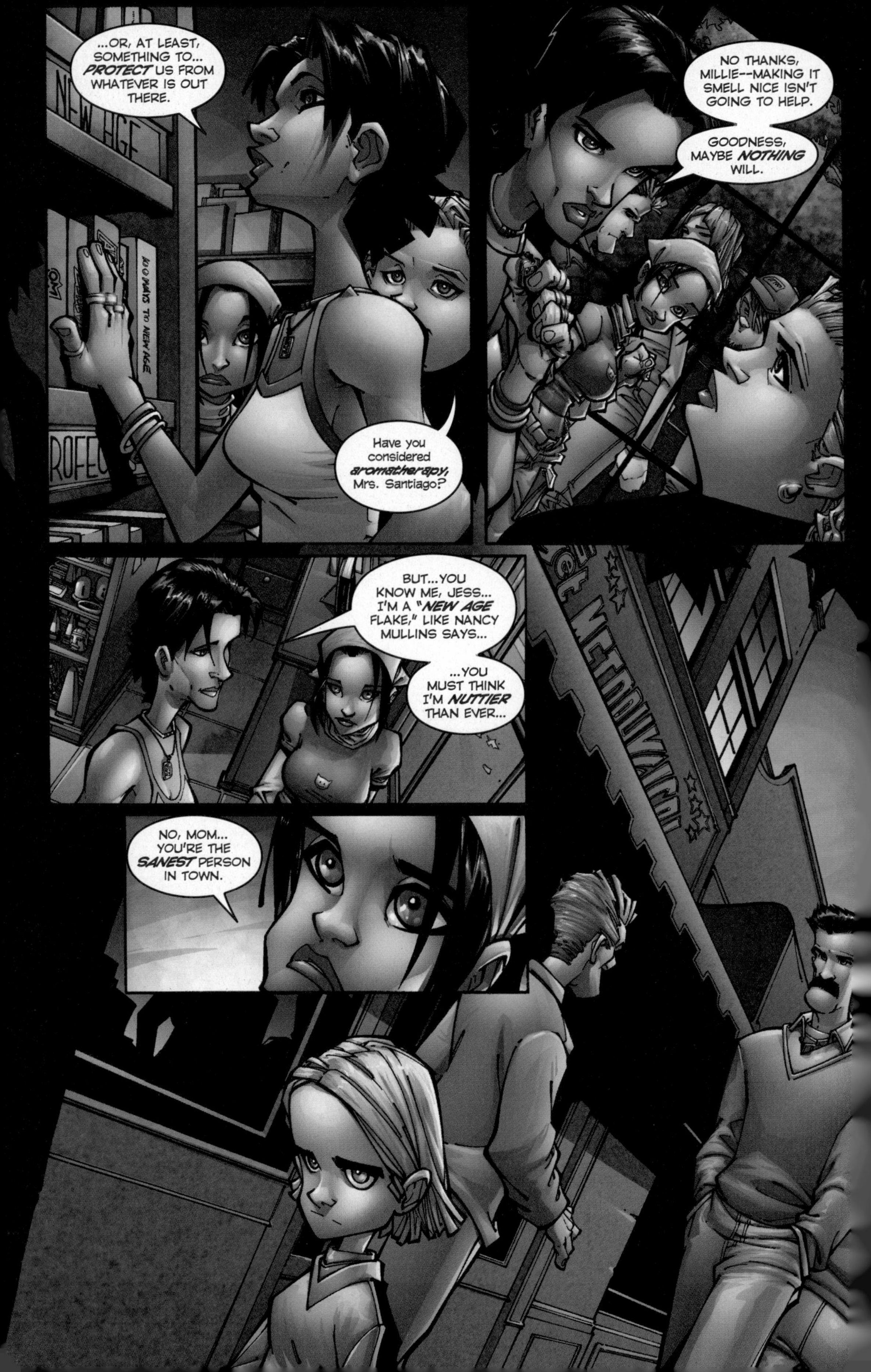
...OR, AT LEAST, SOMETHING TO... *PROTECT* US FROM WHATEVER IS OUT THERE.
Have you considered *aromatherapy,* Mrs. Santiago?
NO THANKS, MILLIE--MAKING IT SMELL NICE ISN'T GOING TO HELP.
GOODNESS, MAYBE *NOTHING* WILL.
BUT...YOU KNOW ME, JESS... I'M A "*NEW AGE* FLAKE," LIKE NANCY MULLINS SAYS...
...YOU MUST THINK I'M *NUTTIER* THAN EVER...
NO, MOM... YOU'RE THE *SANEST* PERSON IN TOWN.

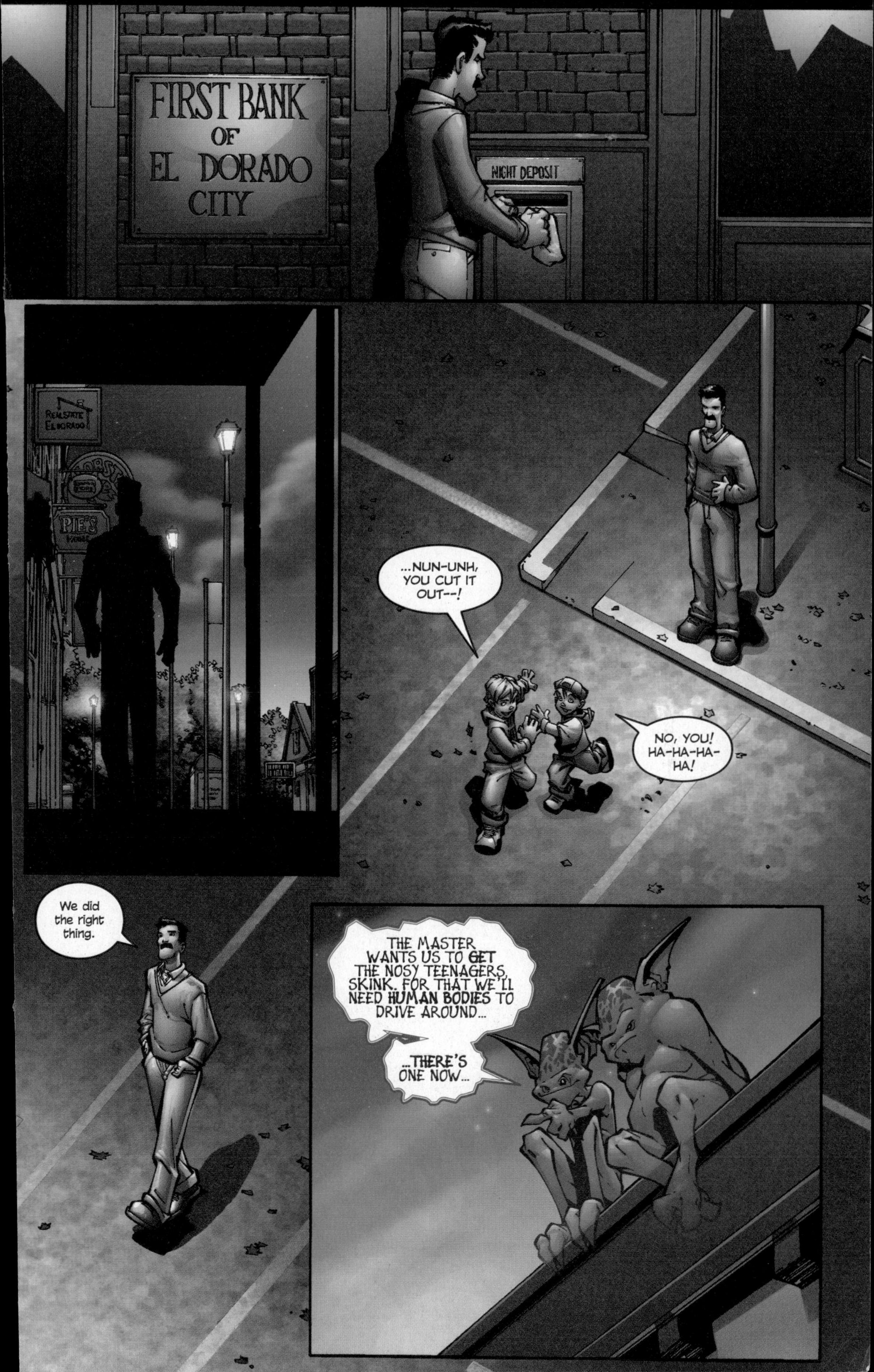
FIRST BANK
OF
EL DORADO
CITY
NIGHT DEPOSIT
PIE'S
...NUN-UNH, YOU CUT IT OUT--!
NO, YOU! HA-HA-HA-HA!
We did the right thing.
THE MASTER WANTS US TO GET THE NOSY TEENAGERS, SKINK. FOR THAT WE'LL NEED HUMAN BODIES TO DRIVE AROUND...
...THERE'S ONE NOW...

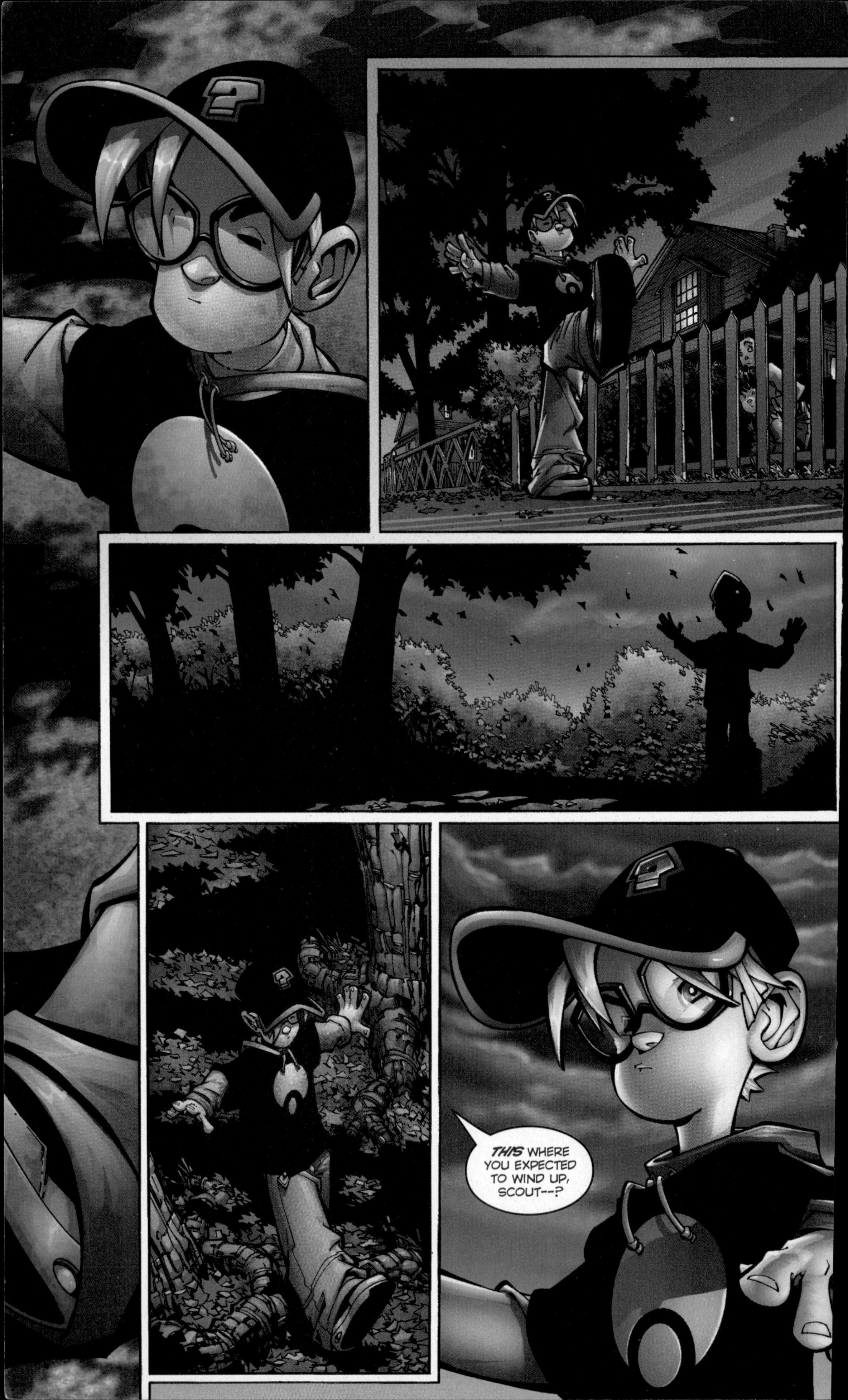
THIS WHERE YOU EXPECTED TO WIND UP, SCOUT--?

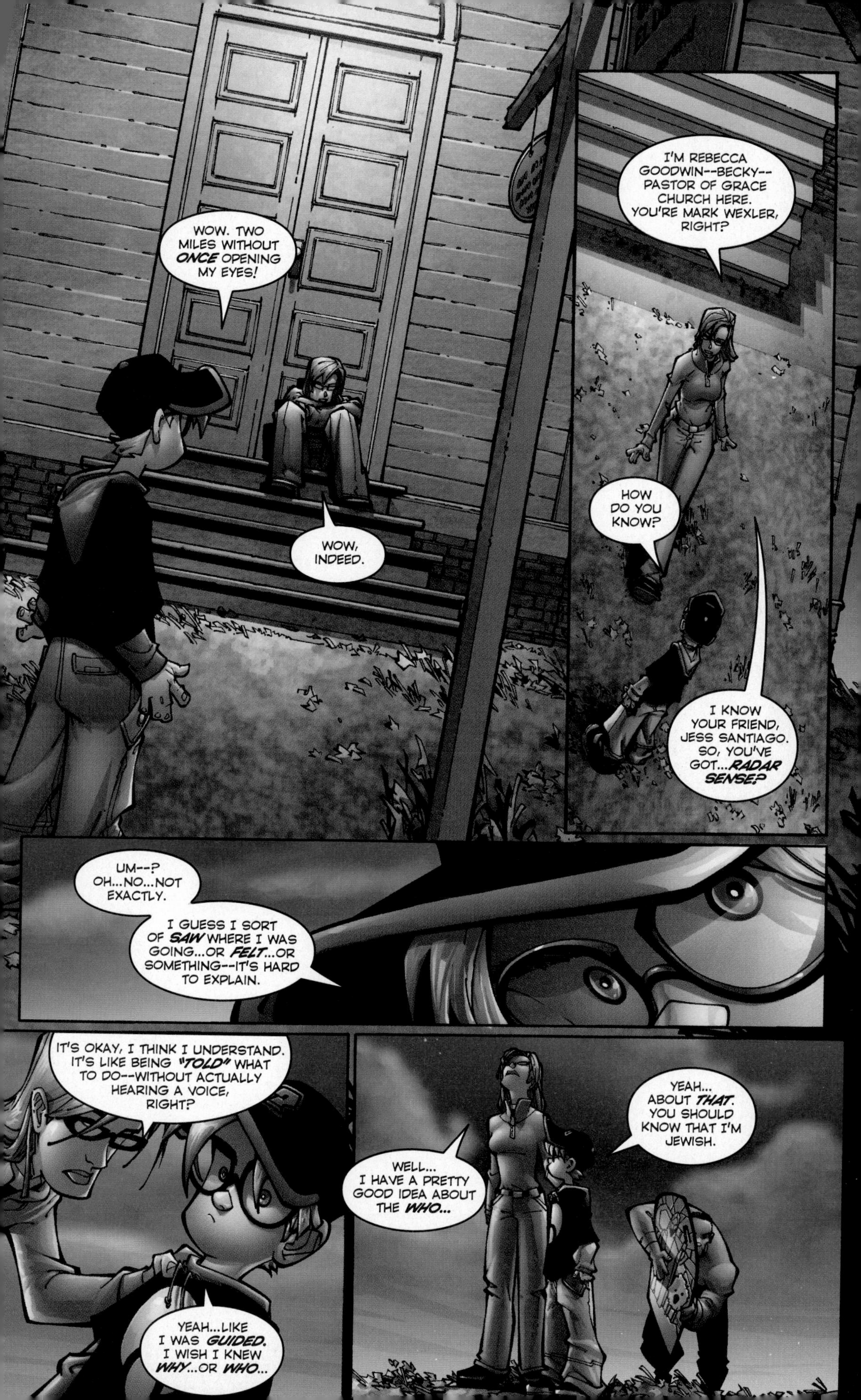
WOW. TWO MILES WITHOUT ONCE OPENING MY EYES!
WOW, INDEED.
I'M REBECCA GOODWIN--BECKY--PASTOR OF GRACE CHURCH HERE. YOU'RE MARK WEXLER, RIGHT?
HOW DO YOU KNOW?
I KNOW YOUR FRIEND, JESS SANTIAGO. SO, YOU'VE GOT...RADAR SENSE?
UM--? OH...NO...NOT EXACTLY.
I GUESS I SORT OF SAW WHERE I WAS GOING...OR FELT...OR SOMETHING--IT'S HARD TO EXPLAIN.
IT'S OKAY, I THINK I UNDERSTAND. IT'S LIKE BEING "TOLD" WHAT TO DO--WITHOUT ACTUALLY HEARING A VOICE, RIGHT?
YEAH...LIKE I WAS GUIDED. I WISH I KNEW WHY...OR WHO...
WELL... I HAVE A PRETTY GOOD IDEA ABOUT THE WHO...
YEAH... ABOUT THAT. YOU SHOULD KNOW THAT I'M JEWISH.

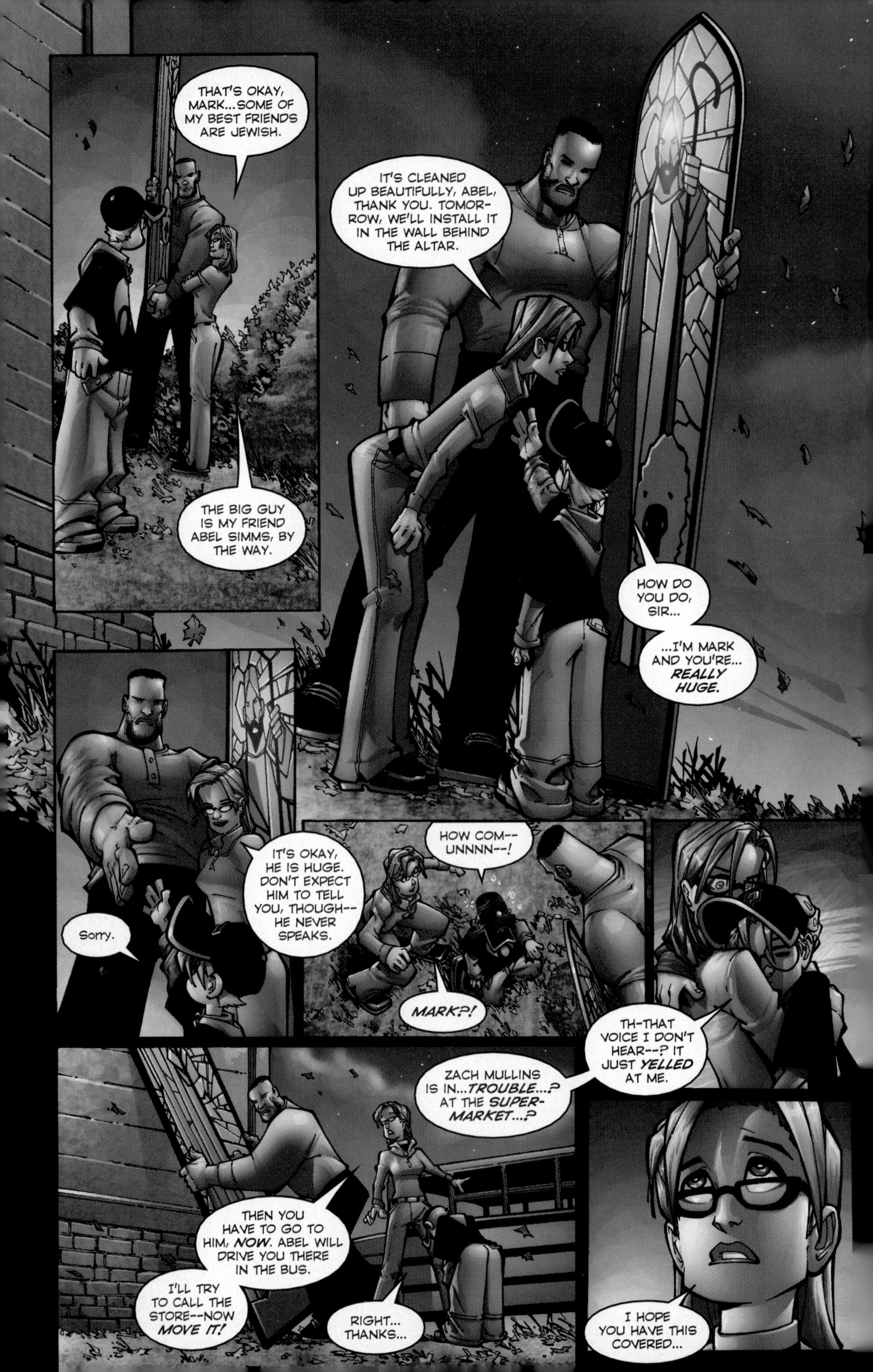
THAT'S OKAY, MARK...SOME OF MY BEST FRIENDS ARE JEWISH.
THE BIG GUY IS MY FRIEND ABEL SIMMS, BY THE WAY.
IT'S CLEANED UP BEAUTIFULLY, ABEL, THANK YOU. TOMORROW, WE'LL INSTALL IT IN THE WALL BEHIND THE ALTAR.
HOW DO YOU DO, SIR...
...I'M MARK AND YOU'RE... REALLY HUGE.
Sorry.
IT'S OKAY, HE IS HUGE. DON'T EXPECT HIM TO TELL YOU, THOUGH-- HE NEVER SPEAKS.
HOW COM-- UNNNN--!
MARK?!
TH-THAT VOICE I DON'T HEAR--? IT JUST YELLED AT ME.
ZACH MULLINS IS IN...TROUBLE...? AT THE SUPER-MARKET...?
THEN YOU HAVE TO GO TO HIM, NOW. ABEL WILL DRIVE YOU THERE IN THE BUS.
I'LL TRY TO CALL THE STORE--NOW MOVE IT!
RIGHT... THANKS...
I HOPE YOU HAVE THIS COVERED...

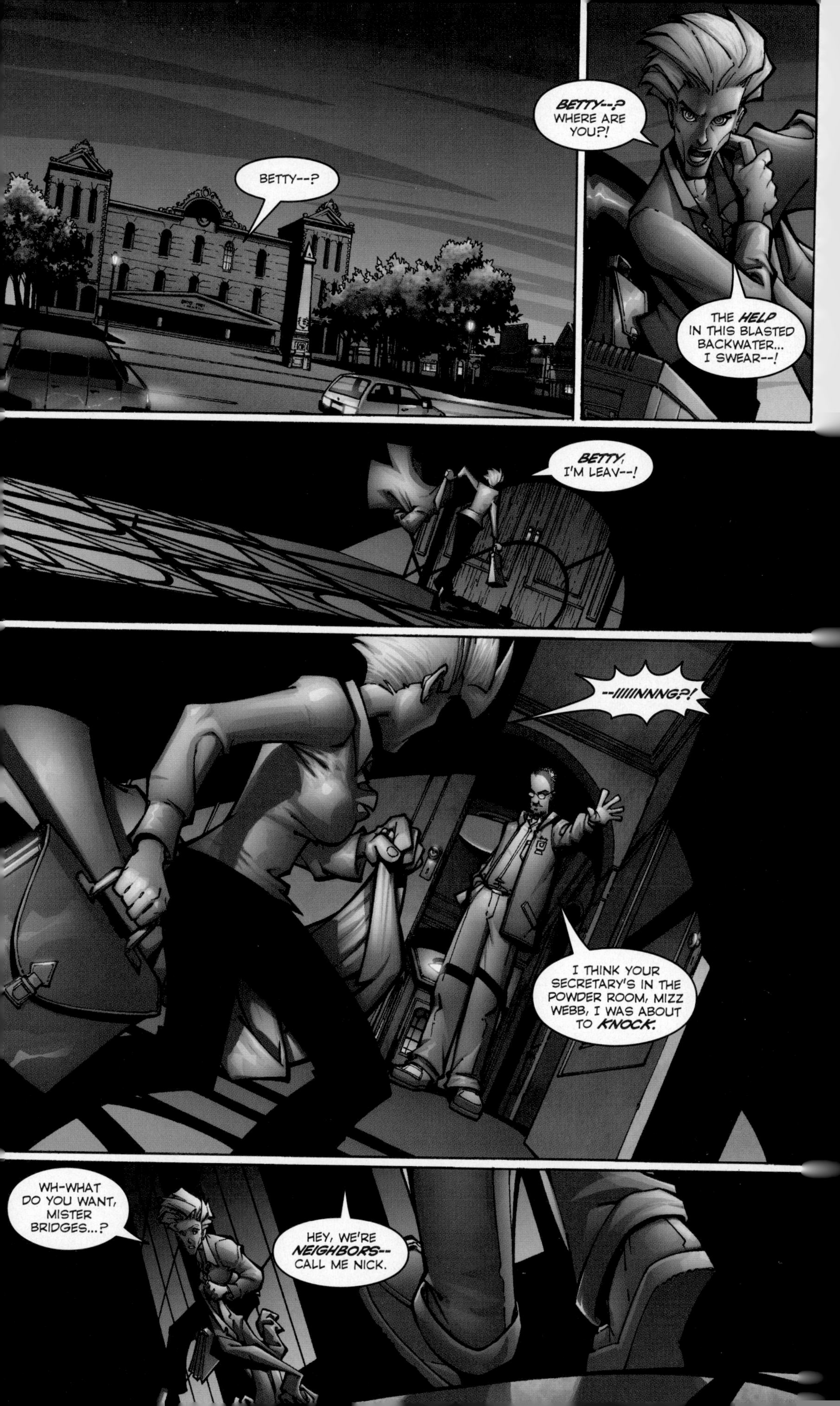
BETTY--?
BETTY--? WHERE ARE YOU?!
THE HELP IN THIS BLASTED BACKWATER... I SWEAR--!
BETTY, I'M LEAV--!
--IIIIINNNG?!
I THINK YOUR SECRETARY'S IN THE POWDER ROOM, MIZZ WEBB, I WAS ABOUT TO KNOCK.
WH-WHAT DO YOU WANT, MISTER BRIDGES...?
HEY, WE'RE NEIGHBORS-- CALL ME NICK.

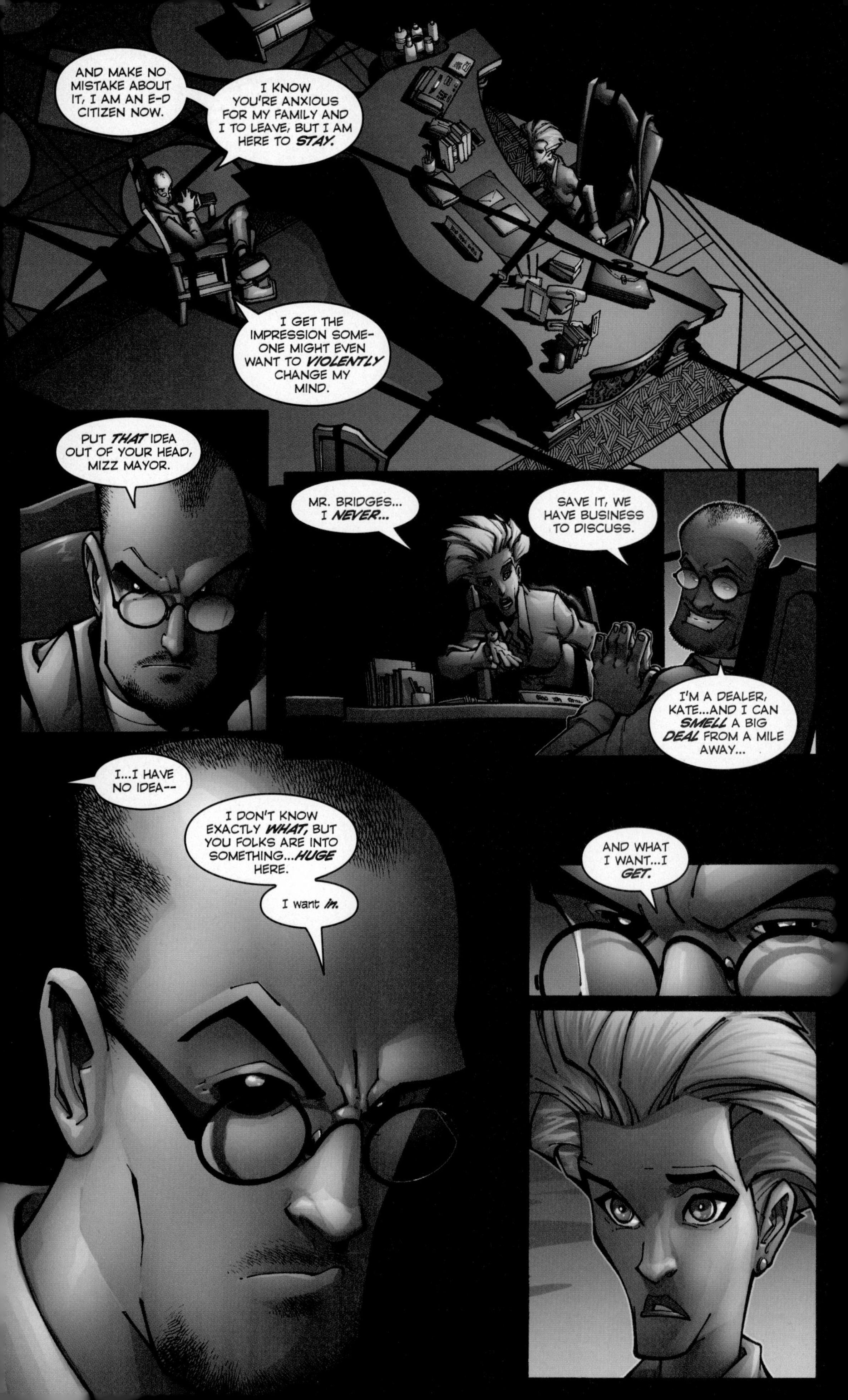
AND MAKE NO MISTAKE ABOUT IT, I AM AN E-D CITIZEN NOW.
I KNOW YOU'RE ANXIOUS FOR MY FAMILY AND I TO LEAVE, BUT I AM HERE TO *STAY.*
I GET THE IMPRESSION SOME-ONE MIGHT EVEN WANT TO *VIOLENTLY* CHANGE MY MIND.
PUT *THAT* IDEA OUT OF YOUR HEAD, MIZZ MAYOR.
MR. BRIDGES... I *NEVER...*
SAVE IT, WE HAVE BUSINESS TO DISCUSS.
I'M A DEALER, KATE...AND I CAN *SMELL* A BIG *DEAL* FROM A MILE AWAY...
I...I HAVE NO IDEA--
I DON'T KNOW EXACTLY *WHAT,* BUT YOU FOLKS ARE INTO SOMETHING...*HUGE* HERE.
I want *in.*
AND WHAT I WANT...I *GET.*

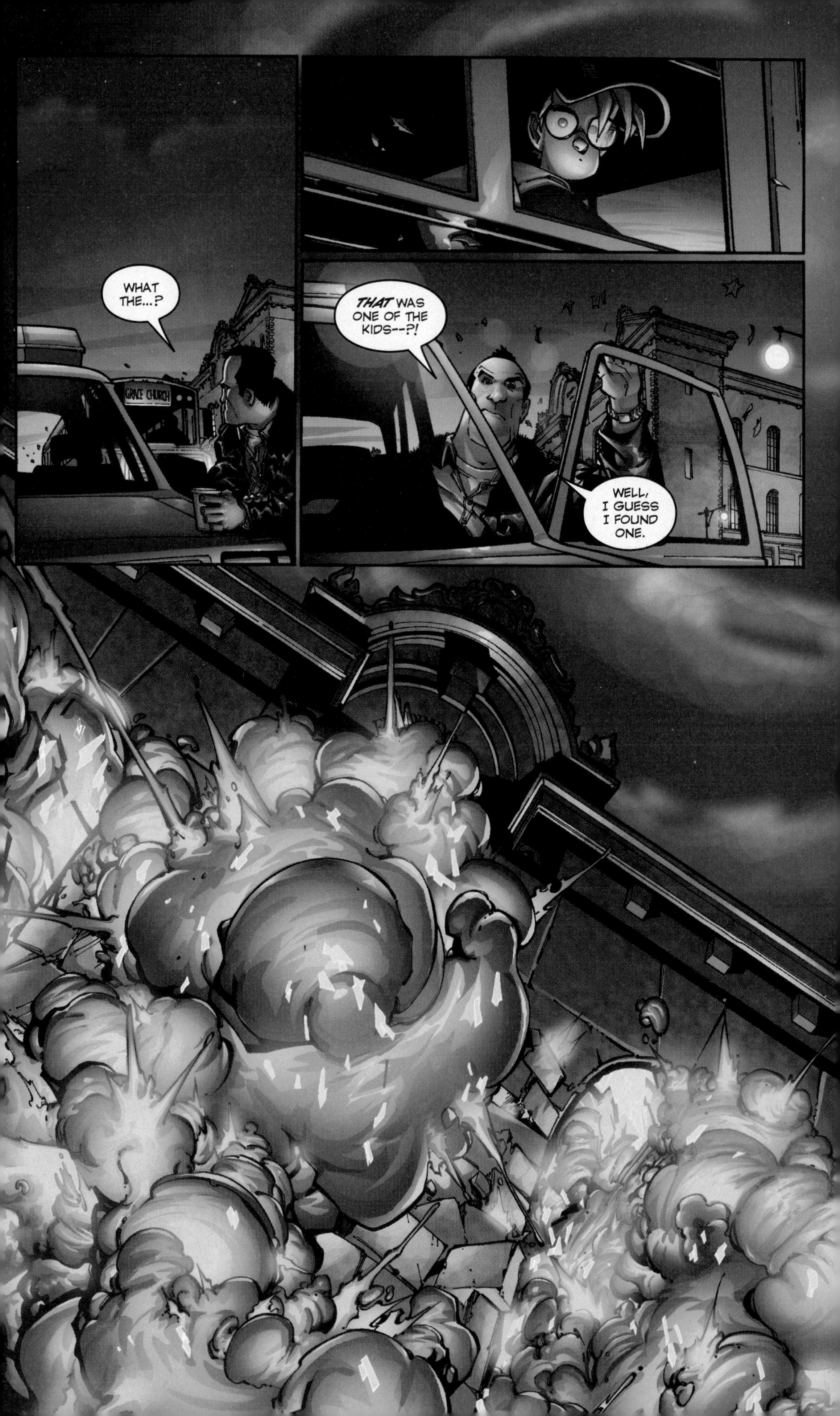
WHAT THE...?
GRACE CHURCH
THAT WAS ONE OF THE KIDS--?!
WELL, I GUESS I FOUND ONE.

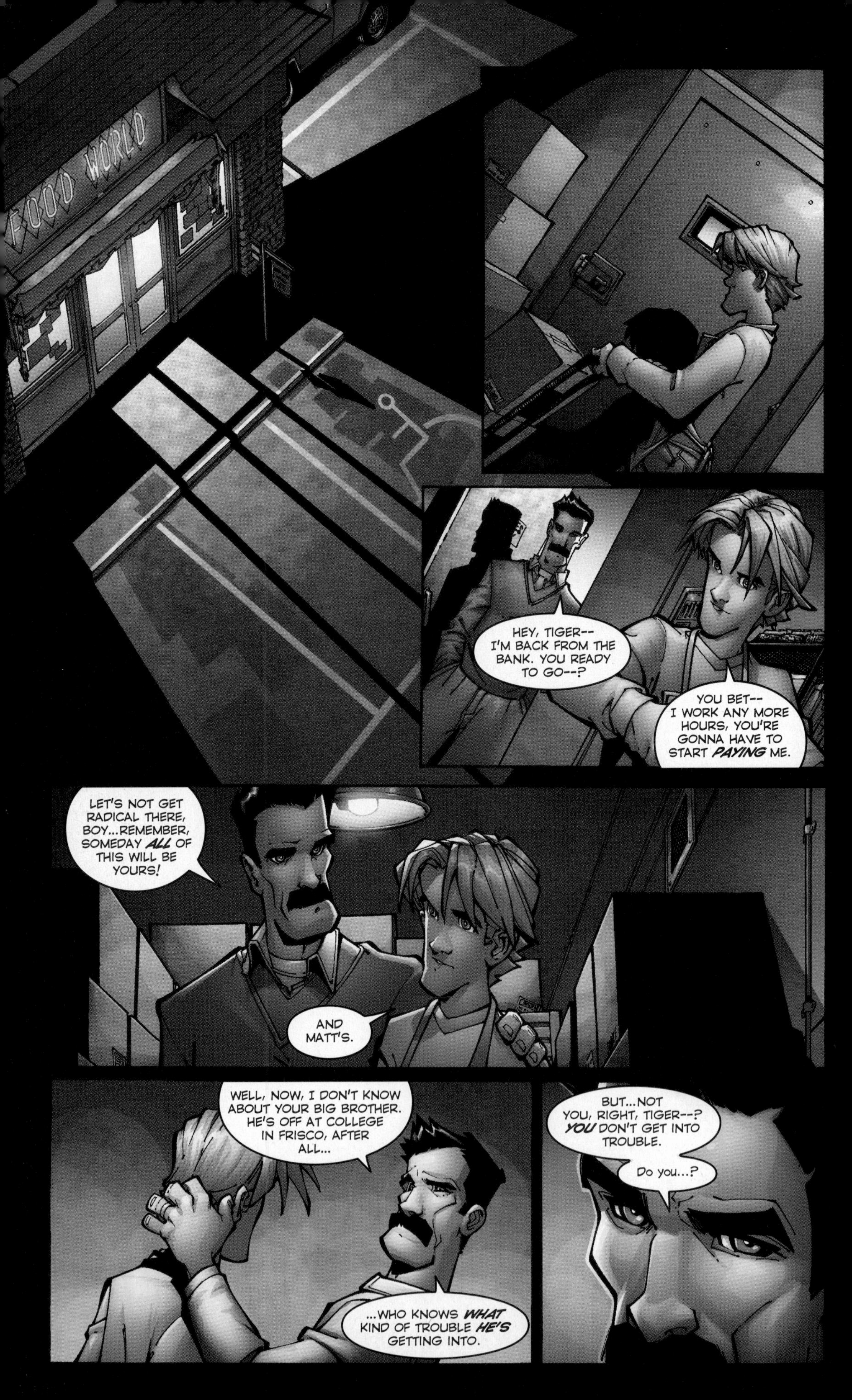
FOOD WORLD
HEY, TIGER-- I'M BACK FROM THE BANK. YOU READY TO GO--?
YOU BET-- I WORK ANY MORE HOURS, YOU'RE GONNA HAVE TO START *PAYING* ME.
LET'S NOT GET RADICAL THERE, BOY...REMEMBER, SOMEDAY *ALL* OF THIS WILL BE YOURS!
AND MATT'S.
WELL, NOW, I DON'T KNOW ABOUT YOUR BIG BROTHER. HE'S OFF AT COLLEGE IN FRISCO, AFTER ALL...
...WHO KNOWS *WHAT* KIND OF TROUBLE *HE'S* GETTING INTO.
BUT...NOT YOU, RIGHT, TIGER--? *YOU* DON'T GET INTO TROUBLE.
Do you...?

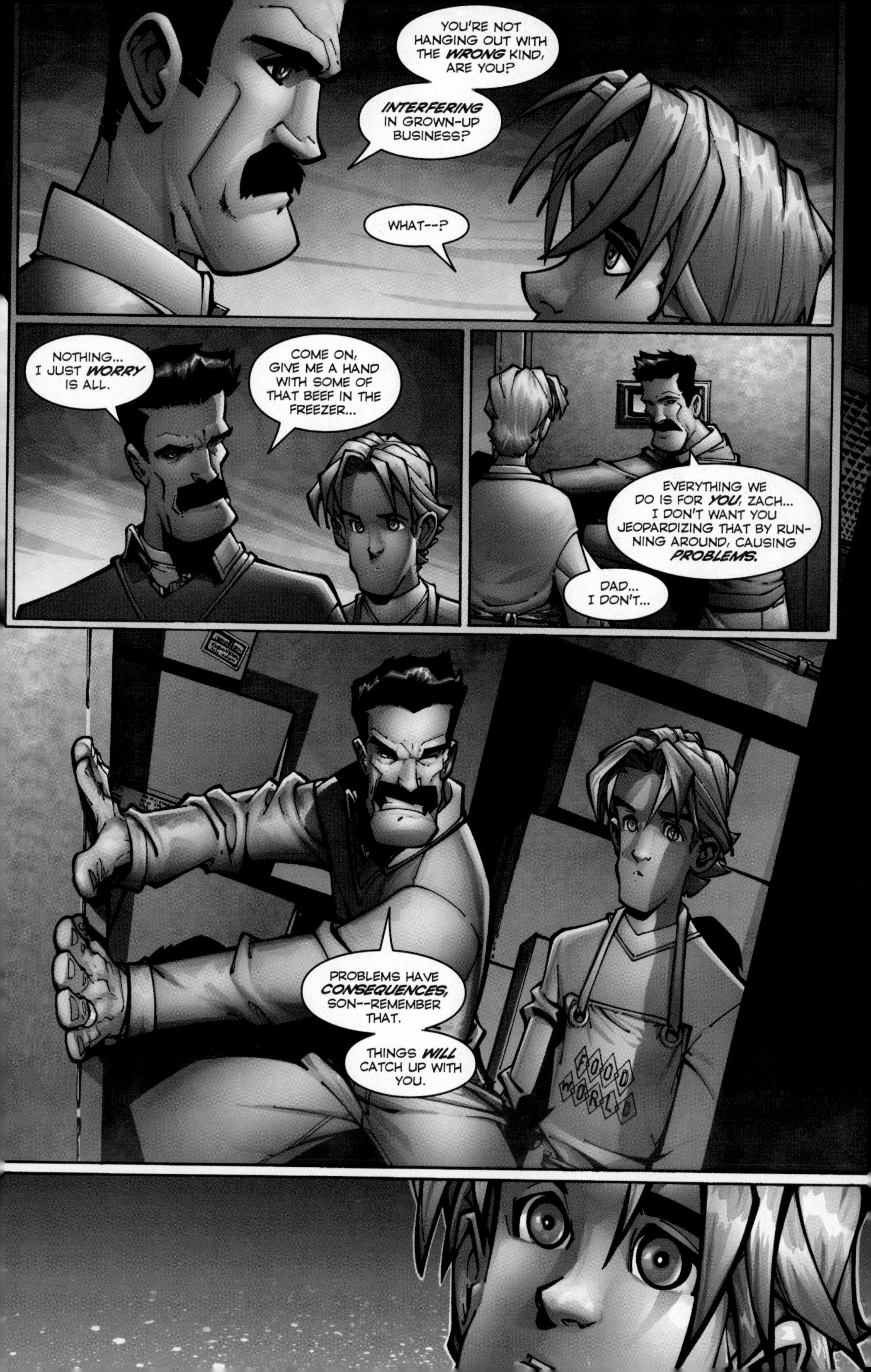
YOU'RE NOT HANGING OUT WITH THE WRONG KIND, ARE YOU?
INTERFERING IN GROWN-UP BUSINESS?
WHAT--?
NOTHING... I JUST WORRY IS ALL.
COME ON, GIVE ME A HAND WITH SOME OF THAT BEEF IN THE FREEZER...
EVERYTHING WE DO IS FOR YOU, ZACH... I DON'T WANT YOU JEOPARDIZING THAT BY RUNNING AROUND, CAUSING PROBLEMS.
DAD... I DON'T...
PROBLEMS HAVE CONSEQUENCES, SON--REMEMBER THAT.
THINGS WILL CATCH UP WITH YOU.
FOOD WORLD

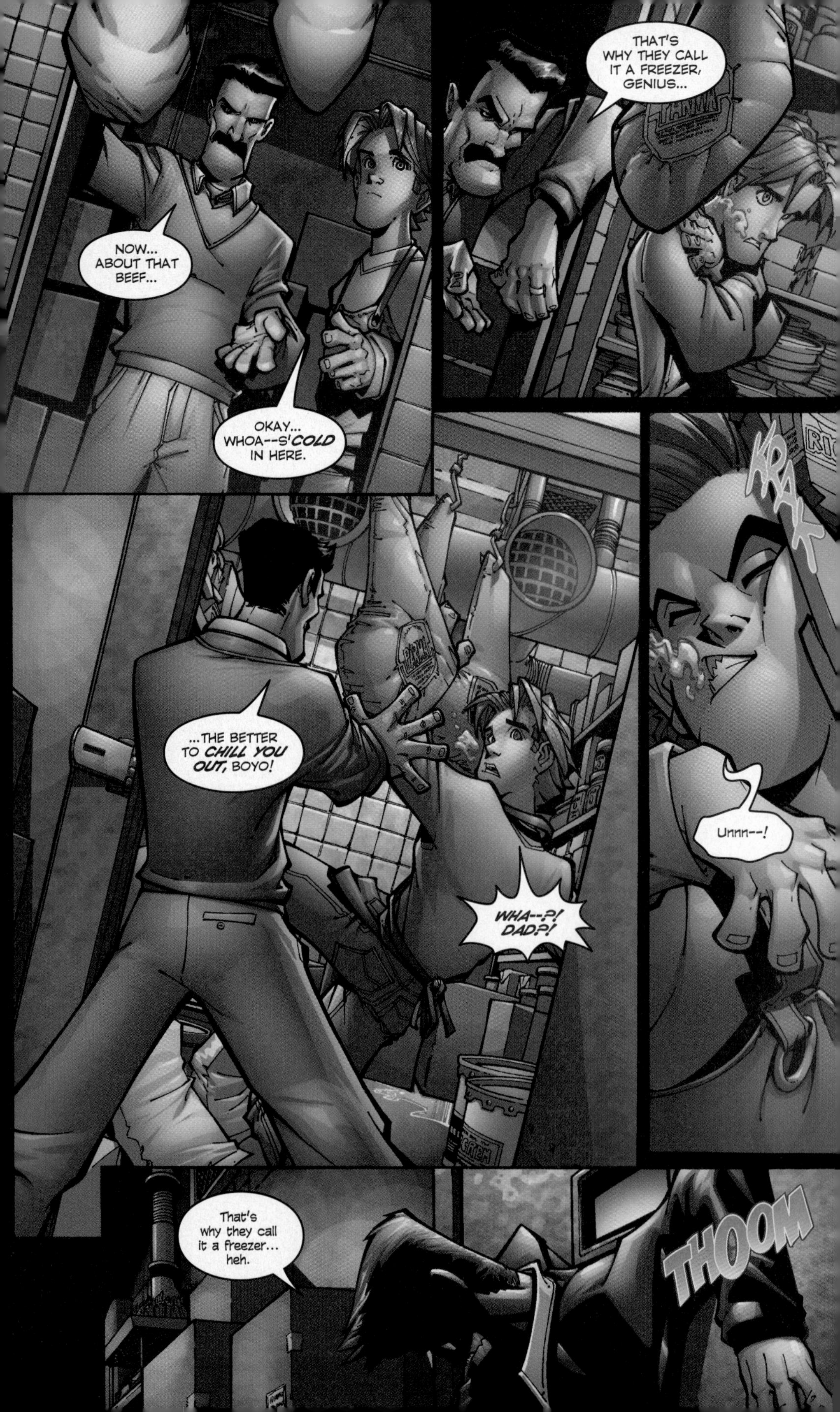
NOW... ABOUT THAT BEEF...
OKAY... WHOA--S'COLD IN HERE.
THAT'S WHY THEY CALL IT A FREEZER, GENIUS...
...THE BETTER TO CHILL YOU OUT, BOYO!
WHA--?! DAD?!
KRAK
Unnn--!
That's why they call it a freezer... heh.
THOOM

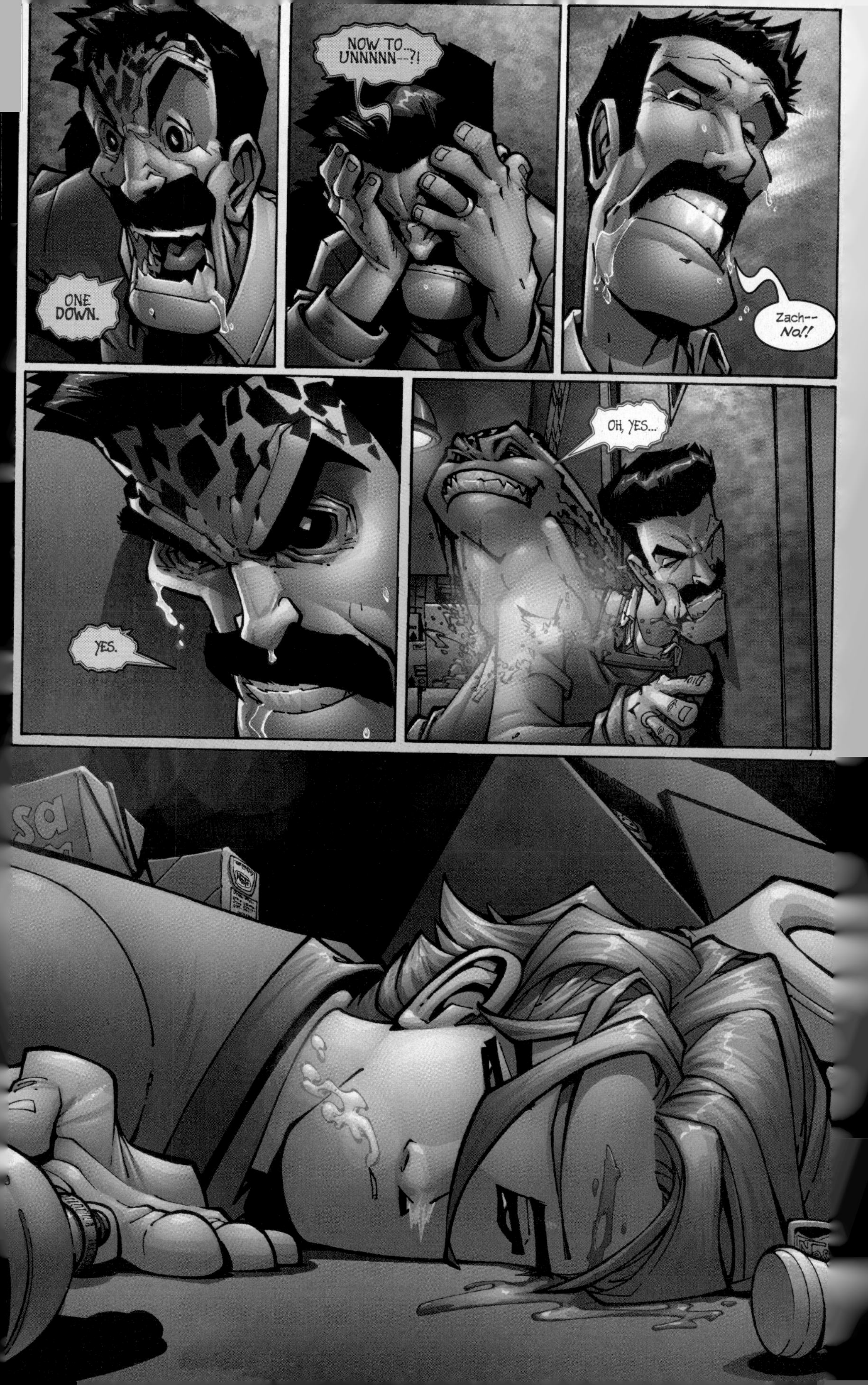
ONE DOWN.
NOW TO... UNNNNN--?!
Zach-- No!!
YES.
OH, YES...

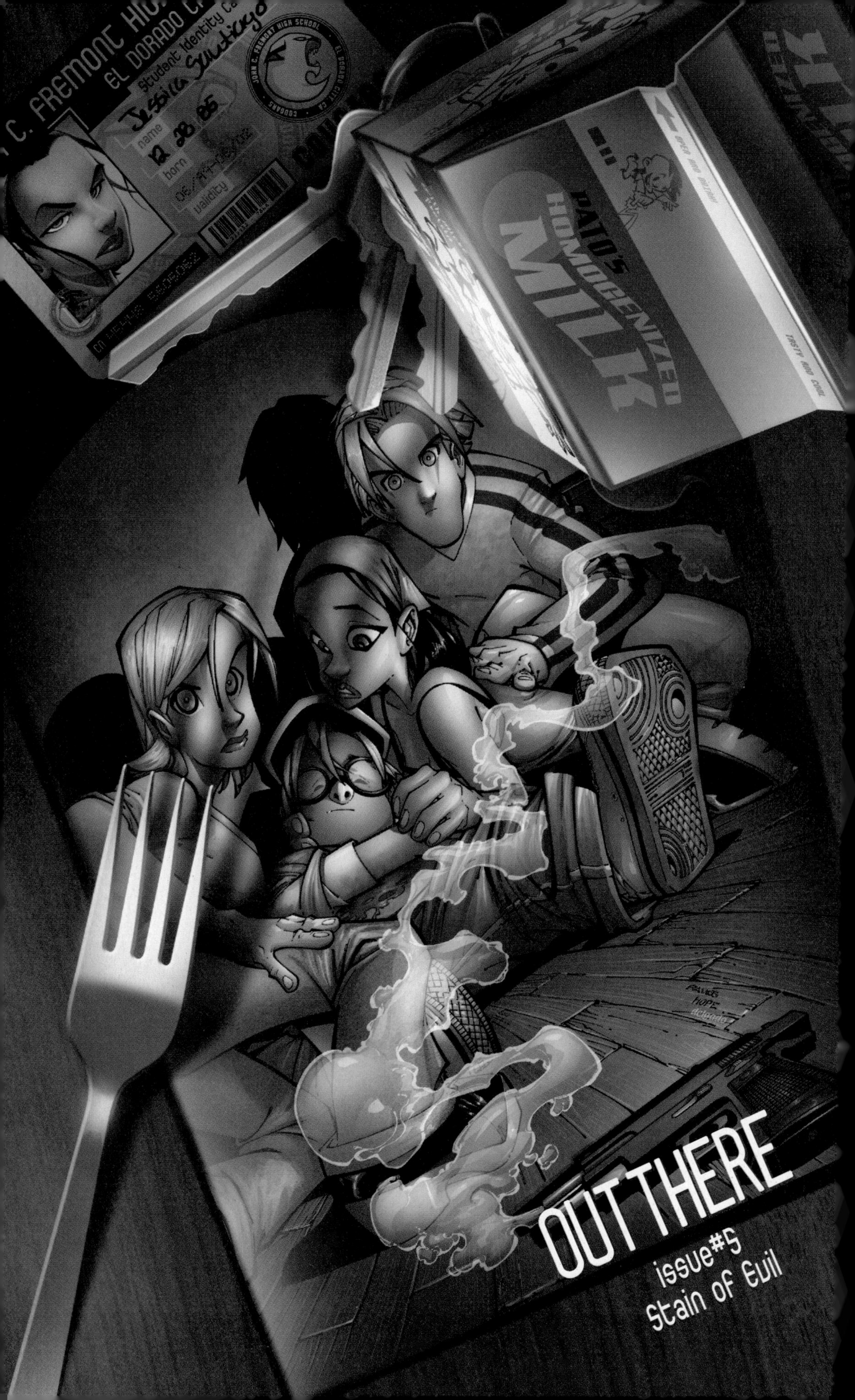
PATO'S
HOMOGENIZED
MILK
OUT THERE
issue#5
Stain of Evil

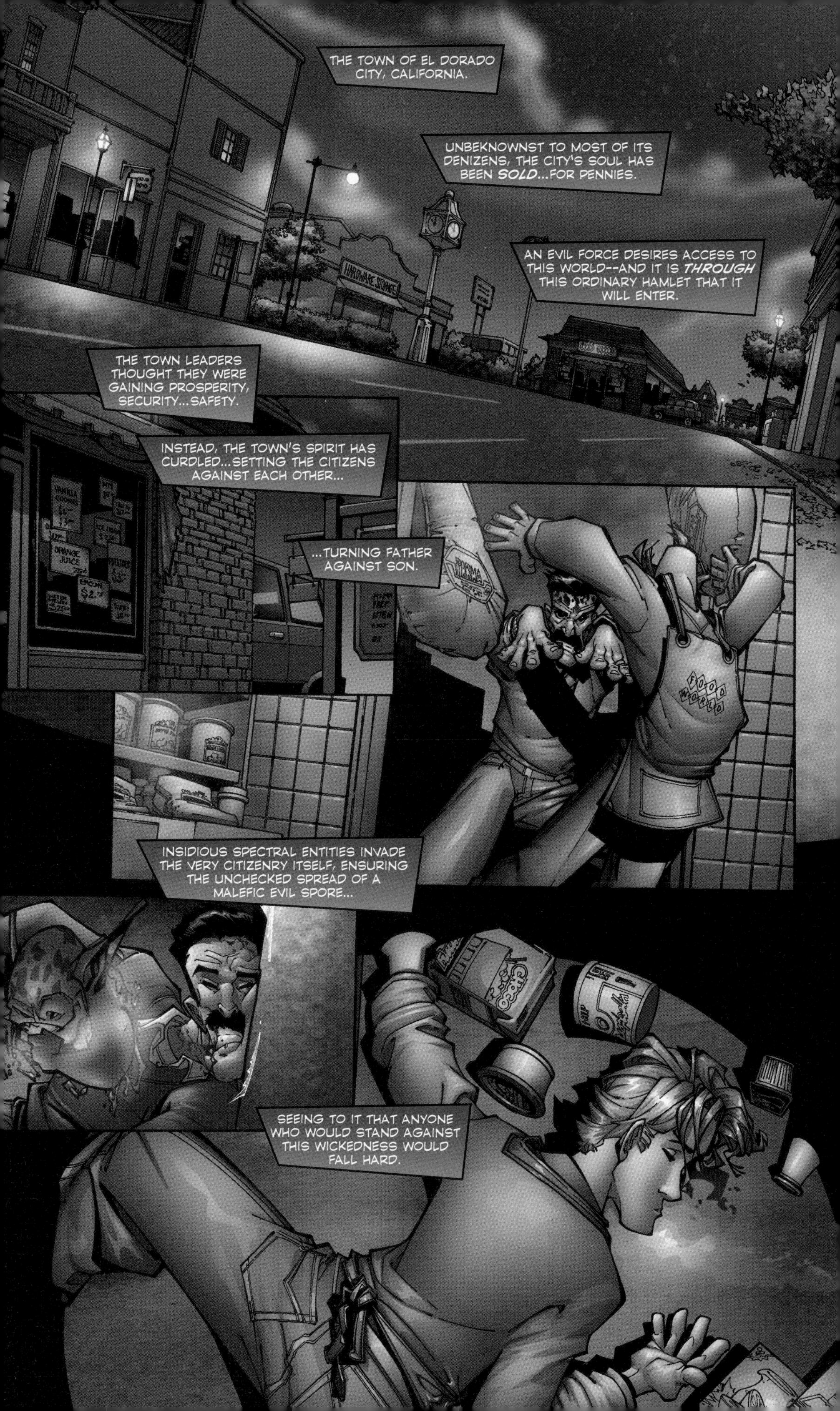
THE TOWN OF EL DORADO CITY, CALIFORNIA.
UNBEKNOWNST TO MOST OF ITS DENIZENS, THE CITY'S SOUL HAS BEEN *SOLD*...FOR PENNIES.
AN EVIL FORCE DESIRES ACCESS TO THIS WORLD--AND IT IS *THROUGH* THIS ORDINARY HAMLET THAT IT WILL ENTER.
HARDWARE STORAGE
THE TOWN LEADERS THOUGHT THEY WERE GAINING PROSPERITY, SECURITY...SAFETY.
INSTEAD, THE TOWN'S SPIRIT HAS CURDLED...SETTING THE CITIZENS AGAINST EACH OTHER...
...TURNING FATHER AGAINST SON.
VANILLA COOKIES
ORANGE JUICE
FOOD WORLD
INSIDIOUS SPECTRAL ENTITIES INVADE THE VERY CITIZENRY ITSELF, ENSURING THE UNCHECKED SPREAD OF A MALEFIC EVIL SPORE...
SEEING TO IT THAT ANYONE WHO WOULD STAND AGAINST THIS WICKEDNESS WOULD FALL HARD.

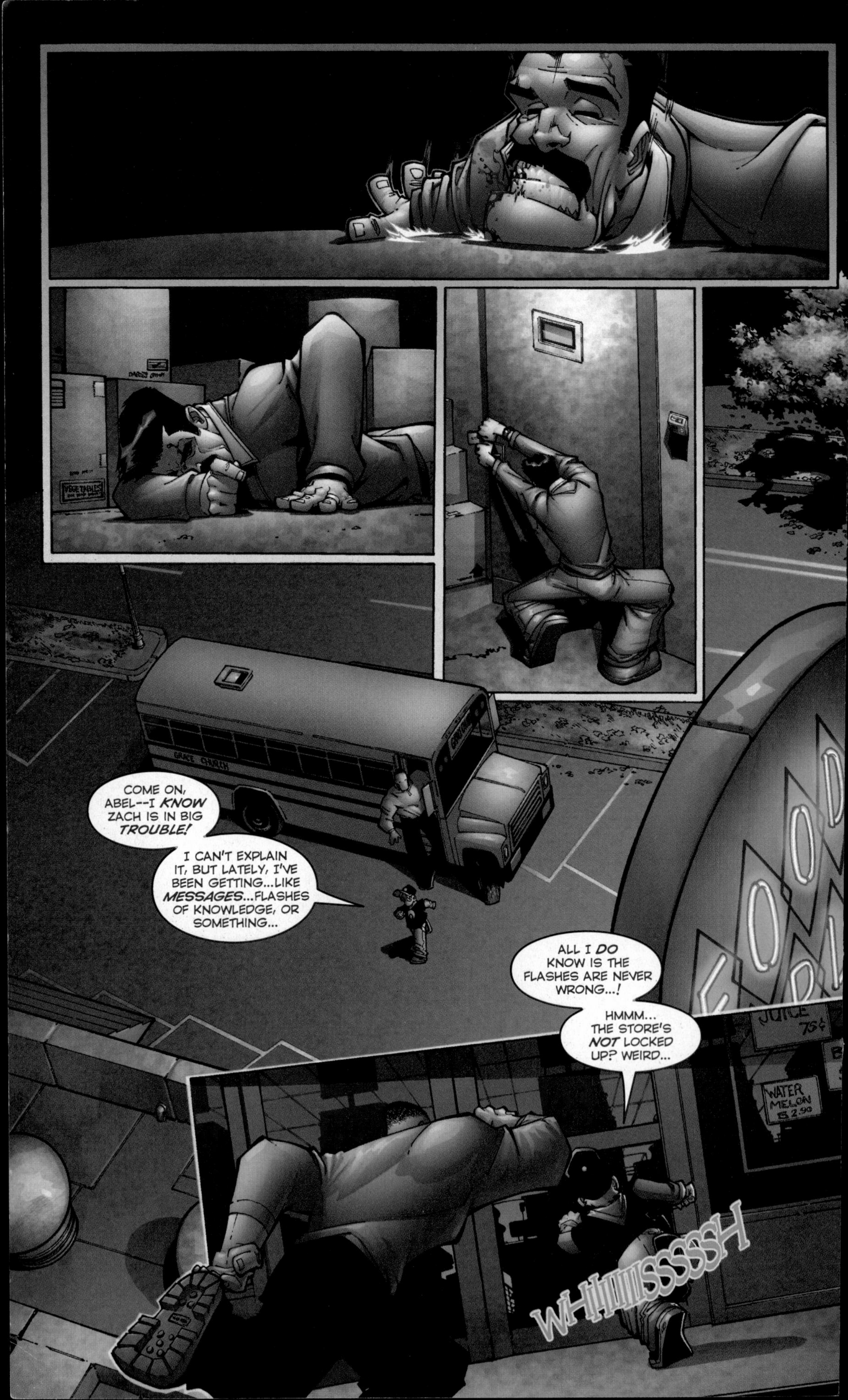
COME ON, ABEL--I *KNOW* ZACH IS IN BIG *TROUBLE!*
I CAN'T EXPLAIN IT, BUT LATELY, I'VE BEEN GETTING...LIKE *MESSAGES*...FLASHES OF KNOWLEDGE, OR SOMETHING...
ALL I *DO* KNOW IS THE FLASHES ARE NEVER WRONG...!
HMMM... THE STORE'S *NOT* LOCKED UP? WEIRD...
JUICE 75¢
WATER MELON
WHIIIIISSSSSH

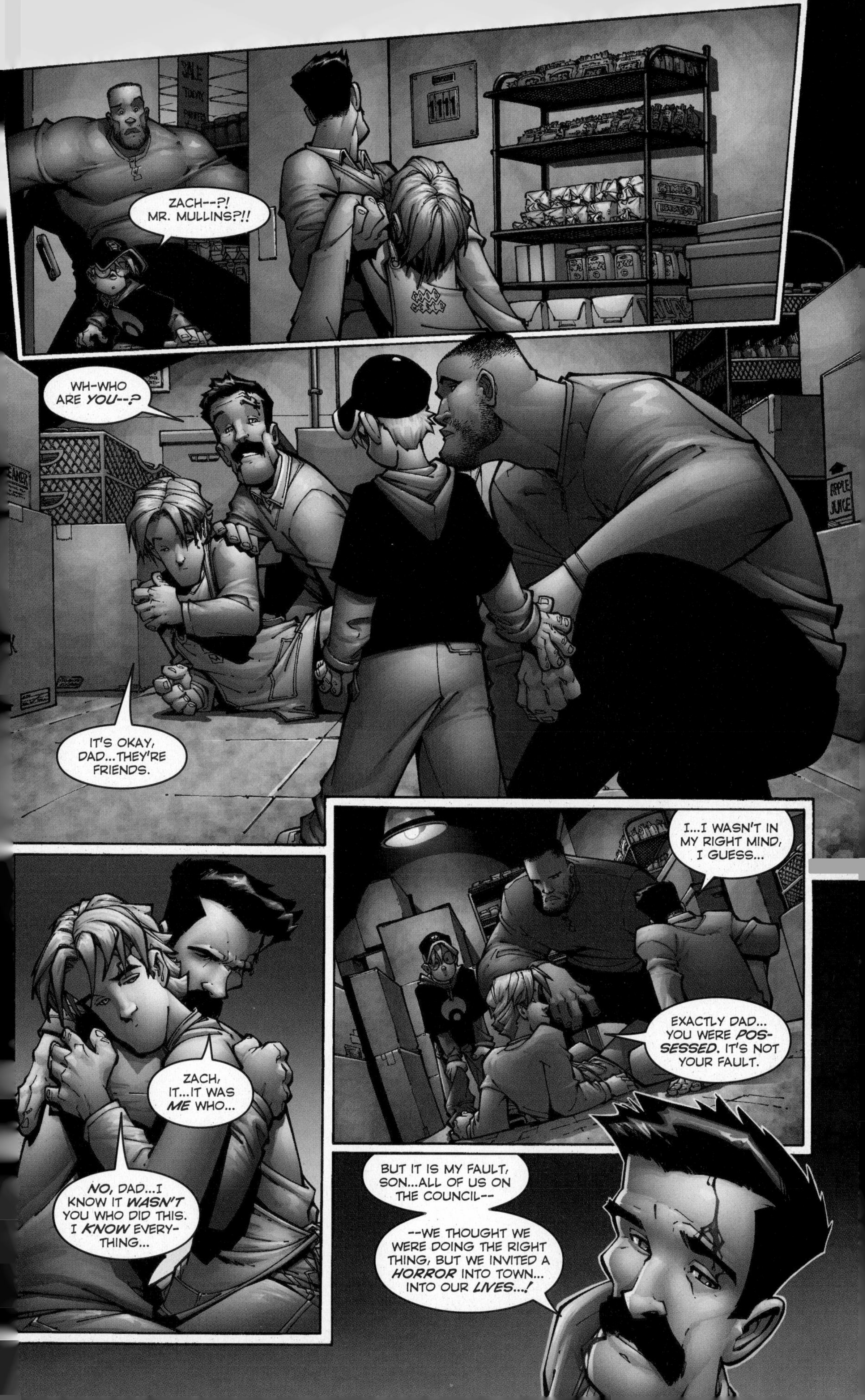
ZACH--?! MR. MULLINS?!!
WH-WHO ARE YOU--?
IT'S OKAY, DAD...THEY'RE FRIENDS.
I...I WASN'T IN MY RIGHT MIND, I GUESS...
EXACTLY DAD... YOU WERE POSSESSED. IT'S NOT YOUR FAULT.
ZACH, IT...IT WAS ME WHO...
NO, DAD...I KNOW IT WASN'T YOU WHO DID THIS. I KNOW EVERYTHING...
BUT IT IS MY FAULT, SON...ALL OF US ON THE COUNCIL--
--WE THOUGHT WE WERE DOING THE RIGHT THING, BUT WE INVITED A HORROR INTO TOWN... INTO OUR LIVES...!
APPLE JUICE

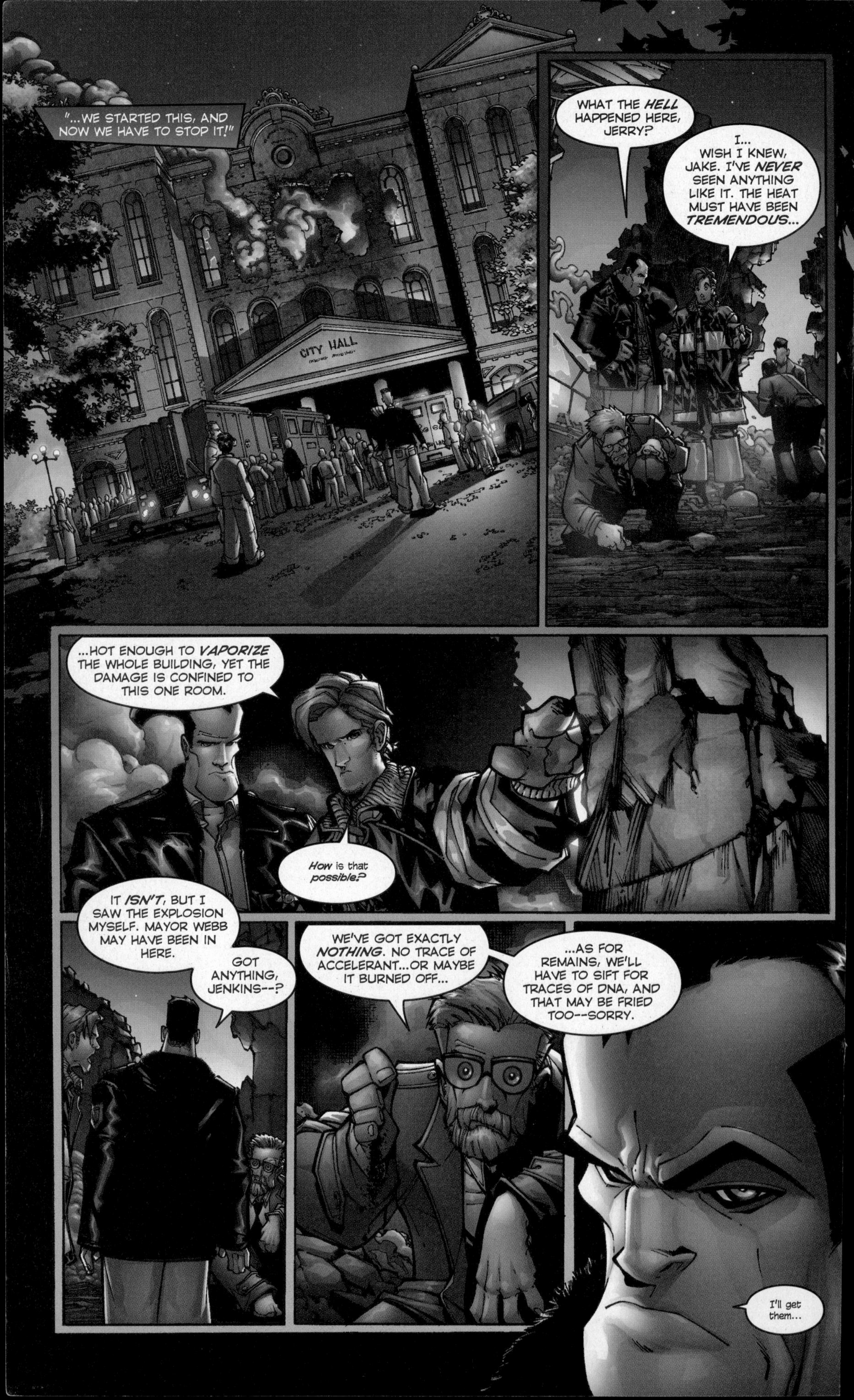
"...WE STARTED THIS, AND NOW WE HAVE TO STOP IT!"
CITY HALL
WHAT THE HELL HAPPENED HERE, JERRY?
I... WISH I KNEW, JAKE. I'VE NEVER SEEN ANYTHING LIKE IT. THE HEAT MUST HAVE BEEN TREMENDOUS...
...HOT ENOUGH TO VAPORIZE THE WHOLE BUILDING, YET THE DAMAGE IS CONFINED TO THIS ONE ROOM.
How is that possible?
IT ISN'T, BUT I SAW THE EXPLOSION MYSELF. MAYOR WEBB MAY HAVE BEEN IN HERE.
GOT ANYTHING, JENKINS--?
WE'VE GOT EXACTLY NOTHING. NO TRACE OF ACCELERANT...OR MAYBE IT BURNED OFF...
...AS FOR REMAINS, WE'LL HAVE TO SIFT FOR TRACES OF DNA, AND THAT MAY BE FRIED TOO--SORRY.
I'll get them...

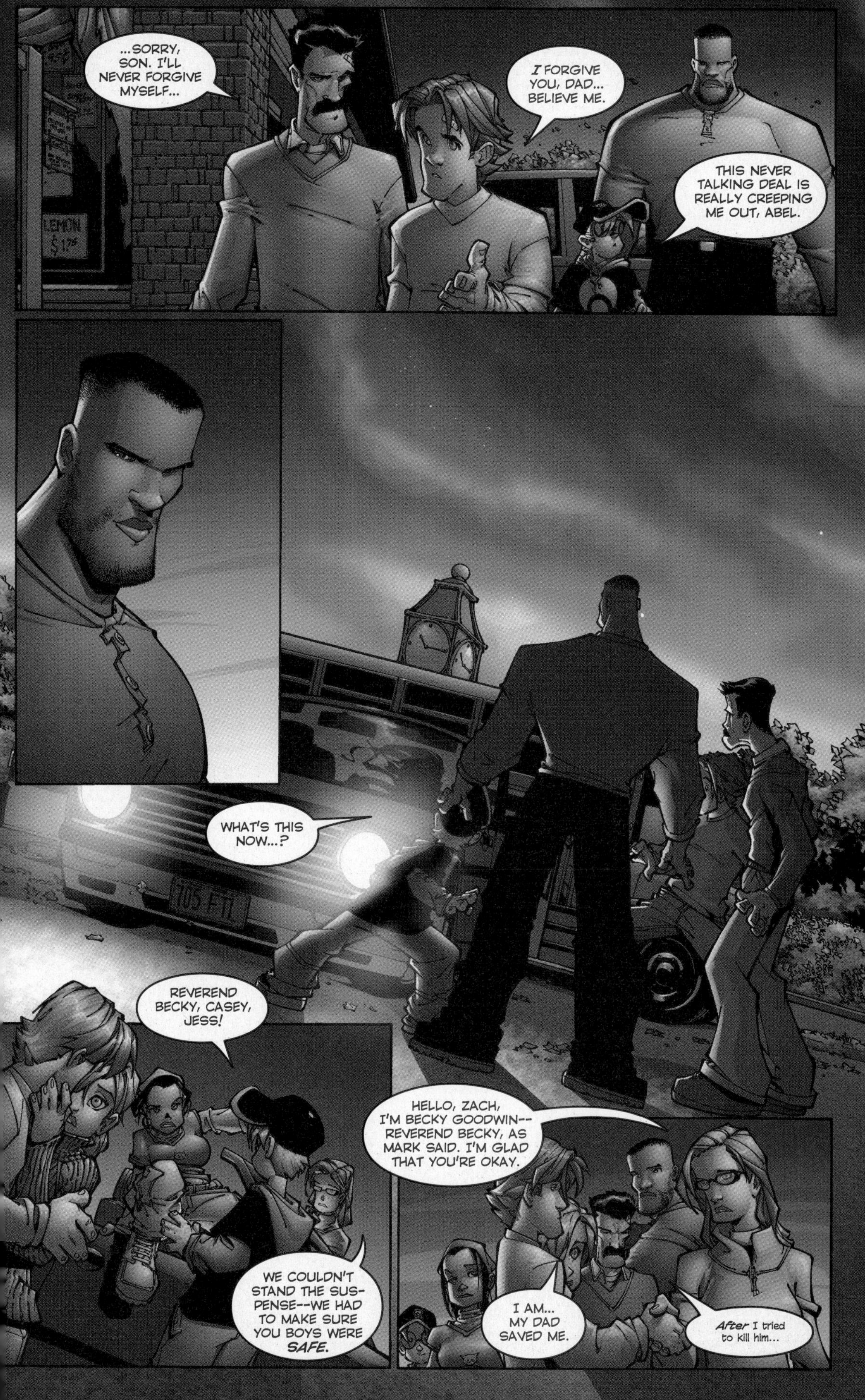
...SORRY, SON. I'LL NEVER FORGIVE MYSELF...
I FORGIVE YOU, DAD... BELIEVE ME.
THIS NEVER TALKING DEAL IS REALLY CREEPING ME OUT, ABEL.
LEMON $1.75
WHAT'S THIS NOW...?
705 FTL
REVEREND BECKY, CASEY, JESS!
WE COULDN'T STAND THE SUSPENSE--WE HAD TO MAKE SURE YOU BOYS WERE SAFE.
HELLO, ZACH, I'M BECKY GOODWIN--REVEREND BECKY, AS MARK SAID. I'M GLAD THAT YOU'RE OKAY.
I AM... MY DAD SAVED ME.
After I tried to kill him...

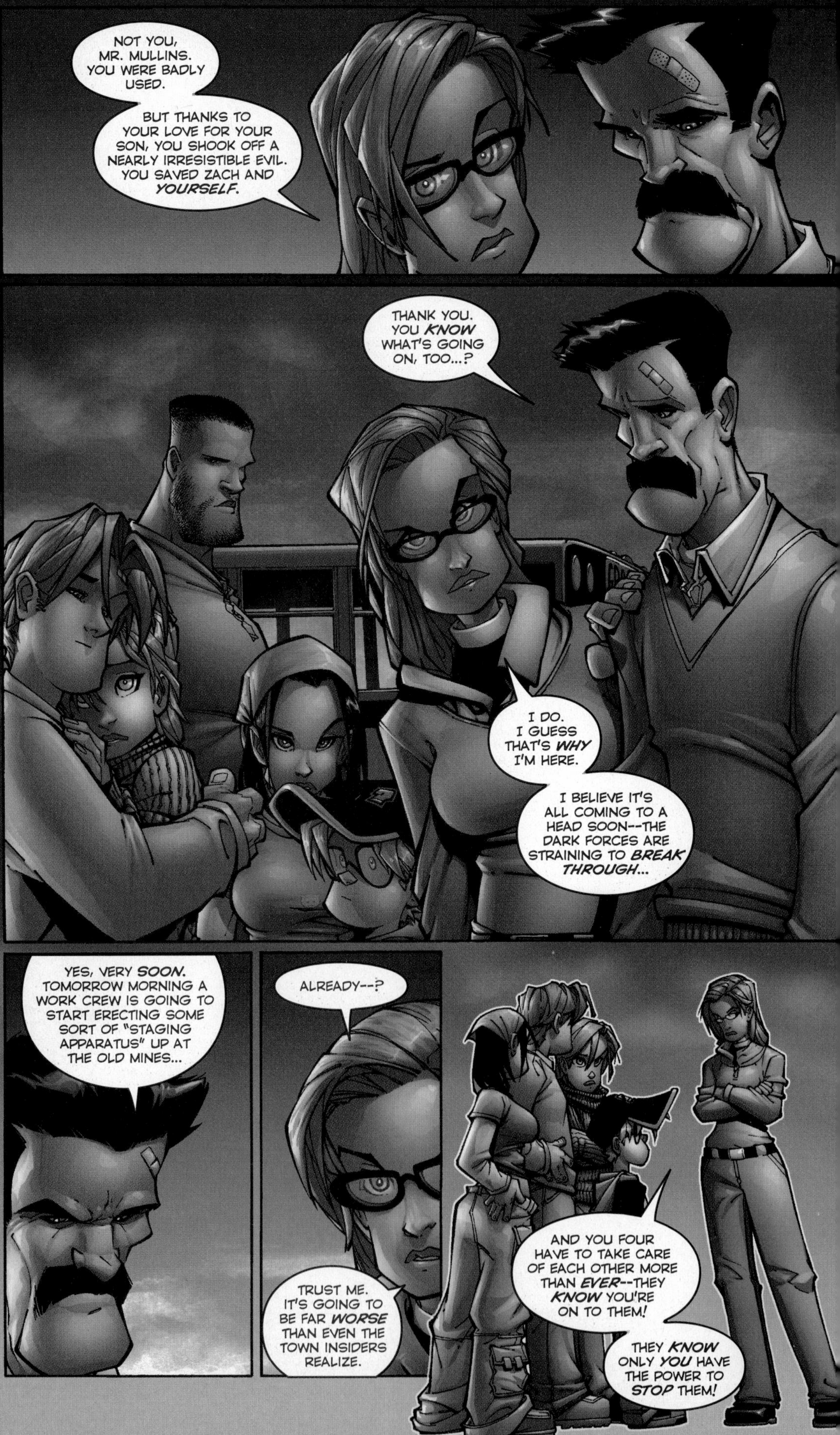
NOT YOU, MR. MULLINS. YOU WERE BADLY USED.
BUT THANKS TO YOUR LOVE FOR YOUR SON, YOU SHOOK OFF A NEARLY IRRESISTIBLE EVIL. YOU SAVED ZACH AND ***YOURSELF.***
THANK YOU. YOU ***KNOW*** WHAT'S GOING ON, TOO...?
I DO. I GUESS THAT'S ***WHY*** I'M HERE.
I BELIEVE IT'S ALL COMING TO A HEAD SOON--THE DARK FORCES ARE STRAINING TO ***BREAK THROUGH...***
YES, VERY ***SOON.*** TOMORROW MORNING A WORK CREW IS GOING TO START ERECTING SOME SORT OF "STAGING APPARATUS" UP AT THE OLD MINES...
ALREADY--?
TRUST ME. IT'S GOING TO BE FAR ***WORSE*** THAN EVEN THE TOWN INSIDERS REALIZE.
AND YOU FOUR HAVE TO TAKE CARE OF EACH OTHER MORE THAN ***EVER***--THEY ***KNOW*** YOU'RE ON TO THEM!
THEY ***KNOW*** ONLY ***YOU*** HAVE THE POWER TO ***STOP*** THEM!

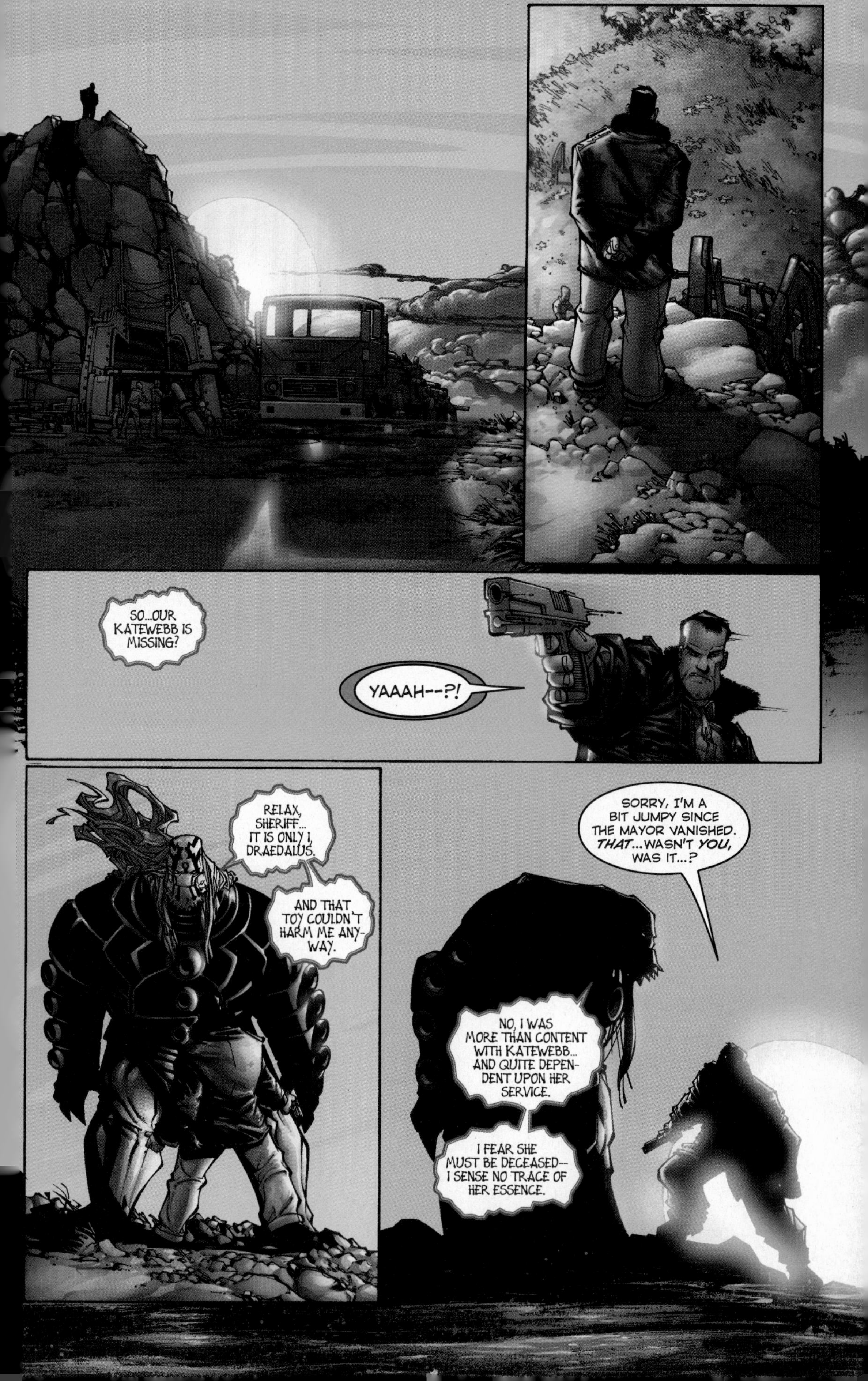

SO...OUR KATEWEBB IS MISSING?
YAAAH--?!
RELAX, SHERIFF... IT IS ONLY I, DRAEDALUS.
AND THAT TOY COULDN'T HARM ME ANYWAY.
SORRY, I'M A BIT JUMPY SINCE THE MAYOR VANISHED. THAT...WASN'T YOU, WAS IT...?
NO, I WAS MORE THAN CONTENT WITH KATEWEBB... AND QUITE DEPENDENT UPON HER SERVICE.
I FEAR SHE MUST BE DECEASED-- I SENSE NO TRACE OF HER ESSENCE.

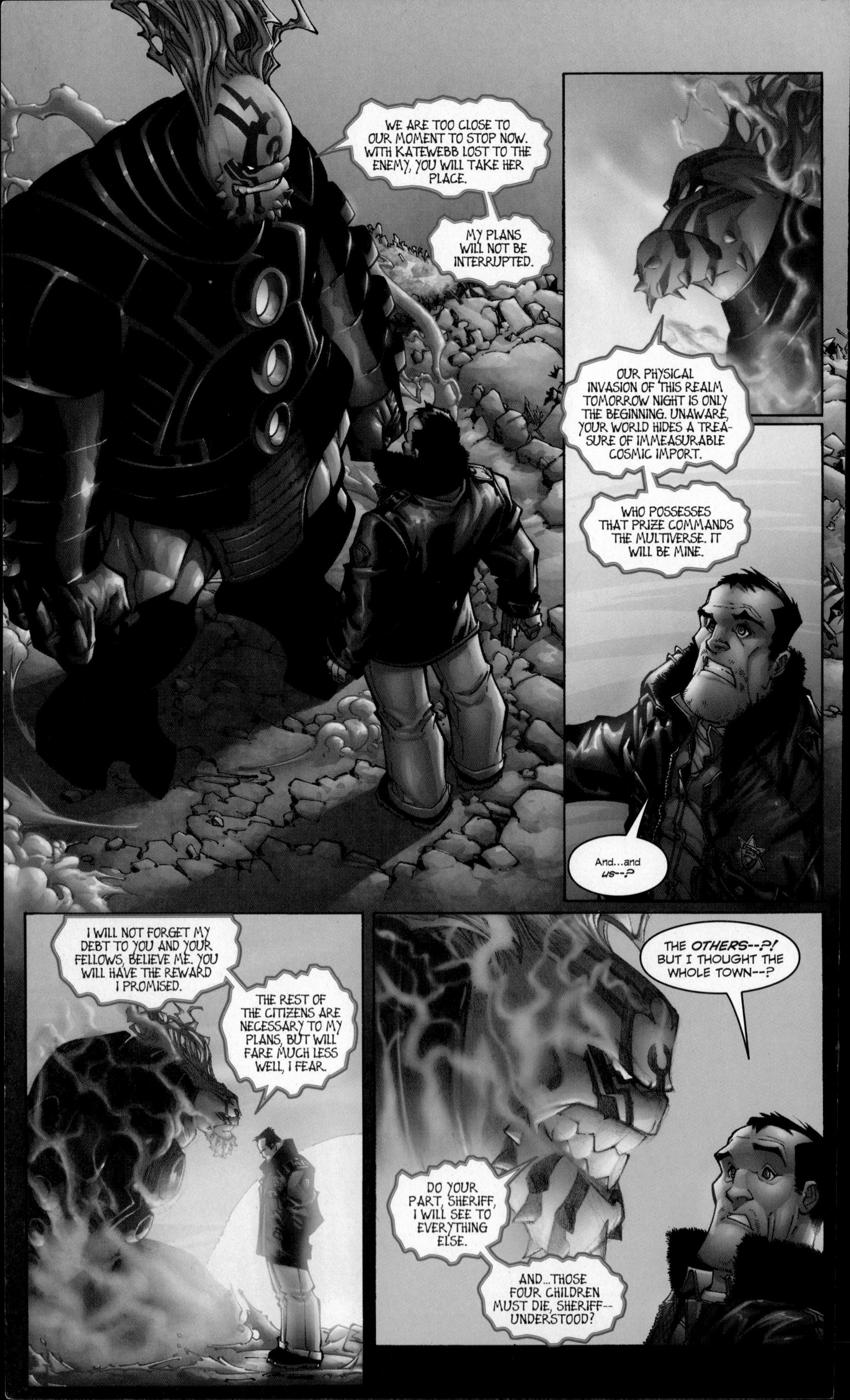
WE ARE TOO CLOSE TO OUR MOMENT TO STOP NOW. WITH KATEWEBB LOST TO THE ENEMY, YOU WILL TAKE HER PLACE.
MY PLANS WILL NOT BE INTERRUPTED.
OUR PHYSICAL INVASION OF THIS REALM TOMORROW NIGHT IS ONLY THE BEGINNING. UNAWARE, YOUR WORLD HIDES A TREA-SURE OF IMMEASURABLE COSMIC IMPORT.
WHO POSSESSES THAT PRIZE COMMANDS THE MULTIVERSE. IT WILL BE MINE.
And...and us--?
I WILL NOT FORGET MY DEBT TO YOU AND YOUR FELLOWS, BELIEVE ME. YOU WILL HAVE THE REWARD I PROMISED.
THE REST OF THE CITIZENS ARE NECESSARY TO MY PLANS, BUT WILL FARE MUCH LESS WELL, I FEAR.
THE OTHERS--?! BUT I THOUGHT THE WHOLE TOWN--?
DO YOUR PART, SHERIFF, I WILL SEE TO EVERYTHING ELSE.
AND...THOSE FOUR CHILDREN MUST DIE, SHERIFF--UNDERSTOOD?

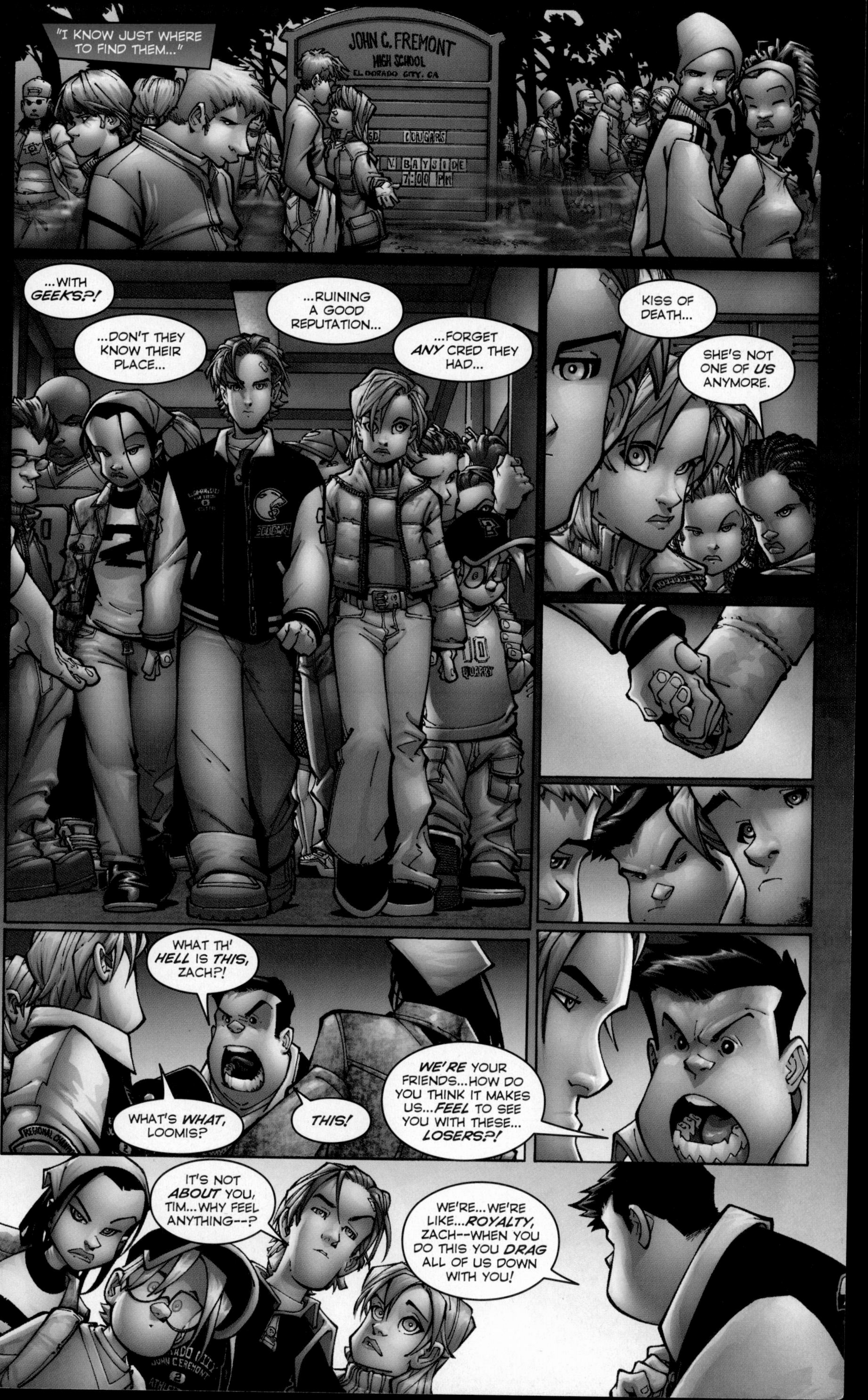
"I KNOW JUST WHERE TO FIND THEM..."
JOHN C. FREMONT HIGH SCHOOL EL DORADO CITY, CA
COUGARS
V BAYSIDE 7:00 PM
...WITH GEEKS?!
...DON'T THEY KNOW THEIR PLACE...
...RUINING A GOOD REPUTATION...
...FORGET ANY CRED THEY HAD...
KISS OF DEATH...
SHE'S NOT ONE OF US ANYMORE.
WHAT TH' HELL IS THIS, ZACH?!
WHAT'S WHAT, LOOMIS?
THIS!
WE'RE YOUR FRIENDS...HOW DO YOU THINK IT MAKES US...FEEL TO SEE YOU WITH THESE... LOSERS?!
IT'S NOT ABOUT YOU, TIM...WHY FEEL ANYTHING--?
WE'RE...WE'RE LIKE...ROYALTY, ZACH--WHEN YOU DO THIS YOU DRAG ALL OF US DOWN WITH YOU!

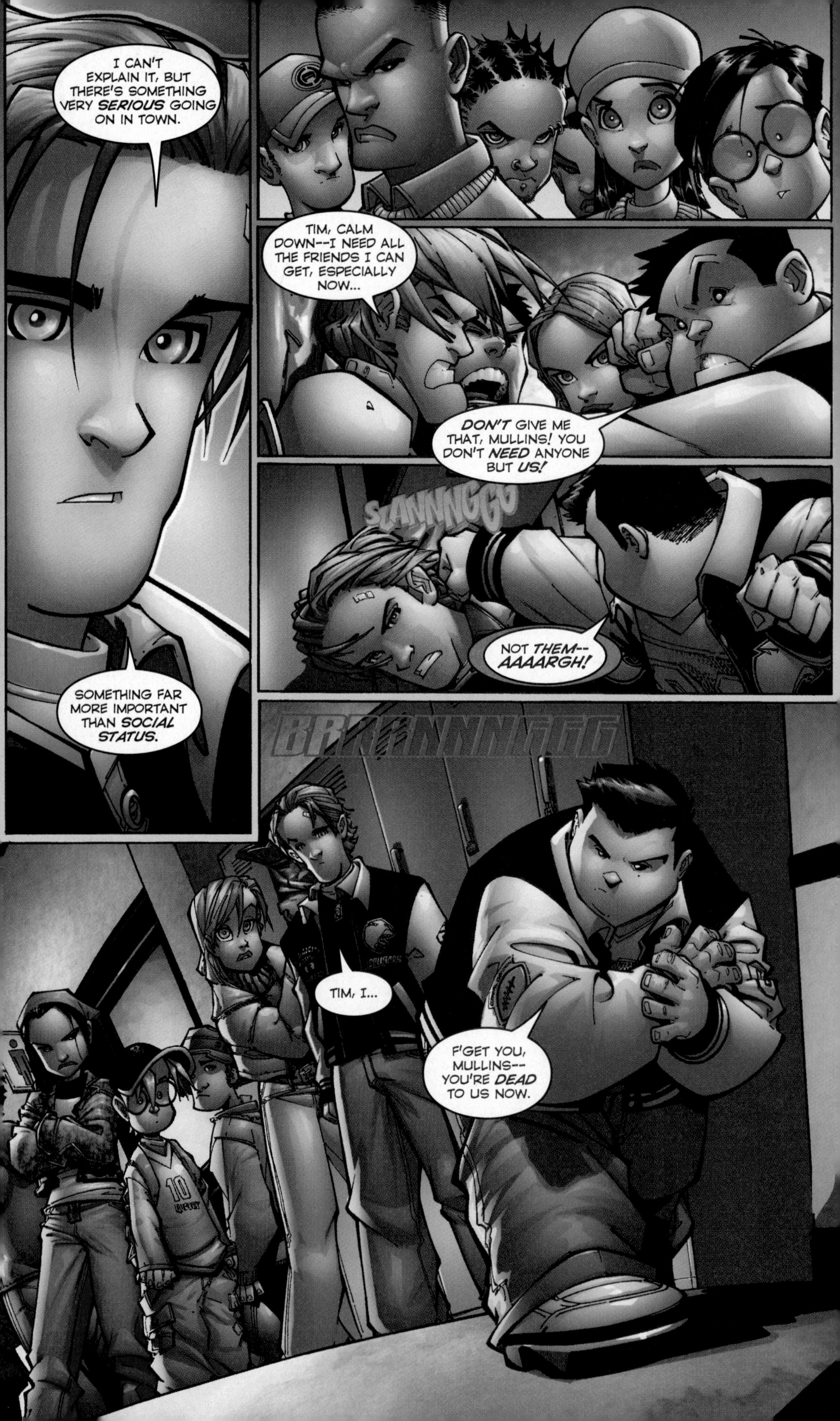
I CAN'T EXPLAIN IT, BUT THERE'S SOMETHING VERY SERIOUS GOING ON IN TOWN.
SOMETHING FAR MORE IMPORTANT THAN SOCIAL STATUS.
TIM, CALM DOWN--I NEED ALL THE FRIENDS I CAN GET, ESPECIALLY NOW...
DON'T GIVE ME THAT, MULLINS! YOU DON'T NEED ANYONE BUT US!
SLANNNGGG
NOT THEM-- AAAARGH!
BRRANNNGGG
TIM, I...
F'GET YOU, MULLINS-- YOU'RE DEAD TO US NOW.

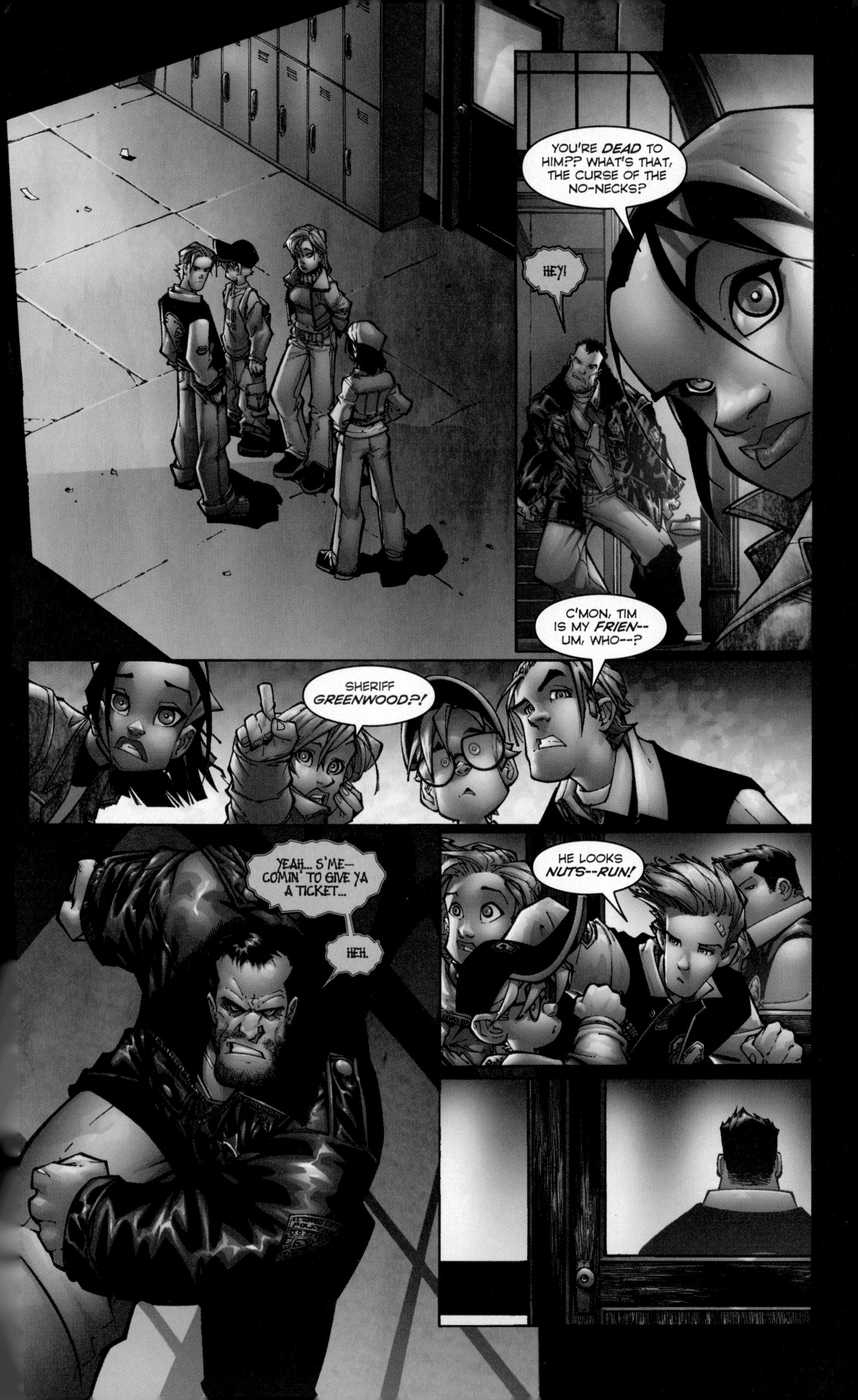
YOU'RE DEAD TO HIM?? WHAT'S THAT, THE CURSE OF THE NO-NECKS?
HEY!
C'MON, TIM IS MY FRIEN-- UM, WHO--?
SHERIFF GREENWOOD?!
YEAH... S'ME-- COMIN' TO GIVE YA A TICKET...
HEH.
HE LOOKS NUTS--RUN!

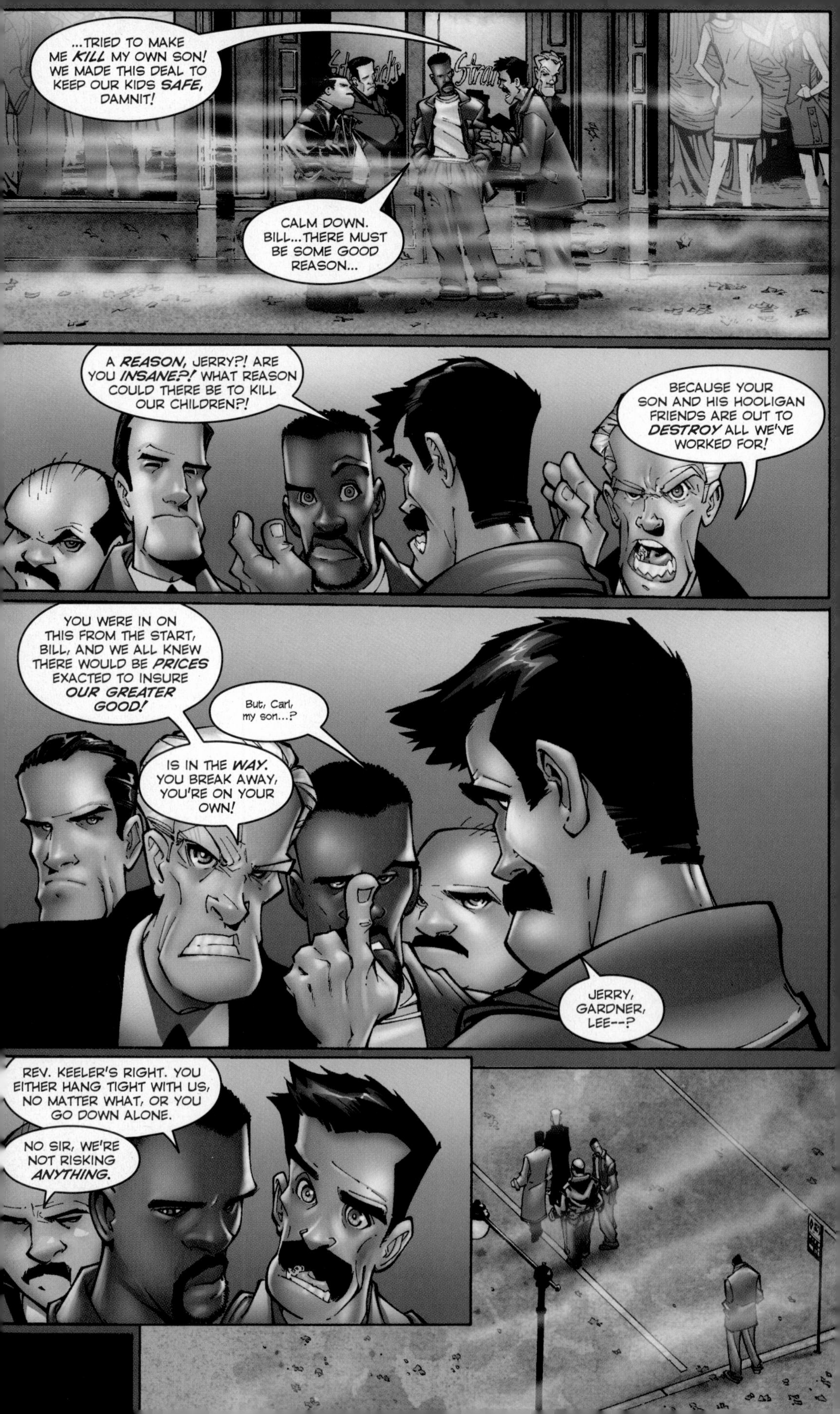
...TRIED TO MAKE ME KILL MY OWN SON! WE MADE THIS DEAL TO KEEP OUR KIDS SAFE, DAMNIT!
CALM DOWN. BILL...THERE MUST BE SOME GOOD REASON...
A REASON, JERRY?! ARE YOU INSANE?! WHAT REASON COULD THERE BE TO KILL OUR CHILDREN?!
BECAUSE YOUR SON AND HIS HOOLIGAN FRIENDS ARE OUT TO DESTROY ALL WE'VE WORKED FOR!
YOU WERE IN ON THIS FROM THE START, BILL, AND WE ALL KNEW THERE WOULD BE PRICES EXACTED TO INSURE OUR GREATER GOOD!
But, Carl, my son...?
IS IN THE WAY. YOU BREAK AWAY, YOU'RE ON YOUR OWN!
JERRY, GARDNER, LEE--?
REV. KEELER'S RIGHT. YOU EITHER HANG TIGHT WITH US, NO MATTER WHAT, OR YOU GO DOWN ALONE.
NO SIR, WE'RE NOT RISKING ANYTHING.

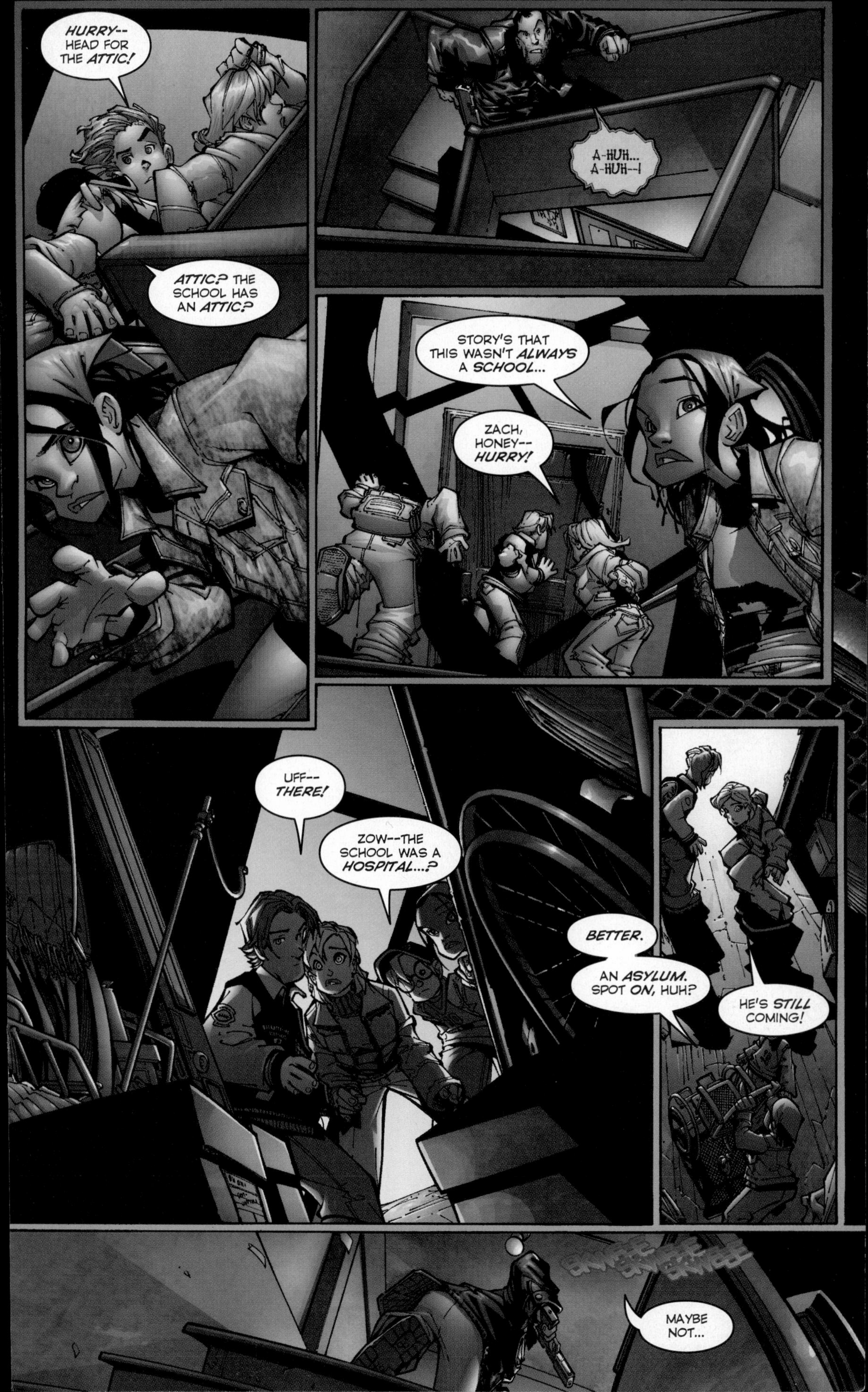
HURRY--
HEAD FOR
THE ATTIC!
A-HUH...
A-HUH--!
ATTIC? THE
SCHOOL HAS
AN ATTIC?
STORY'S THAT
THIS WASN'T ALWAYS
A SCHOOL...
ZACH,
HONEY--
HURRY!
UFF--
THERE!
ZOW--THE
SCHOOL WAS A
HOSPITAL...?
BETTER.
AN ASYLUM.
SPOT ON, HUH?
HE'S STILL
COMING!
MAYBE
NOT...

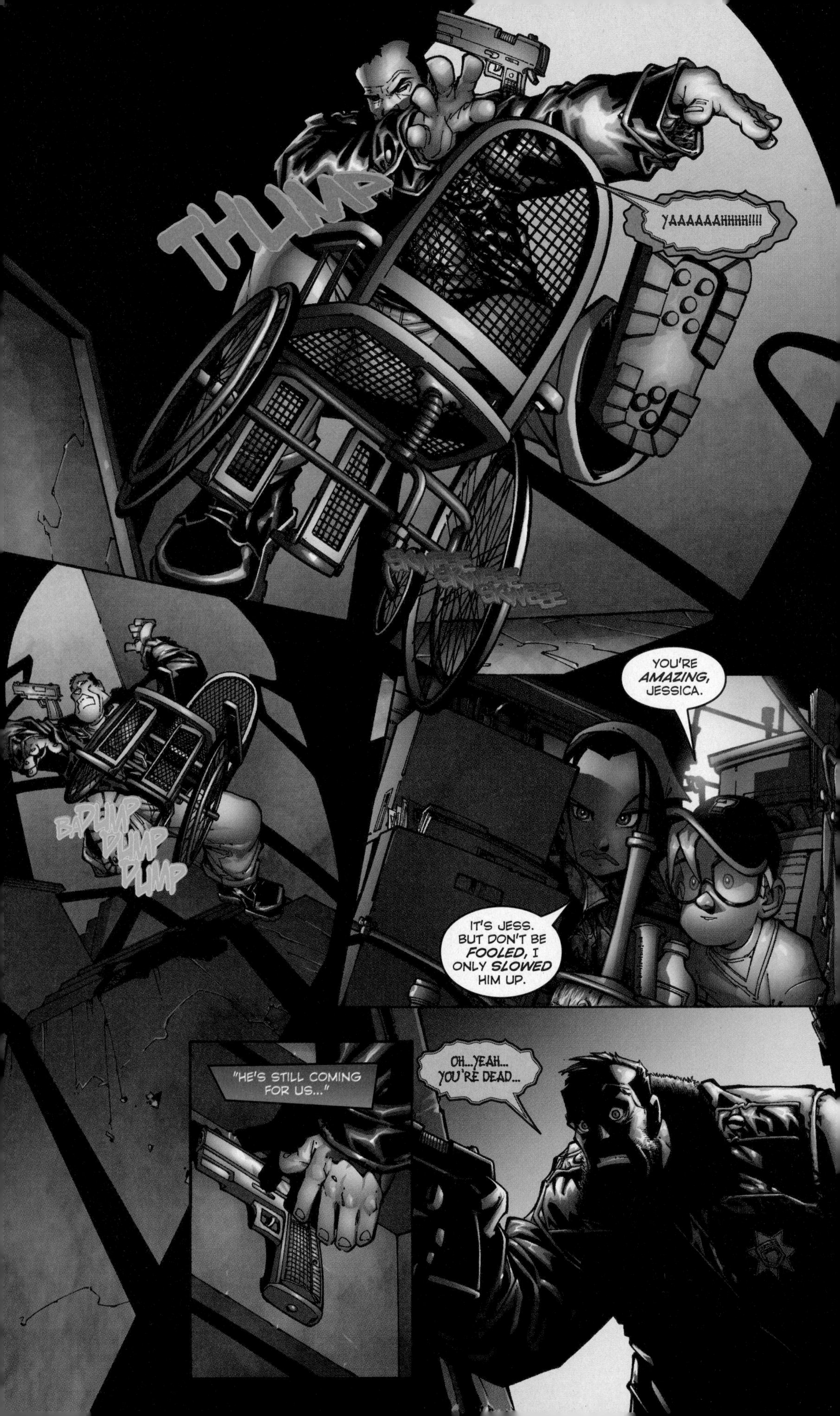
THUMP
YAAAAAAHHHHH!!!!
BaDUMP DUMP DUMP
YOU'RE *AMAZING*, JESSICA.
IT'S JESS. BUT DON'T BE *FOOLED*, I ONLY *SLOWED* HIM UP.
"HE'S STILL COMING FOR US..."
OH...YEAH... YOU'RE DEAD...

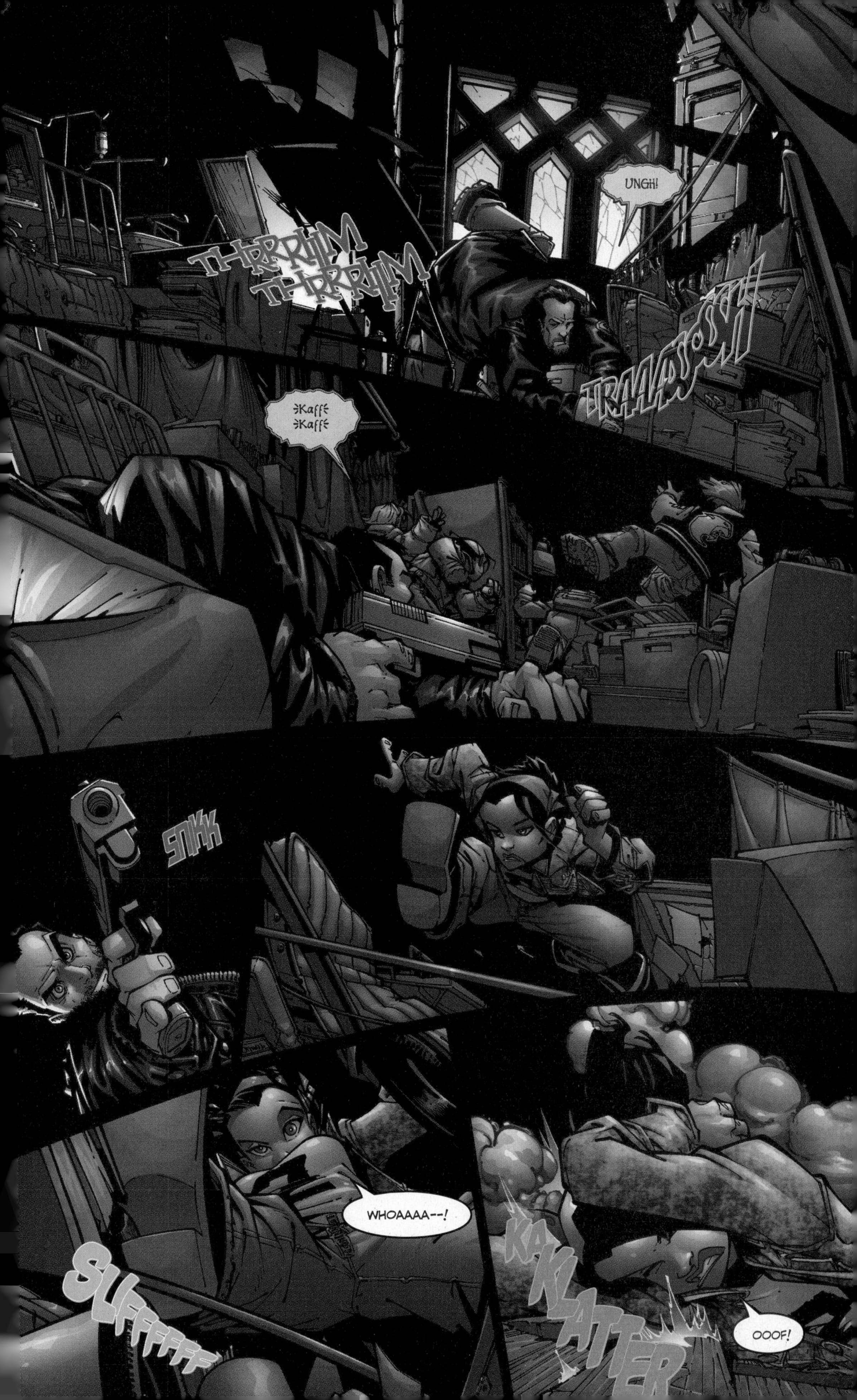
UNGH!
THRRUM THRRUM
TRAAASSSH
Kaff *Kaff*
SNIKK
WHOAAAA--!
SLIFFFFFF
KA KLATTER
OOOF!

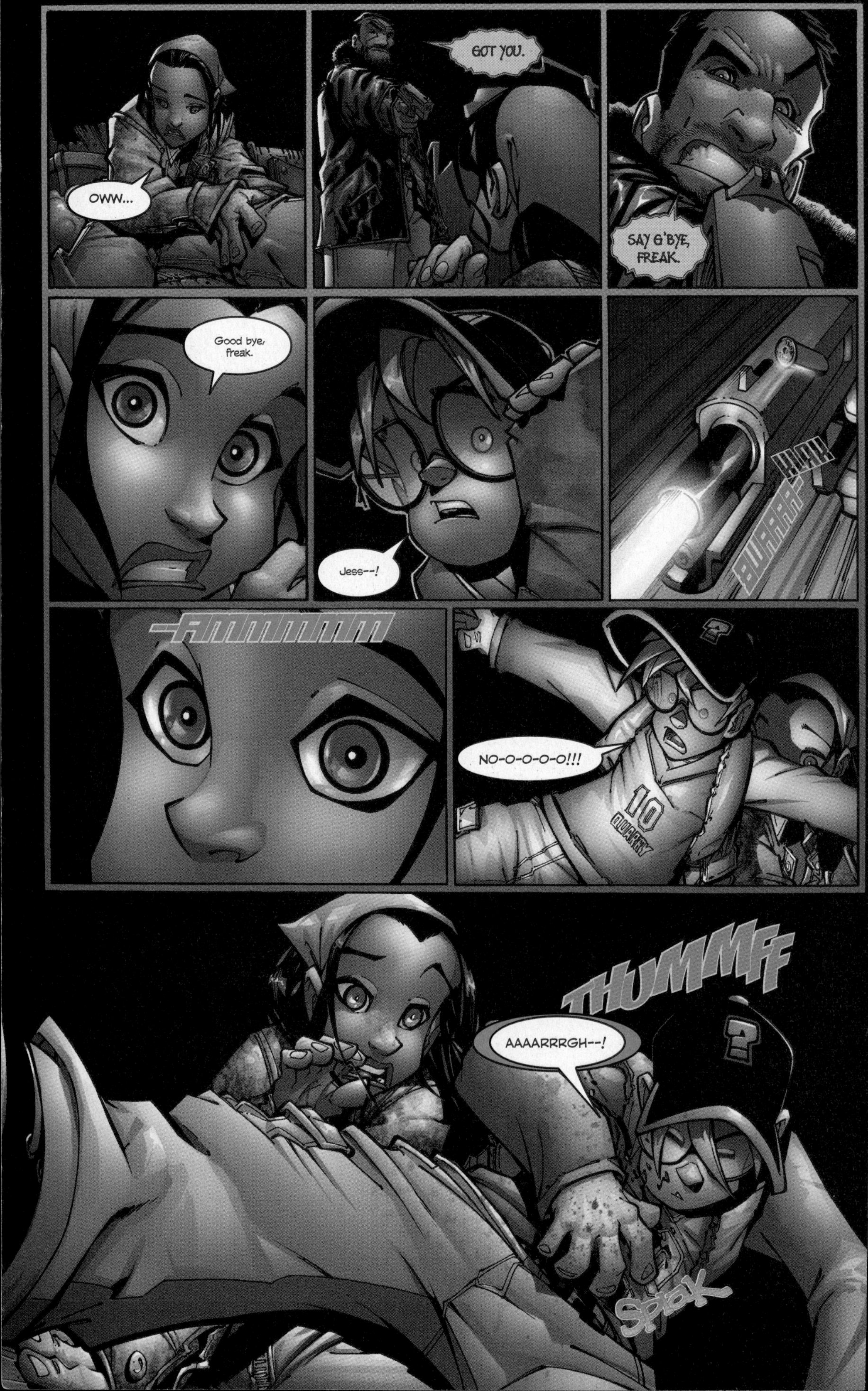
OWW...
GOT YOU.
SAY G'BYE, FREAK.
Good bye, freak.
Jess--!
BWAAAA-
-AMMMMMM
NO-O-O-O-O!!!
THUMMFF
AAAARRRGH--!
Splak

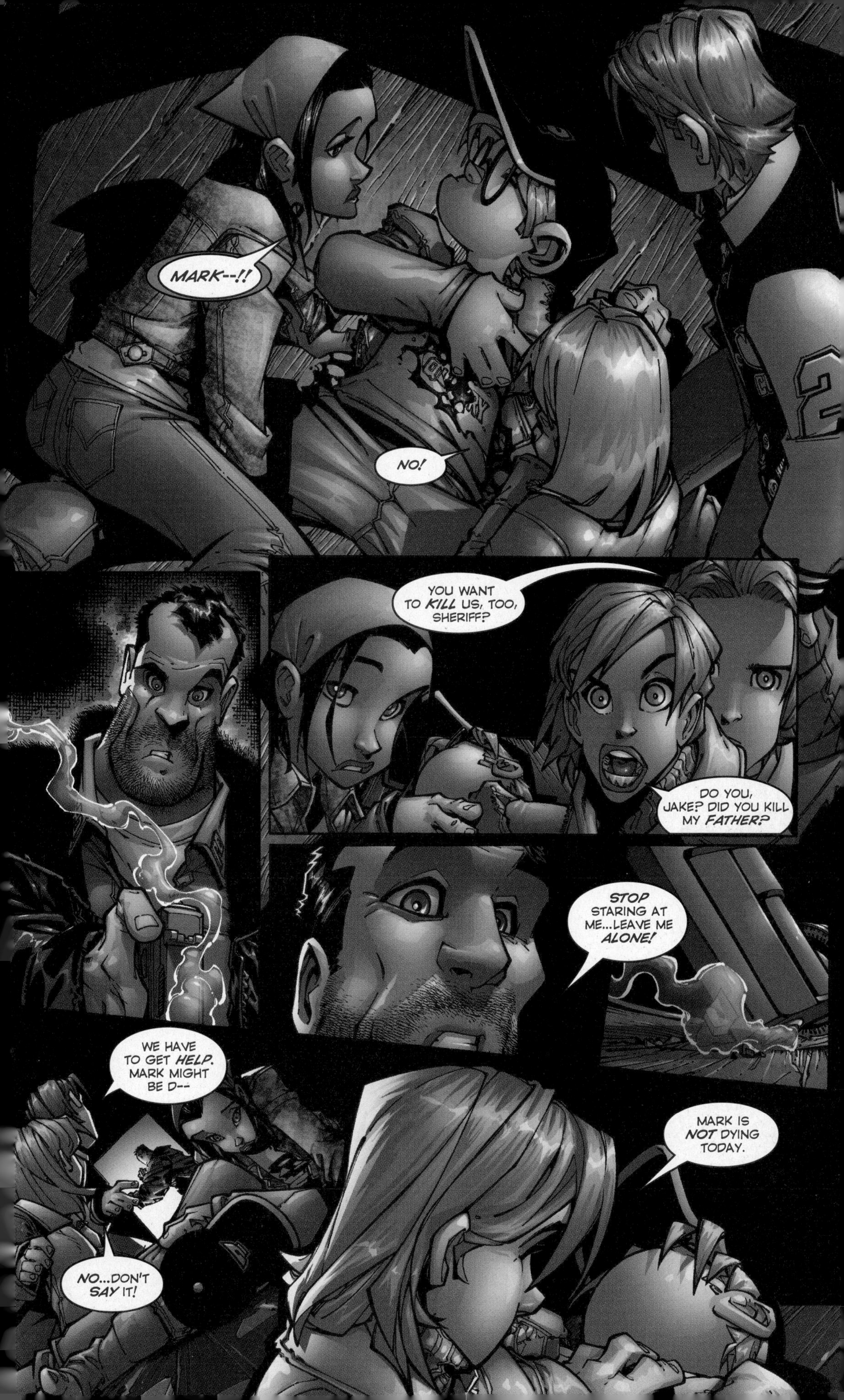
MARK--!!
NO!
YOU WANT TO KILL US, TOO, SHERIFF?
DO YOU, JAKE? DID YOU KILL MY FATHER?
STOP STARING AT ME...LEAVE ME ALONE!
WE HAVE TO GET HELP. MARK MIGHT BE D--
NO...DON'T SAY IT!
MARK IS NOT DYING TODAY.

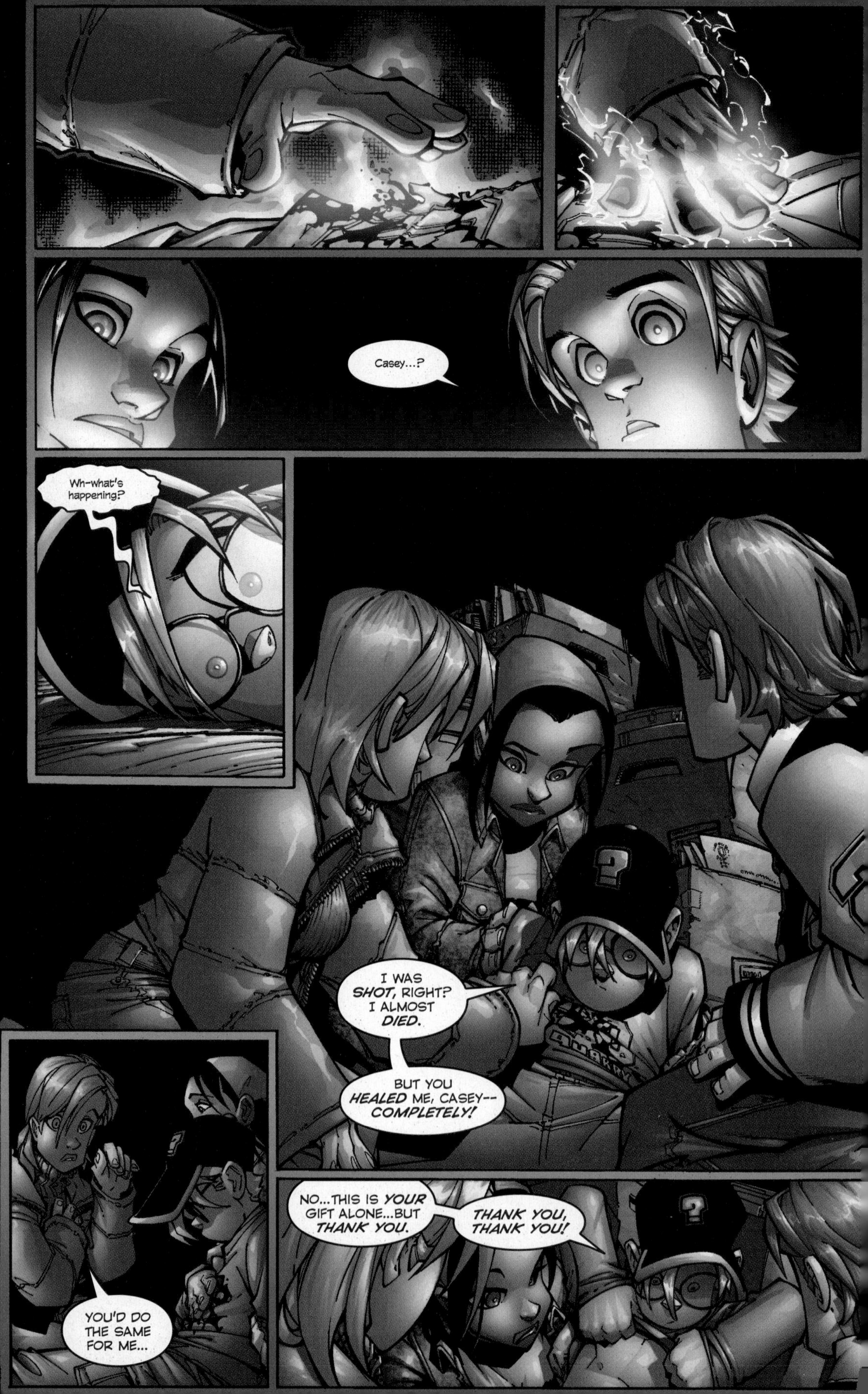
Casey...?
Wh-what's happening?
I WAS SHOT, RIGHT? I ALMOST DIED.
BUT YOU HEALED ME, CASEY-- COMPLETELY!
YOU'D DO THE SAME FOR ME...
NO...THIS IS YOUR GIFT ALONE...BUT THANK YOU.
THANK YOU, THANK YOU!

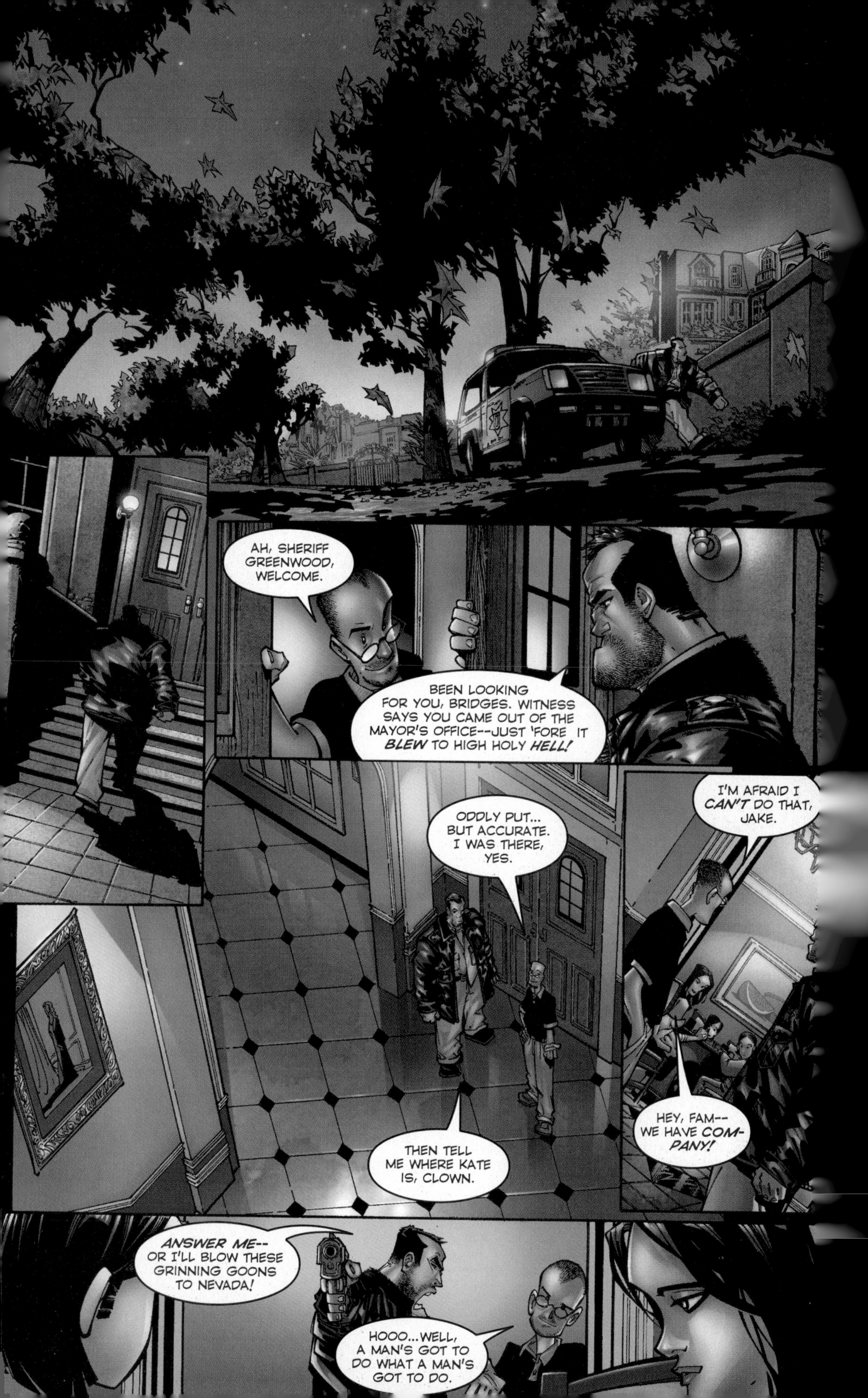
AH, SHERIFF GREENWOOD, WELCOME.
BEEN LOOKING FOR YOU, BRIDGES. WITNESS SAYS YOU CAME OUT OF THE MAYOR'S OFFICE--JUST 'FORE IT BLEW TO HIGH HOLY HELL!
ODDLY PUT... BUT ACCURATE. I WAS THERE, YES.
THEN TELL ME WHERE KATE IS, CLOWN.
I'M AFRAID I CAN'T DO THAT, JAKE.
HEY, FAM-- WE HAVE COMPANY!
ANSWER ME-- OR I'LL BLOW THESE GRINNING GOONS TO NEVADA!
HOOO...WELL, A MAN'S GOT TO DO WHAT A MAN'S GOT TO DO.

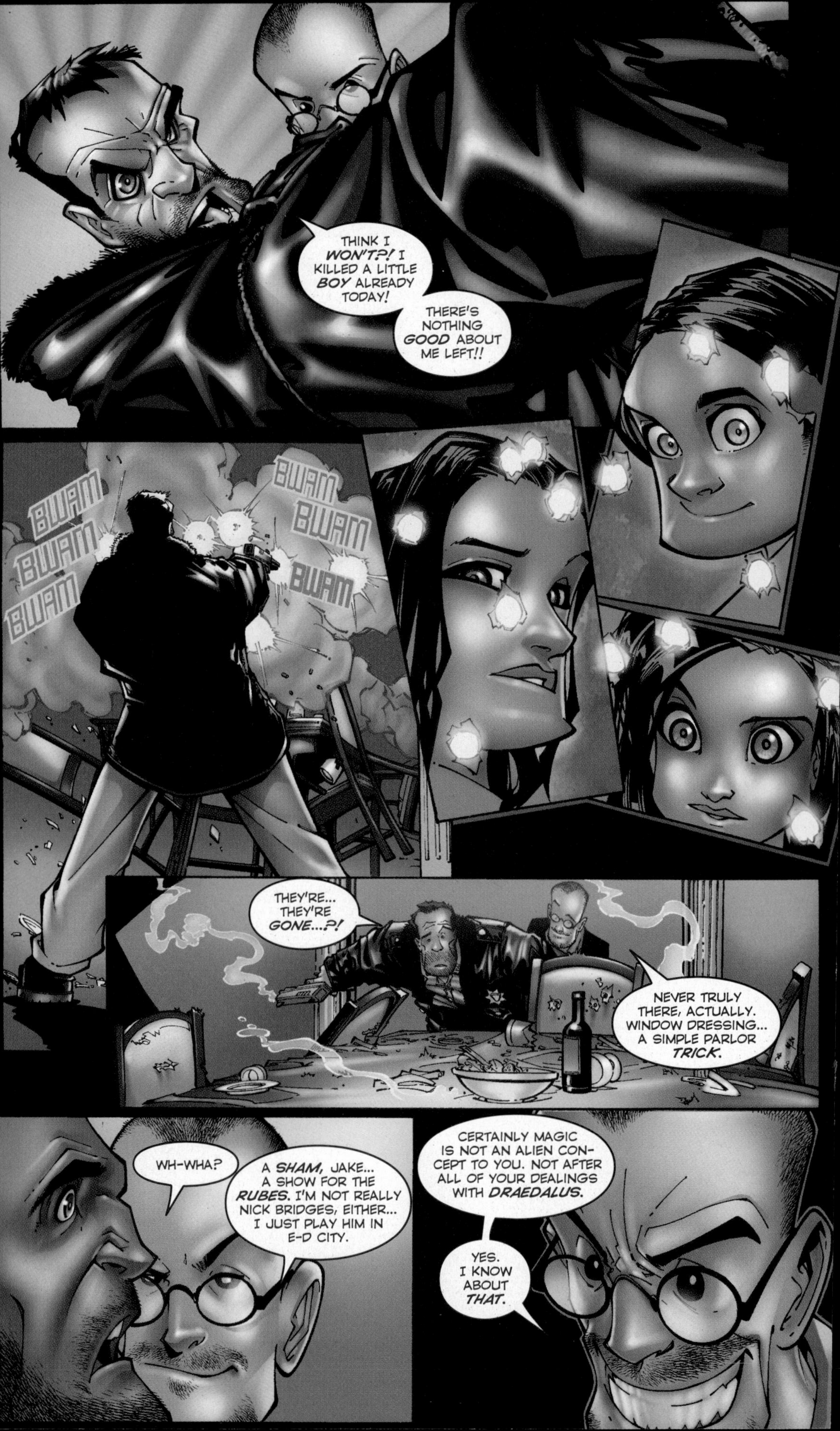
THINK I WON'T?! I KILLED A LITTLE BOY ALREADY TODAY!
THERE'S NOTHING GOOD ABOUT ME LEFT!!
BWAM BWAM BWAM
BWAM BWAM
BWAM
THEY'RE... THEY'RE GONE...?!
NEVER TRULY THERE, ACTUALLY. WINDOW DRESSING... A SIMPLE PARLOR TRICK.
WH-WHA?
A SHAM, JAKE... A SHOW FOR THE RUBES. I'M NOT REALLY NICK BRIDGES, EITHER... I JUST PLAY HIM IN E-D CITY.
CERTAINLY MAGIC IS NOT AN ALIEN CONCEPT TO YOU. NOT AFTER ALL OF YOUR DEALINGS WITH DRAEDALUS.
YES. I KNOW ABOUT THAT.

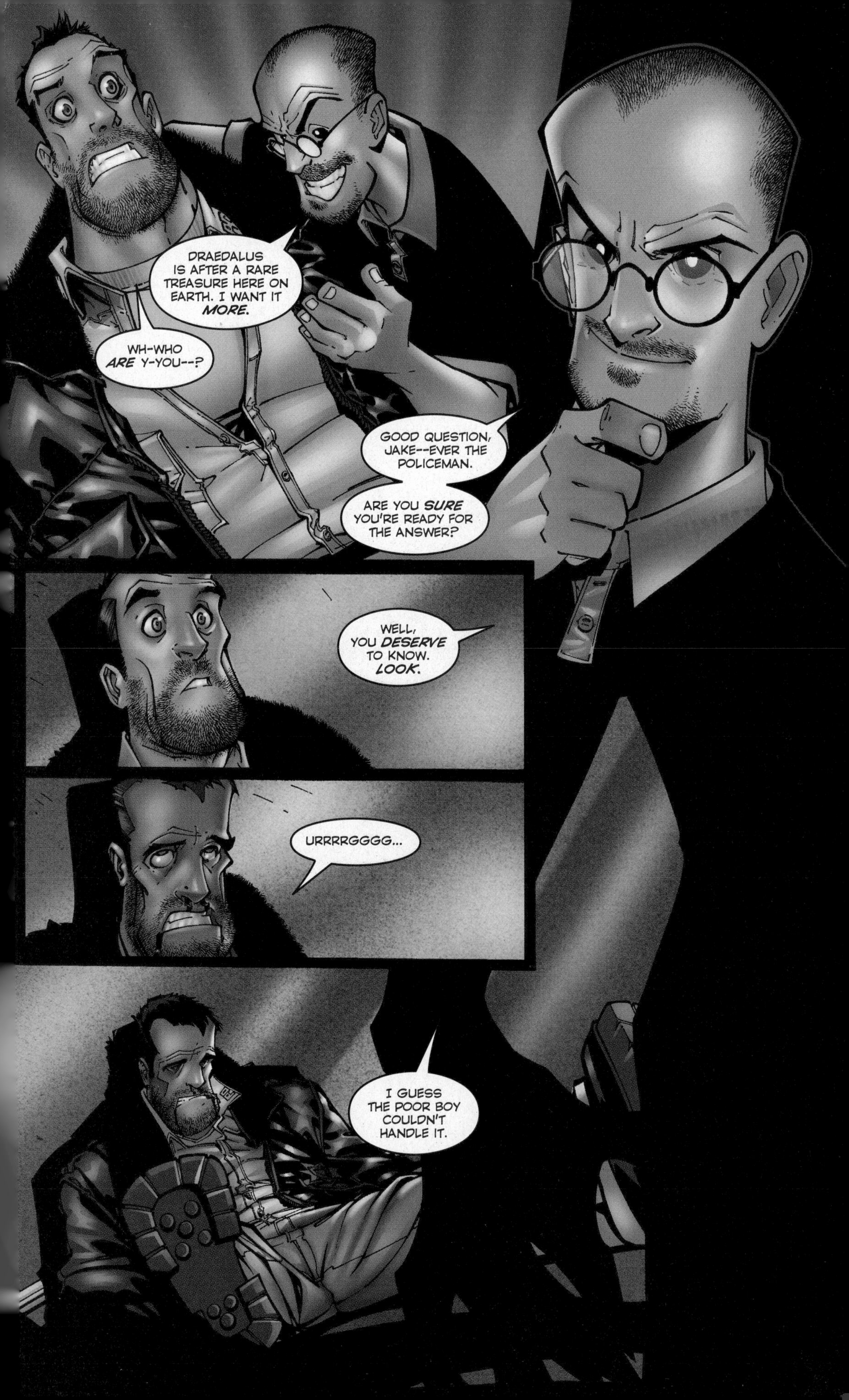
DRAEDALUS IS AFTER A RARE TREASURE HERE ON EARTH. I WANT IT **MORE.**
WH-WHO **ARE** Y-YOU--?
GOOD QUESTION, JAKE--EVER THE POLICEMAN.
ARE YOU **SURE** YOU'RE READY FOR THE ANSWER?
WELL, YOU **DESERVE** TO KNOW. **LOOK.**
URRRRGGGG...
I GUESS THE POOR BOY COULDN'T HANDLE IT.

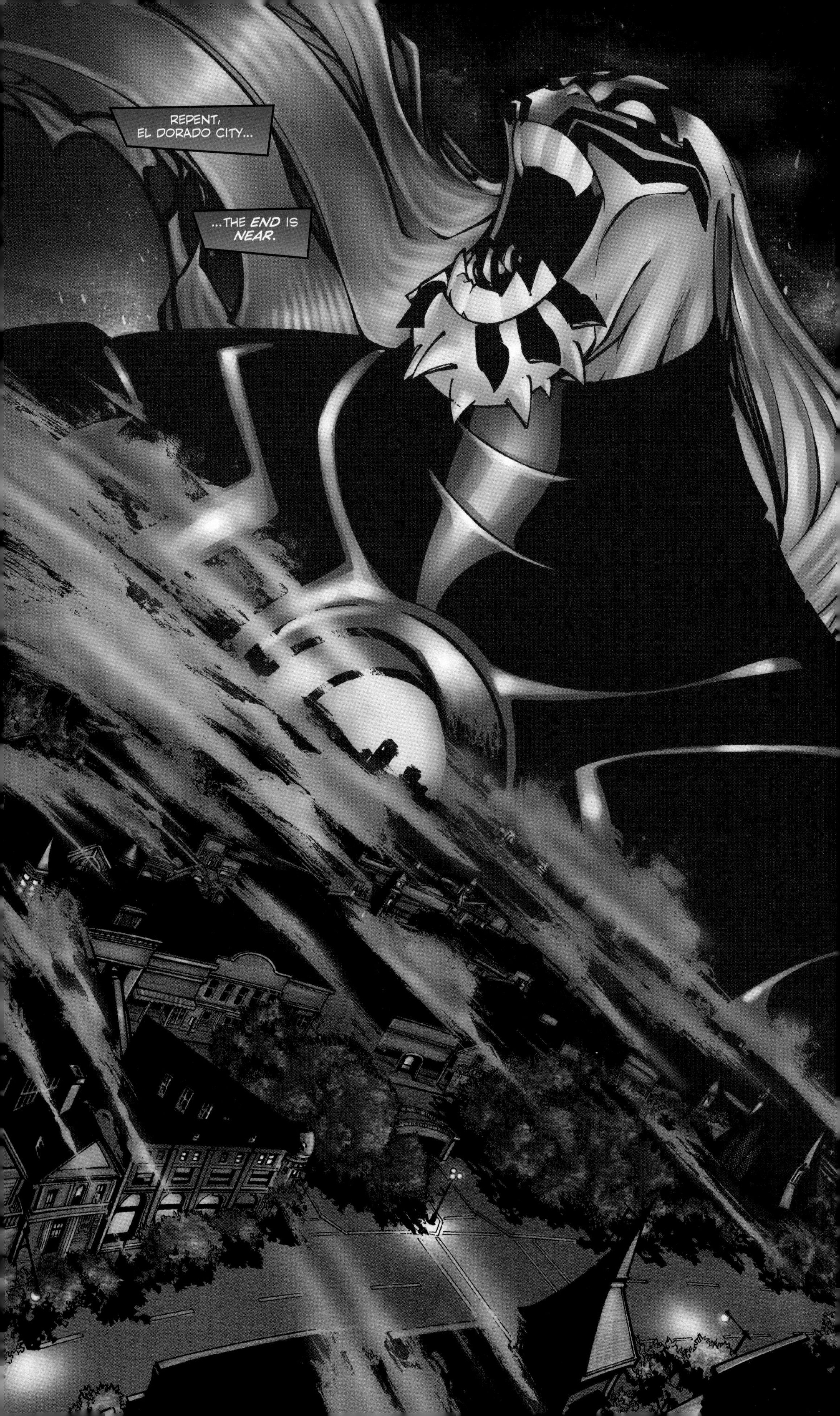
REPENT, EL DORADO CITY...
...THE *END* IS *NEAR*.

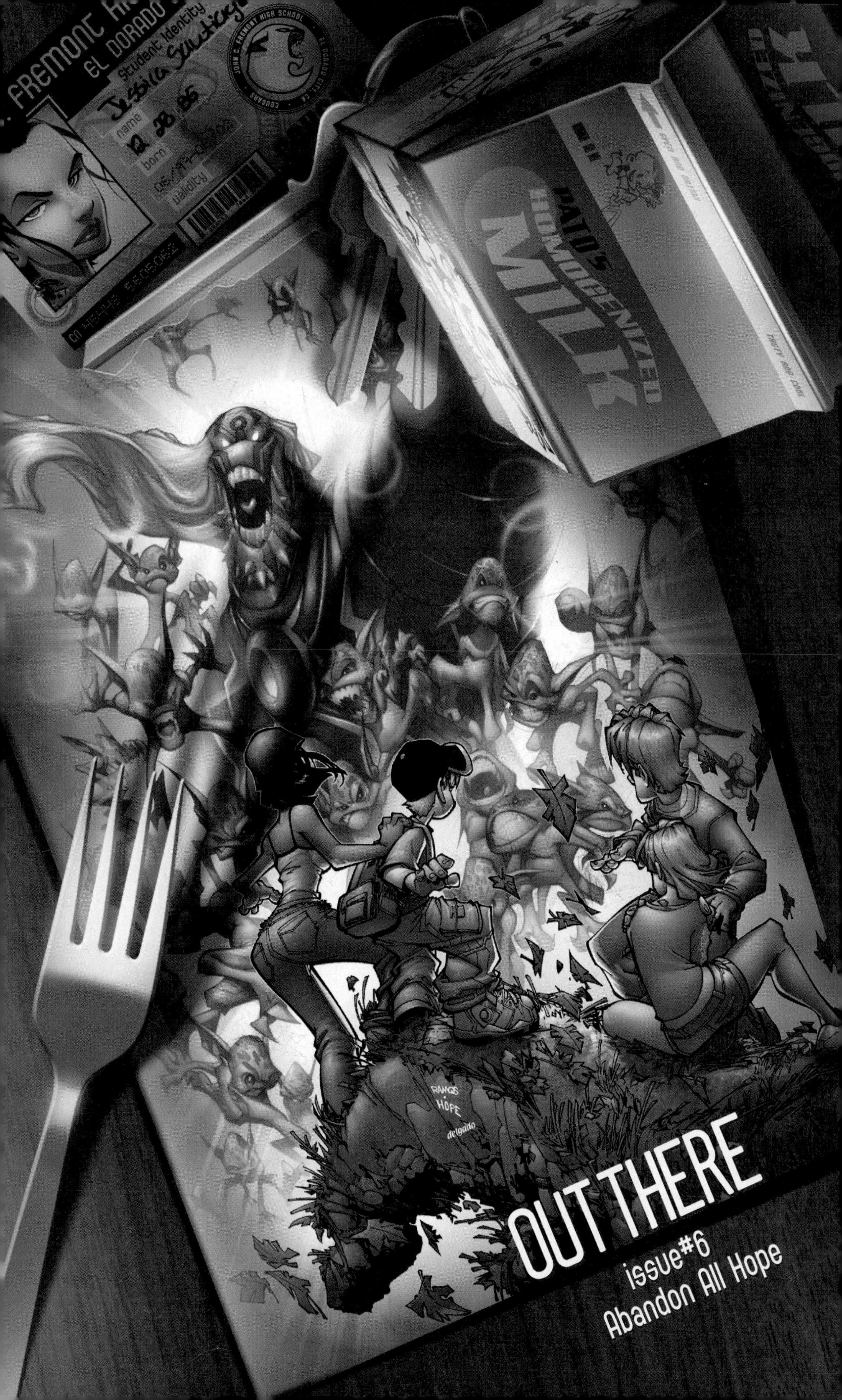

OUT THERE
issue#6
Abandon All Hope
HOMOGENIZED MILK
TASTY AND COOL
Student Identity
name
born
validity
EL DORADO
FREMONT HIGH SCHOOL

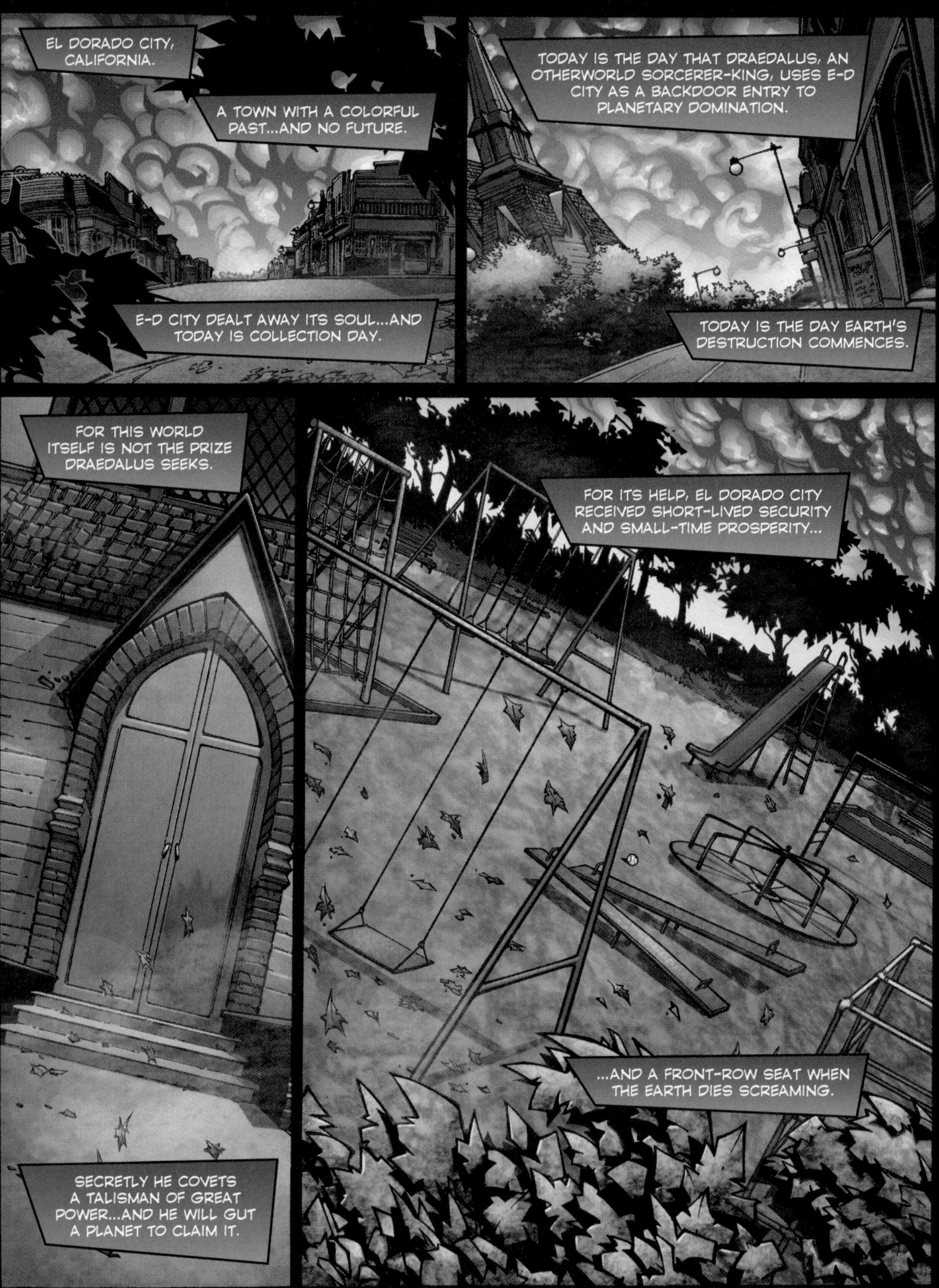
EL DORADO CITY, CALIFORNIA.
A TOWN WITH A COLORFUL PAST...AND NO FUTURE.
E-D CITY DEALT AWAY ITS SOUL...AND TODAY IS COLLECTION DAY.
TODAY IS THE DAY THAT DRAEDALUS, AN OTHERWORLD SORCERER-KING, USES E-D CITY AS A BACKDOOR ENTRY TO PLANETARY DOMINATION.
TODAY IS THE DAY EARTH'S DESTRUCTION COMMENCES.
FOR THIS WORLD ITSELF IS NOT THE PRIZE DRAEDALUS SEEKS.
SECRETLY HE COVETS A TALISMAN OF GREAT POWER...AND HE WILL GUT A PLANET TO CLAIM IT.
FOR ITS HELP, EL DORADO CITY RECEIVED SHORT-LIVED SECURITY AND SMALL-TIME PROSPERITY...
...AND A FRONT-ROW SEAT WHEN THE EARTH DIES SCREAMING.

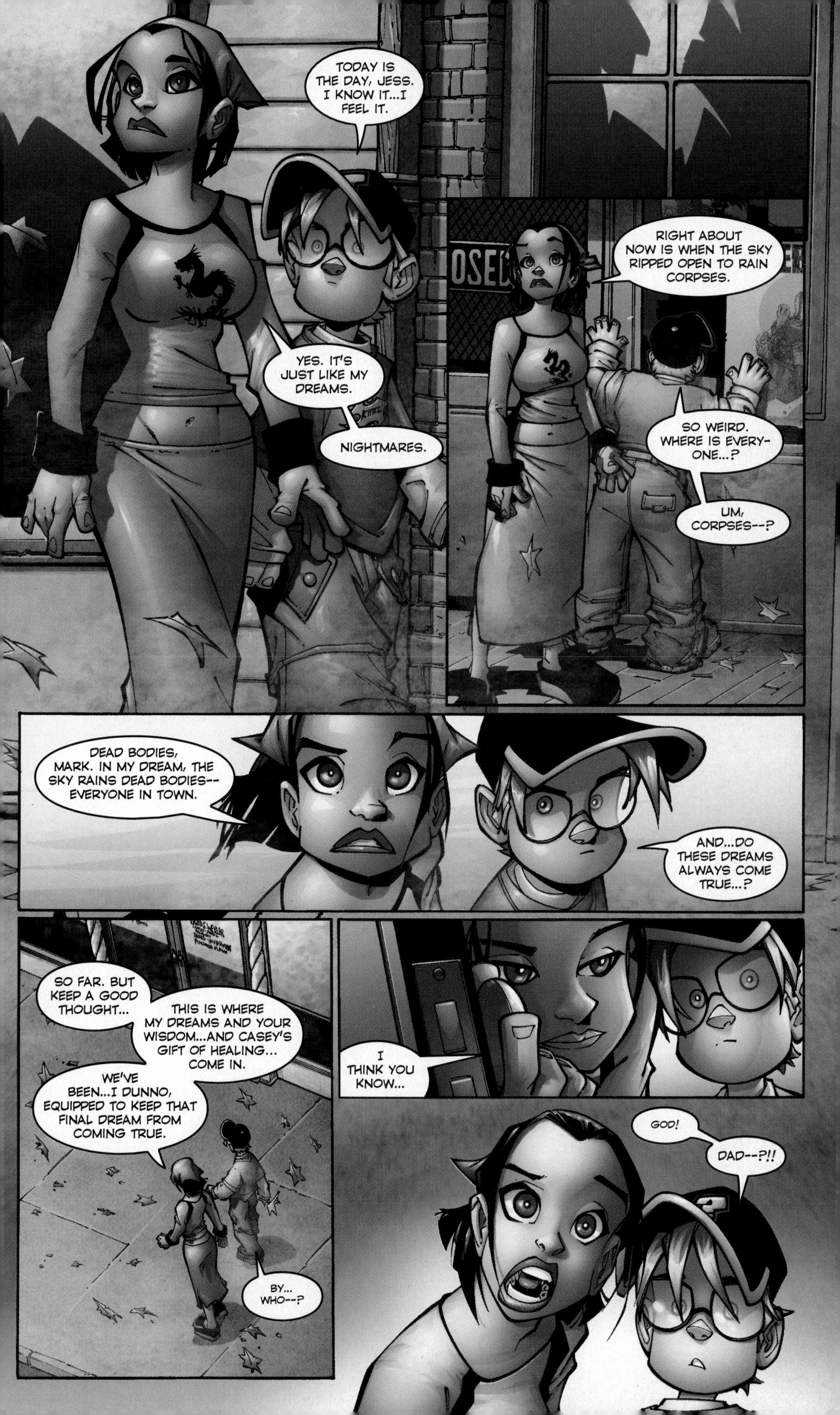
TODAY IS THE DAY, JESS. I KNOW IT...I FEEL IT.
YES. IT'S JUST LIKE MY DREAMS.
NIGHTMARES.
RIGHT ABOUT NOW IS WHEN THE SKY RIPPED OPEN TO RAIN CORPSES.
SO WEIRD. WHERE IS EVERY-ONE...?
UM, CORPSES--?
DEAD BODIES, MARK. IN MY DREAM, THE SKY RAINS DEAD BODIES--EVERYONE IN TOWN.
AND...DO THESE DREAMS ALWAYS COME TRUE...?
SO FAR. BUT KEEP A GOOD THOUGHT...
THIS IS WHERE MY DREAMS AND YOUR WISDOM...AND CASEY'S GIFT OF HEALING... COME IN.
WE'VE BEEN...I DUNNO, EQUIPPED TO KEEP THAT FINAL DREAM FROM COMING TRUE.
BY... WHO--?
I THINK YOU KNOW...
GOD!
DAD--?!!

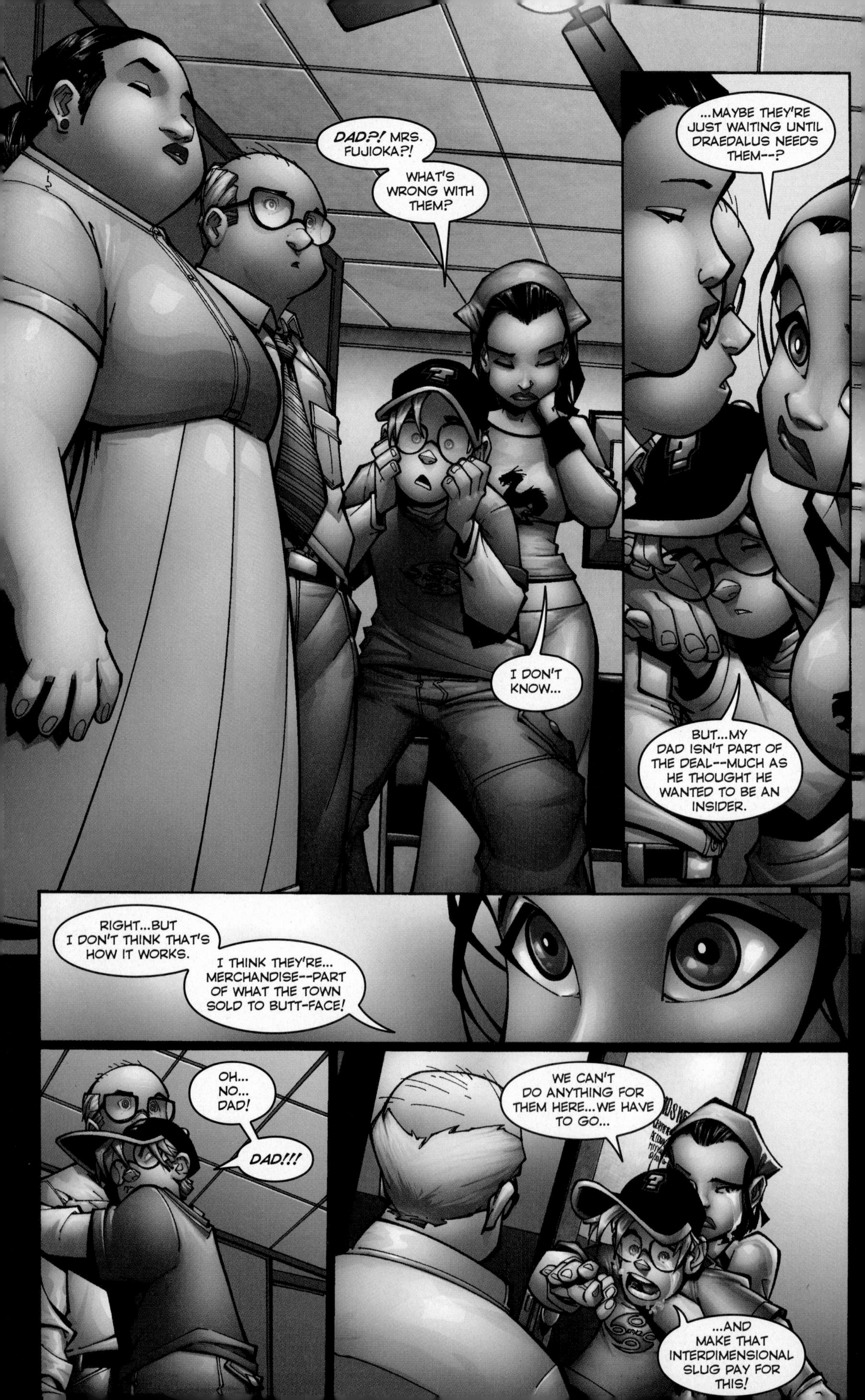
DAD?! MRS. FUJIOKA?!
WHAT'S WRONG WITH THEM?
I DON'T KNOW...
...MAYBE THEY'RE JUST WAITING UNTIL DRAEDALUS NEEDS THEM--?
BUT...MY DAD ISN'T PART OF THE DEAL--MUCH AS HE THOUGHT HE WANTED TO BE AN INSIDER.
RIGHT...BUT I DON'T THINK THAT'S HOW IT WORKS.
I THINK THEY'RE... MERCHANDISE--PART OF WHAT THE TOWN SOLD TO BUTT-FACE!
OH... NO... DAD!
DAD!!!
WE CAN'T DO ANYTHING FOR THEM HERE...WE HAVE TO GO...
...AND MAKE THAT INTERDIMENSIONAL SLUG PAY FOR THIS!

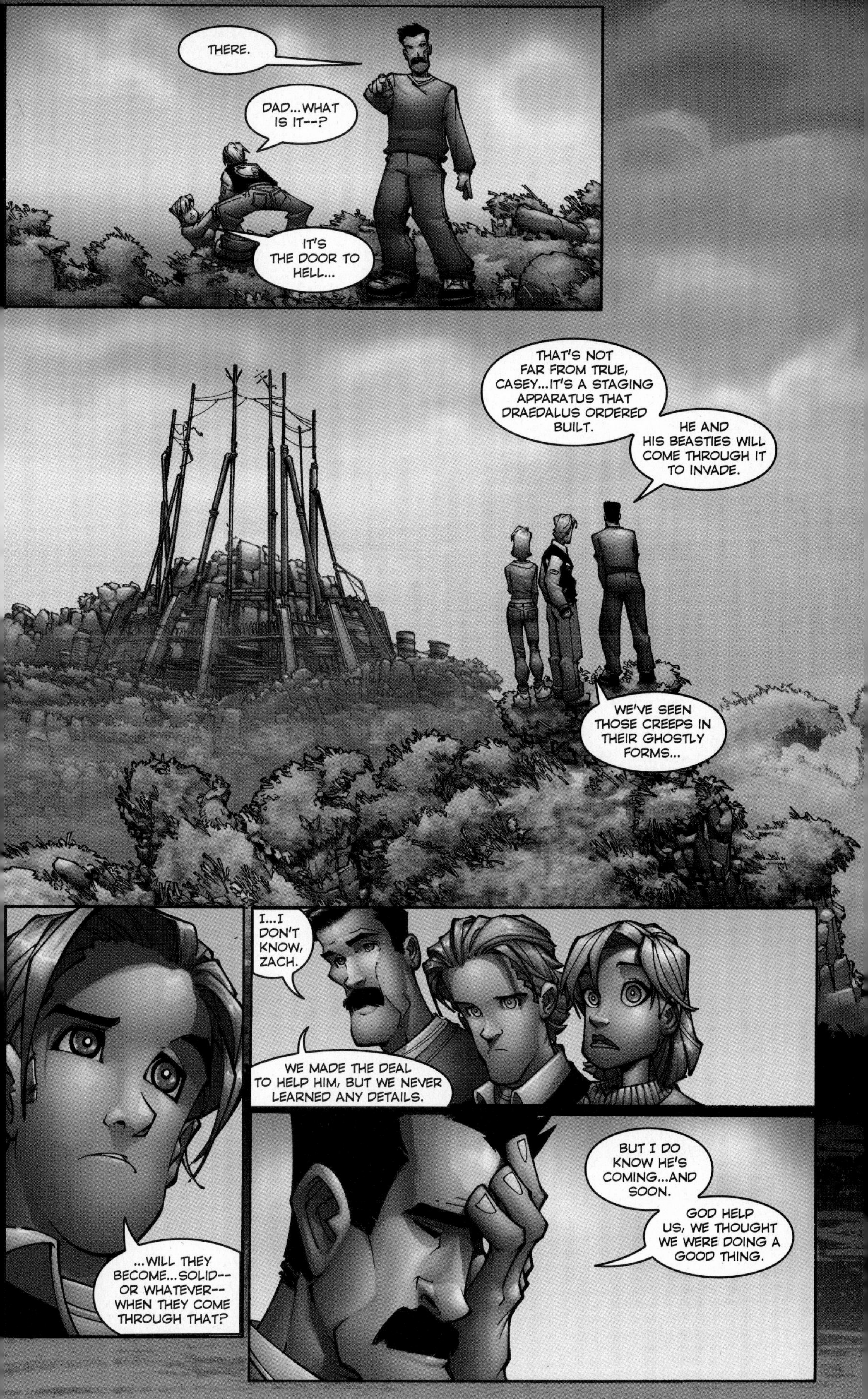
THERE.
DAD...WHAT IS IT--?
IT'S THE DOOR TO HELL...
THAT'S NOT FAR FROM TRUE, CASEY...IT'S A STAGING APPARATUS THAT DRAEDALUS ORDERED BUILT.
HE AND HIS BEASTIES WILL COME THROUGH IT TO INVADE.
WE'VE SEEN THOSE CREEPS IN THEIR GHOSTLY FORMS...
...WILL THEY BECOME...SOLID-- OR WHATEVER-- WHEN THEY COME THROUGH THAT?
I...I DON'T KNOW, ZACH.
WE MADE THE DEAL TO HELP HIM, BUT WE NEVER LEARNED ANY DETAILS.
BUT I DO KNOW HE'S COMING...AND SOON.
GOD HELP US, WE THOUGHT WE WERE DOING A GOOD THING.

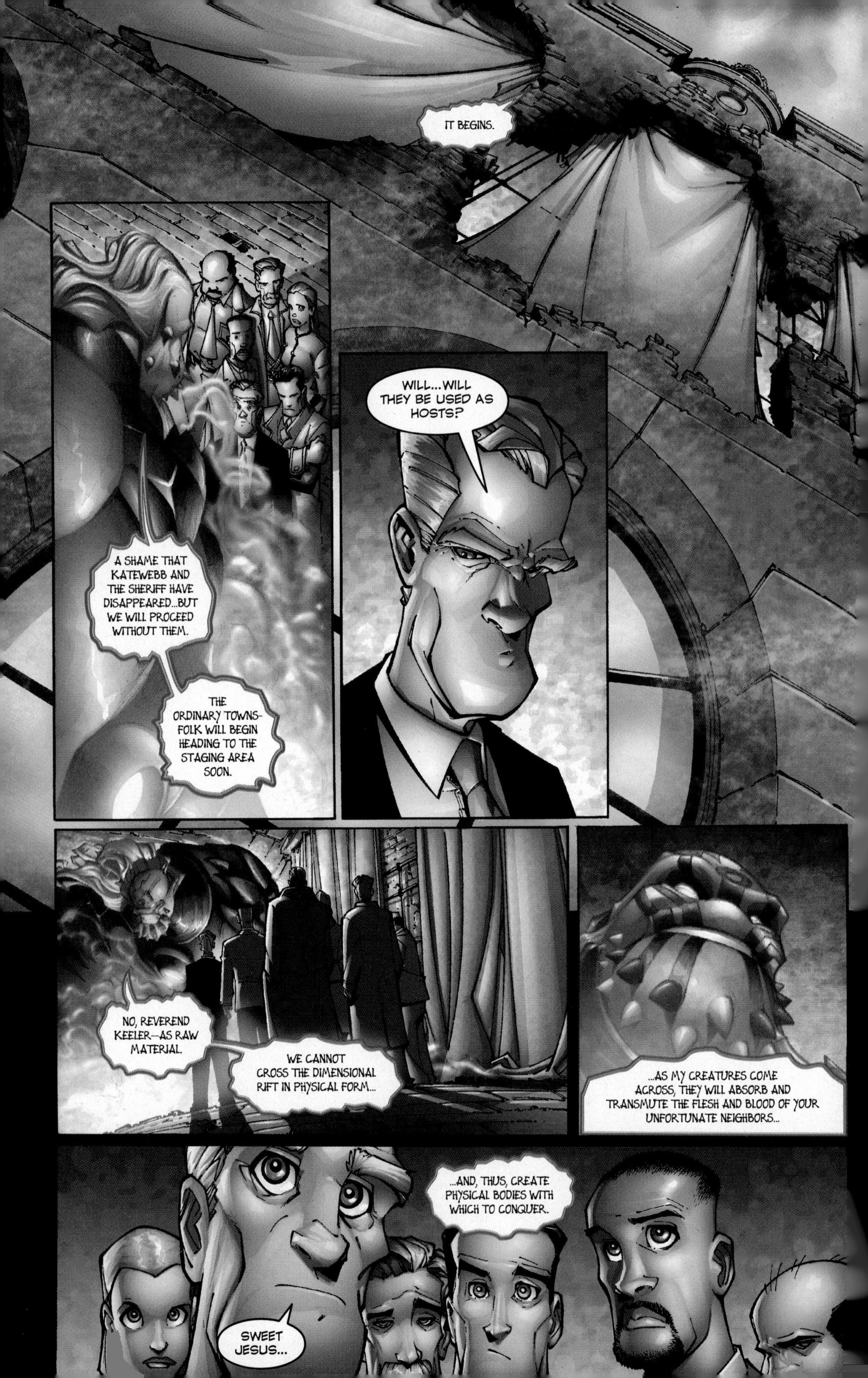
IT BEGINS.
A SHAME THAT KATEWEBB AND THE SHERIFF HAVE DISAPPEARED...BUT WE WILL PROCEED WITHOUT THEM.
THE ORDINARY TOWNS-FOLK WILL BEGIN HEADING TO THE STAGING AREA SOON.
WILL...WILL THEY BE USED AS HOSTS?
NO, REVEREND KEELER--AS RAW MATERIAL.
WE CANNOT CROSS THE DIMENSIONAL RIFT IN PHYSICAL FORM...
...AS MY CREATURES COME ACROSS, THEY WILL ABSORB AND TRANSMUTE THE FLESH AND BLOOD OF YOUR UNFORTUNATE NEIGHBORS...
...AND, THUS, CREATE PHYSICAL BODIES WITH WHICH TO CONQUER.
SWEET JESUS...

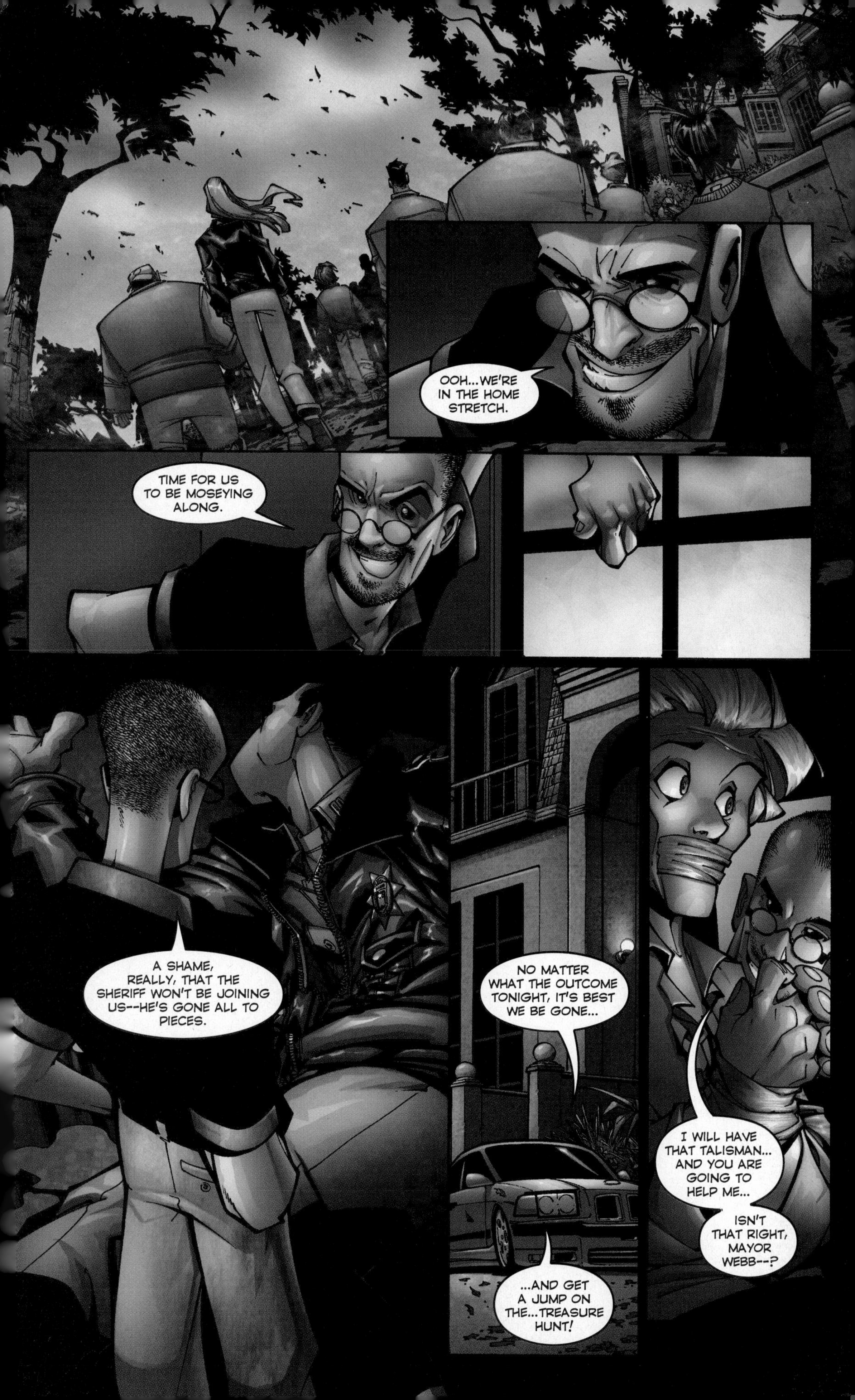
OOH...WE'RE IN THE HOME STRETCH.
TIME FOR US TO BE MOSEYING ALONG.
A SHAME, REALLY, THAT THE SHERIFF WON'T BE JOINING US--HE'S GONE ALL TO PIECES.
NO MATTER WHAT THE OUTCOME TONIGHT, IT'S BEST WE BE GONE...
...AND GET A JUMP ON THE...TREASURE HUNT!
I WILL HAVE THAT TALISMAN... AND YOU ARE GOING TO HELP ME...
ISN'T THAT RIGHT, MAYOR WEBB--?

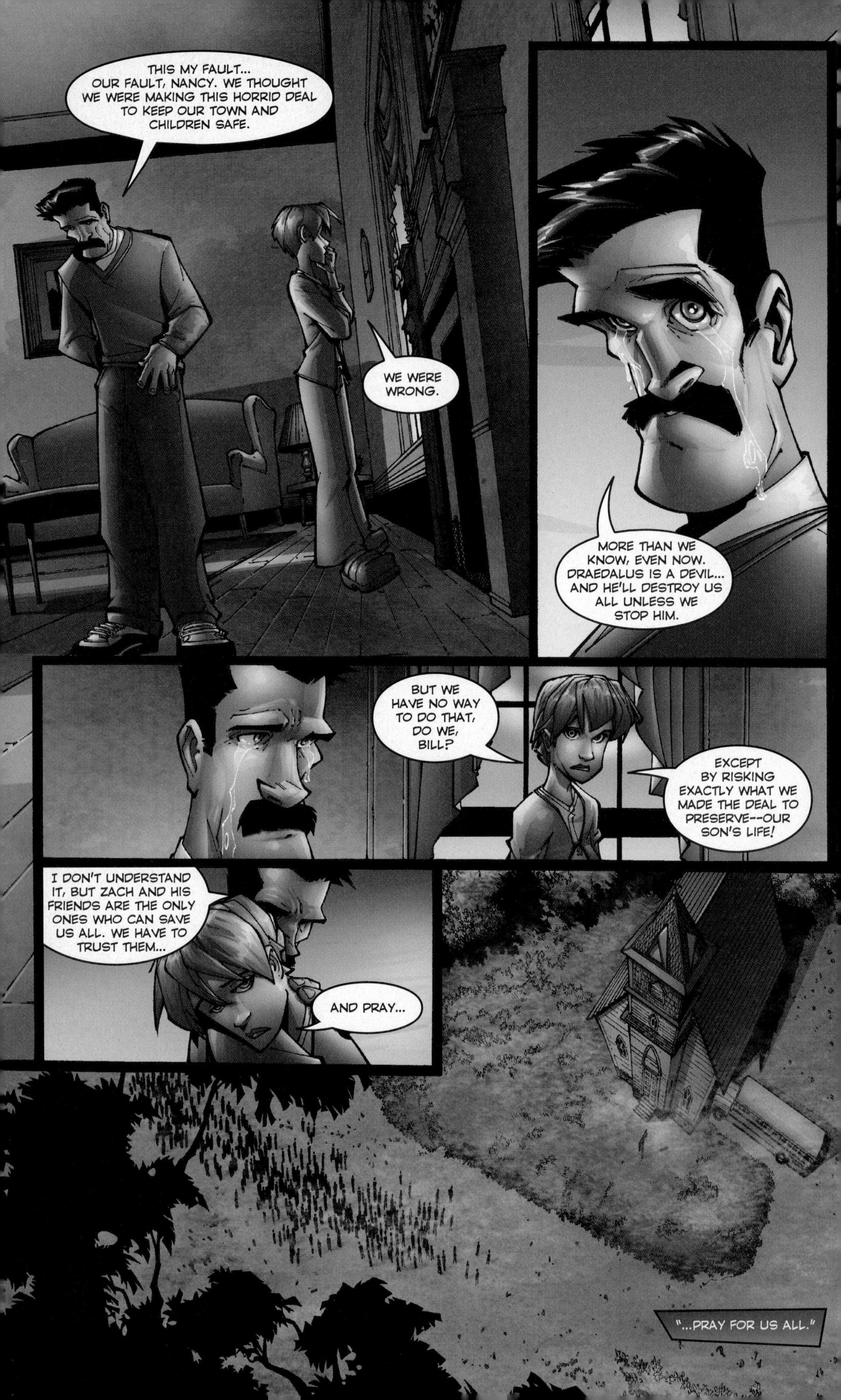
THIS MY FAULT... OUR FAULT, NANCY. WE THOUGHT WE WERE MAKING THIS HORRID DEAL TO KEEP OUR TOWN AND CHILDREN SAFE.
WE WERE WRONG.
MORE THAN WE KNOW, EVEN NOW. DRAEDALUS IS A DEVIL... AND HE'LL DESTROY US ALL UNLESS WE STOP HIM.
BUT WE HAVE NO WAY TO DO THAT, DO WE, BILL?
EXCEPT BY RISKING EXACTLY WHAT WE MADE THE DEAL TO PRESERVE--OUR SON'S LIFE!
I DON'T UNDERSTAND IT, BUT ZACH AND HIS FRIENDS ARE THE ONLY ONES WHO CAN SAVE US ALL. WE HAVE TO TRUST THEM...
AND PRAY...
"...PRAY FOR US ALL."

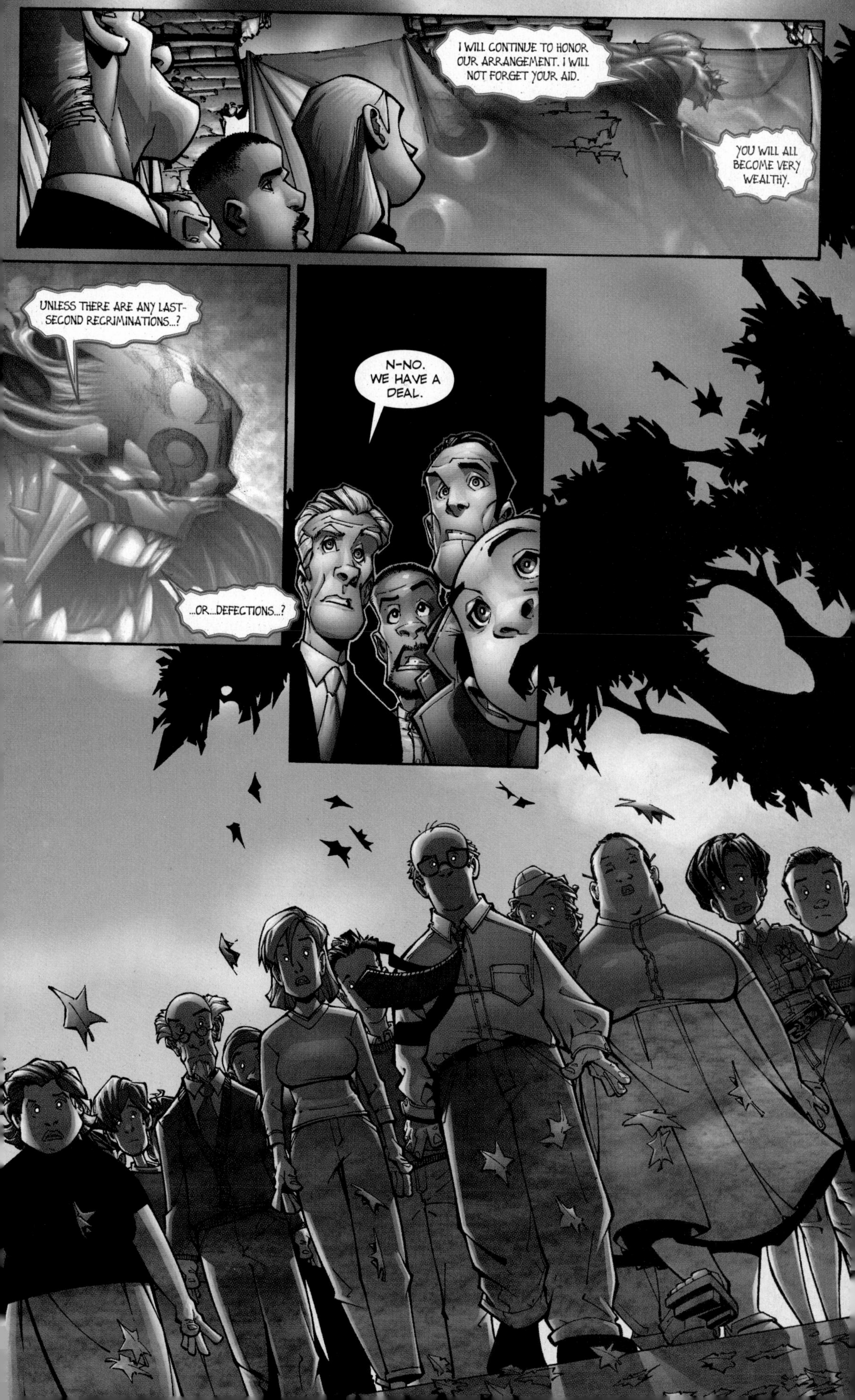

I WILL CONTINUE TO HONOR OUR ARRANGEMENT. I WILL NOT FORGET YOUR AID.
YOU WILL ALL BECOME VERY WEALTHY.
UNLESS THERE ARE ANY LAST-SECOND RECRIMINATIONS...?
...OR...DEFECTIONS...?
N-NO. WE HAVE A DEAL.

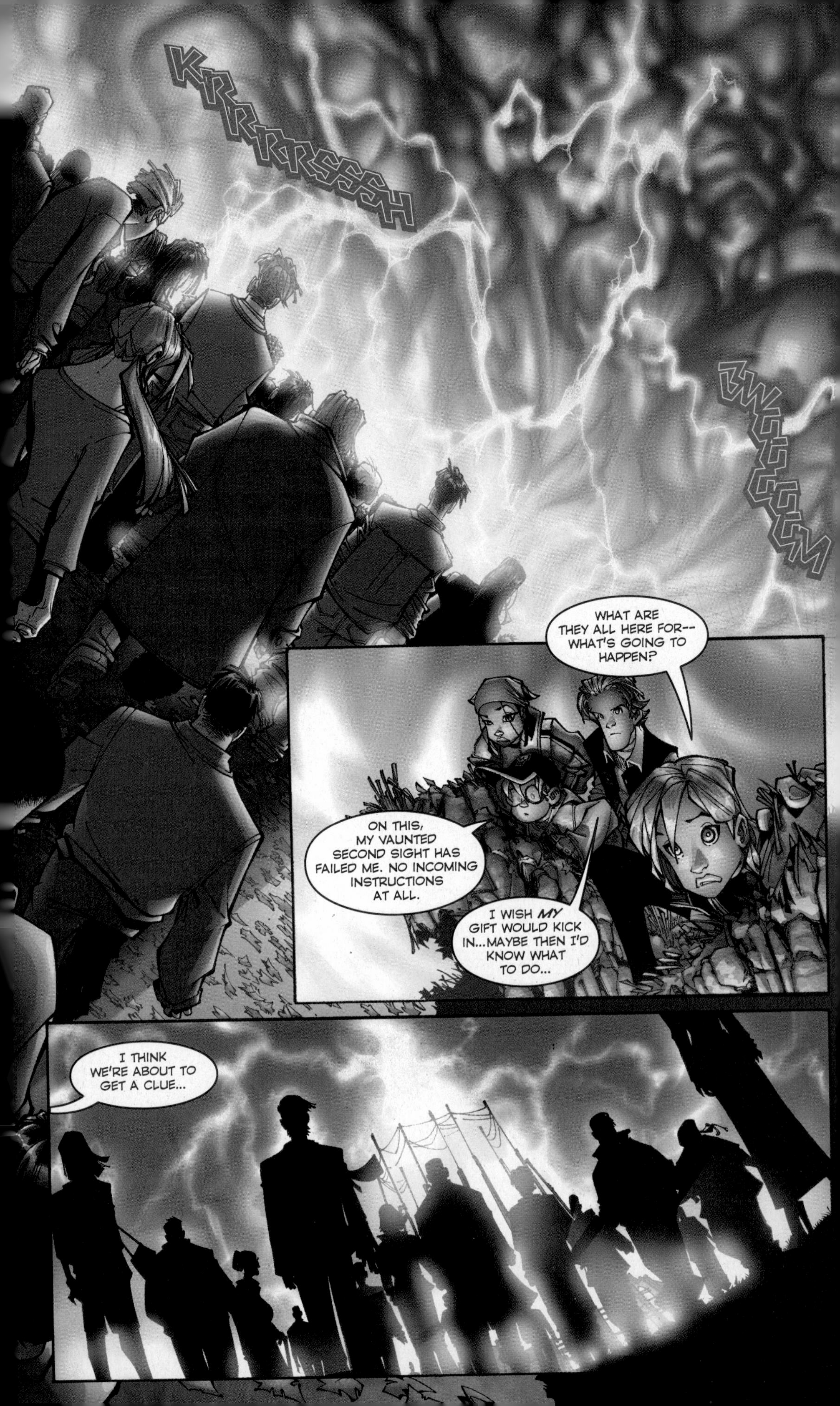
KRRRRSSSH
BWUUUM
WHAT ARE THEY ALL HERE FOR-- WHAT'S GOING TO HAPPEN?
ON THIS, MY VAUNTED SECOND SIGHT HAS FAILED ME. NO INCOMING INSTRUCTIONS AT ALL.
I WISH MY GIFT WOULD KICK IN...MAYBE THEN I'D KNOW WHAT TO DO...
I THINK WE'RE ABOUT TO GET A CLUE...

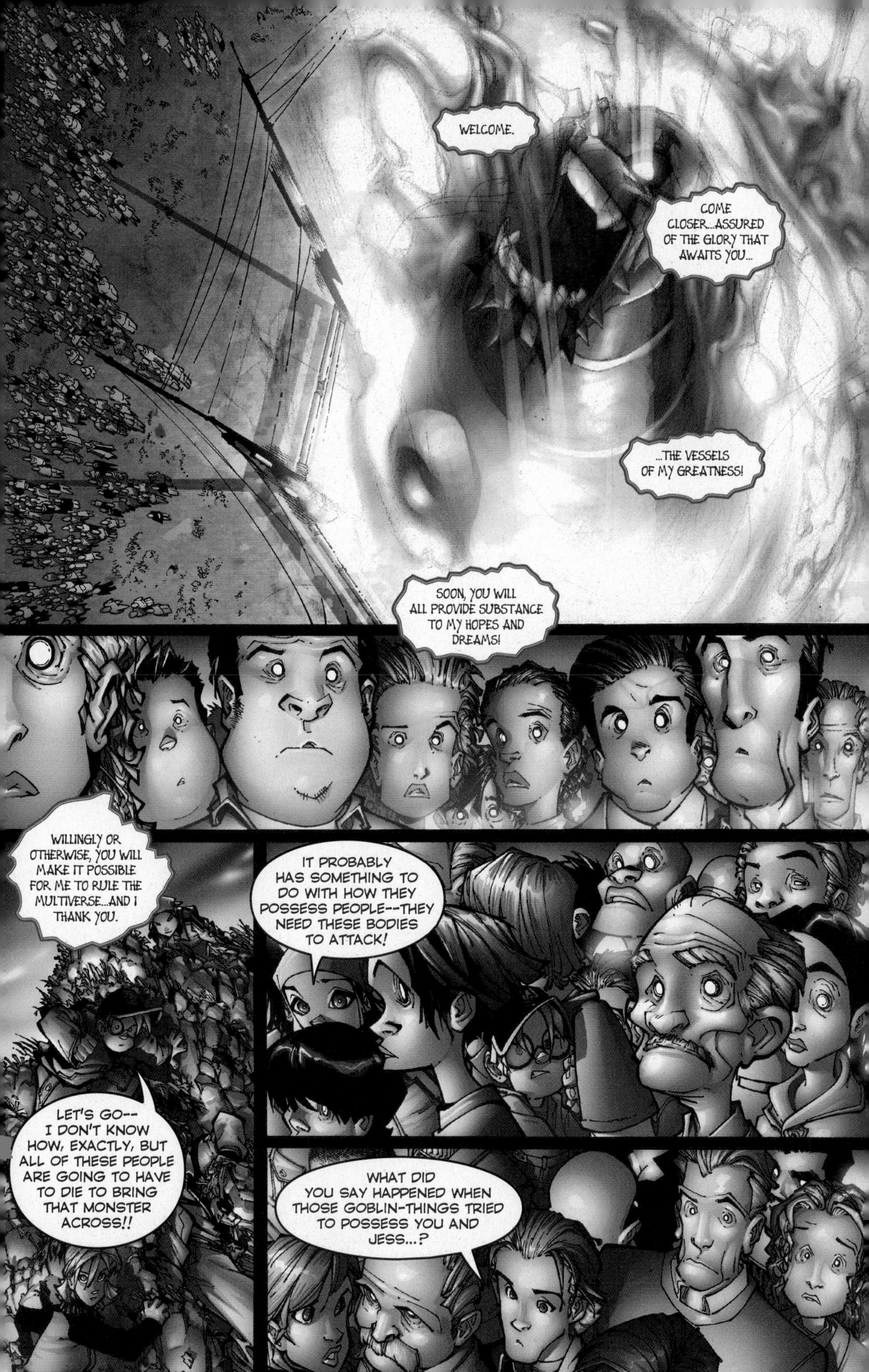
WELCOME.
COME CLOSER...ASSURED OF THE GLORY THAT AWAITS YOU...
...THE VESSELS OF MY GREATNESS!
SOON, YOU WILL ALL PROVIDE SUBSTANCE TO MY HOPES AND DREAMS!
WILLINGLY OR OTHERWISE, YOU WILL MAKE IT POSSIBLE FOR ME TO RULE THE MULTIVERSE...AND I THANK YOU.
IT PROBABLY HAS SOMETHING TO DO WITH HOW THEY POSSESS PEOPLE--THEY NEED THESE BODIES TO ATTACK!
LET'S GO-- I DON'T KNOW HOW, EXACTLY, BUT ALL OF THESE PEOPLE ARE GOING TO HAVE TO DIE TO BRING THAT MONSTER ACROSS!!
WHAT DID YOU SAY HAPPENED WHEN THOSE GOBLIN-THINGS TRIED TO POSSESS YOU AND JESS...?
RIGHT...!

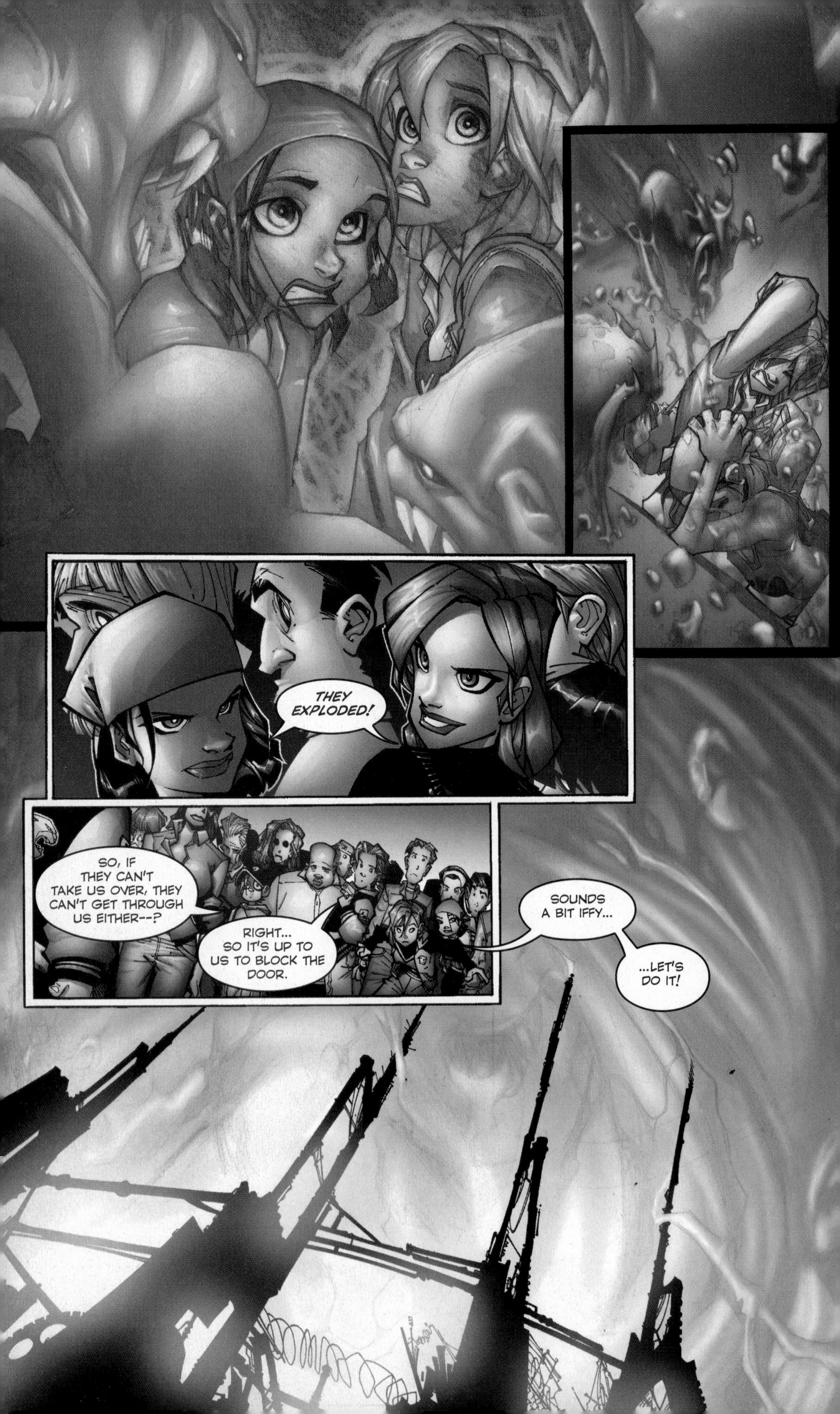
THEY EXPLODED!
SO, IF THEY CAN'T TAKE US OVER, THEY CAN'T GET THROUGH US EITHER--?
RIGHT... SO IT'S UP TO US TO BLOCK THE DOOR.
SOUNDS A BIT IFFY...
...LET'S DO IT!

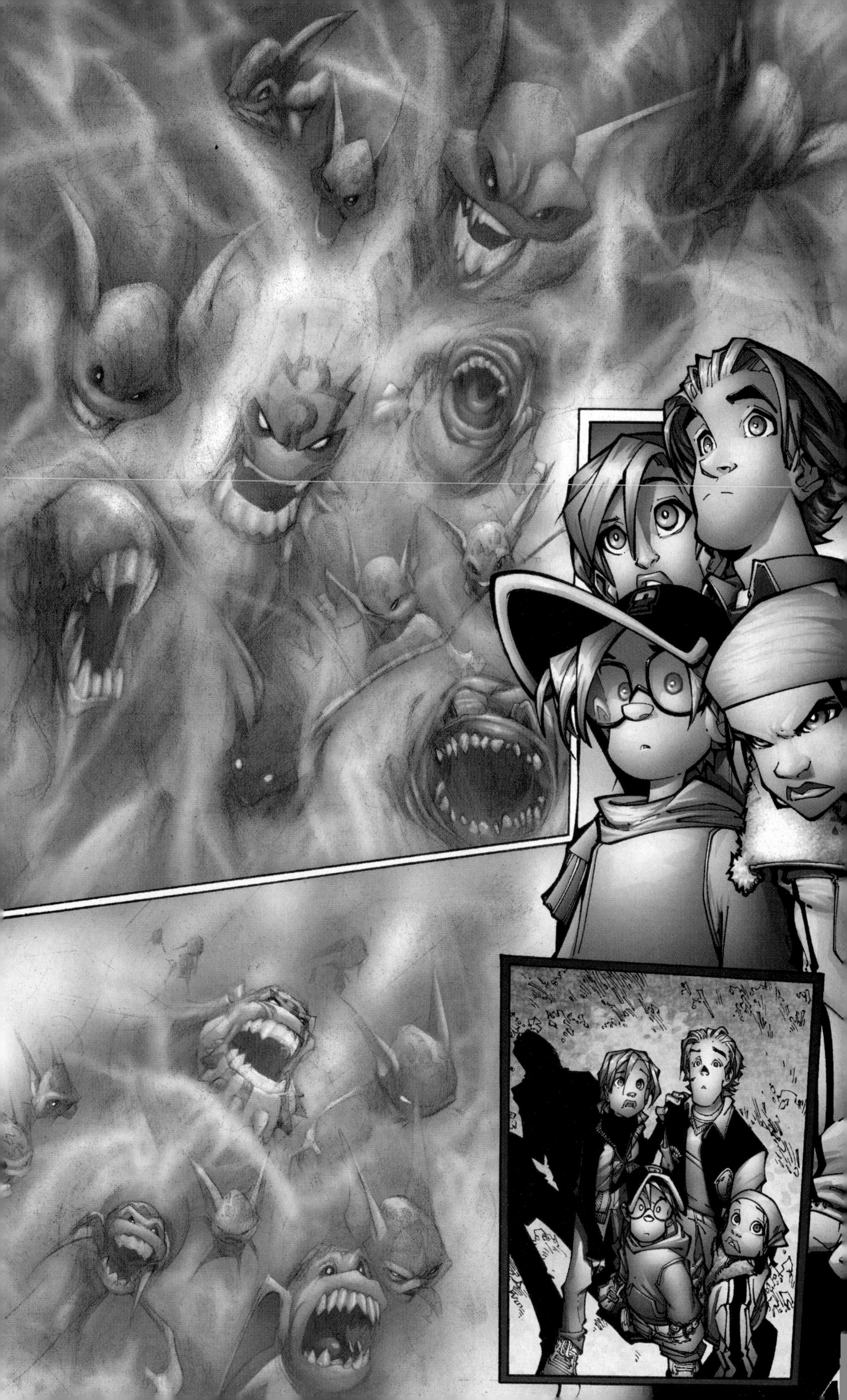

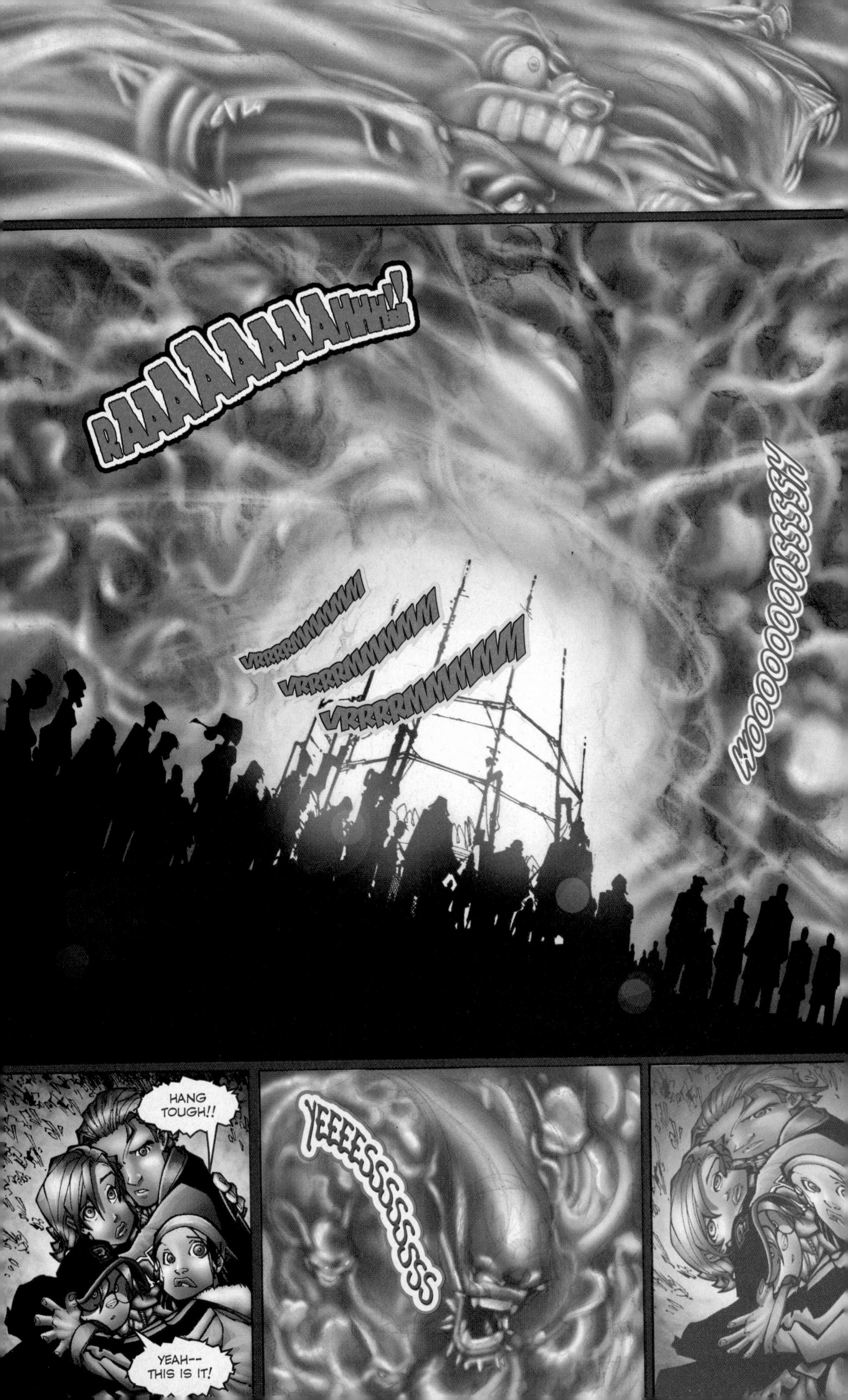
RAAAAAAAAHHH!!
VRRRRMMMMMM
VRRRRMMMMMMM
VRRRRMMMMMMMM
WOOOOOOSSSSSSH
HANG TOUGH!!
YEAH-- THIS IS IT!
YEEEESSSSSSSSS

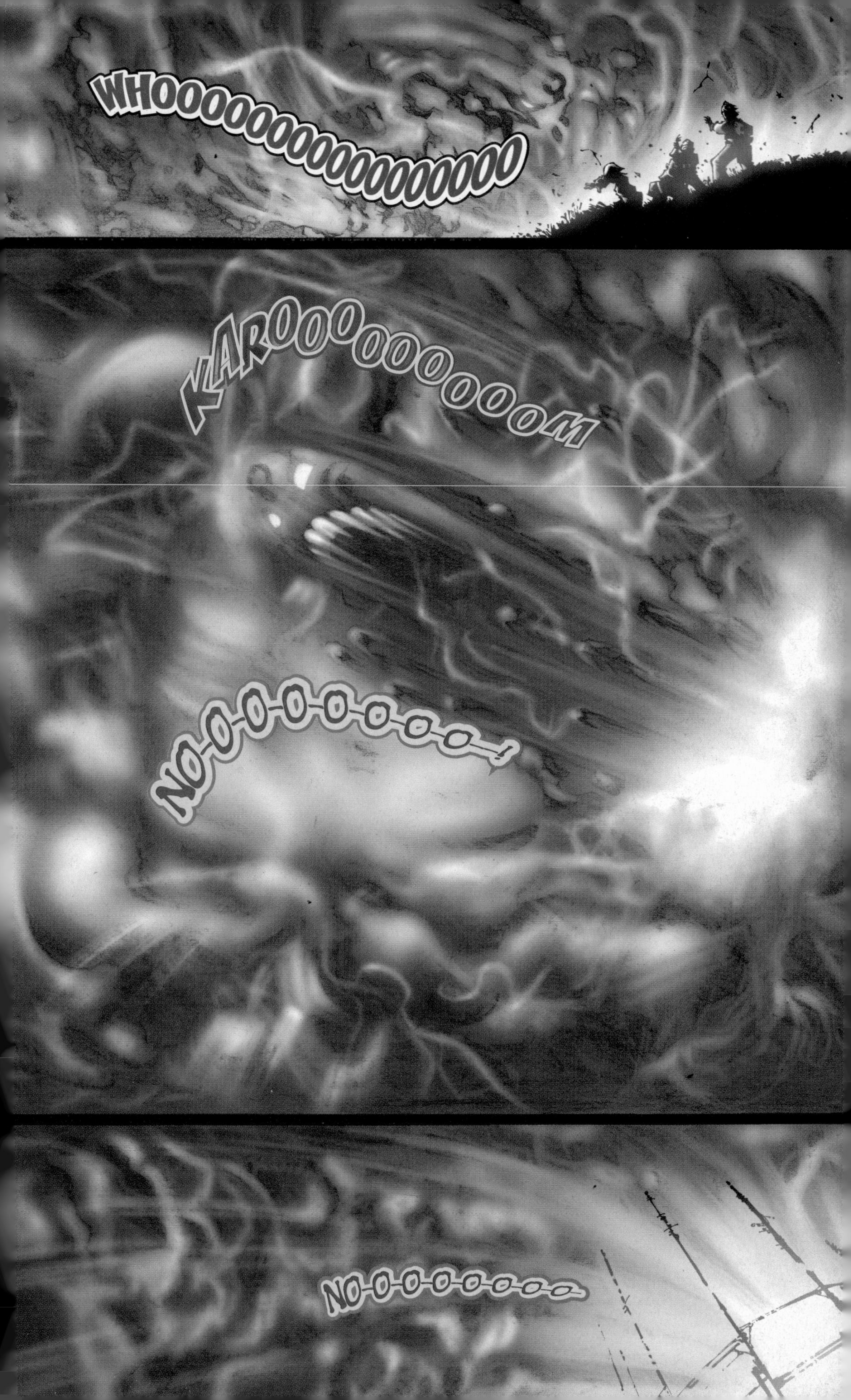
WHOOOOOOOOOOOOOOOOOO
KAROOOOOOOOOM
NO-O-O-O-O-O-O-O—!
NO-O-O-O-O-O-O-O—

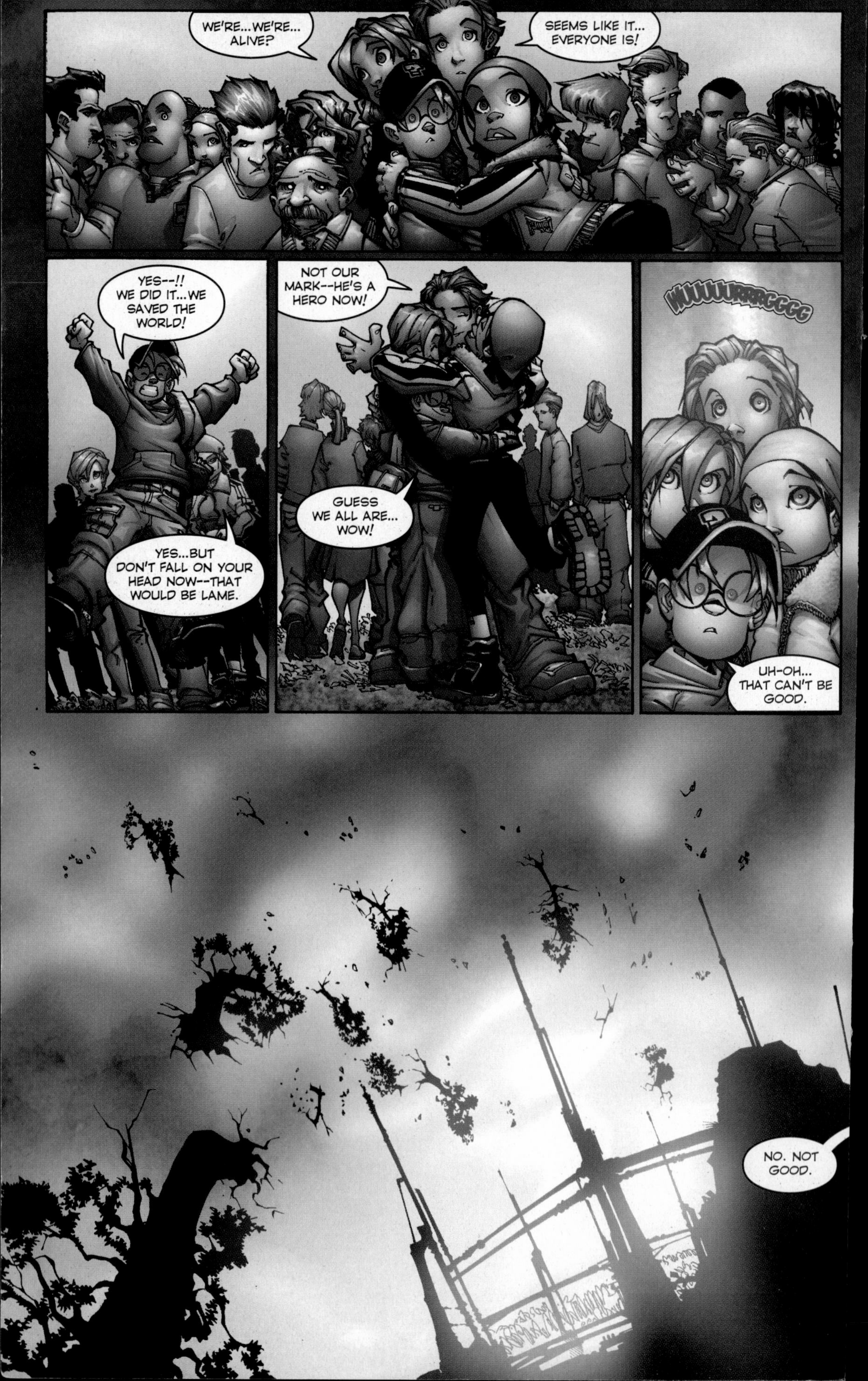
WE'RE...WE'RE... ALIVE?
SEEMS LIKE IT... EVERYONE IS!
YES--!! WE DID IT...WE SAVED THE WORLD!
YES...BUT DON'T FALL ON YOUR HEAD NOW--THAT WOULD BE LAME.
NOT OUR MARK--HE'S A HERO NOW!
GUESS WE ALL ARE... WOW!
WUUUURRRRGGGG
UH-OH... THAT CAN'T BE GOOD.
NO. NOT GOOD.

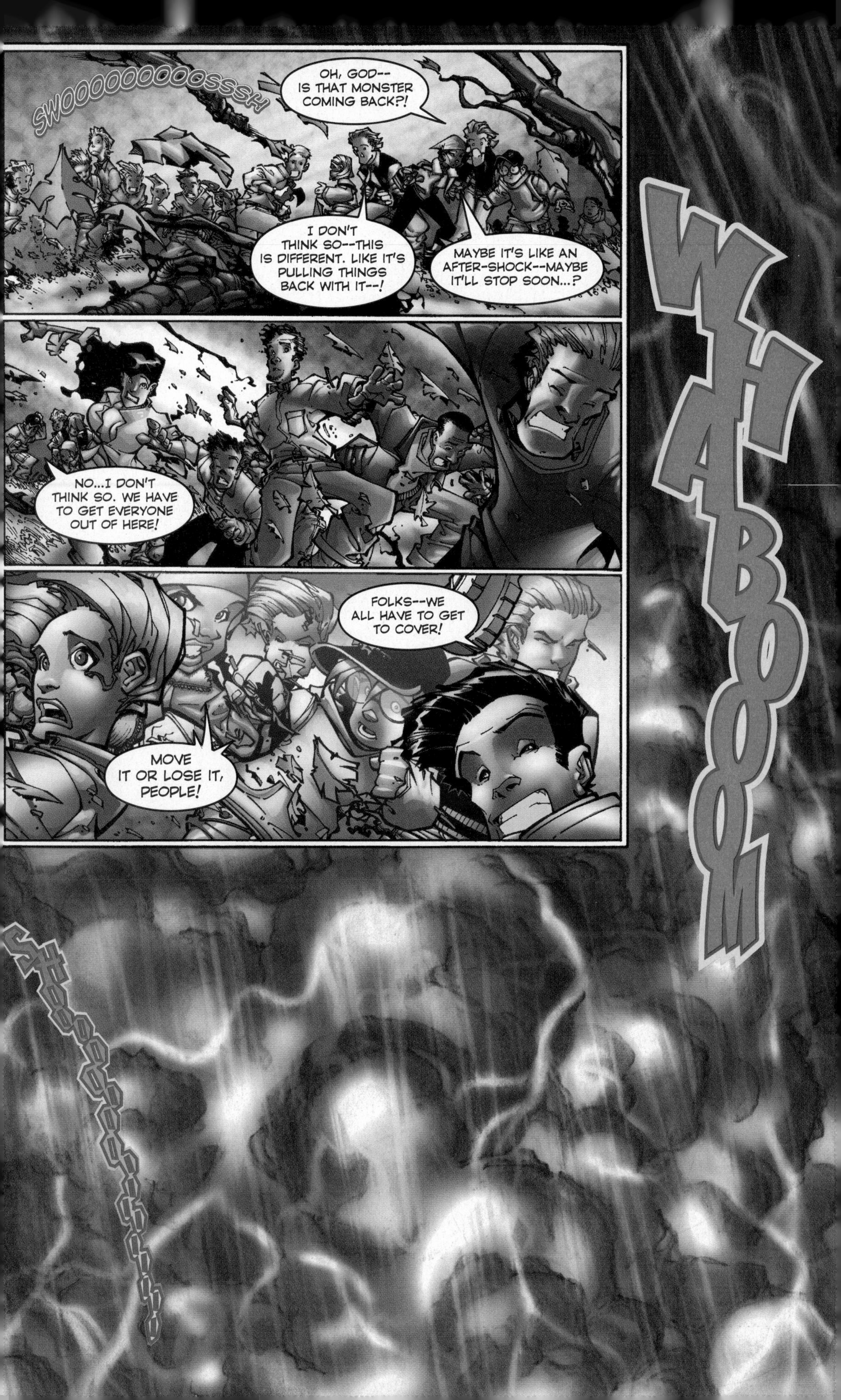
SWOOOOOOOOOOSSSSH
OH, GOD-- IS THAT MONSTER COMING BACK?!
I DON'T THINK SO--THIS IS DIFFERENT. LIKE IT'S PULLING THINGS BACK WITH IT--!
MAYBE IT'S LIKE AN AFTER-SHOCK--MAYBE IT'LL STOP SOON...?
NO...I DON'T THINK SO. WE HAVE TO GET EVERYONE OUT OF HERE!
FOLKS--WE ALL HAVE TO GET TO COVER!
MOVE IT OR LOSE IT, PEOPLE!
WHABOOOM

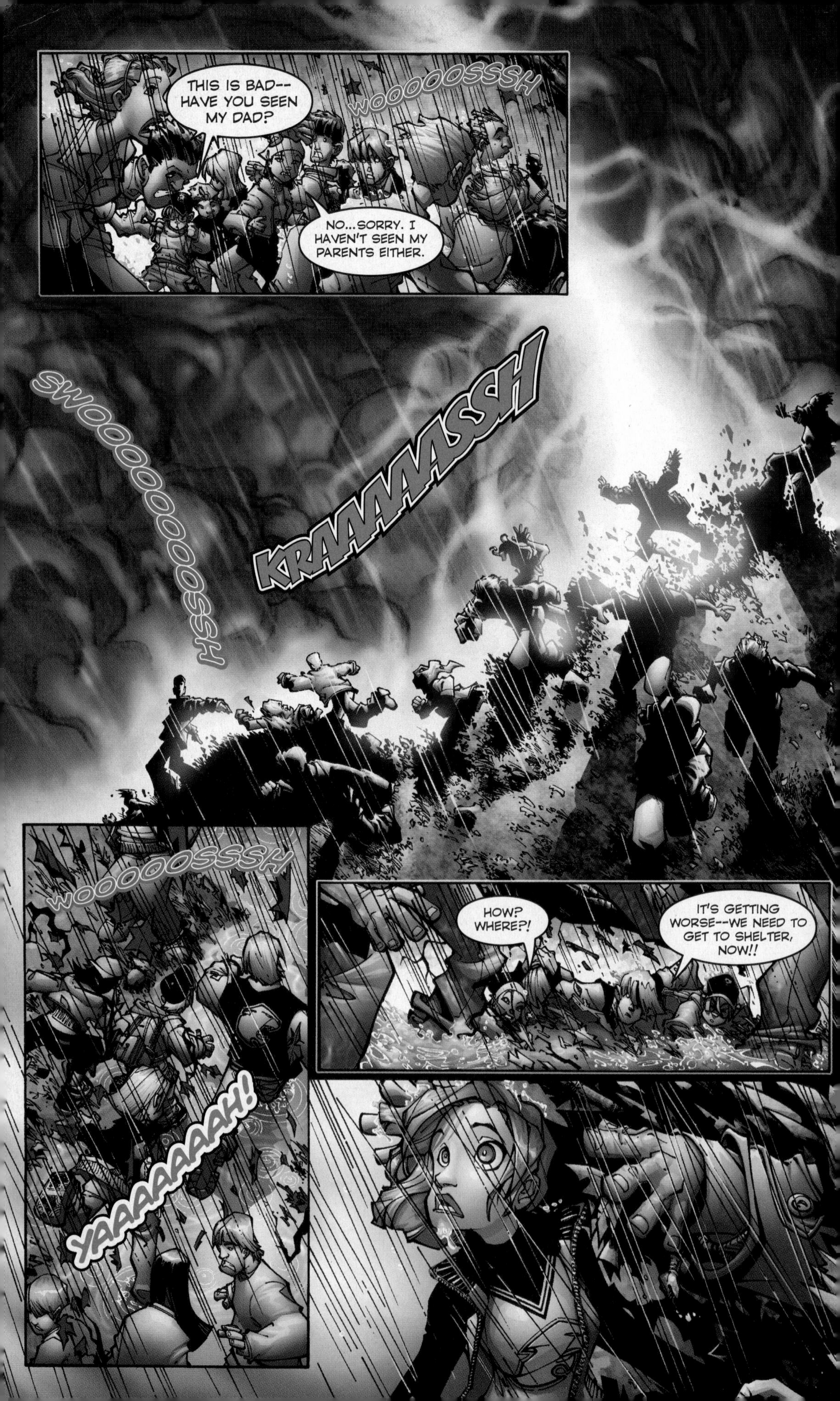
THIS IS BAD-- HAVE YOU SEEN MY DAD?
WOOOOOOSSSSH
NO...SORRY. I HAVEN'T SEEN MY PARENTS EITHER.
SWOOOOOOOOOOSSSH
KRAAAAAASSH
WOOOOOOSSSSH
YAAAAAAAH!
HOW? WHERE?!
IT'S GETTING WORSE--WE NEED TO GET TO SHELTER, NOW!!

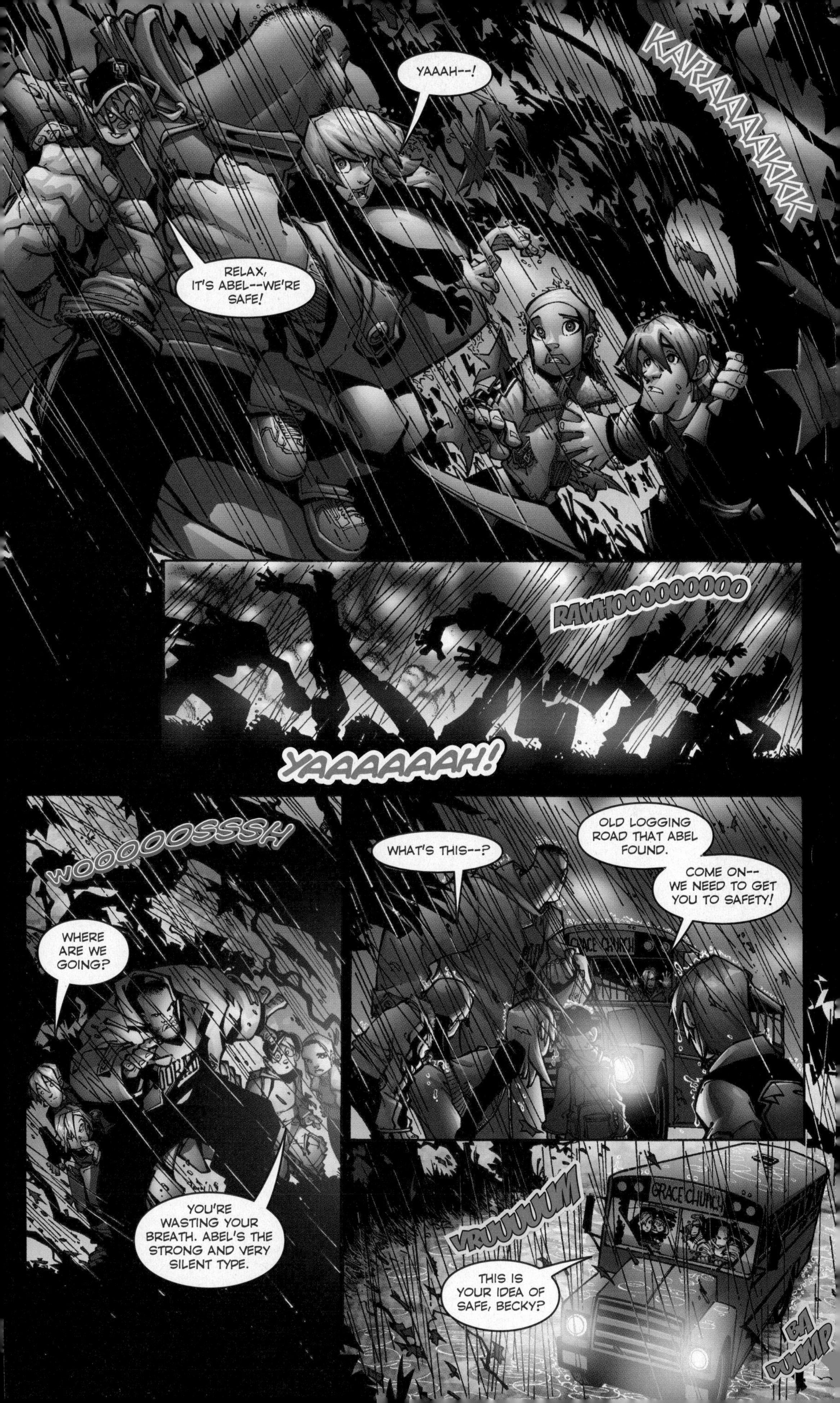

KARAAAAAKKK
YAAAH--!
RELAX, IT'S ABEL--WE'RE SAFE!
RAWHOOOOOOOOO
YAAAAAAH!
WOOOOOOSSSSH
WHERE ARE WE GOING?
YOU'RE WASTING YOUR BREATH. ABEL'S THE STRONG AND VERY SILENT TYPE.
WHAT'S THIS--?
OLD LOGGING ROAD THAT ABEL FOUND.
COME ON-- WE NEED TO GET YOU TO SAFETY!
GRACE CHURCH
VRUUUUUUM
GRACE CHURCH
THIS IS YOUR IDEA OF SAFE, BECKY?
BA DUUMP

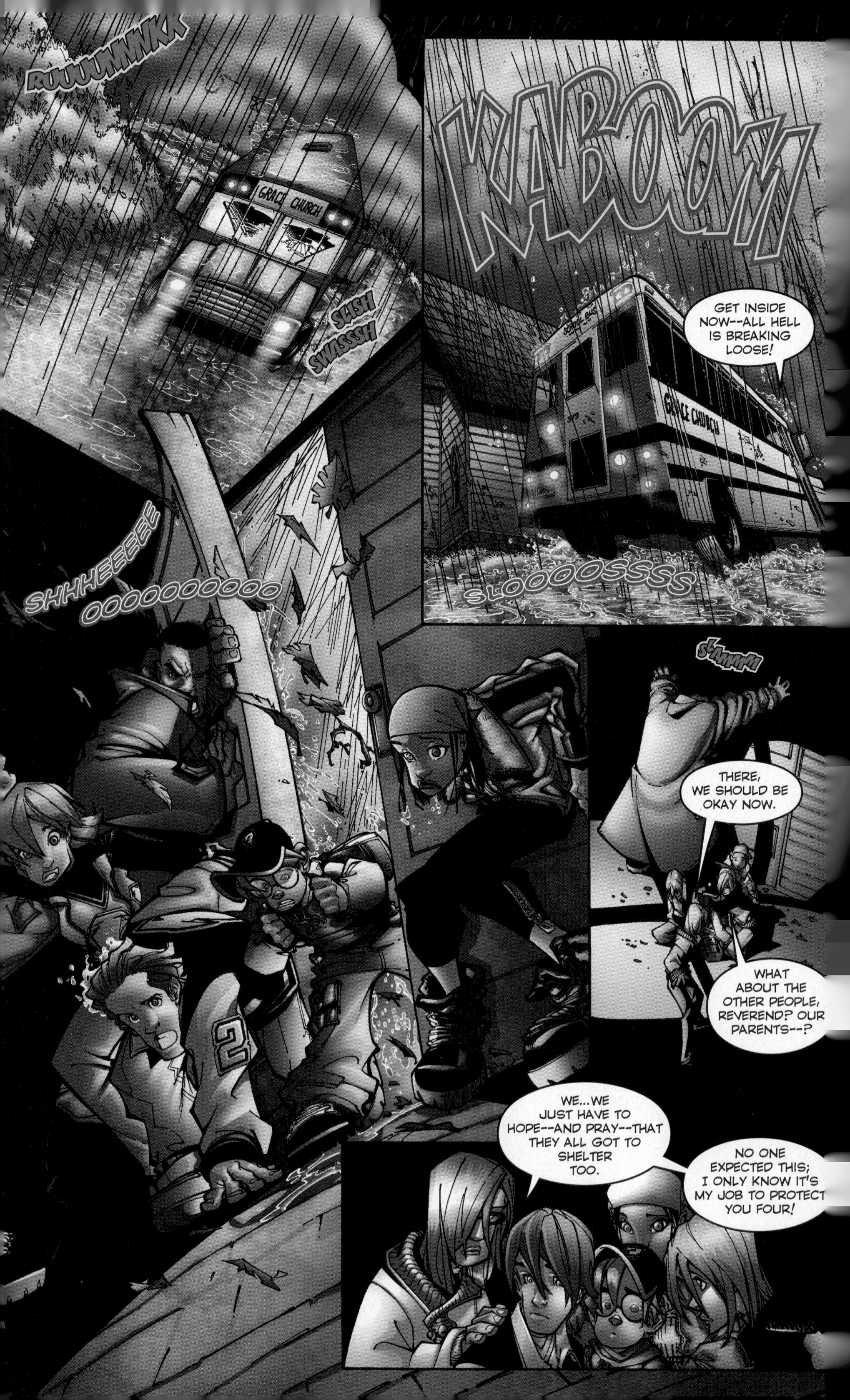
RUUUUMMWKK
SLISH
SWASSSH
KABOOM
GET INSIDE NOW--ALL HELL IS BREAKING LOOSE!
GRACE CHURCH
SLOOOOSSSSS
SHHHEEEEEE
OOOOOOOOOO
THERE, WE SHOULD BE OKAY NOW.
WHAT ABOUT THE OTHER PEOPLE, REVEREND? OUR PARENTS--?
WE...WE JUST HAVE TO HOPE--AND PRAY--THAT THEY ALL GOT TO SHELTER TOO.
NO ONE EXPECTED THIS; I ONLY KNOW IT'S MY JOB TO PROTECT YOU FOUR!

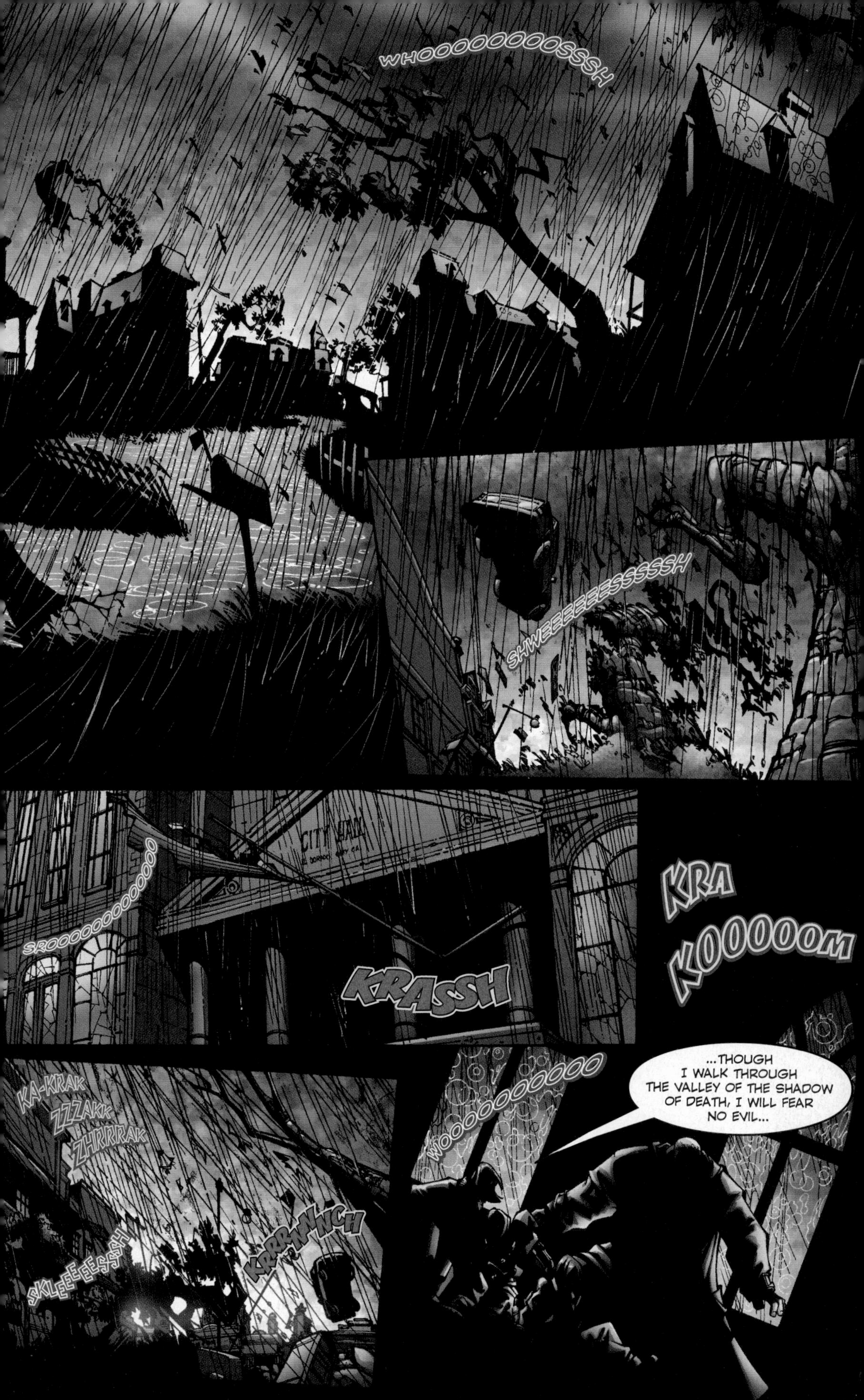
WHOOOOOOOOOSSSSH
SHWEEEEEEESSSSSSH
SROOOOOOOOOOOOOOO
KRASSH
KRA
KOOOOOOM
KA-KRAK
ZZZAKK
ZHRRRAK
SKLEEEEEESSSH
KRRRNNCH
WOOOOOOOOOOOOOO
...THOUGH I WALK THROUGH THE VALLEY OF THE SHADOW OF DEATH, I WILL FEAR NO EVIL...

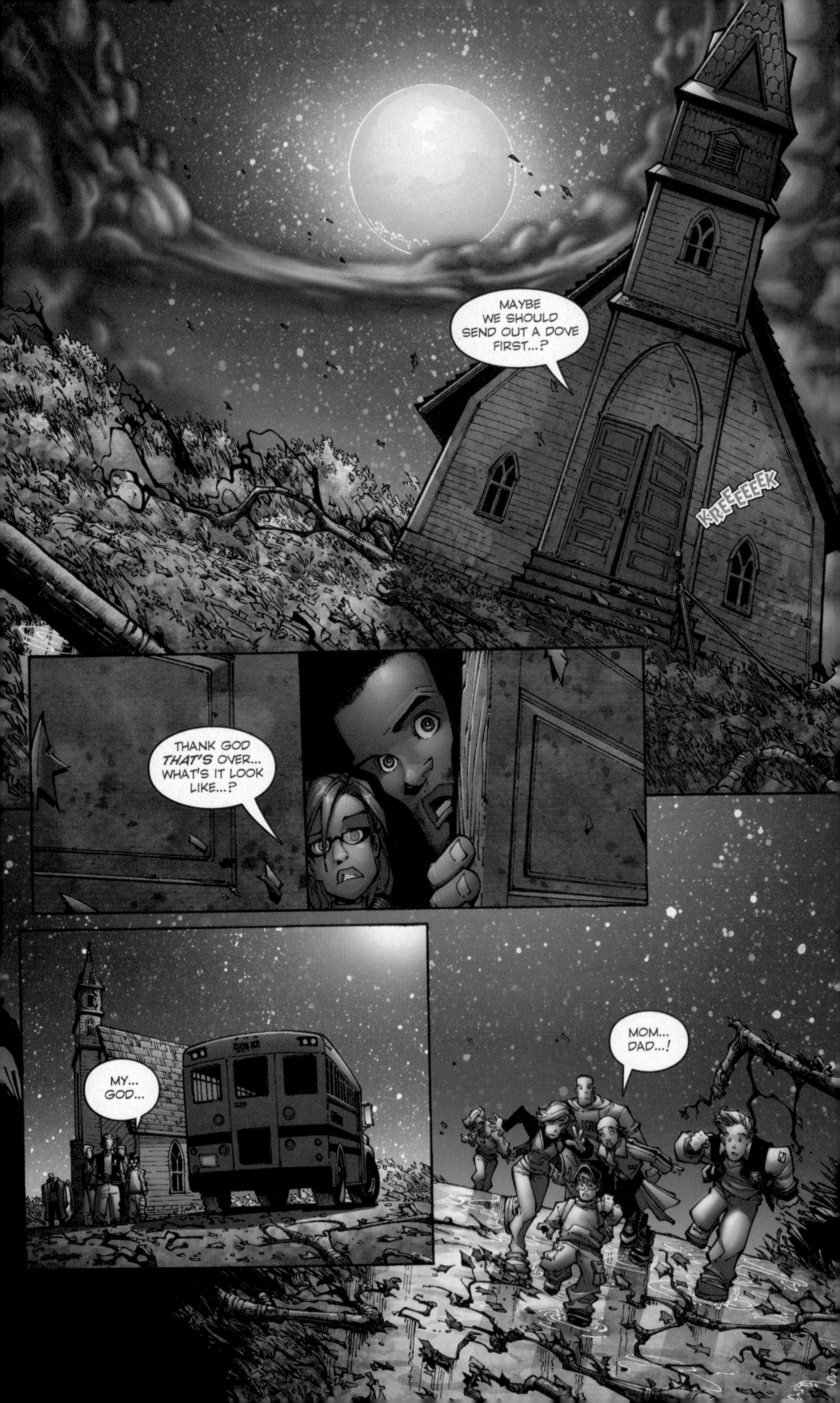
MAYBE WE SHOULD SEND OUT A DOVE FIRST...?
KREEEEEK
THANK GOD *THAT'S* OVER... WHAT'S IT LOOK LIKE...?
MY... GOD...
MOM... DAD...!

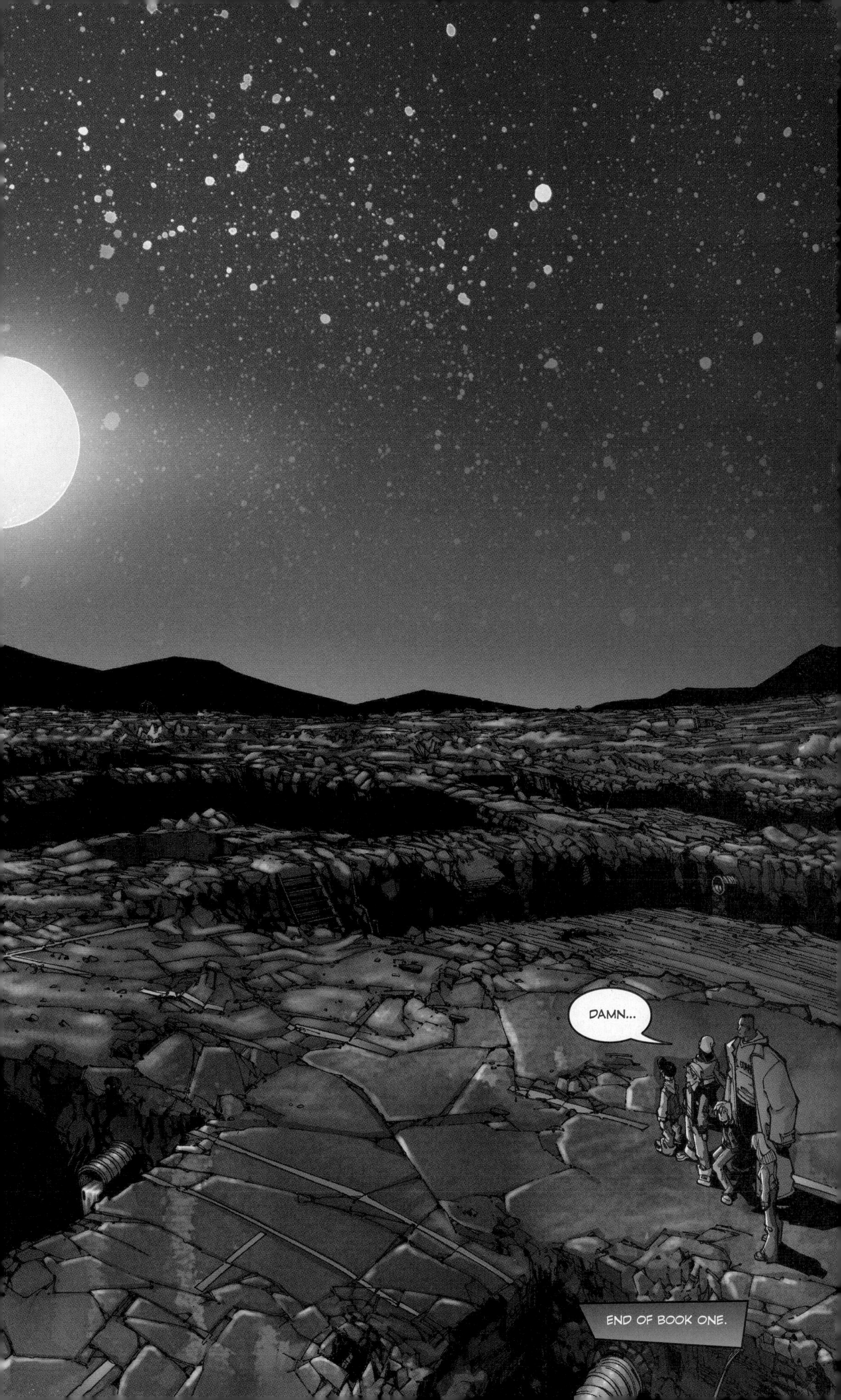
DAMN...
END OF BOOK ONE.

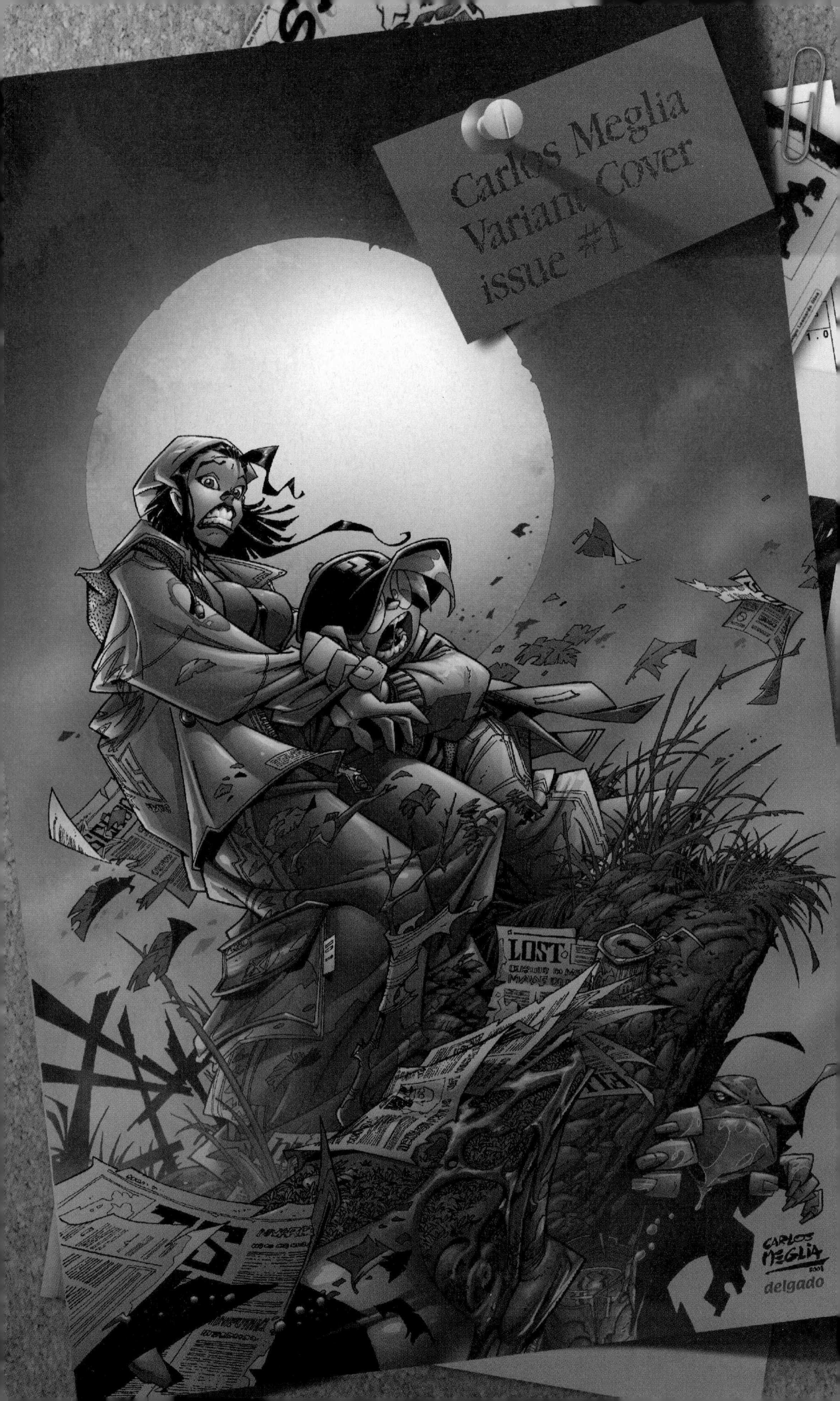

Carlos Meglia
Variant Cover
issue #1
LOST
CARLOS MEGLIA
delgado

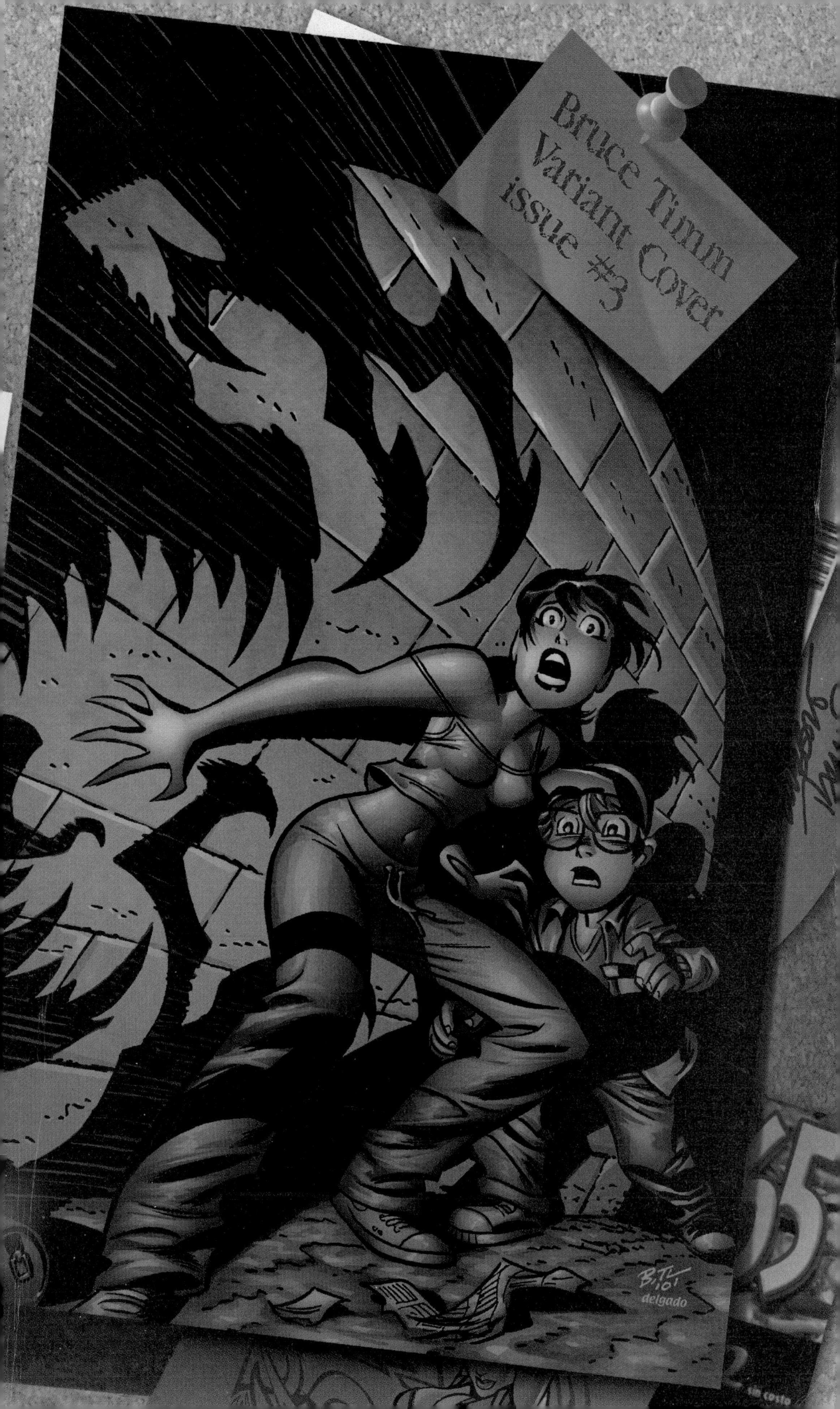
Bruce Timm
Variant Cover
issue #3
B.T. '01
delgado

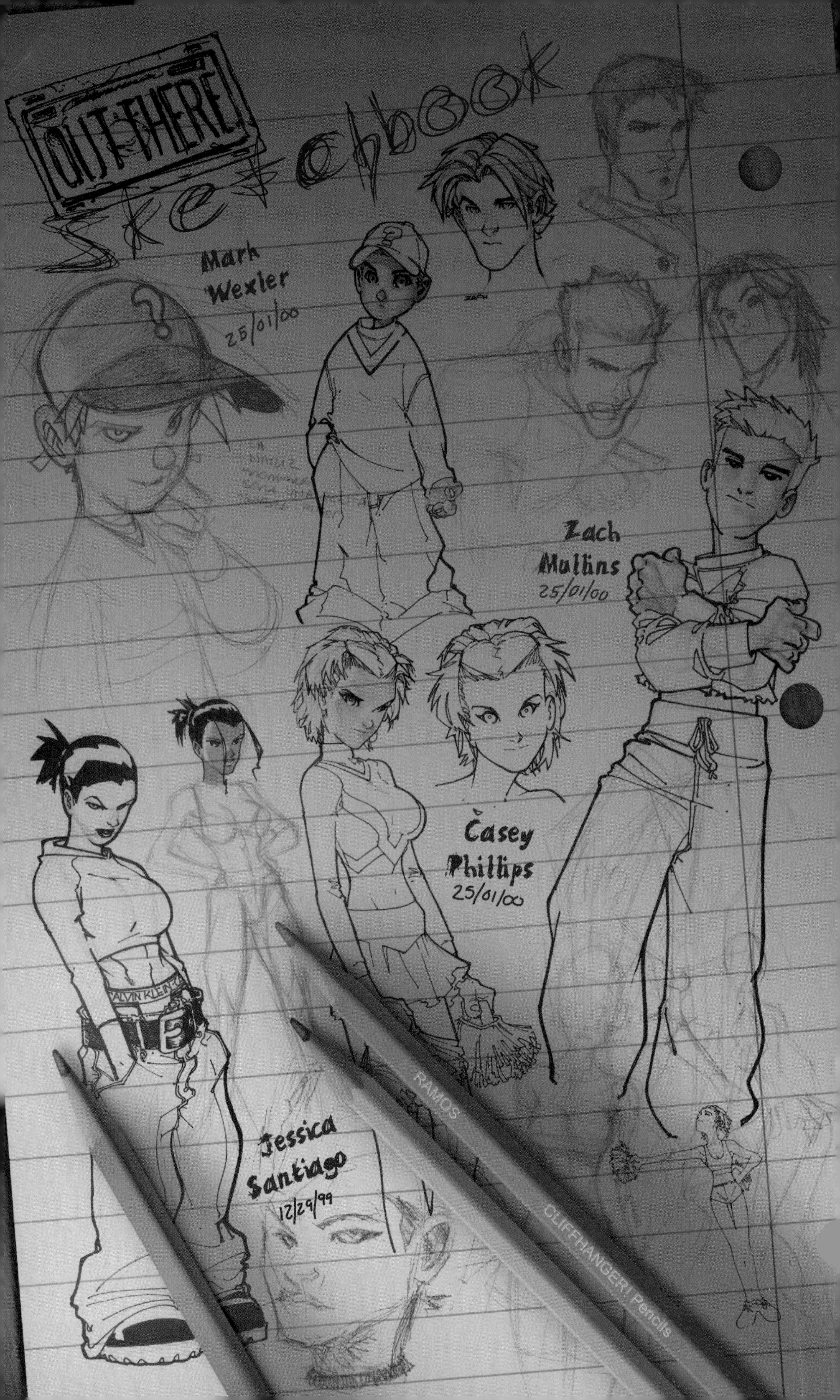
OUT THERE
Sketchbook
Mark Wexler
25/01/00
ZACH
Zach Mullins
25/01/00
Casey Phillips
25/01/00
CALVIN KLEIN
Jessica Santiago
12/29/99
RAMOS
CLIFFHANGER! Pencils

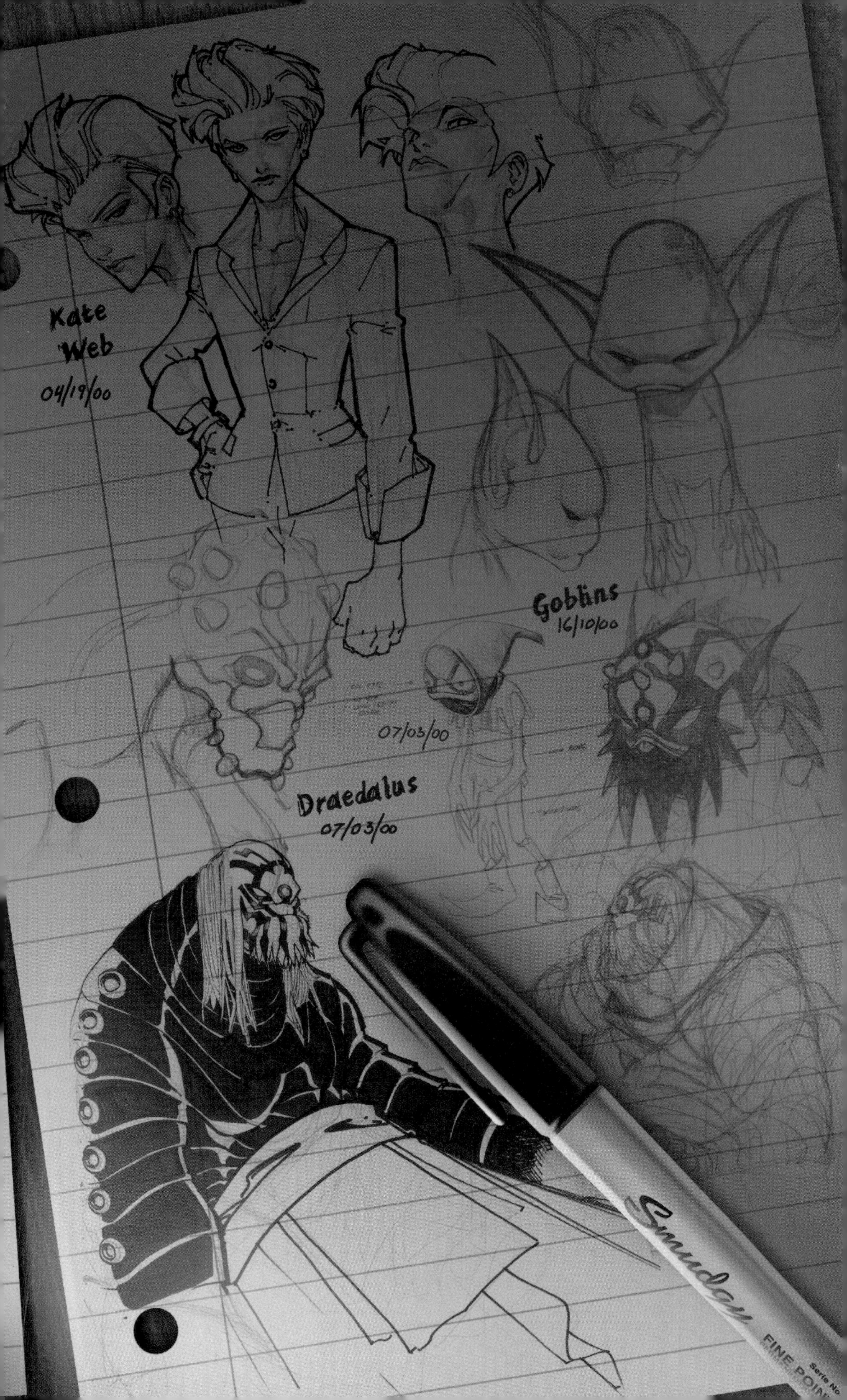
Kate Web
04/19/00
Goblins
16/10/00
07/03/00
Draedalus
07/03/00
Smudau
FINE POINT

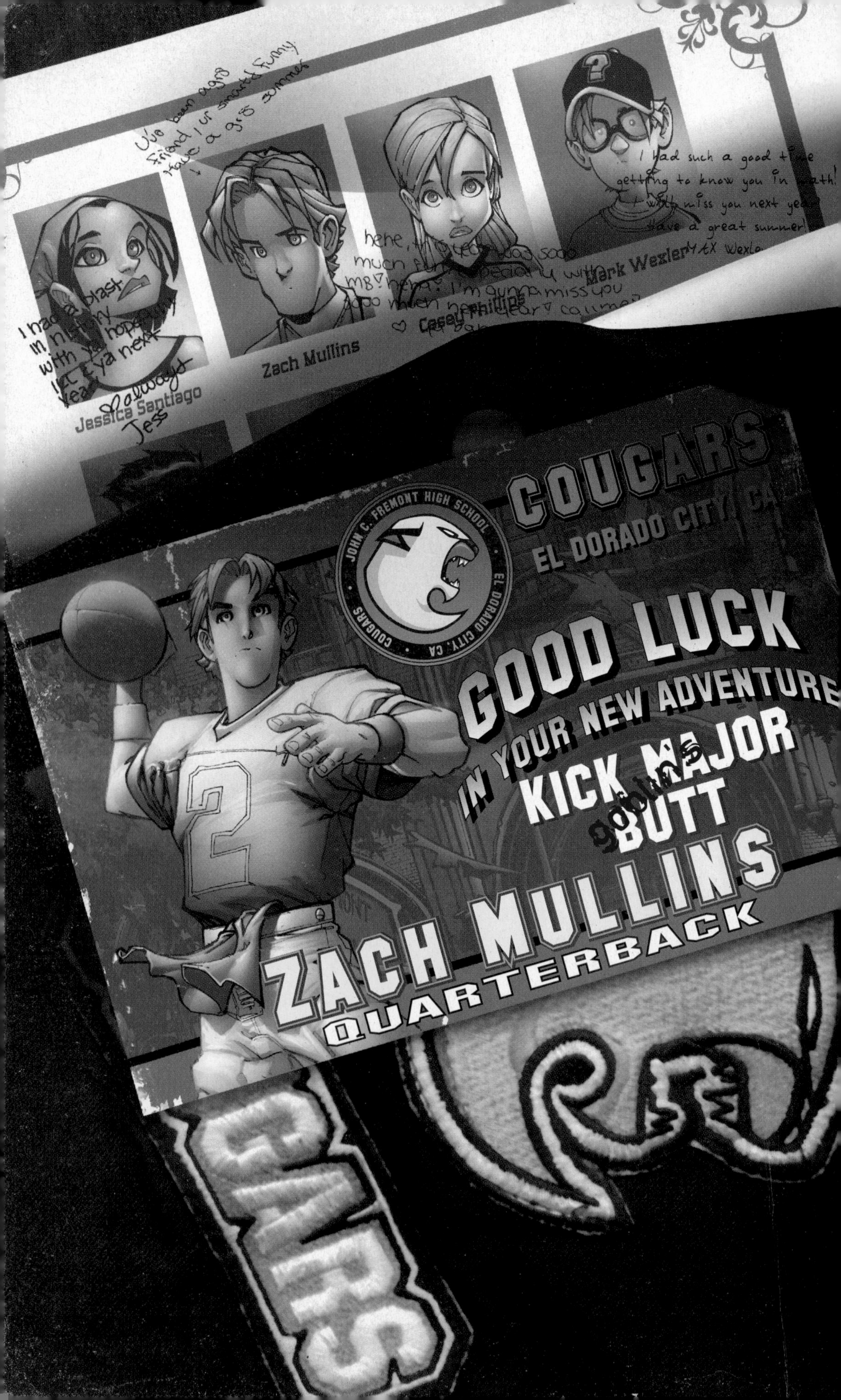

Jessica Santiago
Zach Mullins
Casey Phillips
Mark Wexler
COUGARS
EL DORADO CITY, CA
JOHN C. FREMONT HIGH SCHOOL
EL DORADO CITY, CA
COUGARS
GOOD LUCK
IN YOUR NEW ADVENTURE
KICK MAJOR goblins BUTT
ZACH MULLINS
QUARTERBACK